WHAT WAS THE LOVE OF ONE MAN WORTH?

Was it worth humbling yourself before your new mother-in-law, even as she shot her barbed shafts into you and tried to sabotage your marriage in every way?

Was it worth neglecting the tiny infant daughter who so desperately needed you, and obeying your husband's desire that you not give birth to the new life already stirring within you?

Was it worth sharing the man you loved with other women —trying to shut your eyes to his infidelities when he came from their arms into your own?

Was it worth forsaking all other men—even one as decent and devoted as Paul Carmichael, or as sensually skilled and exciting as Martin Tanner?

"ELEGANT AND SLICK"—*Oregon Journal*

"Complicated human problems, plenty of emotion, and a satisfying escape into a world where impossible dreams come true . . . familiar magic"—*Anniston Star*

Also by Helen Van Slyke and
available from Popular Library:

THE BEST PEOPLE
THE HEART LISTENS
THE MIXED BLESSING
THE RICH AND THE RIGHTEOUS
THE BEST PLACE TO BE

HELEN VAN SLYKE
ALWAYS IS NOT FOREVER

POPULAR LIBRARY • NEW YORK

Published by Popular Library, a unit of CBS Publications,
the Consumer Publishing Division of CBS Inc.,
by arrangement with Doubleday & Company, Inc.

September, 1978

Copyright © 1977 by Helen Van Slyke

Library of Congress Catalog Card Number: 76-51990

ISBN: 0-445-04271-0

Introduction

Everything around her whispered money and taste. Whispered, because the homes of the old-established rich are carefully planned to look just a shade this side of shabby; quietly expensive as though their owners were far too secure to shout their status. Obvious is vulgar; understated is elegant. Be it furniture or feelings. It's as simple as that.

Susan settled herself more comfortably on the slightly frayed Louis XV chaise and plumped the little Porthault pillows in the small of her aching back. She drew a light, hand-woven throw over her legs to protect them from the coolness of the air-conditioned cocoon in which she rested like some delicate, pampered, embryonic butterfly.

The idea of herself as a delicate butterfly made her smile. "Iron butterfly" would be more like it. All the battering blows, the storms of anger and cold winds of despair would have crushed a creature whose wings were gossamer. Hers were not. They'd carried her to heights of joy and treetops of hope. And into valleys of desperation. But they did not fail, even when they faltered.

The merciless July sun scorched the street eighteen stories below, and the huffing, puffing New York traffic set up a symphony of irritable horn honking as screeching brakes were slammed on amid the angry curses of jacketless men in wilting shirts. But she heard and felt none of it. She was cut off from the heat and noise and ugliness of the world outside. She sat alone, rereading what she had written.

My darling, this is a love letter to you.

You will never read it, and perhaps that is just as well. I would not add to the pain you suffered or the lonely moments you endured, locked in the solitude of your personal, hidden hell.

Yet, selfishly, I would wish these words could reach you. Then you would know what you meant to me. What you mean to me still. Today, tomorrow and beyond. I think you do know. For what is transcribed on the heart transcends the petty human limitations of time and space. Apart we are together, you and I. Two who are one. Eternally welded by the links of the love we shared.

I hope you can remember those brief, shining hours. Gratitude is such a tiny word for a life that included your presence. But I am grateful to you. I mingled my tears with yours, echoed your laughter, joined in the delight you felt at your hard-won triumphs. I thrilled to your strength and cursed God for your burdens, wishing I could take them from you, seeking the courage to share and the wisdom to understand Why. Sometimes I succeeded, seeing the bright glimmer of solution in the blackness of the puzzle. Often I was more lost than you, failing you when you needed me most.

But even as I damned the Creator who made you as you were, I adored Him for the very fact of your being. My rage was as nothing compared to the thankfulness for His bringing you into life. My life.

What joy we found in that life! What happiness was allowed two people so alike and so different. Different. That was the word people used to describe you. But you were not different. You were so like the others, yet uniquely yourself. In the bad times you were stubborn and sulky, rebellious and angry, filled with frustration. But in the golden days you were tender and trusting, full of love and warmth and charm. That was the real you: neither angel nor devil, but with irresistible overtones of both.

You were not perfect, my darling. Not even in my enchanted eyes. And yet it seems, in retrospect, the very imperfections that threatened to break my heart were the ones that brought us closer together . . . to share the cruel hurts and savor the dreams that were always just beyond our reach.

The dreams were never to be. Such beautiful dreams. Even as I hoped for their fulfillment, I knew they were no more than the wishful thinking of this grown-up child. But I still believe in dreams, dearest. I've seen them come true for others who love as we loved, and have blind, abiding faith in each other as we did . . .

She stopped reading and stared sightlessly across the room, seeing none of the treasures in it. She saw, instead, the young woman who'd been herself in another time. A determined young woman, wrapped in the ignorant assurance of youth. How supremely confident of the future she'd been. How certain of her competence. No mountain of misunderstanding defied her. No hill of hatred was too tall to level. How could she know always is not forever?

And yet what a vulnerable thing she'd been. So easily wounded for all her façade of self-sufficiency and poise. I was such an incurable romantic, Susan thought. Emotion seemed more valid than experience, for I had so much of the former and so little of the latter. I thought I could deny the truths that offended me, rebel against an older, wiser world that waited, perhaps with regret, to bring me to my knees.

If arrogance is the heady wine of youth, then humility must be its eternal hangover.

I've drunk the wine and found it bitter. Yet I welcome this lifetime of mornings-after.

For they are strangely sweet on the tongue.

Chapter One

Later, when she tried to make sense of everything, Susan realized that the first twenty-two years of her life in no way prepared her for those that were to follow. They had been uncomplicated, eternally trouble-free, naïvely happy in an almost mindless and pleasantly anonymous way.

She grew up, an only child, in a sprawling old house in suburban Bronxville, New York, a gentle Westchester community fifteen miles and twenty-eight minutes on the commuter train from Manhattan. Her parents, Wilson and Beatrice Langdon, were second-generation products of this moderately affluent area, childhood sweethearts who'd married in 1939 and produced the delicate blond, brown-eyed daughter a year later. Wilson had enlisted in the Air Force in World War II, though as a married man with a child he might have been exempt, and Susan carried dim memories of a father in uniform returning hale and handsome to the big house on Sunset Avenue. She had no traumatic recollection of the war or of Beatrice's anguish all through that terrible time. Her father and mother, it seemed to her, had always been there, loving her and each other, fitting gracefully into the Edwardian atmosphere of the village whose stable population was only about six thousand.

It had been the best of worlds. Near enough to New York to let a little girl enjoy the ease and freedom of "country living," with playmates and tree-houses and neighborhood "secret societies." Later there was golf at the Siwanoy Country Club and tennis at the Bronxville Field Club. She dated local boys and brothers of her classmates at Sarah Lawrence College, joined the Junior League, made a modest debut as befitted the daughter of a vice-president of the Chase Manhattan Bank, and, in 1962, at the age of twenty-two, got a job on *Vogue* as assistant to the Features Editor. ("Probably," she would say later, "on the strength of the fact that I come from the same town in which Kate Douglas Wiggin wrote *Rebecca of Sunnybrook Farm*. And Dorothy Thompson practically *commuted* to Berlin from Bronxville in the '30s!")

In any case, she adored her boss, Kate Fenton, loved the fashion magazine's zany atmosphere, made friends with other young women very much like herself who could afford to work for the glamour of the job rather than the modest salary. Her father subsidized her earnings when, after a year, she guardedly suggested she'd like to share an apartment in Manhattan with one of the other assistant editors. The Langdons hated to have her leave home, but they were realistic about it. Young women like Susan were entitled to freedom. Besides, they had faith in their daughter. She was a cheerful, levelheaded, knowledgeable young person, unlike so many young people in the '60s. They had (thank God) no worries about drugs or radical movements or other rebellious tendencies. She'd left their house, but the ties of affection and respect were strong, the contact continuous and their daughter's obvious delight with her new world was a constant source of pleasure for Wil and Bea Langdon.

But there were troublesome things about her independence that Susan kept from her parents. Liberal and understanding as they were, the "generation gap" existed. She did not want them to know that she was no longer a virgin, though she was not silly enough to believe that they did not suspect. Her "affairs" since she'd left home had not been casual. She was not a

10

promiscuous girl. In many ways, she was surprisingly innocent and stubbornly idealistic, always believing herself in love, never accepting the popular attitude that sex was only an exciting temporary adventure. She could not separate the physical from the emotional, could not take love-making as a quick, insignificant encounter. She had slept with only two young men and secretly expected, in each case, that the relationship would be long-term and "meaningful." When it was not, she was heavyhearted and angry with herself for her old-fashioned outlook and her inability to handle sex in the matter-of-fact fashion of the 1960s. Almost apologetically, she discussed this "weakness" with her roommate and best friend, Evelyn Maxwell, a young woman of her own age and approximate background who also worked at *Vogue*. Evie was less sentimental, more experienced, yet gentle and understanding.

"Look, Sue, you've got to understand how *men* feel these days. We've declared our independence, financially and socially. They expect we've also taken the male point of view about our physical needs. This isn't your mother's day when sex, for girls like us, was an undeclared proposal of marriage. You meet a fellow, you dig each other and eventually you end up in bed, enjoying it. For a night or several nights or a few months. But it doesn't mean you're going to be with him for a lifetime, or that he loves you. Or that you should talk yourself into believing *you* love *him*."

Evie was right, of course, Susan told herself. She remembered Professor Higgins' song in *My Fair Lady* . . . something about "Why can't a woman be more like a man?" Today a woman could be. She had to be. It was outmoded, stupid to believe that intimacy between people need be more than a healthy, therapeutic release. Sex was more honest, more satisfying than the fumbling, frustrating "heavy necking" of her high school and college days. She was no longer a skittish teen-ager or a chaste debutante. She was a woman, with a woman's needs. Where was her perspective, her humor? Why did she make such a big deal of "giving

11

herself"? Even the expression was wrong. Victorian women "gave themselves." A hundred years later their great-granddaughters took as much as they gave—and accepted the pleasure for what it was, without guilt or foolish hopes.

But she never really believed what she finally was logically obliged to accept: that passionate words and acts were momentary things. She didn't believe it then or for the rest of her life. The sense that her body and the sharing of it involved dignity and self-esteem stayed with her always. And those who knew her best knew Susan would never truly think otherwise.

Kate Fenton was one of those. Her assistant did not discuss these feelings with her superior at the magazine, but the Features Editor had developed an unusually personal attachment to and understanding of the young woman who'd been "handed to her" by the personnel department. Susan was unlike the long line of empty-headed, indifferent creatures who'd preceded her in the job. For one thing, she took it seriously and wanted to learn. She had perception and imagination, along with a willingness to work hard and an intuitive awareness of what interested the readers of *Vogue*. These were the same traits on which Kate prided herself. She's me as I was twenty-odd years ago, Kate often thought. But she won't end up like me, married to her job, though she has enormous potential. She's not one of those bored little idiots who drift through the halls of this magazine, marking time between their coming-out parties and their rigidly prescribed marriages to "suitable" young men. Susan could be a good editor. But, Kate thought cynically, she'll probably throw it all away for some young broker or banker who'll set her up in a house in Scarsdale and limit her mental capabilities to planning dinner parties for his clients. Oh yes, she'll marry. But I hope it's to someone who appreciates her. Not one of those selfish young studs I hear her talking to on the phone. Not one of those arrogant, overbearing males with whom she's

12

been so enamored in the past two years, and who obviously let her down.

There was no need for Susan to tell Kate how she felt about her "romances." Kate knew. She'd been the same when she was in her twenties—open, giving, believing the "sweet talk" that always came to nothing. Realization had come early to Kate. She liked men. She simply didn't want to marry, and she refused the chances she had. For twenty-five years the magazine had been her mate, demanding all the passion and dedication of which she was capable. She was not dissatisfied with the alliance. She'd come a long way from "little Mary-Kate Fenton" of Selma, Alabama. She'd dropped the Southern accent along with the first half of her name, had become a power in social and artistic circles, on a first-name basis with the great of the theatre, the concert halls, the "salons" of New York and Paris and Washington, D.C. She was known for her sophistication and her brittle wit and widely quoted among awed junior members of the staff, most of whom were terrified of her. Susan was not. That was another thing Kate liked about the girl. She was respectful but not fawningly deferential. For the first time in many years, Kate felt she was working with someone who genuinely admired her as a person rather than an "institution." She half-wished Susan would opt for a lifelong career, even while she doubted it. In any case, she was not the type to hang around as an assistant for twenty years until Kate retired and bequeathed her the job. If Susan kept on working it would, sooner or later, be somewhere else. She was too bright not to want a number-one spot of her own, something she couldn't have at *Vogue* as long as Kate Fenton was alive. And Kate Fenton planned to stay alive for a long, long time. She came from a long line of iron-willed Southern women who lived forever, dominating their families while appearing helplessly "female," dictating to servants while oozing benevolence, doing "good works" to satisfy their vanities rather than giving selflessly of themselves. Kate hated her "genteel" back-

13

ground. "I never go south of the Mason-Dixon Line if I can help it," she often said. "For that matter, anything below Fiftieth Street gives me shudders."

Once, when they were lunching together, Susan shyly asked Kate why she'd never married.

"I'm sure you could have. You're so attractive and witty and bright. I hope I'm not stepping out of line, Kate, but didn't you ever want to?"

"Yes, I wanted to. When I was your age and for a few years more I positively wallowed in romantic fantasies—none of which came true. And then one morning I woke up and said, 'Kate, old girl, unrequited love is a bore. You're never going to find that dream man, so forget it.' And I have forgotten it. Love and marriage, I mean. I've had my moments over the years. I still have them and I hope I will until I'm eighty-five and buying the services of some totally insincere but hungry young man fifty years my junior." Kate laughed. "That sounds as tough as I'm popularly supposed to be, doesn't it? But it's true, Susan. At least partly. The other part is that I can't bear making a fool of myself. I detest failure in any form, particularly my own. And I'm too selfish not to fail a husband . . . or I'd pick one who couldn't fulfill all those old Galahad dreams I still carry around. No, marriage isn't for me. I'm not bright enough to make it work." She speared a shrimp savagely, and without looking up from her salad, asked, "Are *you?*"

"I don't know. So far, it doesn't seem that way."

"Unrequited love," Kate repeated. "To you it's still tears and self-reproach. It takes a while to realize it's dreary. Oh hell, cheer up, kiddo! You may yet find that rare and exotic species who knows how to give as well as take. I'm rooting for you, you know. I don't recommend my way of life for anybody else. I hope you find the man you want, even if it means losing the best damned assistant I ever had."

Susan smiled. "You'll never lose me. Even if I find that 'rare and exotic creature' you'll be one of the best friends I ever had—or probably ever will have. I'll always be in your life, Kate. And I hope you'll always be in mine."

"You can lay odds on it." The older woman seemed suddenly embarrassed. "Listen, I want to charge this lunch on the expense account, so let's talk business to make it legitimate. In the editorial meeting this morning, we decided to do a feature on Richard Antonini. I think you should handle it."

"Antonini? The young one? The concert pianist? I heard him last year at Carnegie Hall. He's sensational!"

Kate arched an eyebrow. "So I'm led to believe. And not only at the keyboard. In the dear old South we used to call his kind 'lady-killers.' Well, why not? He's twenty-eight, handsome and a genius. A veritable young lion, from a long pride of lions. God! Papa Giovanni must be nearing seventy and still conducting major symphonies and minor infidelities. Brother Sergio, an upcoming conductor, is following Daddy's footsteps—in *every* way. But the word is that Richard's older brother, Walter, the composer, prefers the company of young men to that of his wife and children. Quite a family."

"Isn't there a sister, too?"

"Yes. Grace or Geraldine. Something like that. No. Gloria, that's her name. She's the ugly, untalented duckling. A big horsy dame who bosses everybody around, including her husband."

"Richard Antonini isn't married, is he?"

"No. He's the only chick Mama Maria has left, and from what I hear she damn well means to hold onto him. I've met the powerful Signora a few times. A combination of Lucretia Borgia and Hitler. Smooth and sinister. Sometimes known as 'the velvet knife.' Maria really runs the show. Manages the maestro's career. Dictates to the kids. And *their* kids. Richard's her baby *and* her favorite. Would you believe at twenty-eight he still lives with his parents in a big house on East Seventieth Street? That's where you'll interview him, by the way. Call him when you get back to the office. I have

15

the unlisted number. Set up a date. We'll get Irving Penn to take the photograph later."

"I'd better bone up on classical music. It's never been one of my better subjects."

"I wouldn't worry, if I were you. Richard's a publicity hound. He'll feed you the answers without the questions. Then he'll probably make a pass at you."

Susan laughed. "You must be kidding! Make a pass at *me* when all the rich, beautiful women in the world are throwing themselves at him? What would he want of a poor girl-reporter like me?"

"Now *that*," Kate said, "is one of the silliest questions I've ever heard you ask."

Chapter Two

From the outside, the Antoninis' town house was typical of the relatively few remaining private residences of the New York rich. As Susan stepped out of the taxi, she took in the kitchen windows fronting the street level, the authoritative sign announcing the watchful private eye of Holmes Protection, the brilliantly shined brass and the forbidding black-lacquered door with multiple locks.

It was, she thought, like a fortress. Of course it had to be. Inside were precious people and, undoubtedly, precious possessions, both of which had to be guarded from the curious eyes of the public and the terrifying invasion of burglars. What was it like to be rich and famous? Fun, she supposed. But also laden with responsibilities, restrictive and probably quite dull at times.

She rang the bell, saw an eye through the tiny peephole before she heard the unbolting of locks and bolts. A pleasant young Chinese man finally opened all but one safety chain and said politely, "Yes, madam?"

"I'm Susan Langdon of *Vogue*. I have an appointment with Mr. Richard Antonini."

The houseman nodded and opened the door.

"Come in, please. This way."

She stepped into a long, mirrored foyer with a black and white marble floor. At its end, through an open door, she could see a huge dining room, heavy with dark, Italian-looking furniture and dominated by an enormous crystal chandelier. To her right was a winding staircase, richly carpeted, and beside it a small private elevator. Quite close by she could hear the sound of a piano.

"Mr. Richard is in drawing room on second floor. You go right up. You wish to take stairs or you prefer elevator?"

"I'll walk," Susan said.

Her guide led the way. With a reporter's instinct for detail, Susan noted the niches in the stairway wall, each with an impressive bronze bust of a music immortal—Chopin, Liszt, Beethoven, Brahms. A benevolent procession of the past pointing the way to the genius of the present. The phrase had a nice ring. She must remember it when she wrote her piece.

The music was louder now, crashing, thundering. At the top of the stairs, the houseman pointed to the closed double doors at the right.

"Mr. Richard working, but he left word he be interrupted." The man raised his hand to knock, but Susan stopped him.

"May I just stand here a moment to listen?"

"Certainly, madam." The impassive Oriental face broke into a small smile. I must look as awed as I feel, Susan thought. But it's magnificent. How many people are privileged to hear Richard Antonini outside the concert hall? She returned the smile. "You needn't wait, unless you're supposed to. I'll announce myself."

When the servant bowed and left, she stood for a full five minutes listening to the music. She had no idea what it was. Something obscure and complicated and thrillingly powerful. Even with her limited knowledge, Susan was sure it was a tour de force, perhaps a seldom-performed selection that the artist would present at his next concert. There was, finally, a pause and Susan tapped lightly at the door, heard footsteps approaching and then was face to face with the most attractive man she'd ever seen.

"Miss Langdon? Come in. Did Chang abandon you?"

"At my request. He brought me up but I wanted to stand and listen for a moment. Until now, I've only heard you from a distance. It was a treat to be this close."

He grinned boyishly. "What did you think?"

"I blush to say that I haven't the faintest idea what it was, but it was breathtaking."

"It was Schumann's Third Piano Sonata, the one he called 'Concerto Without Orchestra.' And don't feel embarrassed about not recognizing it. Few people do—including many professional pianists. I'm going to try it in my next concert. Somehow, people expect me to do unexpected, the 'undiscovered masterpieces' as well as the good old standbys. I do my best to please. But enough of that! I'm keeping you standing in the doorway like an Avon lady! Come in. Have a seat. Would you like a drink?"

"No, thank you. It's a bit early in the day."

"Tea, then? Coffee? Something soft?"

"Not a thing, thanks. I know you're busy. I don't want to take up too much of your time."

Richard gave the crooked little smile she was to come to know so well. "I have plenty of time. In fact, I'm delighted to have company. Gives me an excuse to relax and talk about myself . . . two of my favorite pastimes."

He was utterly disarming. Susan didn't know quite what she'd expected. Some conceited, pompous young man, she supposed, puffed up with his own importance, perhaps overtly condescending about these "tiresome, necessary interviews." She could see now why women fell in love with him. It was not simply his looks or his fame or even the aphrodisiac of greatness that drew them to him. He had warmth, a shade of humility and, thank the Lord, a nice, light touch of humor. She looked around her, wondering how to begin.

"What a beautiful room! Everything's a treasure!"

He followed her gaze. "My parents' doing. They're a good combination. Mother has taste and Father has money." He laughed. "Actually, they were very smart and very lucky. They were buying Picassos and picking up Renoirs before most collectors caught on. In the early days they invested in signed furniture and good art. Now the insurance costs more than they paid for the stuff forty or fifty years ago. Sometimes the maestro threatens to sell it all, including this mausoleum, but of course he won't. Mother wouldn't let him. And he doesn't really want to."

"But who *would* want to? Most people would give their souls to have a house like this! It would be like living in a museum!"

"If that's your ambition I suppose you could rent a vacant wing at the Metropolitan." He sounded amused and Susan realized she was gushing. She was angry with herself for being so obviously impressed; angry with Richard for the easy confidence that took all this for granted and made light of it. He seemed to sense her resentment.

"Don't misunderstand me, please, Miss Langdon. I respect beauty in all forms. I appreciate everything in this room, but most of all I love that big, fat, black lady by the window." He pointed to the grand piano. "To me, she's more interesting than paintings, more subtle than furnishings, more alluring than women with much better legs." The deep, blue-violet eyes turned suddenly serious. "Have you any idea what a miracle a

19

fine piano is? It takes twelve months to make a great one. Longer than it would take you to make a baby, and, if you'll forgive me, the end product is infinitely more beautiful upon delivery." He warmed to his subject. "I think of my piano as a desirable woman—precisely formed, patiently molded, capable of soothing or exciting, responsive only when properly handled and unbearable when mistreated. She has feminine reactions—instantaneous and strong. She hurls and retrieves eighty-eight hammers at more than two hundred and twenty strings in fractions of a second. She has a wrest plank that can hold up under thirty-five thousand pounds of tension, yet she's so delicate that her soundboard is only eight millimeters thick in the middle and five at the edges. To me, she's the ultimate sex object, and controlling her is as exhilarating as making love." He laughed. "Sometimes more exhilarating. But I'm sure the readers of *Vogue* aren't interested in all that technical jargon about pianos."

Susan was scribbling furiously. "On the contrary. It's revealing. Your infatuation with the instrument and your seeing it in sexual terms." She hesitated. "I mean, particularly since everyone says . . ." Her voice trailed off.

"That I'm Don Juan and Frank Sinatra rolled into one? I assure you if half the things that are whispered about me were true, I'd never have time to perform at the piano. I'd be too tired to get out of bed. Not that I don't like women. I do. Very much. Especially bright and pretty ones."

Kate's half-serious words came back to her. When she answered, she sounded very cold, very professional.

"I'm sure you do, Mr. Antonini, but we leave those things to the fan magazines. We're not interested in your personal life . . . at least not the romantic side of it."

"What, then? Shall we have a heavy discussion about music? A Freudian one about my childhood? A boring one about my family?" He was teasing her. "Name your weapons. I'm all yours."

20

Damn the man. He was so sure of himself and yet she couldn't dislike him. She struggled for poise.

"Let's talk about Richard Antonini the person. Not the silly fan magazine stuff, like what you eat for breakfast or what you—wear to bed. Tell me. Are you at all a political creature? How do you feel about Viet Nam? Let's discuss the world in 1964 from a young man's point of view."

It was his turn to sound cold. "What are you really asking me, Miss Langdon? Why, at twenty-eight, I'm not in the Army? You'll be disappointed by the answer. It wasn't money or influence that's kept me out. Not even a conscientious objection. Nothing more glamorous than a bad back that goes out every now and then and drives me up the wall and into a most repulsive brace. As for politics, I find them unutterably boring. Jack Kennedy was a nice fellow and I'm sorry he's dead. But all we had in common were some mutual friends and trouble with our spines."

It was a not-too-subtle rebuff. Susan wanted to ask him what he thought about the morality of the young, the emerging role of women, subjects she'd planned to get into when she wrote this damned profile. But she was not going to get anywhere on that track. She went to safer ground, consulting the list of questions she'd prepared. "Let's talk about the very young you, about how you got into music, and what your day-to-day life is like."

"Good diversionary tactic. Okay. I was born into a musical family. Father, brothers, all top-flight, as I'm sure you know. Climbed onto the piano stool at five and have spent at least five or six hours in the same spot every day since. I still take lessons—don't look so surprised, most pianists do—from a wonderful, miraculous, terrible ogre of a genius-lady on Central Park West. She's the Ilsa Koch of the keyboard and I adore her. When I'm not being a pupil, I'm practicing, either here or in the basement of Steinway Hall. And when I'm not doing that, I'm on the road more than half the year. Life isn't all Carnegie Hall for me. Not yet. It's

21

also tank-towns and cold pizzas—as well as Los Angeles and Boston and Houston and the lush life. And when I'm not traveling and concertizing, I'm giving interviews like this. Or recording. Or accepting paralytically dull invitations to the homes of rich and influential people who can 'further my career.' Or, once in a blessed while, having dinner with a gorgeous lady and sometimes," Richard said wickedly, "scoring in the more vulgar sense of the word."

In spite of her determination to be impersonal, Susan found herself smiling as she wrote.

"You're very close to your family, aren't you?"

"Very. As you see, I still live at home, which is not a case of arrested development but a matter of convenience since I'm in New York so little. I also go upstate to Pound Ridge where we have a big old place on which the brothers and sister and in-laws and offspring converge regularly. I'm an uncle six times and my alarmingly fertile sister is about to make it seven."

"But *you've* never married? Why not?"

"Have *you?*"

"No."

"Why not?"

"Because I've never found anyone who loved me the way I loved him." Susan's frankness surprised her.

"Then you don't have to ask me that question, do you?" Richard said. "You can just echo your own answer." He reached out and took her hand. The fingers were long, slim, the grasp warm and firm. "Susan. May I say 'Susan?' This has become a sparring match, hasn't it? Practically everything we've talked about you could find in a publicity release my press agent could send you. Do you realize we're shy with each other? Isn't that extraordinary?"

"I'm not shy," she lied, defensively. "You're not an easy man to interview, Mr. Antonini, for all your apparent frankness."

"Why not try 'Richard'?"

"All right. Richard. You make it difficult. I don't quite know why, but you do."

22

"I'm sorry. It's not intentional. I want a good story. So do you. Ask me anything you like. I swear I'll answer truthfully."

Susan thought. "Let's go back to the fact that you're not married. Not *my* answer. *Yours.*"

"I probably will marry one day. My parents are happily married. There's a good example for me. Maybe too good. Make of it what you will, for I'm sure it means something, but I have yet to meet a woman with the extraordinary qualities of my mother. I suppose you'd say she's the 'ultimate piano.' How's that for frankness?"

"Not bad." Susan felt in control now, so much in command that she was emboldened to ask another question on her list. "Your extraordinary dedication to music. Is it real or a defense? Family orientation surely has been very important in your life. Competition in a house full of geniuses must be enormous. A father who's a legend. Super-achieving older brothers with more years of fame. Are you trying to prove something to yourself or them? The Antoninis are a dynasty, with a strong matriarchal influence. Aren't you really a self-contained empire like the Roosevelts or the Kennedys?" She stopped, suddenly nervous about such intimate, probing questions. He'd probably order her out of the house. But instead he simply looked thoughtful.

"My dedication to my work is real," he said slowly. "Competitive? Probably, but in a healthy, extroverted way. A dynasty? We've been made to seem so in the press, but I don't think we're that different from many families. Close-knit. Protective of our own. Outside of our work we live quite ordinary lives, like any big tribe. You don't believe that, do you, Susan?"

"No," she said softly, "I'm not sure I do." She glanced at the French clock on the mantel and was amazed to see that an hour had passed. She had enough meat for her story and there was plenty of background. She stood up, put her notebook in her purse and extended her hand. "Thank you for your time. I'll try to do a good interview. For both of us."

23

"I'm sure you will. I'll look forward to it."

He took her to the door and kissed her hand formally. "You're a charming girl, Susan. I hope we'll meet again."

"I'll come to your next New York concert if I can get tickets."

"I'll send you a pair."

"Oh no! I didn't mean it that way. I wasn't hinting!"

Richard smiled. "I know you weren't. You wouldn't know how to be conniving. Perhaps, if I may say so for your own sake, you'd do well to learn."

She slept badly that night. It was not only because she felt she'd done a bad job on the interview. She thought she was well prepared, but she'd handled it so awkwardly that Richard had been compelled to save it for her. That was part of it. It was unlike her to be so unprofessional and she was annoyed. But another part of her restlessness was the ridiculous instant attraction she felt for the man himself. She told herself she was being stupid. She'd never see or hear from him again. Why should she? She was no more to him than a hundred other star-struck reporters, a hundred thousand worshipful followers. And yet she fantasized their falling in love, even marrying and having wonderful children. She saw herself the devoted, envied wife of a young genius, becoming part of the fabulous Antonini clan, catering, gladly, to her husband's needs, traveling with him, being with him and their family in some elegant town house of their own. I must be losing my mind, Susan thought in the dark hours. It's a schoolgirl crush on a movie star—infantile and impossible. And yet she couldn't forget the way he'd looked at her, taken her hand. And the strange remark about their being shy with each other. Was he trying to tell her that he also felt their meeting was important? He'd said he'd like to see her again. And what did all that add up to, for God's sake? Nothing. Absolute zero. Zilch. Yet

24

no man had ever had such an impact on her. She remembered everything about him. The way he moved and smiled, the way his voice sounded when he spoke passionately of his music, loyally of his family, somewhat wistfully of his life. She tried to turn her thoughts away from Richard Antonini the desirable man and focus on what she'd write about him. It had been an interview with odd, indefinable overtones. And it would be difficult to translate into a good, meaty feature.

It was. Susan struggled at her typewriter for three hours the next morning, hating the way the piece kept coming out. Half a dozen times she ripped the paper out of the machine and wadded it into a ball which she threw angrily into the wastepaper basket. She felt Kate watching her, without comment but aware that this was not her assistant's usual easy, fluent style.

At one o'clock, Susan shoved her chair back from the desk and announced she was going to lunch.

"I take it the Antonini assignment is a bitch," Kate said calmly. "What's the problem?"

"I don't know. I can't get the essence of him. When we talked it seemed interesting, even 'intellectual' in spots. But when I try to write it, it keeps coming out like a cross between a fan letter and a Steinway piano brochure. It's terrible. Unprintable. Damn it, Kate, I really want to do a good 'think piece' on him. He's important and exciting and I keep making him sound like a plastic toy!"

"Why shouldn't you? That's essentially what he is. Gifted, yes. Perhaps even great. But still a creation of our times. I'm sure Richard is like all the Antoninis. None of them is real flesh and blood. They're romantic, improbable sex objects. The press and the public hero-worship glamorous people with talent. We expect them to be above us. It's our society's subconscious wish for royalty. With no real kings and queens and princes, we try to turn our matinee idols into regal beings. We long to endow them with superhuman gifts— such as awesome intelligence and infinite wisdom. And

25

all they have, outside of their God-given talent, is a well-cultivated flair for self-promotion. Hell, I told that bunch in the editorial meeting that young Richard wasn't serious feature material! He should be reviewed by our music critic or left to the society columns. I'm not surprised Prince Charming had nothing meaningful to say. I doubt he ever thinks about anything but himself, his music and his women, in that order."

Susan felt unreasonably annoyed. "Then why did you agree to do the feature?"

"Dear girl, I am not THE editor. I am only AN editor. Contrary to what they say in the ladies' room, I do not win all my battles."

"I still think there's something important here," Susan said stubbornly. "He's a thinking, complicated artist with a lot to say. It's just that I don't know how to write it."

"Take a suggestion? Stop trying to make Richard Antonini sound like Adlai Stevenson by Albert Schweitzer out of Marianne Moore. Tell it like it is. He's the gifted, hard-working, moderately intelligent, infinitely charming youngest son of a famous family. Make him human, Susan. Make every woman want to mother him. Play up his 'loneliness' and his little boy appeal. Give him the other-worldliness that's already his image . . . the dreamy, sensual bachelor, the idealistic child-man, the dedicated artist. Goop it up with culture and charisma. He has enough of both, and that's what people want to believe in. It's an unbeatable combination . . . the kind dreams are made of. And it'll make a piece that will be the most tear-stained page in the October issue."

"I can't be phony about him."

"Who's asking you? On the contrary, I'm advising you to tell the truth—not gloss him over with the veneer of cerebral greatness which is what I suspect you're struggling to do." Kate looked at her sharply, suddenly aware. "You were really taken with Antonini, weren't you? Susan dear, you're only twenty-four but I

26

thought you were much too worldly to be snowed by that practiced professional charm. Was I right? Did he make a pass at you? Is that what this is all about?"

"Good Lord, no! He was a perfect gentleman."

"And you wish he hadn't been."

"Yes. No. I'm not sure. Anyway, what does it matter? Even if he noticed me, it would only be more of the same. I'd make a fool of myself as usual. Especially with a man like that." She felt a need to unburden herself. "Do you know, Kate, that I thought about him all last night? I even imagined what it would be like if we fell in love. Now *that* is crazy, even for me! I spend one hour with a charmer and I'm daydreaming myself into a lifetime romance! Next thing you know I'll be putting his picture up on my bulletin board—the way the secretaries all have photographs of Paul Newman!" She managed to laugh. "Okay. I feel better. I think I can get Antonini out of my head and onto paper after lunch. Join me? I might go wild and have a Bloody Mary to drown my sorrows."

"You're on," Kate said. "I'll even pay."

They came back at three o'clock, a little high and a great deal more relaxed. They glanced at the messages their shared secretary had left on their desks. The second one Susan picked up made her catch her breath. Wordlessly, she handed it to Kate. It was marked 2:25. Kate read it aloud.

" 'Mr. Richard Antonini called. Would like you to dine with him this evening at La Caravelle. Please call him at home.' "

"I don't believe it," Susan said. "It must be a joke."

"Played by whom? It's not my kind of thing. Besides, I was with you, remember?"

Susan didn't answer.

"You're going, of course."

"If I were smart, I wouldn't. I'd stop this whole thing right now, before it starts."

"So?"

Susan smiled. "I never was too bright."

Chapter Three

He'd been pleased but not surprised when Susan returned his call and accepted the dinner invitation.

"Lovely," Richard said. "I'm glad you're free. Give me your address and I'll pick you up. About eight?"

She gave him the number on Fifty-second Street and then added, "Just have the doorman ring up and I'll come right down."

Afterward, she wondered why she'd done that. She wasn't ashamed of the apartment. It was no Antonini mansion, but it was attractively furnished and suitable for two young working women. And it wasn't that she didn't want him to meet Evie, who was equally presentable and the last girl in the world who'd try to steal a roommate's date. I suppose I want to feel as though I'm stepping out into a whole new world, Susan thought. Like Cinderella taking the coach to the ball. I want to drift down and find Richard waiting for me. She hoped he'd be in a chauffeured limousine. She always said that owning one was her ultimate wish. Not sables or yachts or forty-kàrat diamonds, but her own private car and driver. She used to kid about it with her mother. "When I become rich and famous that will be my first important acquisition. Think of the advantages. You never have to own a winter coat, right? And I know it would add ten years to my life if I didn't have to worry about catching cabs, running from one corner to another like some crazed creature!"

Bea Langdon had smiled. "It's not a bad ambition, but you'll need a better-paying job or a rich husband to realize it."

Remembering, Susan told herself that she had gotten neither and was unlikely to. The few times she'd gone to business dinner-dances as the guest of rich manufacturers, she'd reveled in the luxury of a big black Cadillac, knowing it was waiting at the curb no matter what hour they left the party. She'd love it if Richard Antonini provided the same elegant touch, even if it was equally temporary and she was sure it would be. They'd have one pleasant evening and he'd be on his way. She had to be sensible and believe that.

She wondered why this celebrity-bachelor had asked her out at all. Susan underrated her appearance, her charm, her unstudied sensuality. She was unaware of how extraordinarily attractive she was, and also how few totally alluring women there really were in this world. As she dressed, fretting over the appropriate thing to wear, she wished she'd had the will-power to refuse this last-minute invitation. It would have been smarter to play hard-to-get. Not be available on such short notice. Pretend her engagement book was so full she couldn't fit in a date with Richard for another week at least. That's the way the clever girls would have done it. But she never was clever about men. She persisted in believing that she could be honest and let a man she liked *know* she liked him. It never worked. She'd found that out. Still, she couldn't change, couldn't stop hoping that someone, someday, would understand and appreciate the foolishness of this eternal game-playing between the sexes.

A few minutes after eight the house phone rang and the doorman announced that Mr. Antonini was waiting. She started to leave immediately, calling good

29

night to Evie, who was dressing for her own date. "See you later," Susan added.

Her roommate came to the door. "*Will* you?"

Susan paused in the act of pulling a little black silk shawl around her. It was a hot June night but restaurants were always arctically air-conditioned. "What do you mean, '*Will* you?' I may be late, but you're usually *later*."

"I meant will you be home *at all?*"

"What kind of a dumb question is that? I'm just going out to dinner with a man I met once!"

"And have been mooning over ever since."

"I have not been mooning! Evie, stop this! You sound as mother-hennish as Kate! For your information, I am not planning to spend the night with Richard Antonini, even if he is after my lily-white body, which I very much doubt."

"Why doubt? You know his reputation. Everybody does. Not that it matters. I think it would be super to go to bed with a celebrity. A nice change from the sweet paupers who usually buy us a hamburger at P.J. Clarke's and want a return equivalent to a diamond bracelet. With Richard you might even *get* a diamond bracelet."

"I don't want one," Susan said crossly. "And I think the whole world's crazy on the subject of Antonini's sexual prowess. Isn't it possible that he simply wants to have dinner and talk?"

"Nope."

Susan gave an exasperated sigh. "Honestly! This is a helluva way to start an evening. I feel like I'm dating Young Bluebeard."

Evie turned away, flapping a languid hand. "I don't see you rushing to the house phone to send him away."

He was waiting on the sidewalk, the door of the hoped-for limousine open.

"Hello," he said. "I was getting worried. I thought maybe you weren't coming down."

"I'm sorry. A last-minute discussion with my roommate."

"No problem. You look sensational. I'm glad to see you again."

She nearly said, with her usual candor, "Why? What on earth made you call?" But for once she resisted, though there was no mistaking the look in her eyes when she said softly, "And *I'm* glad to see *you. Very glad.*"

He liked the way heads turned and eyes watched them speculatively when they walked into the restaurant. He wasn't sure whether it was because they recognized him or because Susan was so beautiful. She stood out in this room of overdressed, overjeweled women. The scoop-necked, clinging black jersey dress showed off her lovely full bosom, her incredibly tiny waist. The dress hugged her, not too tightly but revealingly. For a moment, Richard wished he'd asked her to come to the house for a few drinks before dinner. The family was in Westchester for the summer.

"Signor Antonini!" The maître d' practically fell over himself. "An honor, sir! And Madame. *Bon soir.* Your usual table?"

"Yes, please."

They were led to a corner in the back. Susan was surprised. She'd only been in this ultraswank restaurant for lunch, but she knew the "right place" to sit was in the corridor between the front door and this room. Richard seemed to read her mind.

"Hope you don't mind not sitting up front. I really prefer a little privacy when I dine."

Susan smiled, flattered *he* knew *she* knew about the "best" tables. What he really meant was that he was so secure he didn't need to be stared at in restaurants.

"This is much nicer," she said, settling on the banquette. "I always feel as though I'm eating in a department-store window when I'm in that alleyway."

Richard ordered their aperitifs and, with her agreement, chose dinner for them. Then he sat back and regarded her appraisingly.

"When we met I thought you were pretty. I was wrong. You're beautiful. It's all right to say that, isn't it? Now that we're not 'on business'?"

"I never turn down a compliment."

"Tell me about Susan Langdon," he said.

"Turn-about is fair play? It's your turn to do the interviewing?"

He grinned, a boyish, disarming crinkling of the face. "Sure. Why not? You have me at a disadvantage. You know all about me and I know nothing about you."

"All right, though I warn you it's a boring biography."

She told him about her parents and her early life, her schooling and the "silly little debut." She was enthusiastic about her job and full of amusing anecdotes about her boss.

"That's about it," she said. "See? I told you it was boring."

"Not at all. I think you have a happy life, Susan. Normal. Full of people who love you."

She brushed it aside. "Compared to yours, it's bland. But yes, I'm lucky. Never really wanted for anything. In fact, sometimes I feel overprivileged, as though I don't give enough in return. I should do more active things outside my job."

"Don't tell me you're into a lot of 'do-gooder' stuff!"

"Don't look so scandalized. I'm not, but there's a need for it. The world is polluted, Richard. Not just ecologically, but socially, morally. People are hungry and discriminated against and used! Those of us who have so much have an obligation to make any contribution we can. Not just giving money or going to charity balls. We ought to speak out for those who can't speak for themselves. Really roll up our sleeves and go to work." She stopped. "I'm sorry. I'm doing what my roommate calls my 'soapbox number'—all talk and no action. Let's change the subject."

"You amaze me. I'd have thought you would be more interested in your own future. Most girls are."

"I like to think I'm not 'most girls,'" Susan said, softening the words with a smile. "My classmates are all married by now and most of them have a baby or two. They have mixed feelings about their old school chum: half pity that I'm not married; half envy that I have all this delicious independence."

"You honestly like the independence? Is that the real reason you haven't married?"

"No, I'm too young," Susan teased. Then she sobered. "I believe in the institution, though a lot of people don't these days. But I'm in no rush. And I told you, the famous 'Mr. Right' hasn't appeared. I'd like to be as certain as anybody possibly *can* be—which isn't really certain at all. I hope to get married one day. But if I don't, it won't be the end of the world. Thank God women don't live under those terrible social pressures any more!"

Don't they? Richard said silently. You should know my sister.

"You're a terrific girl," he said.

"Woman," Susan corrected.

"All right. Woman. Girl. Young lady. Business-person. Who cares? You're still terrific. I'm glad we're going to be friends."

"So am I."

He didn't try to make love to her that evening. He was almost more surprised by that than Susan was. It was not that she didn't attract him. She did. Enormously. The fact was, she frightened Richard a little. For the first time in his life, he felt genuinely eager to win the approval of a woman. It wasn't usually this way. In fact, never. Women had always responded to him immediately when he showed the slightest interest, cried a little when he went on to the next adventure but accepted the end of the affair and continued to adore him. For twenty-eight years he remained untouched, never truly in love. He sensed that with Susan it could be different, that it could even lead to marriage, and he wasn't sure he wanted that. Nor did he want to hurt her. *It will be better if I don't see her again*, he decided. *She's too nice, too vulnerable. And I could get involved. It would get in my way. Marriage would stifle me, though it hasn't seemed to inhibit my brothers very much. But I'm not like my brothers. Or am I? Certainly Susan is not like my sisters-in-law. She's not like Gloria either, God knows. Or even Mother.*

They stayed at Caravelle until eleven and then drove to the Carlyle Hotel to hear the pianist at the Café Carlyle. Susan enjoyed every minute of it. Shamelessly, she loved the deference everyone showed Richard. It *was* fun to be famous, with headwaiters sweeping you past dozens of people to the head of a waiting line, seating you at the best table though you had no reservation. It was amusing to have the entertainer wave from his place at the piano and later join them on the banquette in the middle of the crowded nightclub. It was exciting to realize that people recognized Richard and whispered their discovery to the others in their party.

And Richard himself was so dear. He held her hand quite openly, which made her feel proud and important. His touch excited her and she decided she would go to bed with him when he suggested it. She could handle it. It would be different this time. She knew better than to expect that a "seduction," especially by Richard Antonini, would have any long-range significance. That would keep her from being miserable when it ended. She would have had at least one glorious, unforgettable, unregretted night. Evie was right. It would be super to have sex with a celebrity. You didn't have to be in love. Not in this day and age. She had to get over that ingrained puritanical streak. She was grown-up and modern. *How everything has changed*, Susan mused, looking at Richard's handsome profile. *I was*

34

brought up to believe that "nice girls" didn't even *kiss* on the first date. Now I'm quite calmly deciding that there's nothing wrong with immediate intimacy between consenting adults.

Consequently, she was surprised and actually disappointed when they left the club at 2 A.M. and Richard gave the driver her address. He'd told her, during the evening, that his parents were in the country and he was rattling around all alone except for the servants in that big house. She interpreted this as the buildup for their going there. Apparently she was wrong, and she felt an unreasonable sense of rejection. He was literally going to "kiss her off." It was quite clear the attraction was one-sided. Well, so be it, Susan thought philosophically. Probably better this way. He'll be easier to forget if I don't know him that well.

At the entrance of her apartment he kissed her lightly. "It was a great evening, Susan. Thanks for coming."

She summoned all her dignity. "Thank *you*. I had a wonderful time."

"Hope I didn't keep you out too late."

Not late enough, she wanted to say. "Not at all. I adored every minute of it."

They stood awkwardly for a moment, he waiting to see her safely inside the building, she hoping he'd suggest another date. Finally she smiled and went inside, and Richard, with a little half-salute, turned and climbed back into the big car.

She didn't hear from him for two weeks, during which time it was impossible to forget him. Not only did she have to finish and polish the article about him, she also had to make arrangements with the photographer for his portrait session, discuss the layout with the art director, do a hundred and one things that reminded her of Richard. It seemed, too, that every paper she picked up had his name somewhere . . . in the music section in the society pages ("Richard Antonini pictured at the Southampton Junior League Art Show with debutante Ann-Marie Tillingham") and even in the gossip columns where his every dinner date was reported with the importance of some world-shaking event. She became testier and more morose. She'd told Kate about her evening, saying with pretended lightness that it was "fun and platonic," but one morning in a particularly foul mood she literally hurled the *Daily News* across the office.

"Damn! I'm sick of Richard Antonini! Two weeks ago I was hardly aware of him, and now every place I look I see that face or read the name. He gets more publicity than Lyndon Johnson!"

Kate leaned back and lit one of her endless cigarettes. "Ever heard that old cliché about a woman who thinks she's pregnant? Suddenly every woman she sees on the street is pregnant."

In spite of herself, Susan laughed. "You're right. I can't get that idiot out of my mind. I wish I'd never told anybody I was going out with him. I didn't tell many. Only you and Evie and, unfortunately, Mother. At least you two have had the good grace to keep quiet about it, but every time I call home Mother asks if I've heard from him and then I get snarky and snap at her and hate myself for it. I don't know why I'm so uptight about somebody I've seen twice and won't ever see again. It's downright infantile."

"You're playing that favorite female game called wishful thinking," Kate said. "Perfectly natural. You keep imagining how terrific it would have been if something had come of all this. Rich, handsome, famous, unmarried young men do not come along every day. Can't blame you for being disappointed. 'All sad words of tongue or pen' . . . etc., etc. I'm sorry it didn't work out, Susan. At least I *guess* I'm sorry. I'm not sure how hurt you could have been if Richard had decided to play games."

"I know. All my common sense tells me I'm better off this way. And I'll recover faster. But damn it, Kate,

36

he's special. And I really thought he liked me. A lot. He acted as though he did all that evening. How *can* I be so naïve? I'm twenty-four years old, for God's sake! Am I never going to grow up and stop believing in men?"

"Probably not. Some women never do."

"Thanks heaps! *That's* a dismal future to contemplate."

"Torturous, maybe. But not dismal. People who stop getting hurt are only half alive, Susie. They lose their dreams, their illusions, their hope-springs-eternal quality. Look at me. Tough, cynical, self-protective. That's because I developed a hard shell early. You don't want to be like that."

"You're not really like that, Kate. You only pretend to be."

"Want to bet?"

"Well, if I ever run into that egomaniac again, you can bet I'll tell him what he can do with his phony charm!"

"I'll take odds on that one too," Kate said.

The attraction was not, as Susan believed, one-sided. Richard went about his professional and social activities as usual, but every morning he awakened thinking of Susan Langdon. More than once he was tempted to call, and each time something stopped him. He tried to assess his feelings about her. She was beautiful, but not the most gorgeous creature, by far, that he'd ever known. She was brighter than most. And perhaps that was actually a deterrent, for Richard knew quite well that his intellectual capacities were limited. His formal schooling had been negligible. Mostly he'd been privately tutored, with all the emphasis and most of the time spent on his advancement from prodigy to seasoned performer. Susan's seriousness about world affairs and her sense of responsibility were matters he rarely thought of and such talk made him feel inadequate and slightly inferior, new sensations, and not pleasant ones. He honestly didn't know why he was so drawn to this girl. She was sexy in a completely understated way and he knew she'd be satisfying in bed, but surely no more so than a hundred other women. Yet he recognized, without knowing how he knew, that he was already half in love with her. It made no sense at all and he tried as hard to put Susan out of his thoughts as she tried to forget about him. He wished she'd call him and relieve him of the responsibility of instigating the next move. Girls he dated once usually did. But this one had too much pride and dignity. Class. That was the word for it. Without great wealth or background, she was the classiest young woman he'd ever met. She'd be something to own. Richard wondered whether she'd allow herself to be owned, fleetingly or, God forbid, permanently. To hell with it! There was only one way to find out. Two weeks after their only date, he broke down and called her at the office.

"Susan? Richard Antonini."

There was a fraction of silence. Then, sounding almost amused at his announcing himself by his full name, she said, "Hello, Richard Antonini. How are you?"

"Fine. I've been thinking about you."

"Have you? That's nice."

Damn. She wasn't going to make it easy. "I wondered if you were free for dinner tonight?"

He would have felt much more sure of himself if he'd known what inner turmoil those words produced. There was a longer pause this time. Susan felt Kate listening, though the editor pretended to be deeply absorbed in a manuscript. Don't be eager, Susan, she told herself. In fact, be smart and stay the hell out of it all together. You're just beginning to get him out of your head. A few more weeks of not seeing him and you won't feel that desperate unhappiness about "what might have been." That was sensible. That was logical.

"Yes, I'm free," she said.

38

He picked her up, as before, at eight. But this time when the doorman announced Mr. Antonini she asked that he be sent up. He admired the apartment, was charming to a charmed Evelyn, sat for fifteen minutes while the three of them had martinis on the rocks.

"Your driver probably thinks you've been kidnapped," Susan said.

"I'm without driver tonight. I have a cab waiting."

She was aghast. "Why on earth didn't you say so?"

"What difference does it make? He won't leave without us."

"I'll get my wrap," Susan said.

Evie followed her into the bedroom. "Now *that's* what it's like to be rich," her roommate said. "Not to let a ticking taxi meter give you palpitations. He's something else, Susie! And God, is he good-looking!"

Susan smiled. "I think I'm the world's biggest fool to even go out with him again."

"Don't be crazy. What have you got to lose?"

It was another wonderful evening. Another superb dinner, this time at Lutèce, where Susan had never been, not even for lunch. She loved the small, elegant dining room, the captain who, though less obsequious than at Caravelle, was equally impressed. She was fascinated by her menu, which had no prices on it—a "ladies' menu," as opposed to the man's, which listed the outrageous cost of the entrees.

During dinner they talked easily about inconsequential things. It was not until they got to their espresso and brandy that Richard turned suddenly serious.

"I don't know how you managed it," he said, "but you've had me crazy for two weeks. I kept hoping you'd call me."

Susan raised her eyebrows. "Telephones work both ways."

"I know." Suddenly he didn't seem the great celebrity, the confident, spoiled, uncaring darling of the columns. He seemed almost humble, appealingly uncertain. "I hoped you'd call me because I was really afraid to call you. I knew if I saw you I'd get involved. I know what you're thinking. I've been 'involved' hundreds of times. But not like this. Not emotionally. I could fall in love with you, Susan. And I have a feeling that might be terrible for both of us."

"Why?" Her voice was gentle. "Because I'd suffer so when you dropped me?"

"No. Because I don't think I could drop you."

"And that would be terrible?"

"It might be. After it was wonderful."

She didn't understand. She didn't want to. All she knew was that no matter how Richard felt, she was in love, totally and irrevocably. This might all be part of the technique. She didn't care. She sat silently, stirring her coffee, not daring to look at him.

"There's so much about me you don't know," Richard said. "I'm a vain, meteoric, selfish clod who's never been able to remain faithful. Never wanted to. I don't know if I can, Susan. I don't know if I want to try."

The foolishness and wisdom of women in love came to her. Gently, she put her hand on his.

"Why don't we let things work themselves out as they will?" Susan asked. "Don't fret about what may or may not be. Let's enjoy what we have now."

He leaned down and kissed the back of her hand. Then he rose and draped the little black scarf over her shoulders. "Come on, pretty lady. Let's go home."

This time he gave the cabdriver his address. Alternately cursing and laughing, he fumbled with keys and burglar-alarm switches, finally letting them into the foyer. He opened the elevator door next to the staircase she had climbed two weeks before.

"This way, madam," he said lightly. "Fourth floor." He imitated the elevator operator in a department store. "Fourth floor. Bachelor boutique. Superstereos, built-in bars, adjustable rheostat lighting fixtures." He paused. "And king-sized beds."

Chapter Four

"I must say, I've never seen you looking better, Susie," Bea Langdon remarked a week later when Susan went to Bronxville to have Sunday dinner with her family. "Whatever you're doing, it agrees with you."

Susan blushed. What she'd been doing every night for a week was going to bed with the most glorious, exciting man in the world. Her affair with Richard filled her with such joy that she bloomed. Even away from him she could feel the touch of those extraordinary fingers on her body, the warmth of that seeking mouth on her willing one, the ecstasy they shared in that hidden-away room on the fourth floor. She was madly, passionately in love with Richard Antonini. She'd never felt so desirable, so complete, so happy. For though nothing more had been said about the future, Susan knew this was the man she would marry. He knew it, too, though the words remained unspoken. The only specific hint of his "serious intentions" had been the invitation to go to the family house in Pound Ridge for the long Fourth-of-July weekend.

"I'd like you to meet the family." That's what he'd

41

said last night as they lay together in his bed. "Can you go to the country with me next weekend?"

She'd turned on her side, pressing her body against his. "Darling, I'd go to the end of the world with you, and you know it."

He kissed her eager mouth. "Want to know something? I've never taken a girl up to meet the clan before."

They were the most thrilling words she'd ever heard. She thought of them now as she looked at her mother's contented face. If Richard thought his parents' marriage was a good example, hers was equally good, perhaps better. Certainly it was more peaceful. From time to time in the past week, Richard had spoken, seemingly with amusement, about his famous family, and Susan's impression was that everything Kate had told her was true and then some. Temperament and eccentricity were, apparently, the name of the game. He did not go into detail, but Susan read between the lines. He adored his family but acknowledged they were, to put it mildly, difficult. And now she was going to meet them. The idea frightened her. They'd be there for the holiday. She'd get the full impact of them en masse. It was a prospect designed to unnerve even the most self-assured young woman.

"Mother, I've been invited to the Antoninis' in Pound Ridge next weekend. I haven't mentioned it, but I've been seeing Richard."

Beatrice looked interested. "So he *did* turn up again! You were getting so touchy about the subject I stopped asking."

"I know. I'm sorry I was beastly. It's just that I thought he didn't particularly like me, and I was, I don't know, feeling deflated and disappointed and all those stupid things. My ego was bruised for a while."

"And now it's healed." It was a flat statement, not a question.

"Completely. I'm terribly in love with him. And I'm sure he loves me. In fact," Susan hesitated, "I think he's going to ask me to marry him." She looked almost

42

pleadingly at her mother. "That's the first time I've dared say that aloud. I'm superstitious about it. Scared that I'll jinx the idea by mentioning it. It's too good to be true. Richard Antonini in love with me! I can't believe it. He could have any woman in the world he wanted. Why me?"

Bea Langdon bristled. "Why *not* you, for heaven's sake? You have everything—youth, beauty, brains. And he's not a god, Susie. He may be a genius, but he's human." She frowned. "From the little I know about him and his family, *he'll* be the fortunate one if he persuades you to marry him."

Susan laughed. "Darling, it won't take much persuasion. In fact, *none*. More than anything in the world, I want to be Mrs. Richard Antonini. I'm only afraid I can't live up to it."

"Live up to what? Why should you have to live up to anything?"

"You don't understand. They're all gifted. And rich. And famous."

"Notorious" is more like it, Bea thought. Like most reasonably sophisticated people, she'd read and heard a great deal about this news-making family. She might be "only a suburban housewife," but she was not naïve. Where there was smoke there was more than a blaze of publicity. There'd been too much whispering about Richard's father and brothers and their affairs with all kinds of women and men. It was gossip only hinted at and almost indulgently excused because of their "genius," but it formed a picture of emotional instability. What must the wives of Sergio and Walter go through? What, indeed, had Maria Antonini put up with all these years? Bea felt troubled. Susan was not the kind of girl to shrug off a husband's unconventional behavior or retaliate with indiscretions of her own as at least one of the "Antonini women" was reputed to do. She wasn't thick-skinned, as the matriarch of that family presumably was. For all its wealth and glamour, this was not the kind of family Bea visualized her only daughter marrying into. She felt it would be wrong.

43

Susan was too overwhelmed, too willing to see herself in an inferior role, too humbly grateful to be chosen by one of the "elite." And too blindly in love to see the pitfalls.

"Darling," Bea said now, "I do understand how flattering it must be to have someone like Richard Antonini in love with you. He's a great talent and I'm sure he's a fine young man. But don't rush into anything, Susie. You've only known him a few weeks. Your father and I want you to have whatever makes you happy, and that certainly includes the right husband, but make sure that you're not simply dazzled. Marriage is serious business. It isn't all fun and games. You're no child. You're nearly twenty-five years old, with a mind and will of your own. Look at marriage to Richard from all angles, most of all from a selfish one. And never again let me hear you even *indicate* that you have to 'live up' to anything except your own standards!"

Susan knew what her mother was trying to say. To an outside observer she must, indeed, sound like a fatuous fool. But Bea didn't understand. She didn't know Richard—his tenderness, his concern for her happiness. In this week of intimacy I've come to know the real person under the veneer of the "spoiled brat," Susan thought. I know he needs me. I know I can make him happy. I know that life with a man like this won't be easy, but I'm mature and experienced enough to handle it.

She put her arms around her mother, comforting her as though their roles were reversed and Bea the anxious child.

"There's nothing to worry about," Susan said. "I know exactly what I'm doing. This is the only man for me, Mother. I've waited a long time for him. And in spite of how I must sound to you, I'm not downgrading myself. You and Dad gave me a good base of self-confidence. Believe me, I *know* Richard will be lucky to get me." She gave a little laugh. "If, indeed, he *wants*

44

me. I could still be wishful-thinking. He hasn't asked me to marry him, after all. I only *think* he will."

"And if he doesn't?"

Susan made a theatrical gesture of mock-despair. "No problem. I'll just kill myself."

The effort to clown her way out of a serious discussion did not deceive Beatrice. If Richard didn't marry her, Susan wouldn't literally kill herself, but if there were such a thing as a broken heart she'd have one. I want so much for her, Bea thought sadly. Everything beautiful. So does Wil. Lord, please make it right. Don't let this love destroy her. Don't even let it hurt too much.

Maria Antonini replaced the telephone receiver in its cradle and went into the library, where Giovanni was intently studying a score. She stood for a moment looking at him. He was so deeply absorbed in the music he wasn't even aware of her presence. Nearly seventy, Maria thought, and still as handsome as the day I met him. More handsome, in a way. For now the thick black hair was snow-white, the heavy, sensual features slightly softened with age and success, the uncertainty of the blossoming genius now replaced by the assurance of immortality. Giovanni Antonini. The maestro. The revered. And I made him what he is. I prodded and pushed and molded an adequate young conductor into a legendary figure. I put up with his erratic behavior, his childish susceptibility to women, his inability to cope with the mundane commercial and financial aspects of his professional life. I bore him four children, including three sons who one day will be as great as he, and whose children will continue the greatness. Because I'll see to it. God knows no one else in this family can.

"Joe," she said. "Joe, Richard was on the telephone."

He looked up reluctantly.

"He's bringing a young woman up next weekend."

Giovanni shrugged. "So? The house will be full, but certainly there's room for one more."

Maria sighed impatiently. Except for music, her husband was irritatingly unaware of the nuances of anything. He honestly thought she was concerned about where this unexpected guest would sleep. Someday he would drive her mad with this total lack of comprehension.

"Of course there's room," she said now. "That's not the point."

Knowing he could not escape, he gave her his full attention. Maria's flashing eyes, the way she tugged at her big diamond ring were signs of agitation he'd come to know all too well.

"All right, my dear. What *is* the point?"

"Richard's never brought a girl here before."

Giovanni looked honestly puzzled. "Forgive me, I still don't understand. He's bringing one now. As the young people say, 'What's the big deal?' "

"You simply refuse to understand your children, don't you? You've never tried to understand any of them. Especially Richard."

Giovanni's quick temper, usually reserved for the browbeaten members of a symphony orchestra and seldom displayed at home, suddenly flared.

"Will you please, for God's sake, tell me what you're talking about? What is this nonsense, Maria, about Richard and my refusal to understand things? What is it you want me to understand?"

"I want you to understand," she said slowly and deliberately as though she were speaking to a backward child, "that Richard obviously has found a girl he's interested in. The first one he's ever brought into a closed-family situation. I would like you to realize that your youngest son may be quite seriously involved with some young woman we know nothing about. He was quite emphatic about all of us making her feel welcome. Quite emphatic indeed," Maria said angrily. "As though we had to be taught manners! I didn't care for the tone of his voice."

At last Giovanni understood. She was frightened that some other woman had become more important to "her baby" than she. She hadn't been upset when Sergio introduced them to Mary Louise or when Walter finally presented Jacqueline. As for Gloria, Maria was unabashedly relieved when their only daughter finally found someone willing to marry her. Even if that someone was an impoverished lawyer who wanted the Antonini influence and money more than the Antonini heiress. Richard was another matter. Maria's attachment to him was more intense, her ambition for him fiercer than for any of the others. It was because he was the late, unexpected, even unwanted child, the result of too much champagne on a New Year's Eve in 1935. For years, except for that night, the Antoninis had not shared a bed. When Richard was conceived, Sergio was sixteen, Walter fourteen and Gloria eleven. Maria had long since decided that sex with Joe was over, that he had strayed once too often, and she wanted no more of him. God knows she wanted no more children! She was a cold woman, frigid, he supposed, and she did not miss love-making. Only the false sentimentality of the night and the unusual amount of wine she drank enabled him to come into her bed and leave the seed that was to be Richard Antonini.

How furious she'd been when she discovered she was pregnant! Giovanni still remembered her rage—at him, at God, at everything except her own weakness. Maria did not admit to weakness in herself. Even in this case she was, in her own mind, a victim of Giovanni's selfish, ungovernable lust, not a fallible human who, for once, abandoned her rigid self-discipline.

And yet, when the baby was born she loved him more than the others. He was more beautiful as an infant, more talented as a child. He came more quickly to fame than his brothers, his career cleverly maneuvered, as Giovanni's had been, by the sharp, shrewd

47

mind of Maria. Richard was her creation and her private and personal possession. For twenty-eight years she had successfully discouraged any serious interest in other women. "Flings" were acceptable, for he was a man, with a man's animal needs. But love and marriage definitely were not.

Poor girl, Giovanni thought. Whoever you are. Heaven help you if Richard really has decided to marry you. Maria will make your life hell.

He tried to answer his wife, tried to make light of what she—probably accurately—read into this unexpected turn of events. He couldn't say what he really thought: that Richard, for all his deference to her, was as stubborn as his mother. If he decided to marry he would do so, despite anything Maria might say. Richard was the only one, himself included, who dared cross Maria. Sometimes he got away with it. Sometimes he didn't. But, perversely, she loved and respected the rebel of the family more than those who bowed unquestioningly to her dictates.

"I wouldn't worry too much, my dear," Giovanni finally said. "This may mean nothing at all. Perhaps Richard would simply like a companion for the long weekend. It must be tiresome for him sometimes, being only a son, brother, in-law and uncle. Don't get yourself upset over imagined problems."

"I never imagine anything. I *know* Richard too well."

He attempted the impossible. He tried to reason with her. "So, what if you are right? What if Richard has found someone? Is that so terrible? She's probably a nice girl. Don't you want him to be happy?"

"Happy?" She turned her eyes, now fully ablaze, on him. "I've given my life to making Richard happy! And his happiness is his music, his career, his greatness! I've devoted myself to his comfort, catered to his every wish, provided everything he needed! There's nothing I haven't done for my son! No woman could do more!"

"One can," Giovanni said softly. "She can sleep with him and give him children."

Maria turned away, furious. "You are disgusting!" she said.

"All right," Susan said, "give me the rundown once more. I want to know exactly who's who, right down to the names of the family dogs."

Richard, expertly maneuvering the Lincoln convertible along the parkway, smiled indulgently. "Sweetheart, I've been over it half a dozen times with you. Anyway, you don't have to be so thoroughly briefed. You're *visiting* my family, not *interviewing* them."

More like the other way around, Susan thought. They'll be interviewing me, all right. It was not the July sun beating down that made her hands perspire. She was terribly anxious about this weekend. "Please," she said. "I don't want to confuse your sisters-in-law or get their kids mixed up. I want to make a good impression."

"As though you wouldn't anyhow."

"I love you for the vote of confidence, but I'd still like one more run-through."

Richard sighed. "Okay. You know about the parents. You know that Sergio's my eldest brother. He's a conductor, too. He's married to Mary Louise Ryan, called Mary Lou. They have two kids—Joseph (sort of named for my father) who's fifteen, and Patricia who's twelve. Walter, my other brother, is the composer, and he's married to Jacqueline, who's always called Jacqueline. She was a Calhoun from New Orleans. Very social. They have two boys—Calhoun, thirteen, and Charles, eleven. All right so far?"

Susan nodded. She was folding a finger under for each name he mentioned, keeping track of how many there were. So far, she'd reached six adults and four children.

"Then there's my sister, Gloria, and her husband

49

Raoul Taffin. He's a lawyer. They live in Pound Ridge year round and Raoul commutes to the city. They *also* have two kids. Raoul, Jr., is five and Maria, named for you-know-who, is three. Gloria and Raoul have only been married six years. My sister was a late bloomer. She was thirty-four when she trapped Raoul and she's been making up for lost time. She's pregnant again, and, God help us, they think it's going to be twins this time!"

"Fourteen people. Plus the two of us. Good grief!"

Richard laughed. "It's not as frightening as it sounds. It's a big place. Twenty acres. And each of us has his own house, so there's hope for occasional privacy."

"Four houses?"

"Six, actually. Mrs. Lowman, the housekeeper, has her own. And then there's the pool house, which can accommodate four guests."

"Is that where I'll stay?"

"I doubt it. You'll probably stay in a guest suite in the big house with Mother and Father."

"I don't suppose I could stay with you?" She made a face. "No, of course I couldn't. That would really blow my image, wouldn't it?"

"It would blow my mother's mind, that's what it would do." He took one hand off the wheel and caught hers. "Will you relax, darling? It'll be a fun weekend. A little frenetic, maybe, but you'll have a good time. We can swim and you can play tennis if you like. And there's certain to be a daily softball game organized by Gloria. She's very big on contact sports."

"In her condition?"

"In any condition. My sister is the outdoorsy type. Always has been. That's *her* claim to fame. That and being fertility goddess of the century. Crazy lady. I think she'll probably end up with nine kids."

"Richard! She's forty years old *now!*"

"Don't think Gloria will let a little thing like that stand in her way. She may not be as unflappable as

50

Mary Lou or as glamorous as Jacqueline, but she's got 'em beat hands-down when it comes to endurance." Richard hesitated. "She also holds her husband on a tighter rein than they do." He gave a false little laugh. "Let me know if Serge or Walter tries to get too friendly. I'll take care of them."

For a moment Susan was speechless. Surely he was teasing. His own brothers try to move in on him? Nonsense. But was he lightly trying to warn her? What they said about the Antonini men must be true, she thought. But not Richard. Never Richard. She responded in the same vein.

"Don't worry. I'll use my karate chop on them. Anyway, my love, I only have eyes for you. Or hadn't you noticed?"

He seemed to relax. "I've noticed. Eyes and other delightful things."

"Lecher!"

Laughing, they pulled into the driveway of the estate and after some little distance up a winding private road arrived at the front door of the main house. "Country" indeed! Susan thought. This is a millionaire's mansion. It looks like it was built for William the Conqueror!

"Nice little place your folks have here," she said wryly, looking at the three-story stone building. "Just a simple, rural, weekend retreat. What are the other houses like—the Petit Trianon and Monticello?" She was being flippant to cover her nervousness and Richard knew it. He gave her a quick kiss before they got out of the car.

"You're such a hick," he teased, shaking his head in pretended despair. "I don't know. I just can't take you anywhere."

Take me home, she felt like saying. I'm going to lose you here. I can't live up to this. I'm a stranger. And scared to death. Then she remembered Bea Langdon's words. Why was she worrying about "living up" to anything? Richard loved her. It was no mere whim to bring her here. He must feel sure she'd fit into the

51

family, that they'd all like each other. Suddenly she felt better. It was going to be all right. This wasn't the end. It was the beginning.

Chapter Five

They were the last to arrive, for Susan, the only one with a "real job," had not been able to get away as early as she hoped. When she and Richard walked into the living room, there seemed to be dozens of people waiting for them, people of all ages, all of them looking appraisingly at her, hopefully reserving judgment. A small woman, not more than five feet two and a hundred pounds, wearing a Givenchy pants-suit, came quickly toward them, hand outstretched in welcome, a "perfect hostess" smile on her lips.

"Mother," Richard said, "this is Susan."

Maria took Susan's hand in both of hers. "I would have known. Welcome, my dear! How chic you look! But of course you would. An associate editor of *Vogue!* I'm delighted to have you here, Susan. Richard has told me so much about you. I've been looking forward to this visit."

Richard could hardly contain his amusement and his surprise. Maria was turning on her charm, had taken her "darling pills" as the family referred to this façade of warmth and pleasure. The act always threw strangers off balance. Only the family knew that when Maria was this cordial she was covering an instant dislike or distrust of the person, or plotting his undoing inside her well-tinted, well-coiffed little head. "Beware of Mother when she gushes" was the watchword in the family. "She's up to no good." Richard had witnessed this polished performance many times, played for all kinds of people, and had always found it transparently funny. But this time there was an added dimension of surprise. He had told her almost nothing about Susan beyond the fact that she worked on *Vogue*. Maria must have gone to the trouble of looking up Susan's title on the masthead of the magazine. He wondered what else Maria had discovered about his "friend" in the few days since she'd first heard of her. Probably plenty. Maria's sources of information were good, from the servants in the town house, who undoubtedly knew of Susan's visits there, to her "social" contacts who probably knew or were the bigwigs at *Vogue*. She smells trouble, Richard thought. And, from her point of view, she's probably right.

Susan was completely taken in by this gracious little woman. She breathed a sigh of relief at the apparently genuine welcome, which was almost as unexpected as Maria's physical appearance. She'd seen candid photographs of Richard's mother in magazines and newspapers, but she was usually snapped at the table at some charity dinner. They didn't show how tiny she was. Susan expected someone big and formidable, almost a Wagnerian type with an ample bosom and a booming voice. From her reputation as a tyrant, Susan had pictured Maria as physically overpowering. The last thing she anticipated was this fragile-looking little lady who seemed so pleased to meet her.

"I'm delighted to be here, Mrs. Antonini. It was kind of you to let Richard bring me."

"A great pleasure, my dear. Come. Everyone is eager to meet you." Still holding Susan's hand, she led her to a giant of a white-haired man. "This is my husband. Joe, dear, this is Richard's little friend Susan Langford."

"Lang*don*, Mother," Richard said. "Not Lang*ford*."

"Of course, darling, how stupid of me! But no matter, really. We're all on a first-name basis here, aren't we?"

Giovanni made a small bow, smiling with real warmth. "And what a pretty friend she is!" The deep, resonant voice still held a trace of his Italian origin. "Welcome to our house, Miss Langdon. You pay it a great compliment."

Susan was entranced by the Old World courtesy and awed at finding herself in the presence of the great artist.

"It's a privilege to meet you, sir," she said. And then, almost shyly, "It's something one dreams about."

The handsome, aging face broke into an impish grin. "My dear child, lovely young women have long since stopped dreaming about me, alas. Except, perhaps, as a grandfather figure with a baton. But you are kind."

Maria interrupted. "Joe, dear, stop monopolizing our guest. Everyone else is waiting to greet her."

Like an ocean liner in the wake of a strong little tug, Susan found herself being steered around the huge room.

"This is my eldest son, Sergio, and his wife Mary Louise." Susan shook hands with a dark, broodingly handsome man and a small blond woman hardly bigger than Maria. "And these are their children." Joseph made a formal bow and Patricia actually curtsied. Susan was amazed. Did children really behave that way any more? Obviously, Antonini children did. Sergio looked like an older, more sardonic Richard. What had Richard said? Oh yes. There was almost seventeen years' difference between the oldest and youngest boys. That would make Sergio forty-five, a most attractive age for men. His wife must be about forty, Susan thought, though she seemed more girlish.

There was only time for a word of greeting before Maria moved her on. "And this is Walter and Jacqueline and Calhoun and Charles, who're being allowed to join us for dinner tonight." The boys, like their cousin Joseph, made "dancing-school bows." Maria smiled. "It's a special treat when I allow the

54

grandchildren to dine with us," she said. "You feel terribly grown up, don't you, Calhoun? And you, too, Charles."

"Yes, ma'am." A dutiful chorus.

Walter laughed. "I'm afraid they consider it a dubious honor, Mother. They have to stay on their best behavior."

Susan smiled sympathetically. "It's probably more fun having dinner without the grown-ups, isn't it?" she asked them conversationally.

Maria allowed a shade of annoyance to cross her face before she answered for them. "They *adore* being permitted to come to table."

My first gaffe, Susan thought. Even though Walter had given her the cue, Jacqueline said nothing. She simply stood quietly by, an unreadable expression on her face. Was it scorn? Boredom? Resigned tolerance? Susan couldn't decide. And then she saw a corner of Jacqueline's mouth turn up ever so slightly, as if to say, "You're right, but it's a hopeless battle." Susan liked Walter and Jacqueline on sight. The second son seemed more gentle, more relaxed than his older brother. And his wife, so extraordinarily beautiful in her remoteness, was, Susan felt, the only woman in this family she might possibly relate to.

She was sure of that when they got to the final pair. "My daughter, Gloria Taffin," Maria said, "and her husband Raoul. Unfortunately, *their* babies are too small to join the dinner party." The way in which it was said was an unmistakable reprimand to Walter and Susan. Gloria was a big-boned woman, nearly as tall as her brothers and physically fit in spite of her obvious pregnancy. She shook Susan's hand with a strong grip. Her husband, slight and handsome, had great elegance and charm. They were a strange pair.

"I hear you have two beautiful children," Susan said. "And congratulations on the upcoming event."

"Thanks," Gloria said tersely.

Raoul was more gracious. "Our little ones are very

55

winning," he said, "but already they are *enfants terribles*. Still, we adore them."

"You'd adore them less," Maria said tartly, "if you didn't have that good English nanny! Thank heavens I could find one for you. Gloria is hopeless as a functioning mother. She's much too busy winning blue ribbons in horse shows." Then she reverted to her assumed softness. "Of course, we're very proud of Gloria's athletic accomplishments. And she certainly keeps all of us on our toes! Even me. The only one she can't convert to the great outdoors is my stubborn husband." She looked appraisingly but affectionately at her daughter. "Darling, you really must be careful of your skin. All that outdoor exposure! In another two years you'll positively have an alligator hide! Raoul, can't you control your wife? The women in my family have always been famous for their good complexions."

Richard spoke from behind her. "If not for their *tact,* Mother dear. Stop nagging Gloria. I think you're just jealous of her trophies. Besides, Susan doesn't want to hear the usual family squabbles the first twenty minutes she's in the house." His tone was bantering but he was annoyed, and Maria, to Susan's relief, subsided with an apologetic little laugh.

"Forgive me, Susan. I never can stop worrying about my children. Even when my babies are grown up and have babies of their own. Gloria understands. I only want her to stay pretty."

There was an awkward silence and then Richard said, "Why don't we all have a drink? I could use one and I'm sure Susan could, after working all day, driving up here and meeting twelve new people."

"Good idea." Jacqueline spoke for the first time, but Maria gently vetoed the idea.

"Richard darling, it's after five, and I'm sure Susan would like to settle in before dinner. Why don't we show her to her suite and meet, as planned, for cocktails at seven? Unless, of course, Susan really *needs* a drink . . ."

"Oh no, Mrs. Antonini. Not at all. I'll unpack."

56

"What a sensible young lady you've brought us, Richard dear," Maria said. "Shall I have one of the maids help you, Susan?"

"No thank you, Mrs. Antonini. I can manage."

❄

In the guest suite to which Maria personally conducted her and left with a warm smile, after checking that she had everything she needed, Susan sat for a moment thinking about her introduction to this house, this family. There was no doubt who was in charge. It was Maria's domain, in every sense. It was always "I," or "my." Never "we" or "our." *I* am delighted to have you here. Richard has told *me* so much about you. These are *my* children. *I* found the nurse for the Taffin baby. It was as though Giovanni did not exist as a husband, only as an artistic possession of Maria's, an extension of herself. Susan could well believe all the things she'd heard about Signora Antonini. Until today, she'd thought most of it farfetched. No longer. From her highhanded manner with her family, Susan could imagine the made-of-steel little woman negotiating with managers, making financial deals, choosing the cities in which Giovanni appeared, the clothes he wore, the hotels he stayed in and the cuisine offered. I've never seen such a dominant woman, Susan thought. With sudden insight she sensed that Maria ran her husband's life and controlled her children, not for their sakes but for her own monumental ego, her insatiable need to be in charge of everything and everyone.

The terrible part was that she undoubtedly was good at it, probably so often right that the family had realized the foolishness, as well as the futility, of trying to buck her. It was easier—and usually wiser—to give in, to pay the homage she demanded, to go along with her in matters from career development to child rearing. What the hell, the children probably said privately, she was spoiled rotten and had been, all her life and theirs. It was too late to start rebelling now. And besides she was so damned competent. She had intelligence and experience and a total lack of mawkish emotion that enabled her to view all problems clinically. The children probably thought they loved her. Susan suspected that it was more awe, even fear. She guessed, from the little she'd seen, that Maria's wrath could be formidable, her disapproval cold and devastating, a plague to be avoided. It seemed clear that "the children" and those they married deferred to Mother and probably reserved any true affection for the kind, smiling father who had withdrawn from all decisions, knowing he'd not be allowed to make them even if he tried. He'd seemed indulgent and tolerant of his wife's complete command of the situation. Certainly he uttered no words of protest. Perhaps he admired her strength. Susan doubted that Giovanni felt much love for his wife, but in his gentlemanly way the world would never know that.

She began looking around her temporary quarters. It was a beautiful suite, done in her favorite pink, white and green. A gay, flowered bedroom with ruffled bedspread, an inviting chaise longue, and an ample dressing table. The little sitting room had its own television set, a painted Italian desk well stocked with writing paper engraved "Six Corners," the name of the estate. There was a pile of new best-sellers on the table beside a deep, comfortable chair and ottoman, a bowl of peppermints and a box of cigarettes next to it. The bathroom was papered in green and white lattice-work paper and equipped with thick towels monogrammed "MSA." Maria's initials. Susan wondered what the "S" stood for. What was Maria's maiden name? Sanford? Sterling? Certainly not Smith. More like "Superwoman," Susan thought, half-amused. Or "Simonlegree." She smiled at her own nonsense. Stop it! she told herself. You're making snap judgments based on twenty minutes of contact and twenty different malicious rumors. Give her a chance. If only because she's Richard's mother.

Susan looked out the window. She could see, at a distance, a series of small houses. Which one is his? I wish I were staying in it with him! I love him so. I wouldn't care if he came from a family of aborigines. She wondered if he were thinking of her now, wanting her as she wanted him.

❈

Richard was, in fact, still downstairs in the same house. After the others had wandered off to change for dinner, Maria detained her younger son.

"Sit and talk with me for a moment, Richard. I haven't seen you for nearly a month since we've been staying up here. Is everything all right at the house? You're not too lonely?"

"Everything's fine, Mother." Was this her way of telling him she knew about Susan's visits to the town house? He waited.

"Your friend is charming. A bit outspoken with the children, I thought, but very attractive."

"You weren't exactly the soul of diplomacy yourself a couple of times. Those cracks about Gloria's kids. And the poor old girl's lousy complexion. Why don't you let her up?"

"My dear, what I say to your brothers and sister is only for their own good."

"Those might be the most awful words anybody ever says." Richard grimaced. "They're a license to lecture." He decided to plunge in. "All right, Mother, let's have it. You don't like Susan. Shall we talk about it?"

"That's utter nonsense. How could I dislike her? I don't even know her."

"Stop acting. The minute she walked in you were snide about how 'chic' she was. And all that going-on about being an associate editor of *Vogue*. Interesting that you checked that out. What *else* did you check out?"

"I haven't the faintest idea what you're talking about. You are a grown man, free to pick your own friends without interference from me. If I said something ill-advised about her appearance, I assure you it

59

was unintentional. After all, entertaining a *Vogue* editor makes one feel quite provincial and dowdy."

If it hadn't been so annoying, it would have been funny. Richard felt himself growing angrier. What kind of idiot did she think he was?

"When you go into that 'I'm just a simple housewife' routine, Mother, it really breaks me up! You're about as provincial as Maria Callas. You're in Paris and Milan and Leningrad much more often than you're in Pound Ridge. As for the 'dowdy' part, you're very simple indeed in your Galanos gowns and your David Webb jewelry. Just the typical American homemaker, 'overcome' by meeting a fashion magazine editor. Hell, you're probably best friends with the wife of the man who *owns Vogue!*"

Maria looked at him speculatively. "You seem overly excited about nothing, Richard. I've met some of your lady-friends before, at parties. I'm sure I treated *them* no differently and you didn't seem so upset . . . Or," she said slowly, "is there something special about your little Susan? I'm not stupid, dear boy. This is the first young woman you've felt impelled to introduce to your family. And for a whole, private weekend at that. Should I read some unusual significance into this visit?"

Until that moment, Richard had not been absolutely sure that he was going to ask Susan to marry him. Sleeping with her was terrific. She was interesting to talk to. And he liked having such a beautiful young woman on his arm. But marriage? He hadn't totally made up his mind whether he wanted that. To anyone. God knows, he was surrounded by discouraging examples. There wasn't an ounce of marital happiness among the whole lot of them. And yet, suddenly, perversely, he heard himself saying, "Yes, you should read something significant into it. I'm in love with Susan. I'm going to marry her."

Even when the words were out of his mouth he wasn't certain it was what he really intended. But it was done. He couldn't back down now. He wasn't sure

60

he wanted to. He did love Susan. As much as he could ever love any one woman. There'd been ten good years of bachelor fun. Marriage might be very pleasant, very comfortable, much easier than hopping from bed to bed. As though Maria were deaf, he repeated his words more loudly. "I said I'm going to *marry* her, Mother."

"I heard you, Richard."

"Well?"

"What do you want from me? Ecstatic squeals of delight? Congratulations and blessings? Or perhaps a simple case of hysterics would suit you better. I don't think I need to point out to you why you've decided to take this foolish step just at the moment when you're on the threshold of your best years."

This was Maria at her most devastating. Cold. Sarcastic. Puzzling. Richard stared at her.

"I'd be interested in your theories. Personally, I thought it was quite normal and natural to fall in love."

"For normal, natural people, perhaps." Maria was entering her persuasive phase. "But you are an artist, Richard. Your talent puts you above ordinary behavior. You know that at this crucial stage of your development, the *last* thing you need is the distraction and responsibility of a wife and probably children! You need to be free to concentrate on nothing but your work. My dear, you're still young. There's plenty of time to think about marriage."

"You still haven't answered my question, Mother. Why do *you* think I'm marrying?"

There was a carefully calculated pause. "This is painful for me to say, Richard, but if, heaven forbid, you should not reach the eminence we all hope and believe you will, the time-consuming demands of a personal life would be a face-saving alibi. If you had a wife, there'd be someone to blame, wouldn't there? As there isn't now, when you're pampered, protected and totally self-indulgent. It will be different when you have a family of your own to worry about. There'll be domestic problems. Boring. Demanding. Your daily life will be quite altered. Even the engagements you accept, the out-of-town appearances you're offered will be subject to your wife's opinions and some consideration of her needs. I think you're frightened, son. Afraid of failure. And looking for an acceptable scapegoat if such unlikely but possible disaster strikes."

He was openmouthed. "That's the most insane thing I've heard you say! Afraid of *failure?* For God's sake, I'm already a *success!* And even if I weren't, you're the last person in the world to single out a wife as a deterrent to a man's career! Look what you've done for Father!"

Maria smiled. "This may be immodest, but Susan is not like me. I can tell. She'll hang onto you, burden you with demands for attention, depend on you for decision-making. You'll be irritated, Richard. And resentful of the intrusion into your working life. She's a nice girl. I have nothing against her. But she comes from a different world. Yes, I've done some checking up. You were right about that. She is the product of a solid, middle-class background, raised, I'm sure, to dedicate herself to a husband, but not necessarily to his work. There is no way she could understand you as I have always understood your father. You may love her. I'm sure you do. But she will not put your career first, above her own view of you as a 'couple,' and don't think for a moment she'll take a back seat to you. She's had a career of her own. Even if she's ready to forget it and start a new one as Mrs. Richard Antonini, she won't be any real help to you. On the contrary, she'll be a hindrance. But then, of course, as I started out by saying, it's always comfortable to have an alibi for failing to achieve what you know you should have."

She'd always been able to shake him with this kind of glib, authoritative double-talk. For a moment, Richard was uncertain. Was she right? Was he subconsciously afraid of failure and looking for the "alibi?"

Seeing the slight hesitation, Maria pursued her advantage. "I know. You're thinking that marriage hasn't been a millstone around Sergio's and Walter's necks. You're wrong. Neither of them has attained the stature they could have if they'd not been forced to give part of every day to wives and pregnancies and stupid, domestic obligations that Mary Lou and Jacqueline persist in involving them in. It takes a very special kind of woman to submerge herself in the interest of art, Richard. A very strong one, willing to abandon her own personality and wise enough to find satisfaction in reflected glory." Maria smiled. "I have no doubt that you're going to be a truly great man. The greatest of all my sons. I hoped you shared that conviction and were willing to make sacrifices for it."

He was silent for a long time. Then he said, "I'm sorry, Mother. You're wrong. I'm not looking for someone to pass the buck to if things go wrong. I'm looking for someone to share my life. Other artists have wives and children. I don't believe what you've been saying. I don't think you believe it, either."

"I have always wanted only your happiness, Richard. Which is the same as wanting your success."

"I know that, Mother. And I promise you'll get what you want. Susan will only enrich the gift."

She was too clever not to know when she was beaten. Richard was so like her. Strong-willed, difficult (impossible, really) to manipulate when his mind was made up. And she could see that his mind was made up.

"Very well," she said. "You're of age. There's nothing I can do to stop your marrying Susan."

"I'd prefer your blessing."

"I can't be a hypocrite. I can only hope my instincts are wrong."

He smiled suddenly. "Wouldn't it be ironic if all this bridge-crossing was a waste of time? I haven't even asked Susan yet. She might turn me down."

"Not likely," Maria said.

No, he thought, it wasn't likely. He'd ask her tonight. He knew what her answer would be.

❊

Dinner was a kind of delicate torture, a noisy meal that left Susan feeling more than ever an outsider. The family seemed to forget that she was there, though she sat at Giovanni's right, with Richard beside her. As they always did when they gathered, the Antoninis threw themselves into a spirited discussion of topics which were far from Susan's frame of reference. "The boys" and Giovanni and Maria did most of the talking and most of it about music. There was a heated debate over the merits of Hindemith's *Mathis der Maler* and Prokofiev's *Piano Concerto No. 3.* Giovanni had a long pronouncement about Berlioz's *Damnation of Faust,* while Maria insisted that Beethoven's *Leonora Overture No. 3* was intensely significant.

Susan, with a layman's limited knowledge of the classics, had understood very little of it, a fact Richard realized. Occasionally, he squeezed her hand in encouragement. Once or twice, she caught Maria looking at her thoughtfully. She must know we're in love, Susan thought. And she's bound to disapprove. The knowledge made her feel weak. What if Maria talked her son out of this romance? She had such power over all her children. No. That wouldn't happen. Why wouldn't she want me for a daughter-in-law? I'm presentable, from a better-than-average background, with a fair share of intelligence and a reasonable education. What more could she want for Richard? Maybe a European princess or the daughter of a rich Greek shipowner, Susan answered herself. She looked at Mary Lou and Jacqueline. They were no better than she. But then, perhaps Maria considered Richard better than Sergio or Walter. Damn. Would this dinner never end?

It finally did and they trooped into the library, an enormous room with heavy oak beams, a vast fireplace and leaded glass windows. A huge concert grand dominated one end and there were floor-to-ceiling bookcases, filled with biographies of great musicians, textbooks, histories of composers, bound scores of symphonies, librettos of operas. This "country house" was more impressive, in its way, than the East Seventieth Street one. It reeked of solid position and "old money," and it was even more forbidding, somehow, in spite of its casual chintz fabrics and the masses of fresh flowers on every table.

They were served coffee and brandy by a white-coated houseman, one of the eight servants it took to run this enormous establishment, under Mrs. Lowman's crisply efficient direction.

Susan found herself standing next to Giovanni. "This is a marvelous house," she said. "Do you spend much time here?"

"Most of the summer. That is, Mrs. Antonini and I do. The children have their own places, of course. Except for Richard. However, we manage to gather regularly for many weekends and most holidays. My wife likes to have the whole family together as often as possible. It's difficult, you see. We are on tour a great part of the time."

"It must be a glamorous life."

The maestro shrugged his shoulders. "I suppose. One comes to take it for granted after so many years." He looked wistful. "In time, one symphony hall comes to look very much like another. Hotel suites have an extraordinary sameness. Even audiences are only bodies who own you, for a few hours, for the price of a ticket. The 'glamour,' my dear, is not without its boredom and its difficulties, as well as its rewards." His eyes twinkled. "As I'm sure you will soon find out."

Susan looked at him sharply. Giovanni lowered his voice. "Mrs. Antonini whispered your little secret to me before dinner. I am very happy, dear Susan. You will make Richard a wonderful wife."

Her surprise and momentary exhilaration gave way to annoyance. The arrogance of it! Richard had told his mother he planned to marry, even before he proposed! Before she could say anything, she heard Richard's voice and saw him coming through the doorway, followed by the houseman bearing a tray filled with glasses of champagne. She'd been so interested in

65

talking to Giovanni, she hadn't noticed Richard leaving the room. Now he stood beside her.

"My dear family," he now said loudly, "may I have your attention, please? I wish to propose a toast. Everyone have a glass? Good! Let us drink to the lovely new lady in our midst. My bride to be. To Susan, the future Mrs. Richard Antonini!"

There was a second or two of silence as the assembled group reacted to this sudden announcement. Then there was a babble of "To Susans" and "Good wishes" as they raised their glasses in her direction. Everyone saluted her except Maria, Susan noticed. The matriarch stood stony-faced and motionless, saying nothing. Richard waited, looking at Susan, a satisfied smile on his face. For a moment, she felt outraged. How dare he be so sure of himself, so sure of her? How humiliating to have one's engagement proclaimed as a *fait accompli* before being privately asked! She flushed with instinctive anger. For a fleeting moment she wondered what would happen if she turned coolly to Richard and said, "I'm afraid you're mistaken, dear. No one has proposed to me yet." But she wouldn't, of course. This was what she had dreamed of from the first moment she'd set eyes on him. He was kissing her lightly now, laughing at her high color.

"Look!" he called to the others. "Would you believe, in this day and age, a girl who can still blush?" He was oblivious to the hurt and anger she felt at this hoped-for moment. "Happy, darling?" he asked in a voice meant only for her ears.

What could she say? He was so pleased with himself, so utterly unaware that he'd deprived her of a precious private moment that could never come again, a moment alone when he would ask her to be his wife. She managed to smile. "Of course I'm happy."

They were crowding around her now, the people to whom she soon would be related. The men kissed her and patted Richard on the back. Jacqueline and Mary Lou hugged her, but Gloria only shook her hand, a

66

bone-crushing grip as opposed to the limp one Maria finally offered. Richard's mother was tight-lipped, too well bred to show her displeasure, too proud to pretend happiness.

"You are getting a wonderful man, Susan," she said at last. "I count on you to make his life perfect."

What about my life? Susan wanted to say. Or isn't that important in the scheme of things? She knew the answer as far as Maria was concerned, and she savored a taste of triumph as she gazed steadily into her future mother-in-law's eyes and said, "I don't hope for perfection in anything, Mrs. Antonini, but I'm sure Richard and I will make each other happy."

"When's the wedding?" Jacqueline asked.

Richard answered for her. "As soon as possible. Right, darling?" He had his arm around her. "Early September, before I leave on the next tour. I want Susan with me."

"Not taking a chance on a long engagement, are you?" Sergio asked. "What's the matter, Richard? Afraid she'll change her mind?"

Richard only laughed confidently. "No way. No way at all."

And no way you've consulted me about that either, Susan thought. I'm not to be allowed even to pick the date of my own wedding. Now stop this! she scolded herself. Remember whom you're marrying! He didn't mean to slight her. It would not occur to him to consult her, or even dream that she might be piqued by having no voice in the matter. He's been so terribly spoiled all his life, so used to having his way. It will take time for him to realize that he now has a partner entitled to an equal voice in all decisions. None of that is important. I mustn't be so thin-skinned. So impatient. He'll adjust, as I will. For now, the only thing to do is go along, and not be so damned sensitive. Love will make the difference. Love will soften and mold Richard and bring out all his potential for sharing.

She smiled contentedly. "September sounds wonderful," she said. She looked across the room. Giovanni gave her a small, approving, conspiratorial nod of the head.

Chapter Six

Bea and Wil Langdon waited impatiently for the train to pull into the Bronxville station that hot Monday evening in July. Susan's mother was visibly agitated and Wil kept patting her hand reassuringly.

"It's going to be all right, darling. You heard how happy Susie sounded when they phoned us Saturday morning. And Richard is a gentleman. I liked the way he apologized for telling *his* family first. It was perfectly natural. After all, they happened to be with the Antoninis when they decided."

Bea was unconvinced. "And is it perfectly natural for him not to come out here with her this evening? My Lord, Wil, we've never laid eyes on him! You'd think he could spare the time to meet his fiancée's parents."

"Now, honey, Susie explained that. He has a meeting with his manager tonight."

"Maybe we're not grand enough for him," Bea said petulantly. "Maybe Susan's worried about introducing her dull family."

Wil laughed. "Come on. That's not like you. You know better. You're just a bundle of nerves. Typical mother-of-the-bride syndrome."

Even she had to laugh at herself. "I suppose you're

right. It just seems so sudden. I wish they'd give it more time. Get to know each other a little better. September! That's only two months away! Who can get ready for a wedding in two months? I don't understand the big rush."

"Yes you do. Richard starts on tour. He wants his wife with him."

His wife. How strange the words sounded, even to his own ears. It was hard to imagine Susie married. And to someone so famous. To him, she was still his little girl, his adorable and adored child. But she was not. She was a woman. She'd waited longer than most of her friends to marry. It was like her, her father thought proudly, to wait until she found the right man. Not settle for some second-rate young squirt with a mediocre job and a dubious future.

And yet, though he'd die before he'd let her know, Wil Langdon shared his wife's reservations. He, too, would be easier in his mind if only they wouldn't rush into marriage after such a brief courtship. He did not wish to admit that they probably knew each other well, physically. Fathers didn't like to think about things like that where daughters were concerned. But even if they were intimate, it didn't mean they really *knew* each other. He was not privy to all the gossip about the Antoninis that reached Bea's ears, but he'd heard enough to make him nervous about the family. Not that he didn't think Susan could hold her own in any situation. She had such poise, such good common sense. But this was the Big League. Things would be expected of her that she might be unwilling, if not unable, to supply. She'll have to make so many concessions, Wil thought. More than most wives.

As though she read his mind, Bea said, "Among other things I can't imagine Susan telling me this morning that they want a big wedding! She's always been vehement about the wastefulness of an elaborate ceremony. 'Downright obscene' she always called those productions that cost thousands of dollars. And now on the phone she says they've decided on a full-scale event with all the trimmings. I'm sure it's not her idea! She must be doing it for Richard's sake. Or his family's. I was really surprised at her rattling on about bridesmaids and receptions as though that's the only way to get married. And it's downright inconsiderate. She could at least ask whether we can afford it!"

"Honey, if that's what she wants, we can afford it."

"That's not the point. She shouldn't just take it for granted. It's so unlike her. Everything is. Imagine marrying a man we've never even met!"

"Now calm down," Wil said. "This is the happiest moment of her life. You don't want to spoil it for her, do you?"

Bea subsided. "No. Of course not. And you know I won't. I'm just uneasy. I don't know why. I simply don't have a good feeling about all this."

He gave her a little kiss. "You'll feel better the minute you see her. Here comes the train. You want to stay in the car?"

"No. I want to be right there on the platform when she gets off. One look at her face and I'll know everything."

Susan stepped off the train. And they hugged and kissed and cried a little before they started for home. Bea listened carefully as her daughter talked nonstop. Susan was keyed up, chattering about the wedding plans. It was natural for her to be excited, but this was almost frenetic, as though she had to convince them and herself that everything was flawless. She's in a panic, Bea thought, alarmed. Happy, yes. But almost deliriously so. Almost frantically anxious to assure them how wonderful Richard was, how she looked forward to a beautiful wedding and a glorious life.

"This is pretty sudden, sweetheart, isn't it?" Wil said when they'd settled in the living room. "Your mother's going to have her hands full putting together a big do in two months. And you won't be much help. You'll have to give the magazine at least two weeks' notice. Maybe more. They've been very decent to you. You can't walk out on Kate tomorrow."

Bea looked at him gratefully. He was trying to help, after all.

"I know," Susan said. "I realize it's an imposition, but Richard starts on a concert tour in mid-September, and we want to squeeze in at least a week to ourselves before then."

"Why not wait until the tour's over and then get married?" Bea asked. "He won't be away more than a couple of months."

"Richard doesn't want to wait. And neither," Susan said almost defiantly, "do I."

Bea persisted. "But, darling, it's really only a short time. It isn't years."

Susan suddenly seemed angry. "For God's sake, Mother, you sound like . . ." She stopped.

"Like Richard's mother?" Bea said gently.

"Well, yes. I'm sorry, Mom. I didn't really mean that. You could never sound like Mrs. Antonini."

They waited, but Susan apparently was not going to elaborate. They sat in silence for a few seconds until Bea finally said, "Well, dear, I know your mind's made up. But why don't we simplify it? A small wedding. Just the family at the church here in Bronxville and a few friends at the club after for a little reception. You always said that's the way you wanted it. And that, at least, we could cope with. You've always wanted to be married quietly, surrounded only by those you love and who love you. It would be nice, Susan. I promise. You know we want you to have a sweet wedding."

Susan looked appealing from one to the other. "Don't you understand? I didn't know when I said those things what was going to happen to me. Don't you understand I'm not marrying just *anybody?* I'm marrying *Richard Antonini.*"

Bea took a deep breath. "Yes, we understand, darling. We really do."

❀

Not then, not until years later, could Susan explain what that Fourth-of-July weekend had been like. She had to live through things much more terrible before she could even discuss the lost feeling she'd had at what should have been her moment of utter joy. When at last she did talk about that visit, she was able to put it into perspective, to see it as a warning she'd recognized and chosen to ignore.

She had been annoyed by Richard's highhanded way of announcing their engagement and setting the date, but in her dazed happiness she'd quickly recovered from this unintended lack of thoughtfulness. It was not until the others had gone to bed and only she and Richard and Maria were left in the library that she felt the first full impact of Maria's strength and her own helplessness. She'd wanted so much to be alone with Richard, but he made no sign of their slipping away together, and his mother deliberately lingered until everyone else had finally drifted off. Then Maria, who'd been almost silent during the evening, decided to speak her piece.

"Sit down," she commanded. "I think the three of us had better have a talk."

Susan expected Richard to tell his mother that it could wait; that they'd like to be alone together now. She'd whispered to him in passing that they had to call her parents right away. But he did no such thing. Obediently, he sank into a sofa facing Maria's big chair, pulling Susan down with him.

Maria looked long and hard at her future daughter-in-law. "As you come to know me better," she said, "you will find that I am many things. Above all, I am direct. Like it or not, I've already told Richard that I do not approve of your marriage in September."

Susan misunderstood. "I know it seems a little hurried, Mrs. Antonini." She tried to make a joke of it, glancing at Richard. "I was a bit taken aback myself, hearing the announcement. But since Richard will be traveling for months, I agree. I want to go along."

"The timing is unimportant. Whether Richard marries in two months or two years is not the issue. Not the basis of my objection. Nor are you, personally, the reason I am against this." Maria spoke deliberately. "He chooses not to listen, but the practical fact is that Richard should not marry for some years. He is at a crucial stage of his career, a time when he needs to give his full attention and energies to his music. For all his 'fame and glory' he is at the threshold of emergence into the world of immortals. Every step, every word must be carefully planned, every rough edge smoothed for him. He needs no emotional or domestic distractions. The artist must be selfish, totally self-involved. Richard has had that privilege since he was five. The results are only now becoming evident. And now he is about to dilute his potential with the demands of marriage."

Susan stared at her, speechless, uncomprehending. For a moment the room was quiet. Richard slouched sulkily beside her while Maria sat erect, allowing her words to sink in.

"I don't understand," Susan said finally. "You think I'll be a *handicap* to his career? That's incredible!" She felt anger rising. Anger at Mrs. Antonini's words. Anger at Richard's silence. "How could you believe such a thing, Mrs. Antonini? Don't you know that because I love Richard so much, because I have so much respect for his talent I would never, never do anything to distress or disturb him? On the contrary, marriage will give his work more feeling, more depth. He's not a priest, after all! He's a man!"

Maria smiled condescendingly. "I have never expected Richard to be celibate. He can have all the women he wants. Including you. But they need not carry his name. Or his children. They should not burden him with all kinds of unforeseen problems. A wife could make unwise utterances which might embarrass him in the press, or even create awkward social situations unsuited to his image. I know," she went on, "you don't think those things are possible. You believe you will be a valuable addition, the 'good woman behind every great man,' the proverbial 'power behind the throne.' Richard thinks so, too. Right now. But you're both wrong. His brothers' wives have done nothing but distract them, impede their advancement. What makes you think you'd be different?"

As Richard had earlier, Susan made the obvious comparison. "How can you, of all people, say such things? You who have been so important in your husband's career?"

"I was trained for my role, Susan. My father was a famous concert violinist. I grew up in a household where my mother's every thought and plan revolved around her husband's future. I know discipline *and* self-sufficiency. I know music is all. I recognize that the home of an artist is like a shrine, in which the idol must be protected and served. You think I dominate. No. I protect and serve at the expense of any possible desire for personal recognition. I live only through my husband's genius and that of my sons. I've learned to keep my mouth shut in public, and forego affection in private. Can you do the same?"

Susan's chin went up. "I may not do it your way, Mrs. Antonini, but I will be as supportive of my husband as you've been of yours. Or your mother was of hers. I'm not stupid. I'm untrained in this kind of thing, but I understand what is required of Richard's wife." Her voice softened. "And I can't believe you won't help me learn to be an asset rather than a liability."

"Don't count on any help, Susan. Not from me or anyone. The rules for the life you're choosing can't be taught."

Richard stirred. "All right," he said, "now that you two have gotten everything off your chests, can we put an end to this? I'm damned tired of sitting here listening to both of you discuss me as though I weren't in the room. Susan, you've heard Mother's opinion. And Mother, you've made your speech. Nothing has changed, but I hope you ladies feel better for it. As for me, I'm going to bed. Being the middle of a tug of war is exhausting."

Maria rose with dignity, looking at Susan as though to say, "See? See how impatient he is? How totally unconcerned with the important 'little things'?" At the door, she paused. "Since you are both determined, I shall say no more. Over the weekend we can discuss the details of the wedding, Susan, and of course I shall write to your mother."

When she left, Richard pulled Susan into his arms and kissed her. "Sorry about all that," he said. "There's no stopping Mother when she gets her teeth into something. You were great, honey, but I think you can see that a long debate with La Belle is an exercise in futility. You'll learn what the rest of us know: you just let her go on and on and then do what you intended in the first place."

She tried to be as blithe about it as he, but she was troubled. She hadn't expected Maria to welcome her with open arms, but this quiet, fierce opposition was more than she'd bargained for. What if Maria was right? What if lack of freedom would somehow hamper Richard's career? Suppose he did chafe under these new bonds? She'd not be able to bear it. But that wouldn't happen. It couldn't. They loved each other too much.

"I'll truly try to be the wife you deserve," she said. "I know there'll be enormous responsibilities, but you'll always come first." She was trembling. Richard held her close.

"Hey, you really *are* upset, aren't you?"

She nodded her head against his chest.

"Well, don't be. All that barking has very little bite. You'll see. You'll fit right into this family, just as Mary Lou and Jacqueline have. We're not a bad group, once you get used to us."

She needed more than the sound of his voice, the feel of his arms around her. She needed the closeness of him at this moment, the love-making that blotted out all the worrisome realities, the passion that enveloped her when they were together. "Can't we go to your house for a while?" she asked meekly. "I don't want to be alone."

He ran his hands along her body. "You tempt me greatly, madame, but let's cool it for this weekend, okay? We'll be back in New York Monday, away from all the alert eyes and ears that might inhibit my performance!" He laughed. "Darling, we have years in which to make love!"

She'd gone quietly to bed, but she lay awake thinking about Maria's words. There was so much she didn't understand, including Richard's parting words.

"We should call my family, darling," Susan had said. "And by the way, I've always wanted a small, quiet wedding. All right with you?"

"Fine with me, but I don't know whether we'll get away with it. Let's leave all that for tomorrow, sweetheart. I'm bushed and you must be, too. It's been quite a day." He gave her a quiet kiss and was out the front door before she could ask more questions. It was as though he was running away from an unpleasant subject.

She did not tell her parents of this brutal conversation with Maria. The Langdons would have been outraged. Better to let them think the Antoninis were delighted, as Richard told them on the phone next morning. She supposed most of the Antoninis were, if not exactly delighted, at least philosophical. Throughout the weekend, they treated her with offhand acceptance, not making any great effort to be warm but not making her feel unwelcome, either. No, that wasn't true. Gloria did overtly make her feel unwelcome. On Saturday afternoon when she joined the group at the pool, Richard's sister sarcastically remarked on Susan's beautiful, expensive new bikini.

"Well, will you look at Miss Vogue!" Gloria said. She was wearing a beat-up old white jersey tank suit that made her enormous stomach even more obvious. "Who are you expecting, Susan? Some of your fashion-photographer pals?"

The others smiled tolerantly at Gloria's biting remark. Apparently they were used to their sister's tart tongue, but Susan didn't know how to answer such rudeness. She felt herself blushing. It was an uncalled-for snub, and she was thankful when Richard came to her rescue.

"Your eyes are turning green, Glo," he said. "With that front bulge of yours, no wonder you're jealous of anybody without an extra ounce of fat."

"*You* should be *dying* of jealousy in that case," Gloria answered. "Yours is all between your ears!"

"*Touché,*" Sergio said. "That'll teach you not to meddle with The Mouth, Richard."

They were all so easy, so casually cruel to one another. Even Richard was unperturbed as he joined in the general laughter. They were used to this give-and-take that spared no one's feelings. Apparently they were secure enough to find insults funny among the family. Only Jacqueline was not amused.

"That's a smashing swimsuit, Susan," she said. "Don't pay any attention to these clods, just because they think it's smart to go around looking like a bunch of Salvation Army rejects."

Susan looked at her gratefully, but she noticed that Jacqueline, like the others, was wearing the kind of nondescript bathing outfit affected by people with generations of money and social standing behind them. Only the middle class really bothers much about "smart" clothes. When you're really confident, Susan thought, you don't give a damn. So I'm "overdressed." So what? I may not know much about being a snob at poolside, but damn it, I can show them up in the water!

Without a word, she stepped up onto the diving board and executed a clean, graceful arc into the pool. Effortlessly, she swam six lengths, knowing she looked good, pleased that they were all watching intently.

She'd been on the swimming team at school and loved it, had spent hours practicing her dives and her long, smoothly co-ordinated strokes, never dreaming that one day this special skill would come to her rescue.

Richard was impressed as he offered his hand to help her out of the water.

"You're really good!"

Susan smiled. "Surprised?"

"Not really. It's just one more thing to admire."

Even Gloria was grudgingly complimentary, but the brief moment of glory was soon forgotten. At all other sports, Susan was a disaster. In the softball game she couldn't hit a thrown ball when she was at bat or catch one when she was in the outfield. She knew nothing about touch football and wisely declined to participate in the rough-and-tumble game. Fortunately, Richard played neither baseball nor football. He and Susan sat on the sidelines as Sergio, Walter, Gloria and their older children roughhoused tirelessly throughout the afternoon. Jacqueline detested all strenuous activity and said so.

"You don't like games, either?" Susan asked Richard. "Your family seems to specialize in organized mayhem."

He laughed easily. "I was never allowed to go near 'contact sports.' Mother wouldn't permit it." He held out his hands. "These are supposed to be quite valuable. The private nightmare of all pianists is a broken finger."

"Of course. For a moment I forgot."

"I can't even play a game of tennis. Some of the others are going to have a go at a game this afternoon. Want to join?"

Susan shook her head. "I'll be the cheering section."

Later, she and Jacqueline watched Walter and Gloria play a fierce, driving doubles match against Maria and young Joseph. Richard wandered off to the piano. His mother looked like a girl on the court, her small, trim body moving swiftly to return shots even her grandson couldn't reach.

"She's amazing," Susan said.

"Which one? Maria with her years or Gloria with her belly?"

"Both of them. Where *do* they get their energy?"

Jacqueline lit one of her endless cigarettes. "I suspect it comes from sheer meanness. Or maybe they take out their frustrations in physical fitness. Who cares? I don't. You mustn't either."

"I could never be that competitive."

"Good. We don't need another one in the family."

Susan glanced at her. She seemed perfectly relaxed. Only the chain-smoking was a sign that Jacqueline was not as much at ease as she pretended.

"Was it hard, getting used to the family?" Susan asked.

"Not particularly. But then I haven't gone out of my way to try to make them love me. They don't respect anybody whose veins do not course with rich Antonini blood. That definitely leaves out Mary Lou, Raoul, me . . . and you."

Susan understood the friendly, tacit advice. Jacqueline was saying, "Don't try to become one of them. Accept your place as an in-law. Get along. And don't make waves." Somehow the few words of simple acceptance made it easier to swallow the bitter pill that came on Sunday: the total take-over of her wedding plans. It happened after Mrs. Antonini returned from church. She was the only one who attended, and she found Richard and Susan lounging in chaises on the lawn, contentedly browsing through the New York *Times*. Maria pulled up a chair.

"Since you'll be leaving late this afternoon, I think we'd better discuss the wedding. There are a great many plans to be made and very little time to make them."

"It will take a bit of doing," Susan agreed politely, "but I'm sure we can manage. It will be a very quiet, simple ceremony."

"Quiet? Simple?" Maria looked at her as though she was mad. "For Richard? My dear Susan, I don't think

79

you understand. This marriage will not be buried in the society section of the newspapers. It will be big news. Surely you don't expect a celebrity to be married as anonymously as a shoe clerk! There are important guests to be asked, press coverage to be arranged. I'd think St. Thomas's would be the suitable church. You *are* Episcopalian, I believe? And the reception at the Colony Club, I suppose?"

"Mother, Susan *really* wants a modest wedding at her own church. She told me so again this morning. What difference does it make? After all, it *is* the bride's prerogative to have the kind of ceremony she wants."

Bless you, darling, Susan thought. But Mrs. Antonini was scandalized.

"What difference does it make?" Maria echoed. "Richard, have you taken leave of your senses? If you have no regard for what your family wants, then at least consider what you owe your public! You are an internationally known figure. You cannot simply skulk off to some little Bronxville chapel! How would it look? People would think you were marrying a nobody! They'd probably conclude we didn't approve! There'd be all kinds of unsavory gossip we couldn't control. No. It's impossible. If you insist on rushing into this marriage, then at least let it receive the attention suitable to your stature."

Susan waited for him to refuse, but instead he seemed to be considering.

"Well, you may have a point. Tell you what. Let's compromise. Since you don't like our timetable and Susan doesn't like your conception, maybe we all have to give a little. Mother, you be graceful about the date and we'll go along with the dog-and-pony show." He turned to Susan. "That seems fair, doesn't it, darling?"

She stared at him in disbelief. He was overriding her wishes to suit his mother, his public and, probably in truth, himself. Is this how it will always be? Susan wondered. Will I be on the outside of every decision, large or small, giving way to the demands of public life

80

and the power of Maria Antonini? If I start this way, can I ever turn back?

"No, darling," she said almost in a whisper, "it *doesn't* seem fair. You know how I feel. I'm not an untouched eighteen-year-old who comes trembling down the aisle in virginal white. It's hypocritical and pretentious. I've always hated the idea of a big wedding, even when I was very young. And I'm not a child-bride. I'm an adult, marrying an adult." Her eyes went to Maria. "Mrs. Antonini, I do realize how important Richard is. But this is my wedding, too. I don't wish to have it arranged by concert managers and press agents. It's a very personal and private thing, not a publicity stunt staged for the newspapers and the curious stares of strangers. Please understand. Both of you."

She was trembling as she stopped speaking. She knew she was fighting for something much bigger than the details of a wedding. She was in a struggle for independence—from Maria, from the Antonini name, even from Richard himself, who was beginning to consider the various aspects of this event as clinically as he would plan a concert. And she knew she was going to lose this battle as she would lose many more in the future. She knew it, even as she spoke. She saw the answer in Richard's face as he weighed the matter.

"Susan, love," he said finally, "I know how you feel. I happen to agree with you. But Mother *does* have a point. She's been through this before. It would look odd if we didn't give the world what it expects. Sweetheart, my publicity is something you're going to have to learn to live with, annoying as it is. And it starts for you the day we announce our engagement. Let's be practical, shall we? I know you're too intelligent to be inflexible. *How* we're married isn't what's really important. All that counts is that we'll *be* married. You do see the reasoning. I know you do. And it'll still be your show. A bit fancier than you'd planned, I realize, but you'll still be the star."

I don't want to be a star, she thought. I just want to marry you, and if I refuse to do it your way—your

81

mother's way—I might not be able to marry you at all.

She nodded, finally, reluctantly.

"That's my girl!" Richard said. "I'm sure your parents will approve."

"If they don't wish to undertake the cost of a big wedding, Susan, Richard's father and I will, of course, be willing to . . ."

Susan could have slapped her. "That won't be a problem, Mrs. Antonini," she said coldly. "Thank you all the same, but my parents are well aware that the obligations are the bride's family's." At the moment, she was the most dignified of the three. "They wouldn't have it any other way," she said proudly.

Maria nodded. "Very well. I'm glad you see the necessity for this."

Susan didn't answer. I wish I *couldn't* see it, she thought. One of the things she would like to change in herself was this damned ability to look at both sides of almost any question. She wished she could be more opinionated, less open to reason. People who could were infinitely less confused, probably much happier. She could understand, rationally, why Richard's wedding probably *had* to be elaborate, but she wondered what would have happened if she'd refused to go along with that fact. The question was academic. She *was* going along. She'd try to believe it was for the best. She'd even try to sound convincing to her mother and father when they heard of her change of heart.

Chapter Seven

It was clearly impossible to put together, in a few short weeks, the kind of spectacular wedding she visualized for her son, but Richard's mother did it. Maria was used to accomplishing what other people thought hopeless. She had the drive and determination. She also had money, influence and "personnel." Once she faced the fact that she could not stop this marriage, she took it on as a personal project, enlisting Richard's manager, Paul Carmichael, and Richard's press agent, Gerry Carter, as full-time aides.

To Susan's amazement, and that of the Langdons, St. Thomas's was magically booked for the ceremony on unprecedentedly short notice. The Colony Club—to which Bea Langdon did not belong but Maria Antonini did—was reserved for the reception. Printers were bullied into getting out, overnight, engraved invitations which Maria's social secretary addressed and mailed, keeping a careful count of the RSVP acceptances which came back with the speed of a summons to the White House. Caterers were instructed, florists contacted, a fleet of limousines engaged, police barricades arranged for, to keep back the curious who would gather outside the church.

The Sunday after Susan's visit to her parents, her picture, taken by Bachrach, ("the *only* suitable portraitist," Maria said), appeared in the *Times,* under the headline "RICHARD ANTONINI TO WED."

Beatrice was furious when she saw it. She had unwillingly but realistically turned over all the details, including the announcement, to the "professionals."

"I simply couldn't do what they can," she'd told Wil. "Not in eight *years,* much less eight *weeks!* It must be nice to have such clout." Now she rattled the paper angrily. "There's no doubt whose wedding *this* is, is there? I thought it was customary to feature the *bride's* name."

"Now, honey, you know none of this matters as long as Susie's happy."

"I know." Bea's eyes filled with tears. "I'm being petty. It's just that I always thought her wedding would be something we'd all put together with pleasure. I wasn't prepared for this three-ring circus."

"Sweetheart, don't fight it. You still have plenty to do. My God, the presents that are pouring into this house already! Cataloguing them will be a career in itself!" He looked at the array of silver tea services and porcelain demitasse cups and tissue-thin crystal goblets. "They're collecting a king's ransom of gifts from personal friends. Can you imagine what it will be like after this announcement? You'll be up to your ears in lists of who sent what!"

She wouldn't be comforted. "Any reasonably intelligent eighth-grader could do that. I'm surprised Mrs. Antonini hasn't sent one."

He tried again. "Come on. Stop pouting. In spite of their overwhelming efficiency, there are things only you can do. Look how quickly you got together that list of guests to be invited 'on the bride's side.' You stayed up two whole nights!"

"Big deal. I can imagine what the Antonini list will be like."

"All right, what about the really important things you have a say in? The wedding gown, for one. You and Susan go to Bendel's tomorrow to get that, don't you? And the bridesmaids' dresses?"

"On her lunch hour, for heaven's sake!" Bea said. "Why does she have to give Kate Fenton a whole

84

month's notice? She's going to be absolutely exhausted, going to all the prewedding parties and working full time! And why doesn't she move home right away? It would be better to pay her share of two months' rent to Evie Maxwell and come back here to live until she's married."

Wil's patience began to wear thin. "Darling, it would be even more exhausting for her to commute right now. You know that! Take it easy. She'll still have a few weeks to herself after she leaves *Vogue*. You two will go trousseau-shopping and apartment-hunting and all those nice mother-daughter things."

"Apartment hunting," Bea repeated. "That's another ridiculous thing. They should be moving into their own place as soon as the tour is over. Not coming back to the fourth floor of the Antonini town house!"

Her husband counted to ten. "Okay. I agree with you. But it would be hard to find a place in a month. Staying with Richard's parents is only temporary. Maybe you and Susie *will* find the right apartment before she's married, but there's not much time. When they come back in December you and she can start looking in earnest."

"You know what I think? I don't think they're *ever* going to have their own place. I have a hunch Mrs. Antonini means for them to stay right there. She wants to hold onto Richard any way she can, even if it means putting up with his wife."

"Now why do you say a thing like that? You haven't even met Mrs. Antonini."

Bea was quiet for a moment. "I don't know. I just feel it, from the few things Susan says. And from the way Richard talked about his mother when the four of us had dinner last Thursday. She has an abnormal hold on that young man."

"Abnormal?"

"I don't mean anything *terrible*. Not incestuous! But he obviously thinks she's the Oracle of Delphi! Heaven help Susan. Your everyday, run-of-the-mill mother-in-law is enough to take, without having to cope with

85

such a paragon. And from what I hear, the sister and in-laws also excel in everything from child-rearing to the three-minute mile! Not that I don't think Susan isn't as good as—or better than—any of them. But she'll have her hands full."

"Richard will take care of her," Wil said. "He's a strong character in his own right. And he adores Susie."

"Yes," Bea admitted. "I liked him. More than I thought I would. There were no 'airs and graces' when he came here." She finally smiled. "I am being silly. I know that. My nose is terribly out of joint."

"Your nose is beautiful. Like the rest of you. Of course, you're a little weird," Wil teased. "Most mothers would cut off their right arms to see their daughters making such a brilliant marriage. Admit it. Aren't you the envy of the Friday-afternoon bridge club?"

"Idiot!" But he was right. It was only human, after all, to take pleasure in your child's achievements. And becoming the fiancée of one of the world's most eligible bachelors certainly had to be rated as no mean feat. Bea's friends were wild with envy.

Kate Fenton had different worries. Along with the reservations she and Beatrice shared about the Antoninis, Susan's boss was not convinced that her promising young associate could be happy "doing nothing." She said just that to Susan when she was told of the girl's plans to leave the magazine.

"You love working," Kate said. "You like being important in your own right. What the hell will you do with your time?"

"A million things! I'll be getting our own place ready, when we find one. After we're settled, I probably can do some volunteer work while Richard's busy during the day. And, of course, there's all the traveling. He tours half the year. There's no way I could hold down a full-time job even if I wanted to."

86

"I suppose not. Not if you plan to go everywhere with him. What about children?"

"Not right away. We've agreed to wait a couple of years."

"Good decision," Kate said noncommittally. "You still could do some writing, Susan. Free-lance features or articles for me. Even for other publications. I hate to see you give up the one piece of yourself that's your very own."

"I might try. Later. Thanks, Kate. It's a good idea."

She knew Kate was happy for her, yet troubled about this totally new character she was about to assume. Susan could understand. She privately felt some of those misgivings. But nothing was perfect. It would be a difficult adjustment but she didn't doubt she could make it. She was sorry Kate had refused to be her maid of honor. The woman had looked startled and then burst out laughing when Susan asked her.

"Me? Maid of honor? You must be kidding! That's all you need—an aging spinster doddering down the aisle ahead of you, dressed in some outlandish rig and holding a bunch of flowers! Get Evie or one of your other friends, for God's sake! It's ridiculous!"

She didn't realize how hurt Susan was until the girl said, almost inaudibly, "It doesn't seem ridiculous to me. You're my dearest friend."

Kate was filled with remorse. "Susie, I didn't mean I wasn't honored by your wanting me. It might be the best compliment I've ever had. But my dear, that kind of role is for someone your own age. Now if, God forbid, I were married and could be your *matron* of honor, that might be different. But this just isn't a suitable role for me. I'll be right up front, on your side of the church, cheering. By the way, who are your attendants?"

"Well, I guess I'll ask Evie to be maid of honor since you won't. I'm having Richard's sister and his two sisters-in-law as bridesmaids. I'd planned on Evie as the fourth. Now I suppose I'll ask one of my old college chums."

As she spoke, she realized that she had almost no close women friends. Not that she didn't like women. She had simply drifted away from the Bronxville group and except for Evie hadn't been that close to any young women in New York. It had been easy and (inadmissible thought!) probably politic to ask Richard's female relatives to attend her. It went along with his brothers and brother-in-law being ushers and Paul Carmichael his best man. Who is the fourth usher? Susan wondered, surprised she didn't know. It'll be interesting to see whether Paul and Evie like each other when they meet. They're both very attractive and unmarried . . . She paused, smiling at herself. I'm thinking like all my newly-wed friends whose devout mission in life is to get everybody else married. Matchmaking was a diversion she'd always scorned in others. And here she was mentally doing the same thing. It was a switch, but not the only one. Whoever would have thought Susan Langdon would hold still for this incredible production of a ceremony? She could hardly wait for it to be over and she could be alone with Richard. They'd have only a week before Boston and his first concert of the fall season. They'd rented a fully staffed house on Cape Cod for their honeymoon, a wild extravagance since they had to take it for the whole month of September and would spend only seven days in it, but it was what they both wanted—someplace secluded and quiet, yet close enough to Boston so that traveling time would not cut into their precious free days. Susan had, however, protested the houseful of servants.

"I can take care of us for a week," she'd said. "I'm no Julia Child, but I can keep us fed. Please, Richard. We don't need a bunch of retainers underfoot. Certainly not *this* week, particularly!"

"Darling, I don't want you in the *kitchen* on our honeymoon." He'd smiled endearingly. "Or any other time, for that matter. From here on in, your full-time job is wife and lover, mistress of *me*, not of the *house*."

He meant it well and Susan did not argue, but it was

another glimpse of things to come. She *wanted* to be mistress of her own house. They'd require help, of course, but not a huge staff.

"When we have our own apartment, I'll be mistress of that," she said. "Even if I'm only supervising a cleaning lady."

"One thing at a time, baby."

Sometimes he didn't understand Susan. She should have been thrilled at the thought of the luxury she was about to enjoy. She'd never known what it was like to be rich and waited on. It was as though she resisted the idea of having nothing to do. You'd think she'd be delighted to realize she could hire anybody she wanted for anything. Instead, she seemed troubled by the prospect. He was glad they couldn't rush into a place of their own. It was a good thing they'd live in his old bachelor quarters for a while. Susan would have a chance to get used to life in a big household, find out how to give orders to servants, learn from Maria how the well-oiled machinery of "gracious living" worked. Cleaning lady indeed! What was she thinking of? Even when they found their own place it would have to be something spectacular, a triplex, or maybe a town house, something that would require at least three in help. Susan was acting as though she saw them in a one-bedroom apartment with a dining area attached to the living room. Well, that was nothing to worry about for now. It would be months before they even considered their own establishment. There was the fall tour and a recording session scheduled for December and then the holidays. After that they'd be off for another series of recitals lasting well into the spring. With luck, he could postpone the departure from Seventieth Street for at least six months. Maybe more. Maybe even for a couple of years, until they had a child.

He supposed he'd misled Susan. She and her mother were looking for an apartment. No matter. They wouldn't come up with anything that suited him.

The 4 P.M. wedding was as storybook-beautiful as any ever seen by the hundreds who packed the church, the other hundreds who peered at the famous guests from behind police lines set up on the sidewalk, and the millions who gobbled up every gushing detail of the ceremony and reception on the six- and eleven-o'clock TV news that night, and in papers across the country next day.

Susan was glorious as she came toward the altar on her father's arm, regal in her ivory satin and lace gown with a little tiara of pearls holding her veil and a small bouquet of cream-colored roses crowning the white prayer book that Bea Langdon had carried at her own wedding twenty-six years before.

Gloria, Jacqueline, Mary Lou and Barbara Dudley, a childhood friend of Susan's, walked sedately down the aisle preceding Evelyn Maxwell, the maid of honor. In front of them were the ushers—Richard's brothers and brother-in-law and his young nephew, Joseph, Sergio's fifteen-year-old son. Susan had been surprised that the boy was chosen as the fourth usher.

"I thought you'd pick some old friend," she'd said to Richard when he told her.

"Thought I'd keep it in the family," he'd answered.

That wasn't true, Susan realized. The truth was that Richard had no close men friends except his manager. How strange that neither of us has contemporaries who are not related either to our families or our jobs. Even Barbara had been an almost "desperation" choice. Richard's background and mine are so different, Susan thought, and yet we're so much alike. Loners, really. He's been too occupied with music all his life to form any "outside attachments"; I've drifted away from my early ones. She hadn't seen Barb in nearly two years, not since her fourth bridesmaid's own wedding to Stan Dudley. She'd been surprised, rightly so, when Susan had asked her to be a member of the wedding, but she accepted with pleasure. The two had been inseparable as children, had gone to college together and then drifted apart when the one married and the other moved to New York and a job which absorbed her time and interests.

Susan's attendants were lovely in their ecru chiffon gowns, their arms full of yellow roses. Evie's dress was café-au-lait color, a dramatic touch between the bridesmaids' pale dresses and Susan's creamy satin. All the flowers in the church were in the bride's favorite tones—masses of yellow roses and trees of freesia, pale orange tulips and lemon-colored carnations. They gave the church a golden glow accented by hundreds of candles, and they filled it with the fragrance of springtime-past. It was like a beautiful oil painting, this stately parade, a moving masterpiece splashed with sunlight. Even the noticeable pregnant Gloria looked soft and serene, her floating gown for once diffusing the stocky outlines of the woman's figure.

In the front pew, Bea sighed with pleasure at the sight. And woman-like, she was glad she'd "gone overboard," as Wil insisted, in the choice of her own gown.

"You're the mother of the bride," he'd said. "The most important person there, after the bride and groom. Buy yourself something beautiful, darling. And don't look at the price tag!"

For once, she'd done just that. Her own outrageously expensive Stavropoulos chiffon gown in tones of pale blue shading to green was as beautiful as, maybe more beautiful than, Maria Antonini's gray silk-jersey Dior. True, she did not have the Antonini jewels, but she felt she did her daughter proud. We may not be rich, Bea thought, and this damned wedding is ten times what we can afford, but by God we won't be patronized by anybody! Neither, she thought proudly, would Susan. Watching her approach, so poised and dignified, Bea remembered her daughter's indignation as she recounted her refusal of Maria's suggestion that five-year-old Raoul Taffin and his three-year-old sister be ring-bearer and flower girl.

"I told her, 'No thanks,'" Susan reported. "My God, what does she think this is: The Coronation? Not enough to have a full choir and a fortune in flowers!

91

She actually wanted to have that little boy come down the aisle with my wedding ring on a satin pillow and that baby toddle along strewing rose petals in my path! Can you believe it? Even Richard was with me on that one!" Susan laughed. "He said he was damned if he was going to be at the mercy of a couple of scene-stealers barely out of diapers. I swear, Mother, Mrs. Antonini really *does* think they're the Royal Family!"

Bea had only smiled in reply. It was true, of course, she thought now. This is the wedding of a prince. Pay homage to the son of Maria. She and Mrs. Antonini had met twice, over tea in the town house, to discuss wedding details, and again the night before, when the entire wedding party had been Giovanni's and Maria's guests at an elaborate dinner at home. Like Susan, Bea had instantly taken to the maestro and was charmed by Jacqueline. As for the others, she found them polite but for the most part distant and even in some cases faintly sardonic. There was a great deal of the same almost cruel family teasing that Susan had seen in Pound Ridge, a strange undercurrent of rivalry among the sons and daughter as though each was constantly trying to outshine the others. Maria subtly fostered this, cleverly baiting them, pitting one against the other. What a ruthlessly ambitious woman she is! Bea thought. She doesn't love her children as a mother naturally does; she only wants them to win at everything. Richard was attentive to his fiancée's parents, and Paul Carmichael, whom Bea also liked immediately, was especially warm and considerate. Probably, she thought ruefully, because aside from Evie and Barbara and Stan Dudley, he was the only other "outsider." And even he was no stranger. As Richard's manager, he was as much a part of the family as anyone not born or married into it could be.

"Your daughter is marrying a great man, Mrs. Langdon," Paul had said. "He's the true genius in the family, aside from the Old Man, of course."

She'd smiled. "All I want him to be is a great husband. Susan deserves that."

He'd given her a serious, almost troubled look before he answered lightly, "Of course she does. We all love Susan. Every man here envies Richard his good luck."

Watching her husband and daughter come down the aisle, Bea thought fleetingly of that brief conversation. I hope they do love her, she prayed. But if they don't, don't let them destroy her.

❁

The newlyweds fled the reception as early as possible, taking the limousine a few short blocks to the Pierre Hotel, where they'd spend the night before leaving next morning for the Cape. In the suite, Susan collapsed with a sigh of relief.

"My God, it's only eight o'clock!" she said. "I feel as though it's four in the morning!"

"You didn't eat anything at the reception. Hungry? Want dinner sent up?"

She shook her head. "No. But that bottle of champagne in the bucket looks tempting."

"Let's have some while we're getting comfortable."

While they got into robes, Susan began to laugh.

"What's so funny?"

"I was just thinking how nice it is to be alone—and legal."

"You think a piece of paper is going to make it better?"

"Yes," she said. "Isn't that crazy? But I do."

Richard pulled her to him. "Let's find out how crazy you are."

I was right, she thought much later, lying beside him, fingering the diamond band on her left hand. It *was* better. The best. As close to heaven as I'll ever come. How hopelessly conventional I really am! She hadn't realized it when they'd been in bed before. She'd thought then that she couldn't know greater passion, more eagerness than she had during their affair. But knowing she was Richard's wife made her feel

93

free, uninhibited as she'd never been. And her abandon sweetened and strengthened his desire until they reached heights that left them both speechless with pleasure. It's as though we're discovering each other, Susan thought when they finally separated. She lay limp and satiated, happy beyond description. Then she reached over and began to caress her husband.

"Help!" Richard said weakly. "No more! Not yet!"

"I *was* right, wasn't I?"

He looked very serious. "Yes, sweetheart. Surprisingly, you were. I hope it will always be this good."

"Better," she teased. "On our fiftieth anniversary it'll be *super!* Oh, darling, I love you so much!"

"And I you." He gave her a little slap on the rear end. "Hey, it's nearly nine-thirty. Think I'll call down and see if the first editions of the papers are in."

"You're kidding! Who gives a damn about papers?"

"We had a helluva press turnout."

"I know. I didn't think I'd ever get rid of those funny purple circles in front of my eyes from the flashbulbs."

"You'll get used to it," Richard said. "It comes with the territory."

While they waited for the papers, Susan chattered. "Did you ever see anybody cry as hard as my Aunt Clara? I thought her dress would melt! And your father was so darling. His toast to us was sweet. I'm glad Evie caught the bouquet. I aimed at her, of course. Do you think she and Paul liked each other?"

The doorbell buzzed before he could answer and a bellman handed Richard the *Times* and the *Daily News*. Susan made a face.

"I don't know why you give a hoot about a dumb picture of me in my wedding gown. They'll just run that along with the press release of who attended. I can recite that story to you in advance. The headline will say 'Susan Langdon weds Richard Antonini,' and then there'll be a dreary account of who wore what, and all the other canned information Gerry sent them a week ago. Bor-ing!"

Richard glanced at the papers, smiled, and passed them to her.

"There, my love, is your bor-ing little story."

Susan's eyes widened. She'd expected an important account of her wedding on the society pages, but she'd not imagined it would be treated as news, rushed into print like some major, late-breaking story. The *Times* had a four-column picture of herself and Richard emerging from the church with the heading, "Concert Pianist Richard Antonini Weds." The *News* went all-out, devoting the entire two-page center spread to photographs of the ceremony and the reception. There were not only candid shots inside the church, but pictures of Giovanni and Maria arriving, a shot of Sergio leaving, with Mary Lou barely visible behind him. There was a close-up of the newlyweds cutting the wedding cake and photographs of the great of the music world—opera stars, symphony conductors, violinists, pianists, impresarios. With its usual irresistible urge for puns, the paper had captioned the story "DUET LOOK LIKE A SOLO FOR ANTONINI?"

Susan threw down the pages in disgust. "It's obscene! They make it sound like Barnum and Bailey! It's so vulgar! Kids are dying in Viet Nam and blacks are being beaten up in Alabama, and the best use they can make of space is to report a wedding like it was big news! It reads like a bash at the court of Louis XIV! I'm surprised there isn't a picture of some fat soprano stuffing her face and saying, 'Let 'em eat cake'!"

He was not amused. "It's probably vulgar, Susie, but it's good box office. You're just annoyed because you're surprised. I expected it. You'd better be ready for this and a lot worse when it comes to your precious privacy." Then he softened. "Sweetheart, don't be upset. You belong to the world now, just as you belong to me." He held out his hand, smiling. "You know what happens to bad little girls when they have temper tantrums, don't you? They get sent to bed. And you, thank God, are a bad little girl."

In spite of herself, Susan laughed as he picked her

up and carried her into the bedroom. But it was more than the outlandish publicity that bothered her. The biggest disappointment was that there'd been just the briefest mention of "the bride's parents." For all anybody cared, she could have been an orphan.

In other houses and apartments around New York, other Antoninis sent out for the early editions.

"I do wish Richard would be more careful about camera angles," Maria said. "He *knows* his right side is the better one."

"Perhaps he had other things on his mind," Giovanni answered mildly.

"Jesus, I'm getting fat!" Sergio said.

"Susan looked lovely, didn't she?" Jacqueline asked Walter.

In the guest suite on East Seventieth Street, Gloria threw her copy of the paper in the wastebasket. "No pictures of *us*. As *usual*." Raoul didn't answer. He was already asleep.

Chapter Eight

The week that followed her wedding was one of surprises for Susan, most of them wonderful. Wonderful to awaken beside the man she loved, knowing it was her rightful place. Enchanting to discover the everyday little things that were all part of Richard—what foods he liked and what he hated; the television he preferred ("talk shows" primarily); his fascination with diets and exercise and all forms of physical fitness; his vast knowledge of musical lore. Every piece of trivia seemed a separate, interesting revelation. She did not see them forming a picture of a totally self-involved man, protective of his health and his youthful good looks, scornful and envious of other celebrities, educated only about his own field. She did not see him as ego-ridden and intellectually shallow. Through her infatuated eyes, he was not vain but artistic. His narrowness of interests she interpreted as dedication, his food-faddism as the eccentricity of genius. Even his flashes of male chauvinism seemed excitingly masculine and dominant, and as a lover he was expert and insatiable.

They rose late, breakfasted heartily, took long walks along the ocean, holding hands and stopping occasionally to kiss. Susan felt like the heroine in a soft-focus foreign film, as though she were drifting in the misty atmosphere of some perfect, unreal world. She chided herself for resenting the hours each afternoon when Richard left her for the piano. The first day, she protested when he said he had to practice.

"Oh, Richard, no! Not this week!"

"This week and *every* week, my darling. Can't afford to get rusty, especially when I have a performance seven days from now."

He was perfectly right, of course. This was no businessman on holiday. An artist could not let down for one moment. She tried not to be jealous of the hours he literally shut her out of his life. What a child I am, she thought, wanting every minute of his time, every second of his company. I will aways have to share him with his music. It is the focus of his life. I'm only grateful that what's left over is so intensely, irrevocably devoted to me.

And she *was* proud and grateful the first time she heard him perform after their marriage. It was as though his brilliance was now partly her own. From her seat in the audience in Boston's Symphony Hall, she was so moved that tears literally ran down her face. She wanted to stand up and announce that he was hers, that this beautiful creature at the piano was her adored husband. Susan's eyes and ears and heart devoured him from the moment he made his entrance onstage. She felt she would burst with happiness when the audience stood and cheered, applauding wildly as he entered and faced them with a grave smile and a formal little bow.

He seated himself at the big Steinway, waited, showman-like, for the settling-in-seats to subside, the coughing to stop, the rustling of programs to cease. And then those wonderful hands that excited her began their seduction of the piano. She had heard him play in public before, but it seemed to her that there was new passion in his performance, as though it matched his love-making. There were gentle, caressing motions followed by great slashes of power. She felt the depth of emotion in his approach, the concentration on detail, the melodic shadings, the exquisite intricacies, the whispers of measures and the great surges, like thunder, relating them to his love-making. I've done something for him, she thought, awed. He's never been this great.

At intermission she went backstage, helped him into a complete change of clothing. He seemed to barely notice her as he stripped off his sweat-soaked morning coat and put on everything fresh from the skin out. She'd been amazed, as they left their suite at the Ritz-Carlton, to see how much they carried with them. Richard went to the auditorium in casual clothes and brought another, more conservative "street outfit" to wear when he left past waiting crowds. In addition, there were the two complete sets of formal wear, plus his own special brand of soap, deodorant and cologne, even the blow-dryer he used for his hair and Band-Aids to protect the little finger of each hand.

Susan had laughed. "You look as though you're going away for the weekend."

He hadn't been amused. He hardly seemed to know she was there. He was already temporarily lost to her, deep in thoughts of his work, mentally rehearsing the music. It was the same at intermission. Paul Carmichael was also in the dressing room, acting as Susan did—as a quiet pair of hands, following orders, speaking little, aware that they must not break the intense concentration necessary for the second half of the performance and the encores. She wanted to tell her husband how superb he was, how extraordinary, but she sensed he would not hear her. This was the "performing Richard," as unaware of his wife as he would have been of a paid attendant. She was not hurt. She and Paul smiled at each other, knowing that this Richard was oblivious to everything but his music.

When he finished the final encore—the *Étincelles,* by Moszknowski—Susan unthinkingly stood with the rest, screaming, "Bravo!" as he took his bows and finally shook his head and made a little gesture of apology, as though to say, "I'd go on forever to please you, but I am exhausted."

Reluctantly, they let him go. Then Paul was at her side, protecting her as they made their way through the crowds that swarmed backstage, elbowing aside the throngs of admirers who hoped to get into their idol's presence.

"Excuse us," Paul kept saying. "Would you make way for Mrs. Antonini, please?"

The new words sounded wonderful. There would be many afternoons and evenings when Paul would guide and shelter her, clearing a path with the same polite but forceful request. But never again would she feel what she did that first time. She would come to recognize the more obscure music, anticipate the modest gestures Richard would make as he accepted the hysterical adulation. But she'd never recapture that first magic moment of awareness, that total revelation of Richard's unique gift. In the dressing room she hung back as people surrounded him, kissed him, suffocated him with compliments. He loved it. It was some time before he even saw her. Then, across the room he gave her a smile she interpreted as a special embrace, and she hugged it to her, content.

In Chicago and Minneapolis and Houston and Dallas and San Antonio, Richard repeated his triumphs. He practiced daily on the piano that was made available in each city . . . those concert grands pianists referred to by the numbers assigned by Steinway. When he was in the flower-filled hotel suite he was constantly surrounded by people: local VIP's, patrons of the arts, and the omnipresent press, shuttled in and out by Gerry Carter, who joined them in Boston and expertly manipulated the impossible demands of local papers and TV stations.

At one moment when she and Richard were dressing for a dinner party, Susan, wearing only a bra and panties, said, playfully, "Gerry does a fantastic job, doesn't she? I could almost be jealous of the way she takes you over."

He'd laughed. "She's a terrific press agent."

"So how come she wasn't around when I interviewed you for *Vogue?*"

"I don't know, darling. She's always busier when we're out of town. Maybe she was doing something else that day. Or maybe I had a hunch I'd want you all to myself."

"Now you're telling me you're psychic?" Susan grinned. "You want me to believe you knew I was going to be special?"

He'd come close to her, then, pressing his body against hers. "Could be. I can smell a sexy woman even over the telephone." He pulled the bra away and kissed her breasts. "You're delicious." His hands began to move.

"Darling, stop! We're due at dinner in half an hour."

"The hell with it. Let 'em wait."

✸

She'd be glad to get home, even if home was the Antonini house. The trip was exciting but exhausting. She'd never realized how complicated it was to go on tour with a celebrity, and a demanding one, at that. Richard hated hotel food, so they took full suites with kitchens, which meant that Susan made breakfast the way her husband liked it, fresh and piping hot, not lukewarm from room service. He was fussy about his diet, so Gerry arranged in each city to have a chef come in to prepare other meals which Paul and Gerry usually shared. Occasionally, they went to a party in some elegant private home, but only if the hostess was rich and influential . . . someone who could not be offended because she was "important."

They did not go to many such events and Susan was not sorry. The dinner parties and cocktail receptions were stiff and formal, and though she did not begrudge the fact that Richard was the focus of attention, she felt merely tolerated.

They had, in fact, very little fun for the next three months. When he was not practicing or giving interviews or receiving people, Richard needed rest. He conserved his energy for concerts and his charm for the press and public. He was still sexually greedy, but there were times when Susan felt his mind was somewhere else even when his body was over her own. Still, she was not unhappy. Her response to his touch was instant and as hungry as his. But she found herself restless with too much time on her hands. She did the local shops and museums and art galleries, and when he had time, Paul came with her. She grew fonder of Paul every day. He was becoming her closest friend, her only confidant. A lanky, somewhat rumpled, even-tempered young man of thirty, he was a marked contrast to the spectacular Richard. She was not physically attracted to him, but she loved his company and felt easy with him, to the point where she could discuss things with which she'd never dare bother her preoccupied husband. Things such as the letters that poured in wherever they went. Susan, in her new role as wife/lover/semiservant, had voluntarily taken on the chore of going through the daily mail. It surprised her to find that a classical musician inspired the same kind of manic devotion as a film actor or a rock star. The letters came on heavily engraved stationery and blue-lined pages of schoolgirls' notebooks. Some were pure "fan mail," shy and reverential or overly effusive. But many verged on the obscene, saying what they'd like to do to Richard or have Richard do to them. They were disturbing letters and, of course, never acknowledged.

"I can't believe what people write!" She and Paul were strolling through the Chicago Art Institute. "I've never read such uninhibited propositions! Good Lord, you'd think Richard had his own "groupies'!"

Paul smiled. "He has. The sickies go for *any* celebrity, and to some people Richard's sexier at that piano than Elvis with his guitar. Don't *you* feel that sensuous quality when he plays?"

"Yes, of course. But my God, Paul, you wouldn't think that strangers presumably interested in the classics would have such thoughts about Richard!"

"Why not?" Paul's handsome face darkened. "They're still people who fantasize about being screwed by somebody famous. It's been going on for years, Susie. Since he was eighteen." He paused. "Frankly, I'm glad he's safely married."

She looked at him curiously. "Don't tell me Richard ever *responded* to any of these nymphomaniacs!"

"Honey, he's human, too. You must know Richard had quite a reputation with the ladies."

"Well, yes, but I thought . . ."

"You thought he was an ordinary bachelor, dating your kind of girls and sometimes taking them to bed."

Susan didn't answer. Yes, she had thought that, though she didn't want to think about any of it any more. She knew Richard had been far from a saint. He was attractive, unmarried and full of normal desires, but he was also discriminating and discreet. That's what she'd believed. That was understandable. Forgivable. After all, she'd been to bed with men before

102

she met Richard. But she'd known and liked them, even thought herself in love with them.

"I don't mean to shock you," Paul went on, "but any famous man is subject to temptations the ordinary guy never runs into. Fame as an aphrodisiac works both ways, you know. Anyway, that's over, thank God. He has you now and he loves you very much. Don't pay any attention to the letter writers who're just dying to get on their backs for him. Or any other position he might suggest. In fact, if I were you I'd give up the secretarial duties. Leave the mail to Gerry or to me. We'll send it back to the office to be answered or destroyed."

"Don't be silly. I know it doesn't mean anything. Richard doesn't read it." She smiled. "Not any more."

"Then why should *you?* Or do you dig masochism?"

The words stayed with her. It was naïve to think that Richard could have resisted some of these titillating propositions. What man could turn away from the erotic opportunity to have any kind of sex he wanted, any time, in any way he chose, from people who worshiped him? All right. Forget it. That's past. And Paul was right. Reading all that nonsense *was* masochistic. Turn it off, Susan, she told herself. Your husband is an attractive, sought-after man who was once susceptible. But that's all over. And it was only an ego trip when it was happening. He doesn't need that kind of flattery any more. Nor does he have time or opportunity with me around, she thought wryly, somewhat startled by her own cynicism. Anyway, she still didn't believe that Richard had ever gotten involved with the kind of promiscuous, oversexed women who wrote to him, no matter what Paul implied. Richard could have his pick of the best. I wonder if he ever had an affair with Gerry? Susan thought suddenly. She was a striking divorcée, five or six years older than Richard, and worldly in a way that Susan was not. Gerry obviously was devoted to him, though she'd never given the slightest hint that theirs had been more than a close business relationship. Could you be in love with a man, make love to him and then when he married, turn it off to become the perfect, impersonal employee? It seemed hard to believe. Even Gerry wasn't *that* sophisticated. What kind of crazy thoughts were these? It came from reading that stupid, erotic mail, from watching women make fools of themselves when Richard was in a room, from seeing him be charming and attentive to pretty girls and chic women whose names he could not even remember. She'd never been a jealous woman and she wouldn't start now. But, Susan thought that day in Chicago, I'll be glad when we get back to New York where the spotlight momentarily dims.

The trip also made her realize how anonymous she felt and how much she needed some identity of her own. It was not enough for her to stay docilely in the background all the time. Kate was right. She'd do some writing when she got home. Face it. She got a kick out of seeing her name in print. Maybe she'd look into volunteer work as she'd also considered. The taste of "importance" she'd had on *Vogue,* however minor, was something she missed. Not that she intended to be a "career woman" ever again, but there was no reason why she couldn't be Mrs. Richard Antonini and still achieve things on her own.

They came back to New York early in December, the day before Gloria produced the expected twins whom she named Pierre and Claudette, in grudging acknowledgment of Raoul's dead parents. Susan and Jacqueline went to visit Gloria in Doctors Hospital, where that untypical mother seemed almost disinterested in the whole affair. Even her sisters-in-law's enthusiasm for the adorable twins produced nothing but a yawn and the indifferent response that "they seemed healthy enough."

Over lunch in the Palm Court of the Plaza Hotel, Susan shook her head in wonderment.

"I don't understand Gloria. She acts as though she couldn't care less about those babies. Why on earth does she keep on having children? She doesn't even pay much attention to Raoul, Jr., or Maria. They're always with their nurse, I gather."

Jacqueline nodded. "Don't ask me to play curbstone psychiatrist, but I'll bet you a nickel Gloria will have at least one more."

"For heaven's sake, *why?*"

"Two reasons. She's forty years old and determined to prove that age doesn't matter. And now she's even with Maria. They both have four kids, but Gloria still has time to top her."

Susan stared at her sister-in-law. "You've got to be kidding! About outproducing Maria, I mean. That's insane!"

"Is it? She can't beat her mother at looks or charm or brains. She's not even that much better at sports, when Maria chooses to play well. But biologically she can practice one-upmanship on the old girl. She hates her, you know." Jacqueline made the pronouncement as calmly as if she were saying that Gloria detested spinach.

"Hates her own mother?"

"It may be unthinkable to you, Susan, because you love yours and, more importantly, she loves you. Poor old Gloria's never had anything from Maria but grudging acceptance, and damned little of that. Maria can't forgive her for not being beautiful or talented or both, and she hasn't made much of a secret of it. For all that tough exterior, Gloria's dying for approval. She knows damned well nobody loves her. She wasn't even married for love." Jacqueline gave a brittle little laugh. "I'm not sure any of us was."

Susan didn't answer.

"I'm not saying *Richard* doesn't love *you*," Jacqueline said. "I was talking about Mary Lou and me. She won't admit that her husband is incapable of honest affection *or* fidelity. She just goes her chin-up way, buying clothes and jewelry in the hope that Serge will notice she's alive."

"But if he didn't love her, why did Sergio marry her?"

"Good question. My hunch is he decided at twenty-nine his image called for a wife. Someone presentable, and tractable who'd wipe out the frivolous playboy stigma and make him appear a serious artist, like the father he envies. He'll never hold a candle to Joe as a conductor, but he doesn't know that. He wants to be *more* famous. And Maria's always encouraged him to believe he would be. Mary Lou is part of the picture of 'stability.' Sergio the husband and father. The family man. What a laugh! He travels alone, you know. And in every town there's some cute little thing waiting for him with open legs and a closed mouth. At least, he likes to *think* it's closed. Everybody in the world knows what a tomcat Serge is."

Susan's unspoken question hung in the air. Jacqueline looked at her, faintly amused.

"You're dying to know about Walter and me, aren't you?"

"No, of course not," Susan lied, "it's none of my business. Anyway, I don't believe Walter didn't marry you for love. You're so beautiful and poised and . . ."

"And I was twenty-four years old when I married Walter because I decided it was more glamorous and interesting being an Antonini than an aging post-debutante in New Orleans. I didn't love him, Susan. And he didn't love me. But when I deliberately got pregnant during our 'courtship,' there wasn't much he could do, being who he was. I refused to have an abortion and the Antonini family couldn't tolerate a scandal about their darling budding-genius-composer. So we got married. It hasn't been bad. I like being Mrs. Antonini with a big Park Avenue apartment and a lot of amusing jet-set friends. Walter and I go our own ways, pretty much. We really like each other and the kids. It's an okay arrangement. He has his 'friends' and I have mine. There's been no marital sex in our house-

106

hold for ten years. I have two nice boys and an attractive husband and a not too rapidly shifting roster of lovers. So does Walter. But we keep up appearances. I don't embarrass him and he pays me the same courtesy. If people talk, the hell with them. They can't prove anything, and a little gossip adds to my glamour. Like being married to a bisexual does." She smiled. "Don't look so shocked. Ours is a good deal more honest than most marriages."

"You've never thought of divorce?"

"Thought of it? Once or twice when someone I was involved with began to get to me in more than a physical way. But I always came to my senses. Why should I divorce Walter when we can both have our cake, etc., etc.? The best thing about our marriage is the fact that it's cast-iron protection against making the same mistake twice. Walter and I both know that. We can back off from any entanglement with the excuse that we're already married."

"But aren't you ever jealous?"

"Susan, my dear, jealousy is an infantile emotion. The sentimental indulgence of unrealistic people who fancy that love lasts forever. Look at Maria. Joe had a hundred affairs when, you should pardon the expression, he was up to it. Did she care? Maybe the first or second time. I don't know. But for years she's been much too busy building a musical dynasty to give a damn what Giovanni does—or did—with his spare time. If outside sex made him a better conductor, I'm sure Maria would have acted as procuress. She knows all about her two sons' extramarital adventures, you can bet your life on that. But as long as there's nothing overt and messy, no blot on the family escutcheon by them or the daughters-in-law, she chooses to ignore *that* part of our lives. Thank God for small favors!"

Susan remembered Maria's "speech" the first time they met. Whether Jacqueline knew it or not, Mrs. Antonini did not consider her sons' wives helpful to their careers. Or had she said that only in the hope of discouraging *Richard's* marriage? And would she also ignore Richard's behavior if he followed the example of his father and brothers? Susan shuddered. It was unthinkable that her husband would want to make love to another woman. As unthinkable as her seeking another man. And if, God forbid, Richard ever was unfaithful, could she accept it in the casual way Jacqueline handled her own marriage? Never. She was repelled by what she'd heard. She was not an unsophisticated woman, but Jacqueline's jaded discussion of her own life and that of her in-laws *did* shock Susan. It was decadent. Her sister-in-law was no better than those horrible women who offered themselves by mail to Richard!

No. That was unfair. Jacqueline was honest, realistic. She was a nice woman, strangely enough, though she gave herself no credit for being one. Perhaps she'd even lied about her "deliberate" pregnancy. Perhaps she'd loved Walter and might love him still. It was possible that she was simply making the best of a bad marriage, for her children's sake. What would I do in her situation? Susan wondered. It's wrong of me to judge her. I should judge those men, those Antonini men whose need for blind adulation is stronger than their vows. She tried to match Jacqueline's offhand manner.

"And what about Raoul and Gloria?" she said. "Is that the same kind of marriage?" Susan answered herself. "No, of course it isn't. Not with all those babies coming along every minute."

Jacqueline raised an eyebrow. "It doesn't take long to make a baby. Gloria wouldn't stray. Who'd look at her? But Raoul? My dear Susan, he's an attractive Frenchman with a dreary wife whom he also did not marry for love. What do *you* think?"

I don't want to hear any more, Susan thought suddenly. I want to get out of here.

Jacqueline sensed her distress. "I'm sorry, Susan. I suppose I really shouldn't have gone into all this. But you're family now. It's pointless to pretend. Please don't think this has anything to do with you. Richard's

108

sown his wild oats. He didn't *need* marriage; he *wanted* it. Your life won't be like any of ours. I'm certain of that."

"I am too. I know Richard. And I know myself."

We're both lying, Susan thought. Nothing is certain except my unswerving love for the man I married. But please, God, don't ever let him put my love to that kind of test.

Chapter Nine

In New York, Susan had little time to think seriously about the resolution she'd made in Chicago. The awareness that she would not be content without some degree of independent action remained in the back of her mind, but she was too busy with the holidays to explore the possibilities. Before Christmas, she talked on the phone with Kate and was ashamed to feel pleased when that outspoken woman complained bitterly that she still hadn't been able to find a good replacement.

"You're *sure* you couldn't come back to work?"

"You know I can't, Kate. We leave on another tour in February. I'm dying to tell you about that life! Nobody would believe the experiences of an artist on the road!"

"Maybe you should write a piece about it. Firsthand account."

Susan hesitated. "I don't know. I'm not sure Richard would approve."

"Do it and *then* tell him. I bet he'll be delighted. Forgive me, pet, but he *does* like publicity."

"Let me think about it."

The idea appealed to her and there was enough material to make an amusingly biting story. She'd have to be careful, though, that it didn't reflect badly on Richard. She could be satirical about the rigors of travel, the inanities of the "cultured" people they met, the blatant social climbers and hero-worshipers. Even the incredible fan mail would be a revelation. And Kate was right. Richard did love publicity. Gerry was good at the "artistic" side of it, but no one except the celebrity's wife could tell the "behind the scenes" story. It could be handled with taste, tongue-in-cheek. Yes, it was worth thinking about, once she had Christmas behind her.

Christmas. It was certainly the kind an only child had never known, Susan thought, as she shopped feverishly for gifts. Nine adult Antoninis and Taffins and eight children! Not to mention twelve servants between the town house and Pound Ridge! And then there were her own mother and father, and Kate, Evie Maxwell, Paul and Gerry! Thirty-five presents to be found and wrapped . . . and so many of them doubly difficult because they were for people who "had everything." What on earth did one give the Senior Antoninis? Or, for that matter, the rest of the family?

She was ambivalent about Christmas in the country. There'd been no question that they'd go to Maria's. Richard hadn't even consulted her. He'd simply taken it for granted that Maria would have her "gathering of the clan." The idea of a big family, of the excitement of the children, of a country Christmas, maybe with snow, appealed to Susan's romantic nature. But part of her was sad to be away from her own parents, sad for herself and for them. It would be their first Christmas apart and even the premature celebration on December 23, when she and Richard went to Bronxville, was depressing, for all the attempted heartiness.

Bea cooked a wonderful, traditional dinner and they

110

drank wine and opened their gifts under the same kind of tree Susan had had every year of her life. But in spite of the determined gaiety and the enthusiastic exchange of gifts, there was a wistful look in Bea's eyes and even Wil seemed unusually subdued. Susan and Richard did not exchange their presents that evening. That would be saved for the "real" Christmas. But they gave Beatrice an exquisite strand of cultured pearls with a diamond clasp, and Wil a handsome new set of the most expensive golf clubs.

"Such extravagance!" Bea said. "My dears, you shouldn't have!"

"Richard insisted," Susan bubbled, delighted they were pleased. "Do you really like them?"

"We love them, baby," her father said. "Thank you both."

"I'm afraid our gifts to you don't quite compare," Bea said, "but they come with all our love."

Susan eagerly unwrapped her present. It was a thin gold chain at the end of which was a small gold star inscribed, in minute letters, "Susan-Richard. First Christmas, 1964."

Tears came to her eyes as she kissed her parents. "It's beautiful. And you know what a pushover I am for sentimental things. Thank you, darlings. I'll wear it always."

"Hey, look at these!" Richard said. "You're not the only star in the family, my girl!" He proudly displayed star-shaped gold cuff links. "Thanks so much, Mrs. Langdon, Mr. Langdon! They're beautiful! And I really need them!"

Susan looked at him gratefully. Her parents would never know that he owned at least two dozen pairs of cuff links, gold and platinum, real pearls and diamond clusters. He was being darling, and she loved him for it.

"You went pretty far overboard yourselves," she said, "showering us with gold! We didn't expect all this after the enormous expense of the wedding."

"Sweetheart, your mother and I love you both." Wil

put his arm around his wife. "The best gift is to see how happy you are together." He lifted his glass of champagne. "Here's to marriage. May yours always be as complete and rewarding as ours has been."

They drank solemnly and exchanged kisses. It was a gentle, tender moment. I feel as though I'm taking my vows all over again, Susan thought. And as though Mother and Dad are renewing theirs. Once again, she felt a little pang at the thought of her separations from them at the holidays. Then she smiled, hoping it was a bright, cheerful smile.

"What are you two doing for Christmas?" she asked.

"Going over to the Emersons' for dinner," Bea said. The Emersons were the Langdons' closest friends. "They're having their three children and five grandchildren for dinner that day. It will be a mob scene," Bea went on, "but I'm sure it will be fun."

There was no reproach in her voice, that the Antoninis hadn't asked them. Certainly Richard heard none as he said, "That sounds nice. Christmas is the time for mob scenes, I guess. But Lord knows how we'll get through that madness in Pound Ridge!"

He didn't mean to be unfeeling. He couldn't know how bereft Bea and Wil felt this year. Damn it. Maria *could* have asked them! Susan quickly changed the subject. After all, the Antoninis couldn't ask *all* the in-laws' families. She couldn't expect hers to be an exception.

"As soon as we get back, Mom, you and I will start apartment-hunting again, okay? We sure didn't have much luck in August, but we didn't have much time, either. It'll be almost two months before we have to leave again. I'm sure we'll find something perfect."

"We'll do our damnedest," Bea said, looking at Richard. Did she imagine he avoided her gaze? Did he have no intention of leaving Seventieth Street? If so, Susan was unaware of it. It's probably all in my mind, her mother thought. He's too sensible a young man not to realize that living with one's parents can be a dreadful mistake.

On the way home, Richard took one hand off the wheel and pulled Susan close to him.

"About that apartment business, honey. Don't you think we ought to let it go for a bit? After all, we're off on tour again so soon. Why not wait until we get back?"

There was no response.

"Susie?"

She answered very slowly. "You really don't want a place of your own, do you? I showed you a couple of good apartments before we were married and you found a million things wrong with them. Now you don't even want me to look. I don't understand."

"What's to understand? Of course we'll get an apartment, or maybe a house, but what's the big rush?"

"I don't want to live with your parents. It's as simple as that. We're like children, occupying the fourth floor. I want to run my own house, Richard. Not be a guest in someone else's."

"I'd think you'd be damned appreciative of your easy life." He was angry. "Not that we've been there enough for you to even *know* whether you like it or not!"

"I didn't marry you for an easy life. I married you because I love you and want to make a home for you."

"Well, goddammit, we have a home!"

"No. We only have an address. Your parents' address."

He went stony-silent, both hands on the wheel, eyes straight ahead, concentrating on his driving. The grim set of his mouth was Susan's answer. He has no intention of moving out, she realized. Not now. Not even soon. It's all too comfortable, too easy, too irresponsible. He can have his wife and his mother and his own bed. Life is very uncomplicated this way. He doesn't have to make a decision, except about his work. At least he has that. I have nothing to make me feel important. Not even a house to manage. Or children to

113

raise. My darling is truly a Taurus baby. Stubborn beyond belief.

Her thoughts jolted her into the seemingly simple answer. There was only one way to escape. It was underhanded but necessary. Richard's suite wasn't big enough for them *and* a baby.

Katherine Antonini was conceived in February in a suite in The Everglades Club in Palm Beach during a free weekend, and born in the hotel-like atmosphere of New York's Doctors Hospital in November of 1965, fourteen months after Susan and Richard were married.

Looking at the little pink, squirming bundle they put into her arms at feeding time, her mother no longer felt guilty. Escape from one's in-laws was the wrong reason for having a baby, but now that Katie was here, Susan was so suffused with love for her that she was sure it had been the right thing to do, whatever the motive. She was no longer an excuse. She was an adored and welcomed daughter. Even Richard, once he'd gotten over the shock of Susan's announcement in April, had been satisfactorily enthusiastic about impending fatherhood and was endearingly proud of his beautiful child. He'd even (wonder of wonders!) canceled his November engagements to be in New York with Susan when she was due to be delivered.

Bless you, angel, Susan thought, looking down at her baby. You've changed our lives. In the first months of her pregnancy, Susan was ashamed of her deliberate plot. She and Richard *had* agreed to wait two years before starting a family, and when she told him about "the accident" she was sorry to lie and not very proud of her devious plan. But if Richard had any idea of what was in her mind, he gave no sign of it. He agreed to the necessity of their own place and approved the duplex co-operative apartment she found in June at Sixty-first and Park Avenue. He amiably discussed renovation and decorating schemes with her, fussed over her endlessly, warning her not to "overdo."

There was so much structural work to be done in the ten rooms that they could not move in until late August. Susan, feeling wonderfully healthy, cheerfully agreed to spend the summer in Pound Ridge in "Richard's house," commuting to New York once a week to consult with workmen and decorators and check on the progress of her new home. Things were so good with her and Richard that even Maria's silently furious presence did not disturb her, nor did the "gaggle of Antoninis," as she thought of them, make her feel as insecure and inadequate as they had a year before. In time, she almost forgot she'd done a deceitful thing, just as she forgot Maria's icy reception of the news when they told her and Giovanni, adding that they'd be looking for a place big enough for them and the baby and a nurse.

"I see," Maria said. "Naturally, the fourth floor won't be suitable for you now that you have a family so quickly on the way."

She knows, Susan thought. She knows I deliberately got pregnant to get us out of here. She wondered whether she was blushing. She felt uncomfortable under her mother-in-law's steady gaze, but she said nothing. She would not say she was sorry they'd be leaving. Such a blatant lie would be too obvious.

"My ninth grandchild," Giovanni said proudly. "What shall we have? Another composer or conductor or pianist? Or shall we wish for a beautiful girl?"

Susan reacted immediately. "Why couldn't we have both?"

"Twins?" Giovanni twinkled. "You're going to compete with Gloria?"

She'd laughed. "No, Papa-Joe. But is it impossible for a *girl* to be a musical genius?" She'd easily fallen into the habit of calling him "Papa-Joe" as the grandchildren did. She was unable to call Maria anything but "Mrs. Antonini." For that matter, she'd never been invited to. "There already are some female virtuosos,"

115

Susan went on. "And there'll be many more by the time our child grows up."

The maestro had smiled in agreement. "Of course, of course, my dear. You are quite right. Antonia Brico was the first woman to conduct the Berlin Philharmonic back in 1930. I remember Schweitzer, Klemperer, Bruno Walter, Sibelius all giving their support. Pity, though, it didn't last. I believe she gives piano lessons now."

"What about Lili Boulanger's *Faust et Hélène* that won the Grand Prix de Rome in 1913?" Richard asked. "And how about her sister Nadia? She conducted the New York Philharmonic in 1939 and again for a week three years ago." He was enjoying the little game, pleased to show his father that he, too, was scholarly.

"Quite right," Giovanni said again. "And don't forget Sarah Caldwell up in Boston. Or Rosalyn Tureck. She also led the Philharmonic, though it was from the keyboard, which doesn't literally qualify as conducting. Well, now, Susan. Perhaps your daughter will be a famous musician." He patted her head. "That is, unless you have a son. Then it will be a certainty."

"Maybe she'll be a great pianist, like her father," Susan said. "Don't forget about Gina Bachauer."

"Such nonsense!" Maria snapped. "The musical talents of women lie primarily in their voices. Anyway, it seems rather a waste of time to speculate on the child's future before it's born."

"You have a point, Mother dear. Let's get him *or* her born healthy and then see what happens." Richard was appeasing Maria. "I'll take a chance on the Antonini heritage."

Susan had been ridiculously pleased by her husband's defense of women and Giovanni's contribution to the subject. Maria was more antifeminist than any of them. How strange, Susan thought, when she is such an achiever. But of course it's not achievement for herself she wants. It's for the men in her family.

"I adore you," Susan said that night when she and

116

Richard were in bed. She touched him and felt him respond.

"Shouldn't I be a little careful of you?" he'd asked, almost nervously.

Susan laughed. "Not for months, my darling. And then not for too long!" She patted her belly proudly. "Look. Three months and I don't even show!"

He touched her already swelling breasts. "You do here. And it's marvelous. Maybe I should always keep you pregnant if you're going to be this sexy."

It had been, except for fleeting moments, a wonderful six months, Susan mused now as Katherine greedily attacked one of those full breasts. She loved the apartment, was never bored for a moment, not even when Richard went off in September for six weeks without her. She'd missed him terribly, of course, but it had been fun to catch up with Evie Maxwell and Barbara Dudley for "girl lunches." She had a great deal of time with Bea and Wil, spending nights in her old room in Bronxville and having them stay in town sometimes with her. She'd been able to dine often with Kate, who was still urging her to write.

"I can't do it now," Susan had said again. "I'm much too busy getting the apartment in shape."

"Bull," Kate had said bluntly. "You don't want to. You're afraid Richard won't like it."

"Don't be silly!" She told Kate about the support of women musicians Richard had voiced in the spring. "He's no chauvinist. He'd be *glad* if I did something on my own."

"*That* is what *I* told *you* months ago," Kate reminded her.

"Well, I'll get around to it. After the baby."

Kate shrugged. "How's lovely Maria?"

"All right, I guess. I haven't seen anything of the family since Richard's been away. Except for Jacqueline. We have lunch together often, and talk on the phone nearly every day."

"Nice *somebody* in that family keeps in touch."

117

"I hear from Richard almost every night," Susan said defensively.

"Almost?"

"Yes. My Lord, Kate, he can't call every minute! You have no idea what a frantic thing a tour is!"

"I'd know if you wrote it."

"Oh, shut up," Susan said affectionately.

But it had troubled her that sometimes she didn't hear from him for a night or two. There was always time to make a phone call, no matter how busy one was. She put her uneasiness down to her "condition" and tried to dismiss the things Jacqueline had told her about Sergio's behavior on the road. Maybe I should have gone along, she thought. And then, how absurd to even let such a thing enter my head! Richard wouldn't be unfaithful. Not when I'm carrying his child! Not *ever*! Not every man strayed. She had to be sensible. Men just didn't think about keeping in touch the way women did. They didn't live for a note or the sound of a voice on the phone, for reassurance that they were always in the heart and mind of the beloved.

"You're an ass, Susan Langdon Antonini," she said aloud when these little fears came to her in the middle of the night. "You're a ponderous, slow-moving, dim-witted elephant!" And for the most part, that took care of the uncertainties and she fell peacefully asleep, dreaming of Richard's return and the arrival of his baby.

Chapter Ten

Almost from the day he had learned he was to be a father, a change came over Richard. He was gentle and considerate of Susan during her pregnancy and quite obviously mad about his daughter when she was born. He hadn't been sure, in the first hours after Susan told him, whether he was glad about it. He'd have preferred to wait, and he'd have been happier if they'd decided this together. But his doubts soon turned to anticipation and when he saw Katie his delight was genuine. "Look at those fingers!" he said. "By God, she *is* going to be a musician, Susie! Just like you said!"

When he could, he took to haunting the nursery, playing with the baby under the eagle eye of Bridie Grey, the nurse Susan had been fortunate enough to find. The two women watched with amusement as the famous big fingers placed tiny ones on the keys of the miniature piano he bought as her first toy.

"I wouldn't have believed it," Susan told Kate Fenton. "He's positively dotty about your namesake! I expected him to love her, but I had no idea he'd take to parenthood with such enthusiasm!"

Kate hid her doubts. People did not change so drastically overnight. Richard the selfish lion did not magically become Richard the sentimental lamb. He's showing off, Kate thought, as he always does. He's playing a new and amusing game, preening in a starring role with the supporting actress who's a reproduction of himself and a boost to his ego. But she said nothing, hoping it was true, hoping Richard really had matured with the arrival of this new, dependent life.

Even Paul thought he was witnessing a small miracle. It was amazing how "settled" Richard seemed. In all the years Paul had managed him, he'd seen Richard as the temperamental artist, the petulant ex-prodigy, the careless Casanova, but never as an understanding and incredibly, faithful man. He'd not strayed since his marriage, and though they were on tour for months without Susan, he did not so much as look at another woman.

Even when they started the East Coast tour in April, a tour Susan had planned to accompany, Richard gracefully accepted her unexpected change of heart about making an extended trip. She came to Washington to meet them, but after three days she went home, apologizing that, good as Bridie was, she didn't feel easy leaving Katie alone. Paul expected Richard to be angry, jealous, but he was not. Nor did her husband notice that Susan seemed nervous and distraught, as though she had something terrible on her mind. Paul did, but he didn't comment on her hasty departure. Instead, he said, "Things are a lot different these days, aren't they? You've really become a family man. No offense, but I didn't expect it. That is, I know you. Or I should say, I *knew* you, and I wouldn't have believed . . ."

"That I'd turn out to be a pillar of respectability?" Richard laughed. "Tell you the truth, neither did I. I love Susie, but I never figured to be faithful. I guess the baby's made a difference. I want her to be proud of me. That sounds nuts, doesn't it? A five-month-old kid! As though she'd know! I can't really explain it to you, or myself, Paul. I suppose because Katie's so perfect I'm trying to be better for her sake, and for Susie who gave her to me. I know it sounds maudlin, but for the first time in my life I'm thinking about the future . . . watching my kid grow up, not wanting her to know about me the things I knew about my own father. He's

120

a great man, but it was never a secret that he gave Mother a bad time with women. I think it influenced all our lives. We loved him. We still do. But none of us ever respected him as a father. We didn't listen to him or confide in him. Mother was the one for that. I don't want the same thing for Katie. I want her to have as much faith in me as she has in Susie. And she won't have if I go on behaving like the perennial juvenile. Do you understand what I'm saying, Paul? Susie has become more important to me because she's Katie's mother. And Katie—beautiful, flawless, enchanting Katie—is something I've produced. Susie had her, but it was my seed." He broke off suddenly. "I must sound like a maniac."

"No," Paul said carefully, "I admire you. And I'm glad for all of you."

Richard smiled. "You don't miss the good old days when you and I had a different broad every night? Not that you still couldn't. This mad metamorphosis of mine has nothing to do with you. In fact, I've been meaning to speak to you about that. Don't think you have to tie yourself to me while we're on the road. Hell, man, you're a handsome bachelor! Get out and grab what's right there waiting! Nobody will understand better than I."

"Don't worry about me. I was never the prize package. Who cares about an artist's manager? But if I *wanted* to carry on our old traditions, I would. I know there's plenty there for the taking. Even for me. Being this close to the throne gives me a certain clout with women. Funny. This new life of yours makes sense for me, too. Sooner or later we'd have both worn ourselves out with those mattress gymnastics. I can wait for New York. I have a couple of reliable phone numbers there."

"Have it any way you like," Richard said. "I just wanted you to know that I don't expect you to embrace my voluntary celibacy. With me it's temporary. I still have a sexy wife to go home to."

He had no idea how the words hurt. Paul's longing

for his friend's wife had grown stronger every day and he despised himself for it. He'd known he was in love with Susan from that first tour when they'd spent so many hours together, when she'd been so unsure of her new life. He'd found her a warm, bright human being and every time he saw her, even when she was radiant and content in Richard's love, the hunger grew.

At the beginning, ashamed of his own thoughts, he'd hoped the marriage wouldn't last, that he'd have his chance. He reasoned that a selfish Richard would eventually betray her, or tire of her, or both. And he'd be waiting. But now that unworthy hope had disappeared. The change in Richard seemed real and both he and Susan were happy. Paul tried to be glad, but he envied Richard. No one person should have so much—talent, looks, money, fame, a wonderful wife and now this beautiful child. It's unfair. But at least he appreciates his blessings and that makes it better for Susan. I'm glad she isn't traveling with us very much any more. That means I only rarely have to see her, and that's a good thing. I might accidentally or compulsively let her know how I feel. She'd only be gentle and sorry for me and I couldn't stand that. I couldn't stand her pity.

Susan did not tell Richard her real reason for hurrying home from Washington. Only she and Bridie Grey shared the knowledge of the tragedy that had come to Katherine Antonini and her parents.

Susan became aware of it only two days before she was to leave to join the East Coast tour. The baby's nurse came into the master bedroom that morning and said, nervously, "May I speak with you, Mrs. Antonini?"

Oh, God, Susan thought, she's going to quit. Employees always quit when they came in asking to speak to you. I thought she was happy with us. She adores Katie. Maybe it's money. If so . . .

"Of course, Bridie. What is it?"

"It's Katie, madam."

"Katie?" Susan jumped up, alarmed. "Has something happened to her?"

"No. That is, not exactly." Bridie's sweet Irish face wrinkled up and she looked as though she were going to burst into tears. "It's . . . Oh, God, save us, it's that for the last couple of days . . . I mean, I didn't want to alarm you, madam . . ."

Susan shook her by the shoulders. "What is it? Bridie, what on earth is it?"

"I . . . I don't think she hears, Mrs. Antonini. I think Katie is deaf." The woman began to cry.

Susan stared at her stupidly. Katie deaf? Her baby deaf? No. It was impossible. The nurse must be wrong. Her Irish imagination was playing tricks on her, that's all it was. Susan fought for control.

"What makes you think such a thing?" She was surprised to hear her own voice sounding so calm. "Hush, Bridie! Settle down and tell me about it."

Between sobs, Bridie told her. Two days before, she'd accidentally dropped a heavy pan right behind Katie, who lay on her stomach in the playpen. The baby hadn't looked up or begun to cry as a normal child would when such a loud, frightening noise happened so close to her ear.

"I didn't think too much about it," Bridie said, "but then I began to notice other things. When I shook her rattle behind her, she didn't look around for the noise. When she happened to *see* it she crowed—you know the way she does when she sees something bright colored—but she didn't hear it. At first, I thought it was just because she's so little. But I've cared for babies all my life. I know this is different." Bridie's voice broke. "I know she can't hear."

"You're wrong," Susan said firmly. "Those little tests of yours don't mean anything. Katie's perfectly normal."

"I pray to the good Lord she is." Bridie wiped her eyes. "But you'd better take her to the doctor, Mrs. Antonini."

Without answering, Susan ran to the nursery. Katie was lying in her crib, smiling radiantly at the bright-colored mobile which dangled over it. The sight of her made Susan feel better. There's nothing wrong with this baby, she thought. Bridie's being an alarmist. With Katie's gaze still turned to the ceiling, Susan stood a little behind the crib and clapped her hands loudly. The child continued to look upward. Susie did it again and again, with no results. She felt a sickness start in the pit of her stomach and she literally screamed, "Katie!" Her daughter continued to look up at the mobile, undistracted by the loud voice.

Blindly, Susan picked her up and held her close. Katie clutched at her hair, her earrings, gurgling with pleasure as her mother carried her into her own bedroom and sat in a chair, cuddling her and making little crooning noises. Bridie watched with an anguished expression.

"You'd better call the doctor," she said again.

"Yes. Yes, of course."

Still holding the baby, she tremblingly dialed the pediatrician's office. He was not in, but his nurse was helpful.

"I expect Dr. Ashley shortly," she said. "Is it an emergency?"

"No. Yes. I don't know." Susan was almost hysterical. "Yes, of course it's an emergency! There's something wrong with Katie, and I have to go away to meet my husband in Washington, and . . ." She realized she was babbling incoherently. "I must see Dr. Ashley today! Please! What time may we come in?"

The nurse recognized the panic in her voice. "All right, Mrs. Antonini. Bring Katherine as soon as you can. I'll work you in."

"Thank you," Susan said. "Thank you very much."

Dr. Ashley did not make light of her fears as Susan hoped he would.

124

"I can't really tell about Katherine. Normally, babies begin to hear about thirty-six hours after birth, Mrs. Antonini, but the only way to tell whether this little one has a hearing impairment is to have her scientifically tested." He jotted down the name and address. "I want you to call the New York Eye and Ear Infirmary. I'll ask them to give you an immediate appointment. Their otologists can tell you for sure in an hour. Try not to worry," he said kindly. "It could be nothing. She may respond when she decides to. You remember that old story about the child who didn't speak for seven years? Then one morning at breakfast he said, 'This oatmeal is too hot.' Naturally his parents were delighted and asked him why he hadn't spoken before. And he said, 'Up till now, everything's been *perfect*.' It may be the same thing with Katherine."

Susan couldn't even smile at the well-meant little joke. Instinctively she knew, and no halfhearted reassurance from the pediatrician could dispel the terrible certainty that her baby didn't hear.

Next day the tests confirmed her worst fears. She stood by numbly as the doctors attached metal electrodes to Katherine's hands and feet and administered a series of tiny electric shocks with a machine formidably called a psychogalvanic skin response audiometer. There was much testing with batteries of earphones and twirling of dials and knobs, and Katie cried and the diagnosis was made.

"The child has a slight degree of hearing only in her right ear. Very slight. Almost none at all."

To Susan, the words were a pronouncement of doom. She knew what they meant. Her gay, laughing, alert little daughter was destined for a life in which she would hear nothing. And if she could not hear, she could not speak. Deaf and mute. It was unbearable. Tears slowly began to stream down her face as she stood with a now quiet Katherine in her arms.

"What can we do? Please. Whatever it takes, what can we do?"

The doctor in charge was very gentle. "There are

two choices for the prelingual deaf child, Mrs. Antonini. One is to put her, as soon as she's old enough, into a school for the deaf where she'll be among others like her. She'll learn sign language and be able to communicate through it. The other, which is more difficult, is to try to bring her up in a hearing world. That means, in time, fitting her with hearing aids and trying to teach her to lip-read and speak intelligibly. But I must warn you that if you choose that course of action, it will be your whole life. Yours and your husband's. Katherine will need speech therapists and even more importantly, constant, and I emphasize *constant*, at-home training. You will have to talk, talk, talk. Incessantly. You will say one word over and over a hundred times until she begins to imitate the shape of the word she sees on your lips. It's not an easy thing, I regret to say. I must tell you that most parents find it too frustrating, too heartbreaking, as well as too time-consuming. You and the child would go through torture for years, and even then no one can promise you'll succeed."

"You're telling me we shouldn't even try."

"No, I'm not saying that. Many parents have chosen this way and found it worth all the agony to see their child grow up like other children. It's possible. In all probability, her impairment has nothing to do with her I.Q. That's why we object to the awful phrase 'deaf and dumb.' She is deaf and mute, but she seems bright and chirpy. I'm simply warning you, Mrs. Antonini, that it takes an incredible amount of patience and devotion, an almost fanatic dedication to achieve results. You'll give your life to it. Some people, and no one blames them for it, just can't cope with that burden."

"What about *her* burden, Doctor?"

He shook his head sympathetically. "There is a school of thought that believes the deaf-mute child, like the mentally retarded one, is happier among her own kind. In a way, that life can be less painful for her than one in which she is asked to behave like other children, to compete in areas for which she lacks the equipment. It's a terrible decision for you and your husband.

Think about it carefully, for her sake as well as your own. Your husband is the pianist, isn't he?"

"Yes."

"I think you should take that into consideration. I imagine he travels a great deal. That means most of the burden of training will be on you. Bringing up Katherine 'normally' is an every-waking-hour job that really requires the efforts of both parents. Usually, the mother, at home, works with the child during the day while the father picks up the process at night. Give it a lot of thought before you decide. You have time. She couldn't be put into school or even fitted with hearing aids until she's about two years old. Meantime, why not investigate some of the help you could call on?"

Susan left with a list of books to read and the names of institutions to contact. The John Tracy Clinic in California, founded by Spencer Tracy and named for his own hearing-impaired son, offered on-the-spot training or a correspondence course which helped parents to learn how to handle not only their child but themselves. The Volta Bureau in Washington, D.C., founded by Alexander Graham Bell, also was an organization for the parents of handicapped children, using shared experiences as training and consolation. The same was true of the New York League for the Hard of Hearing, which offered lectures by psychologists, doctors and prominent guests. Eleanor Roosevelt, herself the victim of a hearing defect, had been one of the speakers many years ago.

Susan stayed up all night reading the literature of these organizations. When she brought Katherine home from the testing, she told only Bridie what she'd learned.

"I don't want anyone else to know just yet," Susan said.

"Will you tell Mr. Antonini when you see him in Washington tomorrow?"

Susan looked startled. She'd completely forgotten she'd planned to join Richard. I can't go now! was her first reaction. I can't leave my baby. And there's too

127

much to think about before I tell him about Katie. I must have all my facts marshaled. Even then she realized that she'd already made her decision. No matter what it took, she wanted Katie brought up as a child, not a *deaf* child. But if Richard did not immediately agree, she'd need all the arguments she could muster.

"I'm going to cancel my trip," she said. "I don't want Mr. Antonini upset while he's on tour, and I'm not a good enough actress to keep the news from him if I see him. This is no moment to go away. Besides, I have so much research and thinking to do." She stopped. She was behaving as though she was alone in this problem, as though she had to handle it by herself. As though she was sure Richard would be no help. Katie was also Richard's child and he adored her. What was she thinking of? He had a right to know, an equal voice in the decision. "On second thought," Susan said, "I guess I will go down to Washington. He's expecting me. But I'm not going on with him to Richmond and Atlanta as planned. I'll come home after the concert at Constitution Hall."

On the Eastern shuttle next morning, she rehearsed what she'd say, but by the time the plane landed at National Airport she knew she couldn't tell him. Not now. He'd be heartbroken, distraught, maybe unable to go on with this series of concerts. There's no reason to rush, Susan rationalized. Nothing can be done for a while, one way or the other. I'll keep the secret until he gets home, keep it from him and everyone. I'll have a couple of months to become informed about these children and how to handle them. I can put up a front for Richard for a few days. There are other doctors. Maybe a corrective operation. She swallowed a terrible lump in her throat. Oh, Katie, my precious, beautiful baby, why did this have to happen to you?

For those three days she tried to act as though nothing was wrong. Richard, his mind on his music, did not notice her tension. Only Paul was aware that Susan was deeply troubled about something, and that she was

128

nervous and sometimes so deep in thought that she jumped when she was unexpectedly spoken to.

Whatever the problem is, Paul thought, it's a killer, and she's trying hard to fool all of us. He was sure Richard knew nothing. If he had, the pianist would have behaved differently, probably would have blurted out something to give it away. Susie was going through some kind of private hell and making the awful trip by herself.

Chapter Eleven

Much as she longed to talk to Kate or her mother, Susan stuck by her decision to tell no one of Katie's handicap until she had discussed this wrenching blow with Richard. Keeping quiet about the worst disaster of her life was the hardest thing she'd ever had to do. She wanted to run to Bea Langdon for comfort, to ask Kate's sensible advice, but it would be unfair to Richard. He'd have enough pain without discovering that he was one of the last to know.

Instead, she spent the next two months reading everything she could find on the subject, taking the baby to two more specialists, writing to the Tracy Clinic for information. It was all disheartening. The books she got from the library turned her blood to ice water. They warned that the parents of deaf children sometimes began to hate them for the way they shuffled their feet, made disgusting noises when they ate, behaved more like animals than children. Susan slammed the books shut and refused to believe such possibilities. Unfortunately, she had to accept the fact that Katie's condition was inoperable. She wished she had gone to the Volta Bureau when she was in Washington, but she knew why she hadn't. Going there was admitting that Katie was handicapped, and though she knew that in her heart, she was not yet ready to affirm it by joining one of these groups.

It was still hard to believe, looking at her daughter, that she was anything but perfect. Just as it was nearly impossible to make cheerful replies to inquiries about her, to tell people who asked that "The baby is marvelous!" Susan thought her resolve would melt when Bea came to town and spent happy hours playing with her grandchild, unaware of Katie's condition. But she hung on. Only a few more weeks, she told herself. Then Richard and I will make our plans and it will be easier to break the news to our families when we've already decided on the solution.

When he did return, elated by his triumphant appearances, Richard burst into the apartment full of high spirits, shouting, "Hey! I'm home! Where are my two gorgeous women?" Susan ran to meet him and flung herself into his arms, holding onto him as though she'd never let go, covering his face with kisses. All discipline left her, all the bottled-up control was unleashed. Bridie had been a comfort but no substitute. Only Richard could share the anguish she'd borne alone. Startled by the ferocity of her embrace, he returned her kisses, holding her close and wondering what this frantic welcome meant. At last he disentangled himself and looked into eyes swimming with tears.

"That's even a bigger reception than I expected! I know my homecoming is a major event, but did you miss me *that* much?"

She could barely speak, merely nodded and hugged him again before she said, "Oh, Richard, I've needed you so!"

"Well, I've needed you, too, baby. It's been a long, lonely spring. But I'm home now, and no more traveling until fall. Just a lot of time to spend with you and Katie. Where is she? In the nursery? Let's go see her. How is my beautiful heiress?" He started toward the baby's room, but Susan grabbed at his arm.

"Wait. Please. There's something we must talk about."

"Can't it keep until I've seen Katie?"

"No. It's about her."

He felt the beginning of fear. "What's wrong? She's sick! My God, Susan, don't tell me something's happened to her and you didn't let me know!"

"She's all right, dearest. I mean, she's not really sick." Susan took his hand and pulled him into the living room. "Let's sit down for a minute." She held his hand tightly as she told him the whole story, fighting back the fresh tears as she took him, step by step, over the events that had been her living nightmare since the morning Bridie first came into her room. "So you see, darling," she concluded, "we have an enormous responsibility. It will be hard on us, worse for Katie, but we can do it. I know we can. I've been studying everything I can find on the subject, and there are some marvelous success stories. Girls and boys who've learned to lip-read and speak quite well. Children who go to regular schools, colleges even. Some have married and have children of their own. They lead perfectly normal lives."

He was in the same kind of disbelieving state of shock Susan had suffered earlier. At first he said nothing, simply staring at her, trying to take in what she'd told him. Then the full, terrible impact of it hit him and his face went dead white. "Deaf and dumb," he said. "My child is deaf and dumb!"

"Don't think of it that way. She can't hear and she'll have to be taught to speak and understand, but she can. She will. Thank God we have the money to get her the best speech therapist. We can make it much easier for her than most parents."

"She's deformed. A freak." His voice was hopeless.

"Richard! That's not true! She's the same bright,

alert, happy baby she always was. She'll be a beautiful, cheerful young girl, a lovely woman. She'll have the same kind of life any other child has. It's true. I swear it. She has a handicap. But she has a good mind and if we're willing to make sacrifices it won't matter that much that she doesn't hear. She'll be able to function like other people."

He turned to her, eyes blazing. "Are you crazy? Haven't you ever seen deaf and dumb people, all vacant-looking and unco-ordinated? I can hardly look at them, shuffling along, making grunts instead of words, trying to communicate with their fingers." He jumped up and started out of the room. Susan was frozen with horror.

"Where are you going?"

"To the bathroom. I'm going to be sick."

Unable to move, she waited for him to return. She'd expected him to be devastated, as she had been, but she hadn't anticipated this revulsion, this instant rejection of the baby he adored. It's only the shock, she told herself. He's reacting without thinking it through. Once he realizes how much can be done, he'll adjust to the situation, sad as it is. She remembered her own first days of knowledge. She, too, had been almost insane with grief. That's how it is with Richard, she thought. He can't accept this yet. But he will. He loves Katie so much. When he sees her and we sit down quietly to discuss our plans, it will be all right.

He came back in a few minutes, red-eyed. He'd been weeping, Susan realized. He left the room because he couldn't bear to let me see him shed "unmanly" tears. Her heart went out to him.

"I'm sorry," he said in a low voice. "I don't know what made me flare up like that. I realize you wanted to spare me as long as you could. It must have been hell for you, Susie, all these weeks, knowing and not telling me." He tried to smile. "Let's go see the princess, shall we?"

As Susan had when she was filled with fear, he gathered Katie in his arms and began to talk to her.

"Hello, beautiful," he said. "Your old man's home from the wars. Glad to see your daddy?"

The baby smiled and gurgled, her little head turning from side to side, the big violet-blue eyes, so like Richard's, looking all around the room, her gaze finally coming to rest on her father's face. In an inquisitive gesture, she reached out and put her tiny fingers on his mouth. Richard involuntarily drew back. Susan knew they shared the same sad thought. This is what Katie deliberately would do later when she tried to recognize and imitate unheard words. It was accidental, of course, but it was eerie. In a second, Richard recovered and kissed the little pink fingertips before he put the infant back in her crib.

Arms around each other, they left the nursery. In their bedroom, Richard said, "I still can't believe it."

"I know."

"I talked to her but she didn't hear me. She'll never hear me. She'll never hear voices, or music. She'll be in a world of her own, cut off from us, as we're cut off from her."

"It won't be like that, darling. I told you. It's possible to raise her in a hearing world."

"I don't think so. From what you've told me, it means total dedication to her. There wouldn't be any life for you, and damned little for me when I'm home. You'll never be able to leave her, to travel with me. We'll be prisoners, the three of us, locked in a world of silence."

"But other people have done it!"

"We're not other people, Susan. I'm an artist, in the public eye. Things are demanded of me that aren't demanded of a businessman. And things are demanded of you, as my wife, that aren't required of the average housewife. From what you've told me, the at-home training is as important as the help she can get from speech therapists. That's not the kind of life I can handle."

She knew what he was leading up to, but she had to hear him say it. "What's the alternative?"

133

"You know the alternative. The doctor told you. When she's old enough, she can be sent to a special school for the deaf. Live with children like her. She'll be happier than she would be trying to grow up in a family of healthy, boisterous cousins with whom she can't keep up."

Susan stared at him in horror. "You want to send her away? You want to discard her like some imperfect piece of equipment that needs repair? She's not an object, Richard, she's flesh and blood. Our flesh and blood! No! If you're not willing to do whatever it takes, I am! She's my baby and I want her. I can't just put her out of my life."

He tried to soothe her. "Sweetheart, it will be best for her. That's what I'm thinking of. I know." He paused. "I've never told you this, but we've had firsthand experience. Sergio and Mary Lou had a child between Joseph and Patricia. A little girl, Frances, born in 1950, a year after her brother. When she was three, they discovered she was retarded. She's been in a special school ever since. She's happy there. Mary Lou goes to see her often. She says Frances is content. She looks fifteen years old but her mind hasn't grown past five. She plays with dolls and she can read a little and the staff is very good to her. I was seventeen when they made the decision and I remember how hard it was for them, but they knew it was the only way. She could never be a normal child and it would have been cruel to watch her try to handle herself in a normal family and a normal world. We're going to have to face this with Katie. Much as we love her, we have to do what's best for her."

"No!" It was a scream of pain. "Katie isn't retarded. I don't care if it takes every minute of my life, I'm going to keep her with me." She looked at him, not willing to admit what she suspected. Richard was ashamed of having a child who was not perfect. She was an embarrassment to him. He wanted her out of sight and, if possible, out of mind. He loved her when she was everything he found beautiful, but his love had no room for a child whose presence was an affront to the sensibilities. How could this be? How could this man she adored beyond reason be so selfish, so unfeeling? She could imagine Sergio sending his little Frances away. He was shallow and cold, and she'd never liked him. She could even understand how Mary Lou, anxious to please the family, might have gone along, unprotestingly, with the decision. For that matter, Susan was not sure she wouldn't have done the same, had Katie been mentally deficient and totally beyond help. But Katie was neither of those things. All she asks of us is our time, Susan thought. And Richard is unwilling to give it. He wants to hide her. He's unwilling to admit to the world, as Sergio obviously was, that an Antonini produced a "defective" offspring.

"You think I don't love her," Richard said as though he read her mind. "You think I want her out of the way because I don't want the problems or the publicity. That's not it, Susie. We can't cope. We'll fail and do her a terrible injustice."

"Yes, that's exactly what I think. Not that we'll do her an injustice, but that it will be inconvenient for you. Your damned public might find out, is that it? Or maybe your mother won't approve. You can't stand the idea of some reporter telling the world that you fathered a deaf-mute! 'Do what's best for her!' I know what's best for her. To stay with the parents who love her, to go to school with children who have no such handicap, kids who'll accept her because she's bright and sweet and wonderful." Susan was trembling. "No, Richard. I won't let you send her away. Not even," she said slowly, "if it means leaving you and taking Katie with me."

He stared at her. "You won't do that. You couldn't. We love each other."

"Katie is part of that love. Please see this as it really is. It's no disgrace, Richard." Shamelessly she played on his weakness. "If anything, it would only make people admire you more, knowing what a loving father you are to this helpless child. They'll admire your courage, your determination."

For a moment she thought he was going to buy this obvious ploy. God knows she didn't want to leave him, but she couldn't send her little girl away. She wanted them both. She'd do anything to keep them.

Richard hesitated, mulling over her words, but then he shook his head. "You don't believe me, Susie, but I'm not thinking only of us. I really am trying to do what's best and easiest for Katie." He sighed. "Look. I'm tired. We both are. There's nothing to be done immediately. Let's give this a little time."

It was something. At least a small concession. He'll come around to my way of thinking, Susan told herself. He has to get used to the idea. He hasn't lived with it, as I have. He's reacting from shock, from sadness and disappointment. In a few days he'll see that keeping her with us is the only possible thing to do. Everyone will back me up. I know they will. Mother and Dad. Paul. Jacqueline. Papa-Joe. They'll all see that Katie needs constant love from us. Even Maria, impossible as she is, has a soft spot about "her own." Since Katie's birth, Maria had been, if not cordial, at least more tolerant of Richard's family, even conceding that his baby was one of the prettiest newborn grandchildren she'd ever had. Maria will see that this is not another Frances. For once she'll agree with me.

Blindly confident that things would work out, Susan smiled and nodded. "You're right, darling," she said. "We'll give it a little more time." She held out her arms to him, inviting his love-making. "I've missed you so. I want you so much." Her voice was a seductive whisper.

She expected him to react as he always did, but he turned away. "Not tonight, Susie. I'm done in."

She couldn't believe it. They'd not seen each other in weeks. What was happening? Did he find it tasteless of her to think of sex at this time, as though Katie's future had already begun to affect their intimacy? One thing has nothing to do with the other, Susan thought.

136

If anything, we need the touch of each other more tonight than we ever have. She wanted her husband to hold her, comfort her, as she would comfort him. She wanted an affirmation that their desire for each other could not be dampened, not even by tragedy or the quarrels that unhappiness produced.

"I don't understand," she finally said. "It's been so long. So much has happened."

"Exactly. My God, after the last hour do you really think I can be in the mood for romance?" He wasn't angry. Worse, he was indifferent to her. Is this to be my punishment until I see things his way? she wondered. Is the battle of wills to be fought in the bedroom?

With all the dignity at her command she answered him calmly. "No. I suppose not. I couldn't have made love to you the night *I* found out."

It was a lie. She'd gone to Washington two days after she'd learned about Katie. They'd made passionate love, she in her misery, Richard in his blissful ignorance. We view sex differently, Susan thought. Richard thinks of it only as lusty physical fulfillment when things are going well. To me, it's also spiritual nearness and peace, strength and solace when the rest of the world threatens my very existence.

Richard gave her a perfunctory kiss and climbed into bed, lying as far away from her as possible. They both lay sleepless, staring into the darkness, wrapped in their separate, tortured thoughts.

It was weeks before they made love again, though it was only hours before Susan knew she had lost her battle. She was to find no support for her decision anywhere, not even from her own parents, who were the first to be told.

Bea Langdon looked at them and began to weep with pain for her daughter and her grandchild. Wil had taken Susan in his arms, his own eyes wet, while

Richard stood by, miserable and inarticulate. Only Susan had been able to speak at that moment.

"I've been doing a lot of studying," she said firmly, "and I know we can bring up Katie to be like other little girls. We can get the best speech therapists and in time she'll have her hearing aids. I'll work with her day and night. Other people have done it successfully."

The Langdons looked at Richard.

"I wish I could agree," he said, "but I can't. Susan doesn't realize she'd have the burden of this alone most of the time. I have to work and travel. I can't give this what it takes. At best, it would be a ninety-ten arrangement. I've read everything Susan's gathered about bringing up a deaf-mute child at home. It's admirable, what some parents have done together, but in our circumstances, we're not equipped for it."

Susan waited for her mother and father to dispute this. They adored Katie. They'd see why she couldn't be consigned to a silent, abnormal world. She thought she wasn't hearing correctly when Wil Langdon said, "I suppose you're right, Richard. If yours were a different life, if you could really share the burden, I might feel otherwise, but it's too much for a woman alone, or virtually alone."

"Daddy!"

"I know, sweetheart. I can imagine what you're feeling. God knows what agony you've both gone through! Your hearts must be breaking! But you must also be realistic, Susie darling. You can't run the risk of ruining Katie's life and your own."

"I wouldn't ruin her life! I can do it. I know I can!"

"You're a strong woman," Wil said, "and I know you believe that. Maybe you're right. Maybe you could do it. But what will you do to Richard, to yourself, to your marriage? How can such an undertaking possibly succeed unless both parents are willing and eager to take a long chance?"

Susan was hurt, bewildered. She turned to her mother. "Mom, *you* understand. You'd do it my way, wouldn't you?"

Bea looked tortured. "Darling, I don't know. I have a husband who can always be at my side. That makes a difference."

Susan felt the bottom dropping out of her world. "You both think Richard's right." Her voice was flat. "You really think his way is best for Katie. I wouldn't have believed it."

Bea took her hand. "No one loves that baby more than we do. No one loves *you* more. But you must think of her first, Susan. You're sure you can single-handedly make her a normal child. I'd give anything, anything in this world to feel that way too. But you're speaking from a mother's natural emotions, darling, not from terrible reality. What will you do if you send her to a regular school and her classmates ignore her or laugh at her? How will you heal those wounds? What will you feel when you see an angry child having temper tantrums because she can't hear or make herself understood? Forget your marriage. If it's good, it might even survive the absences and your total preoccupation with this problem. I think it *is* strong enough to survive those things. But think about your little girl, Susan, and what will happen to her. Where will she be when other young girls are going out on dates, giggling on the telephone, falling in love, doing all the things you and your friends did? Will you be able to bear that loss for her? Don't think of yourself, my darling. Don't even think of how you'd die a thousand times every day if you weren't with her. A mother's true love is always sacrifice, willing sacrifice, as long as it's best for the child."

Susan began to cry. "You think I'm being selfish."

"No, sweetheart," Wil said. "You're acting from the most unselfish of motives. You're literally offering to give your life to Katie. What could be more unselfish than that? But if that well-meaning sacrifice only results in forcing a child into a lonely half-world, you'll have destroyed everyone. Susie, baby, it's a terrible decision, but you know you have to make it. You'll be able to visit Katie at her special school, even have her

139

home some of the time. And you'll have other children."

She looked at her parents with momentary hatred. They'd betrayed her. And then the anger was replaced by sorrow. They didn't understand, any of them. They were desperately trying to be unemotional about something that couldn't be treated as a dispassionate problem. They believed what they were saying, but they were wrong.

"If we send her away, I'll never go to see her," Susan said in a mechanical voice. "I couldn't bear it. And I'll never have another child."

"You don't mean that," Bea said, her voice soft with sympathy. "Of course you'll see her. And you'll be glad to see her happy and contented, not torn apart with frustration. As for other babies, you'll have them, darling. It's important that you do. For many reasons."

"No, I'd never risk it again." She looked at Richard and her eyes were empty. "You win," she said. "If this is what my family feels, I know how yours will react." She began to laugh hysterically. "Aren't we all marvelously civilized? So sensible. So intelligent! How could I have been so stupidly sentimental? My God, Richard, I thought your ego was monumental, but mine must be colossal! Imagine my presuming that I could handle this! What an insane idea to entertain!"

She was out of control and the three people with her were frightened. Richard tried to calm her.

"Easy, darling. We're not talking about tomorrow."

Susan looked at him, but he felt she didn't see him. "Oh, but we are," she said. "I want you to take her away right now. There must be a fine, expensive institution that will care for her since I can't. The sooner the better, so we can get on with our lovely, untroubled lives." She was laughing and crying. "What do you think I'm made of? Wood, like your precious piano? Do you think I can stand seeing her for another two or three years, knowing every day brings us closer to the time we'll be torn apart? No, no. Take her. Take her right now so everybody can forget she ever existed."

140

Richard shook her. "Susie! Darling! Stop this!"

Bea was sobbing openly and Wil looked as though he wanted to die. As quickly as Susan's hysterics had begun, they subsided.

"I'm all right," she said quietly. "Just leave me alone. All of you."

She would not go with Richard when he told his parents. She went to bed after the visit to her family and refused to get up. She wouldn't go near the nursery nor allow Bridie to bring Katie in to her. She simply lay there, saying nothing, except to ask Richard, after a week, whether he'd made arrangements for a place to send Katie.

He was nearly out of his mind. The terrible news that had greeted him was compounded by Susan's withdrawal from him, from the world. She refused to see anyone, picked listlessly at the meals the cook set in front of her. She simply lay like dead, staring at the ceiling.

"Yes," he said now, in answer to her question. "There's a lovely school up on the Hudson. They usually don't take children until nursery age, but they'll make an exception for us. It's beautiful, honey. I went up there yesterday. I wish you'd go see it with me."

There was no answer.

"Susan darling, we must get you some help. This thing has been more than any woman could handle. I want to have the doctor in."

"When can they take Katie?"

"Any time," Richard said sadly. "But we don't have to think about that right now. Let's get you on your feet first. Please see the doctor. If not for yourself, for me. For everybody who's so worried about you."

"I'm not the one they should be worrying about."

He kept quiet, but he was running out of patience, unused to dealing with emotional problems of this kind. Nor was he helped by Maria's cold reception of the news. Giovanni had looked mortally wounded, but Maria's reaction had been unreasonable outrage.

"This must come from Susan's side of the family! Nothing like this has ever been known in ours!"

Richard flared up. "What about Frances? I suppose that was Mary Lou's fault?"

"I have no doubt it was."

"Mother, how can you? This is a terrible thing! My child is hopelessly handicapped and my wife is having a nervous breakdown. My God, have you no compassion?"

"Of course I have. I'm bitterly disappointed that Katherine is not normal. And I'm sorry Susan is so weak she can't hold up under the strain. But I fail to see how my carrying on like a madwoman can help things. I prefer to do something constructive, Richard. Such as finding a suitable place for the child. And in one thing Susan is right. It should be as soon as possible."

"What am I going to do about Susan? I think she's losing her mind."

"You'll get her a psychiatrist, obviously. And you'll be sure to keep all of this very, very quiet. I mean *all* of it, Richard."

"Like Sergio did," he said bitterly.

"Precisely. Can you imagine the field day the tabloids would have with your deaf and dumb child and a crazy wife?"

He'd gone home numbly. Two days later Maria used her influence at the place he'd since gone to see. The sight depressed him unutterably. From babies to adults, those who lived there were mute. The terrible silence was all-pervasive. Yet the people seemed cheerful, conversing in rapid sign language, and the surroundings were more than comfortable. It was as luxurious as it was expensive.

In September, when she was ten months old, he and Bridie took little Katie to the place where she'd probably live most of her life.

Susan did not even kiss her goodbye.

Chapter Twelve

It was Kate Fenton who, late in October, finally broke through the invisible wall that Susan had built between herself and the reality she was unable to face. A month after little Katie went away, the baby's godmother barged, unannounced, into Susan's bedroom and stood glaring at the wan, closed-eye figure under the coverlet.

"What the hell do you think you're doing?"

Susan opened her eyes and stared lifelessly at her unexpected visitor.

"Remember me?" Kate asked. "I'm part of the living. You look like a candidate for Morticians' Award of the Year!"

Susan didn't answer.

"No, I take that back," Kate went on. "You're more eligible for the title of 'Woman Sorriest For Herself.' Susan, I'm disappointed in you. I'm more than disappointed; I'm mad as hell at you! You're behaving abominably. Making a lot of innocent people suffer with your self-pity. I thought you had more guts than that. Or if not more guts, at least more consideration. Your poor mother! She's beside herself!"

"I'm sorry," Susan said.

"Are you now? Well, isn't that big of you! Listen, dear girl, you've had one lousy kick in the teeth, but does that give you the right to punish the world? Don't you think all of us who love Katie are in enough agony without going crazy with worry over you?"

"I can't help it."

"Don't you dare say that to me! You don't *want* to help it! If you did, you'd behave like a normal human being instead of a zombie. You'd get out of that bed and start living again. I don't care whether you want to or not, you owe it to the people who care about you, your friends and parents, and, most of all, your husband."

Susan's face darkened at the mention of Richard. "Don't talk to me about him," she said. "If it weren't for Richard, I'd have my baby with me. He's the one who didn't want her here. I think he never wanted her at all. He's probably glad this happened."

Kate sank into a chair. "For God's sake, will you listen to yourself? Have you forgotten how pleased he was when you were pregnant? How crazy he was about the baby? Whether you believe it or not, he did what he thought best, what everybody except you thought best. I don't know if they're wrong and you're right, Susie, but I do know you can't proceed to slowly kill yourself and everybody around you because your vote was overruled. You're not thinking about Katie. You're much too involved in what's happened to you."

Tears began to roll down Susan's face. "That's not true. There's not a moment I don't think about her. I dream of her. I didn't even dare say goodbye to her, Kate. I knew I couldn't let them take her if I saw her again." The tears came faster. "Oh, Kate, what am I going to do? That little thing, that baby, separated from her family, all alone with strangers! I can't bear it! It's wrong. It was evil of Richard!"

Kate felt so sorry for her she had to choke back her own tears. But it wouldn't do to show pity. She had to take a tough line. Solicitous as she felt, she knew Susan had to be shocked and angered into moving again.

"Now you listen to me," Kate said firmly. "You're not the first person this has happened to. Neither is Katie. And you won't be the last. It's tragic, yes. It's a terrible trick of fate. But that's what it is, Susan. Fate. You can't fight it and you can't change it. You have no choice but to accept it. I can guess what you're going through, not only because of Katie's handicap but because you want to take care of her and can't. But you *can't*. If you went back to the doctor who examined her and asked him what your chances are of doing the job alone, of bringing up that child virtually single-handedly, he'd tell you again it's not a one-person job. The kindest thing for Katie is to let her be with trained people who'll enable her to make the adjustment millions of others have. You think only you can help her. Sorry. Not true. You are not indispensable. In fact, in your efforts to help her, you'd probably maim her for life. And then, by God, you'd have *reason* to want to die!"

Susan looked like a whipped child. "You really believe that?"

"I really do. This is the biggest sacrifice you'll probably ever be called on to make. Make it with grace. Make it out of love for Katie, if nothing else."

"I don't know. I still think . . ."

"No," Kate said. "No more thinking. It's time for action. Get up. Get going."

"If only Richard would work with me." It was almost a whimper.

"He can't," Kate said flatly. "What do you want him to do, stay home and give piano lessons? That's not fair. And even if he gave up his career, what kind of house would Katie grow up in? Richard would come to hate you. He'd hate his child. You'd spend the rest of your life in guilty misery, trying to make two unhappy people happy. Is that what you want for this baby you love so much? To have her used as a reason to wreck two other lives? I don't think so. When you reason it out, Susan, you can only come to the same conclusions everyone else has. Let that baby have the life she was born for. In time the pain will ease for you and Richard. It's not as though you've given her up for adoption. You'll be able to see her. Perhaps, when she's older, she can even come home. But for now, she must learn to function within her limits. And so must you." Kate paused. "I'm not big on amateur psychiatry, but any fool can see that right now you hate Richard. You have to get over that hurdle, too. You need professional help. Someone uninvolved to talk to. We'd like you to have some sessions with a good doctor."

She expected resistance, but she received none. Susan didn't even have the will to fight. "All right," she said listlessly, "if that's what everybody wants. But it won't help."

"It won't if you go into it with that attitude! Susan, how much do you expect of people? How long do you think we'll go on tiptoeing around your martyrdom? Even those who love you best are getting impatient. It's a cynical thing to say, but nobody wants to listen to the same old troubles month after month. Not even your parents. And not your husband. For better or for worse, remember? You took a vow to share everything. Let Richard share your grief, and you share his. He has plenty of it. It's his child, too. You've put him through enough. You've put *yourself* through enough."

Susan held out her hand. "Thank you, Kate."

"I'm not shaking the hand of any road-company Camille. Get up and start getting dressed. *Then* I'll shake your hand. Hell, I might even kiss you!"

For the first time, Susan smiled.

The sessions with the doctor went on for many weeks, and if Susan did not come out of them reconciled, she at least began to have a better understanding of herself. She saw that her pity for her daughter was as real as her love. But she also painfully recognized that her own ego was involved. In the family of giants she'd married into, she'd always felt unimportant. Her beautiful baby was a personal triumph, something she did not owe to any Antonini but one. Now she was unconsciously seeing Katie's imperfection as a symbol

146

of her own failures, a reflection of her inadequacy. These were not pleasant things to discover. She was not even sure she entirely believed them, and though she began to behave "normally," there was an unusual reserve, a lingering inability to recapture the old laughing, loving Susie.

She tried hard to become once again the young woman Richard had fallen in love with, but it was not until the next spring, just before he went on tour, that they resumed their marital relations, and even then it was a near disaster.

Richard had wanted her to make the West Coast trip with him, to Seattle, Portland, San Francisco and Los Angeles, but Susan was deep into her sessions with Dr. Marcus, and though she would have been glad for an excuse to end them, Richard agreed it was better that she stay in New York and continue with the psychiatrist.

"He's helping you, sweetheart, isn't he?"

"I suppose so."

"Then we can sacrifice a little more time together, can't we? I hate leaving you, but I expect to return to the girl I love."

"You can't. She doesn't exist any more."

Suddenly he was angry. "Goddammit, Susan, what do you expect of me? I lie here night after night, hungry for you, not daring to touch you, afraid you'll shatter like some piece of glass if I so much as say one wrong word! What about me? What do I have to look forward to?"

He was right. Susan knew what she was doing to him. She still loved him. He'd been wonderful, kind and patient all these months, a different Richard from the undisciplined man she married. If only I could feel, she thought. If only I could desire as I used to.

"I still love you, you know."

"Do you?" Richard asked. "Then prove it."

He moved against her, caressing her tenderly. The response that used to come instantly did not appear and it infuriated him. Uncaring, he tore off her night-

147

gown and threw her onto the bed. Afterward, he was covered with remorse. "My God, how could I have done that? How could I rape my own wife? I'm an animal! No better than my own father! Can you ever forgive me?"

She didn't know what he meant about Giovanni, but instead of resentment, she felt release. "I should be outraged," she said quietly, "but I'm glad you did it. If you hadn't, the gulf between us might have widened hopelessly. You didn't 'rape me,' Richard. You did what was necessary to bring me to my senses. I was afraid to have you touch me. Afraid my anger was still there. It is. But so is my desire. And my love. I've asked more of you than I had a right to. This was no 'violation,' as though you were some sex fiend attacking me in an alley. You're my husband. Thank God you shocked me out of my numbness."

He couldn't believe what he heard. She liked it! Maybe it was true that some women fantasize about sex by brute force. Or maybe Susan had to be brought back to reality with this uncontrollable evidence of his craving for her. Whatever, he wasn't going to probe for reasons. That was the doctor's job.

When he left three days later, it was with a light heart. They'd made love, good, passionate love, every night and morning since. He was filled with well-being, his old confident self again. She came to him willingly now, almost fiercely ecstatic at her climax. And then she held him until he fell asleep, making little sounds of love as she might to a baby. He didn't recognize them as such. He only knew he felt restored and virile. He was a little ashamed that he hardly thought of Katie these days, but he told himself that life had to go on. His life. And Susan's. Things were okay again. His body made her forget, just as hers gave him back his temporarily lost feeling of manliness. Sex, Richard thought. Old Freud was right. It's the basis of everything.

"That's quite a smile you're wearing," Paul Carmichael said when Richard got into the car to go to the airport. "You look like your old, cocky self."

Richard grinned more broadly. "Susie's fine again."

At first, Paul didn't know what he meant. "You mean she's through with the doctor? Will she be joining us?"

"No. Her head isn't back to normal, but everything else is, thank God."

Paul felt a flush of jealousy. You ass! he told himself. She's his wife.

"I'm glad. For both of you."

"You'd better believe it," Richard said. Then he frowned. "Trouble is, it only happened the last few days. I'm like a sailor rescued from a desert island. I don't know how I'll get through the next few weeks without more of that."

This time Paul understood only too well what he was saying. You bastard. We all marveled at the change in you. There's been no change at all. He could almost read Richard's mind. He's like a child who's been very, very good for a long time. Now he thinks he deserves anything he chooses as a reward for that behavior. It's going to be like the old days before he was married. He'll be hellbent on proving himself all over again. Well, he can do it alone. One of us will be ridiculously faithful to Susan.

"Do you think I should see my baby, Dr. Marcus?"

"Do you want to, Mrs. Antonini?"

"I'm not sure. That is, I want to see her, but I don't know whether I could stand it."

"Do you want to see her for her sake or yours?"

Susan thought for a moment. "She won't know me, will she? I'm only indulging myself. Being masochistic."

He didn't answer.

"It's pointless, isn't it? I'm not ready to handle that and it won't mean anything to her."

"I think that's probably true. How are you getting along with your husband away?"

"I miss him."

"What do you miss about him?"

"Everything. His presence. His music. Even his love-making."

"Even?"

"I didn't mean that. I love sex with Richard. Why did I say 'even'?"

"I don't know. Why do you think you did?"

She pondered. "Because that's only a small part of what I think love and life and marriage should be? I don't think it's a 'necessary evil,' Doctor. I enjoy it. It's not something to 'submit' to. Except that once."

"Then why do you think you mentioned it as the third thing?"

Susan was quiet for a moment. "Maybe that's all my life has really been for the past three years. This crazy sex urge of ours. Maybe I thought it was enough. I've been nothing but Richard's bedmate, haven't I?"

"Some women find that enough."

"You mean *I* don't."

"I can't say. Apparently you have some doubts."

"Yes," Susan said slowly. "I have to feel important. My job made me feel important." She swallowed hard. "So did Katie. And now they're both gone. I need something more, don't I?"

"It's worth thinking about, Mrs. Antonini."

Maria slammed the evening paper down in a rage. "I don't believe it," she said. "I simply do not believe it!"

In the gathering darkness of the early evening, Giovanni looked across the living room at his wife. "What is it you don't believe, my dear?"

"Susan is writing a column! Why wasn't I told about this?"

"Perhaps because we've been away," he said mildly. "Let me see. What kind of column?"

150

She handed it to him. "Some trash called 'The Woman's Way.' I thought Gloria was joking when she called this morning to say that Susan was writing regularly for a newspaper. Apparently it started two weeks ago. What on earth would possess that girl to do such a thing?"

Giovanni was busily reading. "Doesn't seem so bad to me," he said. "She writes well. Amusingly. And the material is inoffensive, if this is an example. 'The Private Life of an Idol's Wife.' That's rather appealing. She's simply talking about women who leave careers to marry celebrities." He smiled. " 'Sometimes the second fiddle is the most important instrument in the orchestration of a marriage.' Quite a well-turned sentence, don't you think?"

"No, I certainly don't think!" Maria snapped. "She's making a laughingstock of us."

"Oh, come now," Giovanni said placatingly, "I don't see it that way. Sounds as though she's making a good case for the status of a full-time wife. A refreshing change from all the propaganda about how terrible it is to be married."

"It's trash," Maria said again. "She's such a fool she can't see that they're simply exploiting her name! Richard Antonini's wife is no ordinary 'homemaker.' The world will think she's speaking for him, whatever she writes. It's dreadful. A newspaper column! Whoever heard of such a thing?"

Giovanni couldn't resist. "I seem to recall Eleanor Roosevelt. 'My Day' it was called, wasn't it?"

"Yes," Maria said. "And everyone knew she was using the column to glorify the political policies of that despicable husband of hers. You only prove my point. People read nonsense like this believing it reflects the husband's views. Do you think this column would exist if Susan's name were Smith?"

"I still don't understand what harm it can do. She's not going to write anything damaging to Richard. Maria dear, I'm sorry for Susan. She's been through so much, with the baby and now the doctor. It must be

151

lonely for her, not being able to travel with Richard. At least this gives her something to do."

"What she should do is stop pampering herself! Bad enough she produced a defective child and left the solution up to Richard and me while she lay like a lump in her bed! Not enough that she's still running to psychiatrists, and heaven help us if *that* ever gets out! Now she's going to air her private life so every chambermaid can read what it's like to be married to an Antonini!"

"I think you're making too much of this, my dear. I see it as a good sign. At least she's coming back into the world, poor little thing."

"Poor little thing indeed! She's always been headstrong and scheming." Maria thought of the pregnancy which had gotten Susan her own home. "She's devious and unpredictable. Who knows what she might write about us?"

"Maria, be sensible! She's not writing a gossip column about us. She's taking current subjects and discussing them from the viewpoint of an intelligent woman."

"She's always had you fooled. From the first minute she knew how to flatter your ego. You don't understand women like this. I said she was an unsuitable choice for Richard. But he wouldn't listen."

Giovanni sighed. "All in all, she's been a good wife to Richard."

"That's debatable. She's been a terrible daughter-in-law to *me*. And this column business is the last straw. If Richard were here he'd put a stop to it. Since he isn't, it's up to the family."

He made one last try. "Don't you think it should wait until Richard comes home? You're tampering with a matter that should be between husband and wife, Maria." Not that you don't always, he thought.

"I know my son," she said loftily. "He has no idea what's going on. I'm sure of that. She's taken advantage of his absence to indulge her selfish need for personal publicity. I'll see her tomorrow and straighten her out. Idiot! I could kill her!"

God knows you're trying, the maestro said silently. But it's not Susan's death you really want. It's the murder of a marriage you're plotting.

☸

It was a terrible scene, one that left Susan in despair. Maria phoned and invited her to lunch and she dutifully accepted. They were alone in the library afterward when the older woman got right to the point.

"Susan, I don't know how you ever got into this business of writing for the newspaper."

Unaware, Susan smiled. "It was just luck. I needed something to do, Mrs. Antonini, and my old boss, Kate Fenton, happened to have lunch with a publisher who was looking for a woman to write about today's problems from a female angle. Kate suggested me and to my amazement I was hired. I can't wait to tell Richard! I know he'll be pleased that I'm occupied and interested."

"So Richard doesn't know. I thought not."

"No. I want to surprise him when he comes home." She found herself eager to confide in her mother-in-law. "It's really been a lifesaver for me, having this work to do. I thought when Katie . . . when she went away . . . I thought I didn't want to live any more. I thought I had no purpose." Susan smiled. "This silly little column isn't much, but it makes me feel part of things. It's a first step."

Maria looked at her coldly. "It's a wrong step. And you must stop it immediately."

Susan was uncomprehending. "Why? What's wrong with writing little essays a couple of times a week? It's good therapy. The money isn't important, but it gives me something to think about. Dr. Marcus says . . ."

"I'm not interested in what Dr. Marcus says. Nor in your therapy. I am interested in your husband's career and the possible embarrassment to him."

"I don't understand. This can't hurt Richard."

"Don't be naïve, Susan. In your position, everything you write will be interpreted as a personal insight into your life and your husband's. It's unseemly for you to go about expressing views with which he may not agree."

Susan suddenly understood. It wasn't Richard's agreement that was at issue. It was Maria's angry conviction that Susan was competing with him. That was taboo. *Verboten*. Antonini wives stayed in the background, spoke when they were spoken to, behaved as decorative and decorous appendages. They didn't have careers of their own. Or, except for Maria, even thoughts of their own. At least none that were expressed in public. They stayed out of sight, like Mary Lou. Or lived separate lives, like Jacqueline. They didn't write columns or give revealing interviews or reach for any kind of personal identity. Well, she wasn't going to go along with that. She was a person with a mind of her own. Richard would be the first to agree with that.

"I'm sorry you think I'd ever embarrass Richard or any of you," Susan said. "I hoped you'd give me credit for more taste and intelligence. I even hoped you'd understand this helps fill an important need for me."

"You! Always you!" Maria was angry. "*Your* taste and intelligence. *Your* needs. I don't give a rap about your needs! You have only one obligation: to make Richard's life serene so that nothing interferes with his work. You have usefulness only in that you can try to pick up where I left off and devote your life to his genius. Haven't you worried him enough? Haven't you distracted him to the point where I fear for his career? I won't stand by and let you destroy him with your selfishness. You're making a fool of yourself with this 'job' of yours and you'll make a fool of him with your pushy ways! You must stop this immediately, Susan. No more columns. No more items such as the one I saw this morning in *Newsweek*. No more pictures in *Time*. You are not a public figure to be photographed

154

and interviewed and gossiped about. I'm appalled by what's happened. You are Richard Antonini's wife and you will conduct yourself as such."

Susan was surprised by her own calmness in the face of this tirade. "You seem to have done a great deal of research since you got back from Europe two days ago. How clever of you to have assembled such a dossier. You must give me the name of your clipping service."

"Your levity is as inappropriate as your disrespect. But it is no more than I expect from you. Be as discourteous as you like. I don't care, as long as you stop this unacceptable behavior."

"I don't intend to stop, Mrs. Antonini. Only Richard could possibly make me stop and he wouldn't try. It's innocent and gives me a little pleasure. You're making it sound like a plot to upstage the entire family and harm my husband! How ridiculous! Nothing could be further from the truth. Richard will find your attitude as funny as I do."

Maria was furious. "You're sure of that, aren't you? Very well. Let's find out. Why don't we call Richard in Los Angeles right now and see what he says?"

Susan hesitated. To refuse to call would seem an admission that she doubted his reaction. But this was not something she wished to discuss with him on long-distance, and certainly not with his mother hovering in the background waiting a chance to have her say.

"Well?" Maria asked. "What about it? Shall we call?"

"No. This is a private matter between Richard and me. I'm sticking to my original plan to tell him when he comes home."

The other woman smiled knowingly.

"I'm not afraid to call him in front of you," Susan said defensively. "I just don't think this concerns you." She knew it sounded weak, frightened, and the knowledge depressed her because it was close to the truth. She wasn't sure how Richard would react. She had been, before Maria had delivered her vehement ultimatum. But now Susan wasn't as confident. Richard might agree that her tiny emergence into the public eye was unsuitable. "Do it and tell him later," Kate once said. Had she been wrong? He doesn't like competition any more than his mother does, Susan thought with discouragement. And if she gets to him before I do, she'll certainly persuade him to make me stop writing the column. She flirted with the idea of begging her mother-in-law not to interfere, to let Susan handle it her own way, but that would be as demeaning as it would be futile. I won't beg, she decided. I won't grovel. Not to her or any of them. But even as she wondered how to make Richard see this situation her way, she knew she'd been beaten once again. She was, as always, no match for Maria.

Chapter Thirteen

Jacqueline settled herself comfortably on a banquette in the front room of La Côte Basque and gazed around appraisingly before she turned her attention to her sister-in-law. "This really is a most civilized restaurant," she said. "Say what you will about how Madame Henriette rules it like a benevolent despot, what with all that nonsense about not admitting ladies in pants, you must admit she keeps up her standards. No blue-denimed slobs in here, thank God! Just beautiful people. I do like beautiful people. Even though under those Trigère dresses beat little hearts of pure steel."

Susan looked around as though she'd never been there before, trying to see the assembled lunch crowd through Jacqueline's eyes. They were mostly beautiful. And mostly famous. Albert, the official host, was hovering over a rich and impossible social-climbing widow, making polite conversation about Paris, where she'd soon be buying couture clothes and he'd be ordering his winter supply of fine wines. "Madame" herself was chattering in French to a former Presidential aide of JFK, all the while keeping an eye on the orderly destruction of the "cold dish table" near the door, where the waiters rapidly depleted the artistic array of cold baby lobsters, fresh salmon, artichokes, and *oeufs en gelée*. A famous cosmetician faced them across the room and a film star and her current lover occupied the table reserved for the Duke and Duchess of Windsor when they were in town. It was all elegant and expensive and sleek, the province of a very small and influential segment of New York.

"This is Maria's favorite restaurant, isn't it?" Susan asked.

Jacqueline laughed. "Yes, but I like it nonetheless." Then she sobered. "I hear you had quite a little dust-up with our sainted mother-in-law over that column you're writing. Is that why you suggested lunch—to talk about it?"

Susan was surprised. "As a matter of fact, yes. I do need your advice. But how did you hear about it so quickly? It only happened yesterday."

"Darling girl, everybody in the family has heard about it. Maria was on the phone to Mary Lou and Gloria and me five minutes after you left. Not that that's surprising. She's on the phone to me every day of her life when she's in the vicinity."

"Every day? Maria calls you every day?"

"Like clockwork."

"For heaven's sake, why?"

"To give me advice about the children. What else? You'd think that Calhoun and Charles were hers, with all the instructions she gives about their care and feeding. We all get it. As though none of us had the mental capabilities to run our lives and handle our own

157

children. Do you mean she doesn't call you every day?"

"No. Almost never. Unless it's about something like the column."

"Well, I guess she wouldn't call you at that," Jacqueline said thoughtlessly, "since you don't have children for her to manage." She stopped abruptly. "Oh, Susan, I'm so sorry! How careless of me! For a moment I forgot . . ."

"It's all right."

"No, it isn't. I'm an insensitive boor. How is Katie? Have you been to see her?"

Susan shook her head. "I'm afraid to go. I know she's well taken care of, but I don't think I could stand seeing her being brought up by strangers, no matter how capable, kind and well paid they are."

Jacqueline was silent.

"I've never really discussed that with you," Susan said. "I have a feeling you think I did the wrong thing."

"Not the wrong thing, I don't suppose. That is, I don't blame you for buckling under all the pressure. Maybe it was sensible. Everybody seemed to think so."

"Except you."

"I'm not sure," Jacqueline said. "I keep wondering what I'd do in your place. Of course, the situation's a little different with me. Physically estranged as I may be from Walter, he *is* there. The kids feel as though they have both parents. In your case, with Richard away so much of the time, I don't know." She lit a cigarette. "Hell, I don't know what I'm talking about. We probably wouldn't have had the determination and the patience to cope with an unhearing child either. It must be a monumental job."

"I wanted to do it."

Jacqueline looked at her almost angrily. "Then why didn't you? Nobody could have forced you to send Katie away. It's just like this damned column. Maria's having a fit over it and Richard's going to back her up when he comes home and you're going to give in again.

158

My God, Susan, you can't let them have their way in all things! Where's your backbone? What are you afraid of—losing your husband? You'll lose him anyway, the route you're going. Richard's a bully. All the Antoninis are basically bullies. And the only way to survive in their world is to be as tough as they are. Look at me. I may not be much of an example, but damn it I live my own life in spite of them. And Walter accepts it. He knows they're all going to get back what they give, selfishness for selfishness. Our marriage would have broken up long ago if I hadn't been just as pig-headed as the rest of his 'wonderful family.' I want to stay married. So do you. But you won't if Richard thinks he can use you for a door mat."

"What about Mary Lou? She never crosses Sergio or Maria."

"Don't kid yourself. You ever see Mary Lou's jewelry? In her quiet way, she makes Sergio pay for every fling. A Buccellati bracelet for every extracurricular roll in the hay—that's Mary Lou's method. She acts meek as a lamb, but she's learned how to get her revenge on the Antoninis. She hits Serge where he lives—in his wallet."

"But what about her child? She put Frances in a home."

"True. The difference is, Mary Lou wanted to. She had to, if only for the sake of the son she already had. Remember, Frances is retarded. There's no hope for her. It wouldn't have been fair to Joseph and, as it turned out later, to Patricia to have raised those normal kids in a household with a sister who simply couldn't keep up. And it would have been miserable for poor little Frances."

"That's what I was told about Kate."

"Except you have no other children to worry about. If you wanted to put all your energy into Katie's development you could, without depriving others."

"So you really do think I was wrong," Susan said slowly.

"All right. Yes, I think you were wrong. Something

159

went out of you when you let them take that child away, Susan. It was the beginning of total submission. Now you're at the second step. I know you're going to stop writing this column you really enjoy doing. And for what? To please Maria? To make Richard happy? Bull! You're quitting because you've lost the will to fight."

"I haven't said I was quitting the column."

"Well, aren't you?" Jacqueline softened. "I don't mean to be so hard on you. I know you love Richard. I know his happiness is everything to you. That there's none for you unless he's content. But *you* matter, too. It can't be all giving and no taking. Nobody loves a jellyfish. Sorry, but that's the God's truth. They're drinking your blood, Susan, these damned Antoninis. They'll keep doing it till you're drained lifeless. They'll turn you into a stupid little robot who'll put up with anything. A faceless creature who doesn't make waves. And when that's accomplished, Richard will find you so boring that he wouldn't even *pretend* to be faithful." Jacqueline was so intense she didn't think what she was saying. "My God, from what I hear he's already . . ." She clapped her hand over her mouth. "Oh, Jesus, I didn't mean to say that!"

Susan went deathly pale. "He's already what?"

"Nothing. Forget it. A stupid piece of gossip. You know how people talk. Come on, let's order lunch. I think I'm going to have the rack of lamb. It's divine here."

"No," Susan said. "We won't order until you tell me what you meant."

"All right. Maybe you should know. The word is that Richard's picked up his old affair with Gerry Carter on this trip. They're sleeping together all over the West Coast, I hear. You know, of course, they had a thing going when Richard met you. I'm sorry, Susan. I had no right to tell you, I suppose. But I can't stand your giving up everything *you* want in life while Richard has it all *his* way! This doesn't mean he doesn't love you. It's just another side of his life. He doesn't

160

want to marry Gerry. If he had, he would have long ago. He married you. He didn't have to. He *wanted* to. But now that he's so sure of you, so sure you'll do exactly as he tells you, he thinks he can get away with anything. That's why you've got to be independent. Demand what you want, whether it's your work or your baby or both. Fight him. Make life tough for him. It's the only way he'll respect you. And the only way you'll survive. Believe me. I know the Antonini men. And the Antonini women."

The bottom dropped out of the world. Susan's mind jumped to bits and pieces of the past. She'd wondered about Gerry, intuitively sensing there'd been something there, but supremely confident that it was over. She thought of her newly revived sex life with Richard before he left on tour, of the way he'd demanded her body, of the insatiability of his physical needs. She instinctively knew that once he'd resumed his sexual activities with her, he'd not be content to go for weeks without a woman. Any woman. She'd have to decide now. Make a life of her own, as Jacqueline advised, or devote herself to her marriage, do whatever Richard wanted, travel with him, put career and children out of her mind forever. She wondered why she felt so certain Jacqueline was telling the truth about her husband and his publicity woman.

"How did you hear about . . . about Richard and Gerry? Was it Paul? Has Paul been in touch with you?"

Jacqueline shook her head. "Paul? He'd be the last one to tattle, especially about Richard. Paul's a loyal darling. He may know what's going on, but wild horses couldn't drag it out of him. No, my information comes from a friend of mine in San Francisco. She says the whole of California knows, because Gerry's making sure of it. She was humiliated when Richard dumped her for you. Everybody thought he'd marry her." Jacqueline laughed bitterly. "My God, they sure don't know the Antoninis, do they? Imagine Maria letting Richard marry an 'employee!' Not that he ever intend-

161

ed to, but Gerry kidded herself that he did. Anyway, I suppose this is her revenge, proving she can get him back any time she wants him, even on this basis. Or maybe she loves him. I don't know, Susan. I'm only sure of one thing: Richard's reverting to his old role as a naughty spoiled brat and you'd better nip this in the bud."

"But how? By doing everything he forbids me to?"

"Exactly. Get your baby home. Rehire Bridie and in a year or two you can start teaching Katie to live in the real world. Even without Richard's participation, I believe you can do it. Meantime, keep on with the column. Who cares whether he and Maria hate the whole thing? Try being selfish for a change. It's the only way you'll make it." She shook her head. "I have some nerve, handing out this gratuitous advice. You'll probably hate me, and I'd be sorry about that because I'm really terribly fond of you, Susan. You're the best thing that's happened to the Antoninis in years. You're the only one in the whole damned family I can relate to. And, if you'll forgive the immodesty, I rather think that goes both ways."

"It does," Susan said. "Even at this moment." She tried to laugh. "It's not easy to be fond of someone who knocks the props out from under you, but I suppose it's better. At least now I know I have to decide what to do." There was a muffled catch in her throat. "Maybe I should leave him," she said sadly. "Maybe I should divorce him, get a job, bring Katie to Mother's."

"You don't want to do it that way," Jacqueline said. "And you don't have to. You can make this work. Remember you're dealing with a man, not a superbeing. He's like all men, complete with the irresistible urge to see exactly how far you'll let him go. Like a child testing your patience. He knows damned well you'll hear about Gerry. Maybe in an infantile way he'd like you to. I'll bet he really wants you to be the independent, no-pushover young woman you used to be. I don't pretend to read his mind. Right now I could cheerfully murder him. And yet, I like him. In fact, of all the brothers I think he's probably the only one really worth saving." She beckoned for a menu. "If I haven't entirely spoiled your appetite, shall we order lunch?"

One look at his face when he came into the apartment told Susan that Richard already knew about the column. Whether Maria had called him or whether he'd seen it in the paper or heard about it from a friend, she didn't know. It didn't matter. He barely said hello, didn't kiss her, slammed into the bedroom and began taking off his traveling clothes. Susan followed him silently.

"Would you like a drink?" she asked.

"I'd prefer an explanation."

"I presume you mean about the column."

"Exactly. What the hell do you think you're doing, Susan? Are you crazy? I have to deal with the press every day of my life! What kind of position do you think this puts me in, when my wife is one of them? I simply don't understand you! You're not well enough to travel with me, but you're in such good shape that you can take a stupid job writing a bunch of idiotic drivel! Who put you up to this? That damned, meddlesome Kate Fenton, I suppose. Or was it your shrink who thought you should have an 'outside activity'?"

"Kate got me the interview," Susan said quietly, "but I got the job on my own. Obviously you know your mother doesn't approve."

"You bet she doesn't! And she's dead right! It's embarrassing beyond belief! You'll quit it. And right away."

Susan felt her anger rising, but her voice was under control. "And what will you quit, Richard? What will you give in return?"

He stared at her. "What does that mean?"

"Don't pretend. I know about Gerry."

He turned his back to her and fiddled with the buttons on his shirt. Finally he faced her. "All right. You've heard. Goddamn people's big mouths! I'm sorry. I didn't mean it to happen."

She didn't answer.

He became suddenly defensive. "In a way, you know, you're just as much to blame as I. You should have been where you belong, with your husband. Not skulking around New York, crying all over that bloody Marcus and letting that bitch Kate Fenton con you into doing something stupid! You should know, of all people, that if you'd been around I wouldn't have needed anybody else to screw!"

The coarseness of it made her cringe. "Is that all you need? Someone to screw? Funny, I thought it was love you wanted. Tenderness. Something more than you can get from a call girl . . . or even a press agent. Apparently I don't matter to you as a wife. I've been part servant, part mistress. For a little while I was also part of your ego when I was carrying your child. And now you want me to be a combination of legal whore and watchdog, is that it? You want me to give up everything I want in order to tag along after you and make sure you stay out of any bed but mine. Well, I won't do it, Richard. I'll go with you, gladly, anywhere, but not as a deterrent to your tomcat instincts. I can't make you faithful to me unless you want to be, so don't stand there and tell me it was my fault you were with Gerry or God knows who else! You could always find a way to cheat on me if you wanted to, even if I shared every room in every hotel suite from here to Timbuctoo! Don't try to transfer your guilt to me by saying I'm to blame because I wasn't where I belong. Where *do* I belong, Richard? On a scale of one to ten, would I rate a possible seven . . . maybe one step above your manager and three steps under your piano tuner, your mistress and your mother?"

For once, he was openmouthed, struck dumb. And then in one of those meteoric changes of attitude he came toward her and tried to take her in his arms.

Susan pulled back. "No. No more getting everything

164

you want that way. Let's straighten this out right here and now. You speak of the embarrassment of my writing a column. What of my humiliation having the world know you've picked up with your ex-mistress? What of the abuse I've taken from your mother? What about you and your family taking our child away against my wishes? What is a little job compared to all this, for God's sake? How dare you come in here giving me orders about the only thing I've done on my own in the past two years?" She was erupting with anger. "You're killing me, Richard, and I don't want to die! I did once, but no more. I intend to live, hopefully as half of you. If not, I'll live on my own."

He couldn't believe this was his adoring, obedient Susan. And yet he liked it. This was the spunky, sure-of-herself young editor he'd found so attractive, the only woman worth marrying, the one he'd felt had Maria's strength tempered with compassion.

"I don't want to kill you, darling," he said quietly. "I want you to live forever, with me. I'm sorry, Susan. I'm truly sorry about the thing with Gerry. It just happened. I didn't plan it. I was so happy when I left you. I suppose I was still hungry, and you weren't there. I'm not blaming you," he added hastily. "That was a stupid thing to say. I was wrong. I beg your forgiveness and I promise it won't happen again." He paused. "As for the column, perhaps I'm making too much of it. If it makes you happy, what the hell. How much harm can it do? I trust your taste and discretion. Who knows? Maybe it will be helpful." He smiled. "They say Eleanor's column was the most useful propaganda FDR ever had. What's good enough for a President should be good enough for me."

Now it was her turn to stare. Jacqueline was right. Her beloved was a bully and only understood those like him. How quickly he would trade his objection to her writing for her "forgiveness" of his lapse of faith. How easy it was to get one's own way if you stood your ground. More than standing your ground, you had to attack. The knowledge saddened Susan. It was not

165

the way she thought, and she resented the necessity for it, but there was too much at stake not to press her advantage.

"There's something else, Richard," she said.

"What's that?"

"I want to bring Katie home."

His reaction was violent and instantaneous. "No! We're not going to go through that again. It's out of the question. Everyone has told you so. I won't have you giving up your life to a hopeless cause."

"It's my life. You have yours." She was amazed at her own strength. "I want our child here. I'm going to bring her home, whether you agree or not. If it's too painful for you, I'll try to spare you as much as I can and I won't ask you to help. I won't neglect you, Richard. I love you. I want us to be happy. I'll plan things so I can travel with you some of the time." Susan paused. "And when I can't, I'll try to trust you. Again."

"You're really making me pay for one stupid lapse, aren't you?" His tone was bitter.

"It's not a question of payment. Or vengeance. I think I've known all along that I was trying to play a role I wasn't suited for."

"What role is that?"

"Jellyfish," Susan said, remembering Jacqueline. "Nobody loves a jellyfish."

Bea went with her when they drove up to get Katie. Susan's mother was worried about her. Worried about how thin she'd become this past year, more worried still about the grim set of her daughter's mouth, the unreadable expression in her eyes. Susan, who'd always been so gay, so outgoing, now seemed, if not bitter and cynical, something closely approaching that frame of mind. And she'd been so uncommunicative of late. Even when she called to ask Bea to go with her to the school where Katie lived, she hadn't explained. She'd merely said tersely, "I'm going to get Katie. Will you come?"

Bea hadn't hesitated. Of course she would go, in spite of her reservations about this move. She would do anything for her child. Lie, steal, even kill, she supposed. It crossed her mind that even now she might be part of a "kidnap plot," that Susan was taking her baby over Richard's objections. Not that such an action really would be kidnaping. Susan had as much right to remove Katie as the Antoninis had to put her there. But her daughter's tense attitude on the drive upstate increased Bea's feeling that the decision was not one made happily or in accord with her husband.

As they crossed the George Washington Bridge, Bea glanced out of the car windows, looking right and left, up and down the Hudson River. It was so beautiful in this area, so near tumultuous, dirty Manhattan, and yet one felt a million miles removed, as though the serene countryside had not changed since the Dutch created their settlements in the seventeenth century. She loved the quiet, peaceful vista of mountains, the winding roads with signs that pointed to towns called Garrison and Fishkill and Cold Spring. It was remote and lovely.

"You have the directions?"

Susan nodded. "Bridie remembered them very well. She went with Richard."

"Bridie gave you the directions. I see. Then Richard doesn't know you're doing this. I rather thought not." Bea sighed. "Susan, is it wise to bring Katie home without his approval?"

"I don't care what's wise. I know what I'm doing. You were wrong, all of you, to agree with him. I know you meant well. I don't blame you or Dad or Kate. If anyone's to blame, it's I. I didn't put up a fight. I was too much in shock. Now that I'm all right I know what must be done."

She explained her plan to her mother. Bridie had been re-engaged to look after the baby. When Katie was old enough she'd start with a speech therapist. There'd be constant, meticulous training for years to

167

come, but Susan was determined to make it work. "I've signed up for the correspondence course at the Tracy Clinic. I'll find the right prenursery school for her, one with normal children. I know what I'm in for, but it's the only answer. Katie has her rights and I'm going to see that she gets them. I have to. I brought her into the world."

"I," Bea thought. All this without Richard's co-operation. Worse, with his disapproval. She thinks she can do it alone. She's gambling her marriage, her child's future, even her own sanity. And yet I understand. I'd probably do the same. It's not possible to be coldly clinical where your baby is concerned.

She felt such sadness for Susan and Katie. She even pitied Richard. He'd been through hell in that awful period of discovery, and it was not he who insisted the child be sent away immediately. It was Susan who, in her anguish, had made that hasty decision. But now that it was done, Richard was determined to stick by the heart-rending choice, still believing it the only viable alternative. What will this do to the two of them? Bea wondered. How far apart have they already drifted?

As though Bea communicated her thoughts, Susan suddenly said, "I may leave Richard, Mom. I may have to."

"Darling, no! You love each other. He'll adjust to having Katie home if that's what you truly want."

"It isn't just Katie." Susan's whole body tensed. She wanted to tell her mother about Gerry, but she couldn't bring herself to do it. "It's . . . well, a lot of things. He doesn't really want me to do the column, though he finally agreed. He doesn't need me, but he doesn't want me to have any life of my own. I don't know. We don't seem to share anything lately."

"That will change," Bea said. "You've both been through a terrible, stressful time. And there's been too much separation. That's no good for any marriage. Promise me, Susan, that even when you have Katie back you'll still arrange to travel with Richard as much as possible. You're wrong, dear. He needs you. You need each other."

"Do we? I wonder."

The owner of the school for the deaf was surprised to hear that Mrs. Richard Antonini had arrived. In all the months since Mrs. Giovanni Antonini, the child's grandmother, had made the arrangements with him, Mr. Pomeranz had never once laid eyes on Katherine's mother. The father, the famous pianist, had brought the baby, had looked as though he were in actual pain as he left her, had seemed, understandably, near tears.

"It's kind of you, Mr. Pomeranz, to make this exception. I know you normally don't take children before school age, but my wife is ill and we thought it best that it be done at once."

"I understand, Mr. Antonini. Your mother explained the circumstances. Katherine will have her own quarters and a special nurse until she's old enough to be with the others. We've never done this before, but you may be assured that we will give your daughter the best of care." He did not mention the enormous "contribution" Maria had made over and above the exorbitant annual "tuition." It had been sizable enough to make Pomeranz more than willing to bend his rules. Since that day, no one had come. Mrs. Antonini, Sr., telephoned occasionally and so did the child's other grandmother, Mrs. Langdon. Brief conversations in which they ascertained that the child was well. Other than that, silence. Until today, when the receptionist announced Mrs. Richard Antonini. Surprised and vaguely troubled, Mr. Pomeranz hurried out of his office to meet her.

Susan introduced herself and her mother.

"We've spoken on the telephone," Bea said. "I'm Mrs. Langdon. Katherine's grandmother."

"Yes, yes, of course. Happy to meet you both. Very happy to know you, Mrs. Antonini. You've come to see Katherine? That's fine. You'll find her well and happy."

Susan shook her head. "I haven't come to see her, Mr. Pomeranz. I've come to take her home."

"Take her home? But Mrs. Antonini said . . ."

Susan interrupted him coldly. "*I* am Mrs. Antonini. My mother-in-law does not speak for me. I'm removing Katherine. She belongs at home."

"But your husband told me this was a permanent arrangement."

"You are mistaken. It was only until I was well again. Now, if you'll be good enough to show me where my daughter is, we'll be on our way."

The owner hesitated. The twenty-five-thousand-dollar "gift" had been made with very explicit instructions. It was all highly irregular, this sudden change of plan. And, for that matter, how did he know that this cool, beautiful young woman was who she presumed to be? He'd never seen her or the woman who allegedly was Mrs. Langdon. They might be impostors, kidnapers intent on stealing the baby! He'd be responsible! My God, Pomeranz thought, I could be in terrible trouble! The Antoninis were influential people. Even if this *is* the child's mother she might be taking Katherine against her husband's wishes. I could be charged with neglect. Maybe sued. My school taken away. My license revoked. A few frozen seconds ticked by before he answered.

"Mrs. Antonini, this is all very sudden. I've had no instructions to release your daughter."

"What instructions do you need?"

"Well, that is, you were not the one who made the arrangements or brought her. I really feel . . . I mean some authorization . . . I'd have thought we'd have had notice . . ." Pomeranz was stammering, wondering how he could ask this woman to identify herself.

She did it for him.

Susan's voice was approving and sympathetic when she answered. The cold, hostile attitude disappeared and she smiled kindly. "You need to be sure of who I am. Of course. You should be. I'm delighted you're so cautious. For all you know, I could be here to kidnap the baby." She fished her wallet out of her handbag. "Here's my driver's license, Mr. Pomeranz. And a bank card with my picture. And here's the best proof of all. It's a photograph of me holding Katie only a couple of months before she came to you. My husband took it. I'm sure you recognize us both."

The man examined everything carefully. She was who she claimed to be, all right. But that didn't mean the family wanted the baby released to her. The wrath of the Antoninis could still come down on his head.

"I'm sorry," he said placatingly. "I didn't mean that I doubted your identity, but we have to be very careful."

"Naturally. I told you I approved of that. Now, may we see Katherine?"

"Of course. Right this way."

He led them up the winding, carpeted stairway, wondering how he could reach someone who would authorize this curious development. Perhaps he could stall the woman long enough to reach her husband or her mother-in-law.

"Katherine has quite a few things," he said. "It will take a few minutes to pack them. Perhaps meantime you'd like to inspect some of the classrooms and play areas? That is, you might wish to have your little girl return here when she reaches school age?"

"No," Susan said. "She'll be going to regular nursery school with hearing children."

"I see. Well, in any case, you'll excuse me for a few minutes? There are certain release forms for you to sign. I'll see to it." He paused outside a closed bedroom door. "Katherine is in there with her nurse. I'll be back right away."

Pomeranz scurried down the hall. Susan and Bea looked at each other with the same thought in mind: he was going to telephone Richard or Maria.

"Let's move fast," Susan said.

Bea hesitated. "Susie, don't you think we should

171

visit now and come back later for Katie after you and Richard have talked more about it? It seems a lovely place and they obviously are very conscientious. Perhaps . . ."

"No. I've come for her and I'm taking her home."

She opened the door and moved swiftly to the playpen where a smiling Katie was engrossed in inspecting a pink plush elephant. At the sight of her, Susan's determination strengthened. She was so beautiful, so charming in her serious study of the little toy. Ignoring the startled nurse, Susan scooped up the baby and held her close, hugging and kissing her, laughing with joy.

"Hello, angel," she said. "Hello, my darling. Mummy's here. We're going home. Isn't that wonderful? Katie's going home!"

Katie smiled and grabbed for Susan's earring. The nurse was on her feet, reaching for her charge.

"It's all right," Susan said. "I'm Katherine's mother. We're taking her with us. Mr. Pomeranz is getting the release papers. We're to meet him in his office."

Without another word she strode out of the room, carrying Katie, a worried Beatrice at her heels. Susan headed directly for the front door.

"Susan! Are we going to leave like this? Aren't you going to sign the forms?"

"There aren't any forms, Mother. You know that. He's stalling until he reaches Richard or Maria, and when he does, he won't let Katie leave. Come on. Hurry up. I want to be out of here before Pomeranz tries to stop me."

"Darling, you're crazy! What will Richard say?"

Susan glanced at her briefly over her shoulder as she opened the front door. "He'll say just what you said: that I'm crazy. Only he'll mean it."

172

Chapter Fourteen

It hadn't been easy, but it hadn't been as drastic as Susan expected. Yet the blind determination that fortified her when she went to get her baby slowly weakened as she and her mother drove back to the apartment in uneasy silence. Silently she rehearsed what she'd say to Richard, tried to think how to defend herself against Maria's inevitable, angry participation. When she let herself in her door she felt terribly alone and frightened, and she hugged Katie tightly, as though "they" would drag the child out of her arms by force.

Bea had offered to come in with her, but Susan shook her head.

"Thanks, Mom, but I have to do this part alone. It's between Richard and me. I'm so grateful to you for going with me, but I have to face the rest of it by myself."

She'd stood for a moment, watching her mother walk slowly down Park Avenue toward her own car. At the corner Bea turned and looked back and then made a "thumbs up" gesture of encouragement. Susan nodded and managed to smile, thinking, God bless her. She does understand.

The apartment was very still as she walked in. Perhaps Richard isn't home, she thought hopefully. Perhaps Mr. Pomeranz couldn't reach him. She prayed for a little more time, dreading the moment she'd have to stand up to him, but as she went toward the nursery,

173

Katie toddling beside her, he opened their bedroom door and stood silently looking at her.

"So you did it."

"Yes. I know you're angry, but I had to. Don't be too hard on Mr. Pomeranz, Richard. Please. He tried to keep me from taking her. I don't want him to suffer for this."

He exploded in a mirthless laugh. "Pomeranz! Who the hell cares about Pomeranz? Who's even thinking about that little nobody at a time like this? Susan, in God's name, what have you done? I thought you were just beginning to accept the inevitable and now you're starting all over again!"

"I could never accept it. At first it was almost bearable because it was unreal. I knew it and wouldn't believe it. But now I know I was right all along. Katie belongs with us. She's worth every bit of pain and sacrifice." She held the child by the hand. "Look at her, Richard. Look at your daughter. She's as much a part of you as your arms or legs. You can't amputate her from your life."

He stared down at the little face, saw the dark, curly hair, the big, trusting eyes, the features so like his own. "Oh, Christ," he said, almost like a prayer. "Susan, you know we can't. We can't handle this." But even as he protested, she heard his surrender.

"Yes we can, darling." Susan's voice was joyful. "I swear to you I'll make it right for all of us. We'll forget everything that's happened. Everything. It will be better than ever for us. I won't neglect you for the baby, I promise. There's room for both of you, enough love to go around." She pushed Katie gently into his arms. "Hold her, dearest. She needs her father as much as I do."

He took Katie reluctantly, remembering the delight he'd felt when she was born, recalling the first months before they knew. How changed he'd felt then! How much he'd wanted to be the father of this beautiful little girl, to be close to and proud of her. And now it couldn't happen. They'd never have the parent-child

174

happiness he'd imagined. She'd never hear. Not his voice or his music. And if she spoke it would be gutturally, in nasal tones offensive to his ears. Involuntarily he shuddered, thinking ahead, hating himself for lacking the kind of blind faith Susan had, unable to believe, as she did, that this helpless little thing could be what her mother dreamed. He should insist, right now, that Katie go back. But he couldn't. The depth of love in Susan's eyes wouldn't let him. She had to have her chance, even if it was only for a little while. Gently, he stroked his child's head.

"All right," Richard said sadly. "We'll try."

Susan, weeping with relief, put her arms around both of them. "Thank you, dearest. Thank you. You'll never regret it."

I wish I were sure of that, he thought as he kissed her. I wish I could believe that this demanding child will never come between us.

For almost a year, he nearly did believe it. Despite Maria's outrage, Gloria's scorn for his "weakness" and Sergio's older-brother advice based on the experience with his own Frances, Richard defended Susan's choice. He also found a new kind of peace in her return to "normalcy," her renewed sexual passion for him, and he was aware of the extra effort she made to ensure he was not disturbed by the mute presence of Katie. Strengthened by Paul's approval of his actions, fortified by Jacqueline's compliments and the Langdons' gratitude, he almost came to believe that the situation was manageable. Once again he returned to the voluntary faithfulness he'd chosen after Katie's birth. Even when, on rare occasions, he made a trip without Susan, he entered into no intimacy with other women. Gerry had departed even before Katie came home, given a handsome severance the very day after Susan had told him she knew about the resumption of the affair. He'd been so guilty then, so remorseful that he never wanted to see his publicity agent again. Susan had not commented on the dismissal. Gerry had understood.

"I knew it couldn't last," she said. "Susan was bound to find out, and you care about her too much to hurt her again." She couldn't resist a cynical smile. "At least with me."

"With *anybody*," Richard had said firmly, and believed it. There was no lover like Susan when she was happy, no one who satisfied him so completely and who was so obviously satisfied in return. There were even long stretches when he nearly forgot about Katie's handicap. She was walking but had not yet reached the "talking stage" and to all outward appearances she was a contented, cheerful busy child, secure in the devotion of her mother and her nurse. He did not spend much time with her, so she was not a constant reminder of the imperfection he hated in all forms. For all that he saw of her, she might almost have been away at the school. Unconsciously, he refused to think what would happen when she was fitted with hearing aids, when the speech therapy began, when she went "out into the world." For now life was good. He was playing better than ever, his ego gratified by public acclaim, his physical needs well taken care of by his wife, his position as "best in the family" confirmed by his growing reputation over Sergio and Walter. Even Maria was less sharply critical of his actions, though she reinforced her disapproval by barely speaking to Susan and never coming to see her granddaughter. The first summer after Katie's return, the Richard Antoninis took a house in Southampton. By tacit agreement, they knew they could not spend months in Pound Ridge with the child Maria refused to acknowledge. Instead, with little discussion, Richard went alone to his parents' house for occasional visits. He would simply say, "I think I'd better go to Mother and Father next weekend." And Susan would nod, answering merely, "We'll miss you, darling. Give everyone our love."

In a sense, though she bitterly resented Maria's stubborn refusal to see Katie, it was almost a relief not to be in the midst of the supercharged Antoninis. Susan appeared, dutifully, at dinner in New York when they were invited to the town house or to Walter's and Jacqueline's, but those times were rare and she got through them without great distress, even though her mother-in-law's presence was like a cold wind that chilled her to the bone. Giovanni was always dear to her, asking after Katie, making it plain that he felt no "stigma" in having a grandchild unlike the others. Susan was grateful to him, as she was grateful to Jacqueline, for making her feel welcome. Sergio and Mary Lou, like Gloria, sided with Maria. They thought Susan a fool for insisting upon raising a "deformed" baby, and Richard an ass for allowing it. When the family was all together she was almost pointedly ignored. She no longer cared, and made less effort than ever to be part of the conversation. She'd come a long way from that first, anxious weekend when she'd so desperately wanted to be accepted by Richard's famous family. She had her husband and child now. Her own home. The friendship of Jacqueline and Kate Fenton. And the unswerving support and devotion of Bea and Wil Langdon.

She'd given up writing the column which had been such a bone of contention. She told herself she didn't need that "ego trip" any more, and it was a small enough concession for Richard's reluctant compliance with her much more important wish. She said so to Kate one afternoon after an elegant lunch at Quo-Vadis. They strolled down Madison Avenue, looking in the window of boutique after boutique, pausing to inspect Jolie Gabor's spectacular jewelry shop, dropping into Boyd's, the only place in New York where one could get any kind of domestic or imported cosmetics, browsing through the little gift and card shop near Fifty-eighth Street, picking up always-needed birthday greetings and "get well" cards like two secretaries on their lunch hour.

"This is such mindless fun," Susan had said as they

came out into the sunshine clutching their little paper parcels. "I don't envy you, Kate dear, having to go back to the office and face deadlines."

"Don't you? I thought you enjoyed doing that column."

"I did. But Richard hated the idea. And he's been so patient about Katie, the least I can do is do something to please him. He was so relieved when I quit, and it doesn't matter that much to me. Not any more."

"Not since you've decided to spend your whole life being slobberingly grateful to your husband for allowing you to keep your own child, and his?"

"Kate! That's cruel!"

"Sorry. But it's true, isn't it? You've really abdicated any identity of your own. Pity. Hate to see a good mind go to waste. No need for it. For God's sake, Susan, you don't have to repay Richard for something that's as much his doing as yours! You didn't create Katie singlehandedly and you shouldn't feel the sole responsibility for her! All this nonsense about 'pleasing Richard.' I never heard such rot! He should be down on his knees to you in gratitude for putting up with his family and his temperament and his infidelity."

Susan stared at her, amazed.

"Oh hell, don't look so surprised. Everybody knew he was back with that trashy Girl Friday of his last year. At least he had the good taste to get rid of her professionally as well as personally."

Susan flushed. "He was going through a terrible time, Kate. You know that. You saw how I was."

"Bull. He was just plain horny and you know it. I don't say you shouldn't have forgiven him. Gad, if every wife divorced an unfaithful husband there wouldn't be a marriage left in America. I just say that all the 'bigness' hasn't been on Richard's side. Not by a damn sight. So if you really wanted to write that column, you shouldn't have stopped. In fact, I think it was a lousy idea to stop. You're living in too small a world now, Susie. Your whole life is Richard's comfort and Katie's

178

future. That's not enough. Not for someone as vital and interested in things as you."

"I have my interests. You named them."

"Okay. I'll shut up."

"No. I'm glad you always speak your mind to me and I can speak mine to you. It's terribly important to have a woman to talk to. I know I can say anything to you. You and Jacqueline. She was the one who told me about Gerry. I've never even mentioned it to Mother." Susan paused. "I'm not kidding myself, Kate. I don't know what will happen now that Katie's intensive training has begun. Up to now she's been no problem to anyone. But from here on . . . I don't know. I've got to give myself to both of them. It's been easy enough for me to travel sometimes with Richard. The baby didn't even miss me when I was away. But now that the daily teaching has started, how can I leave her? And if I'm not with Richard . . ."

Kate finished the sentence for her. "There may be another Gerry or a string of Gerries."

"Yes. But I have to take that chance."

"You still seeing Dr. Marcus?"

"No. He helped me a lot but I don't need him any more. He gave me strength and some understanding. I doubt I'd be sane today if it weren't for him, and for you who insisted I go see him." She looked pleadingly at Kate. "It's going to be all right, isn't it, Kate?"

"You want soothing lies?"

Susan shook her head.

"Then how can I tell you it's going to be all right? Nobody knows. The only thing I know is that you will do what your heart tells you. That's the way you are, Susie. Incredibly durable in some ways, pathetically hurtable in others. And incurably romantic in this calculating age. You'll blunder through, my girl, I have no doubt. But the path you've chosen, like our wonderful city streets, is not without its neck-breaking potholes. Try not to fall into too deep a one."

❁

That fall, the nightmare of turning Katie into a functioning person began. A woman weaker than Susan, one less fiercely determined, would have admitted defeat, but from somewhere Susan found a superhuman kind of strength created out of love for her child and, admittedly, a stubborn refusal to admit that nearly everyone thought she'd taken on an impossible task.

There were days, many of them, when Susan herself wearily thought it impossible. Katie had, for such a small child, a strong will of her own. At the doctor's advice, Susan had given her a doll fitted with two hearing aids like those she now wore. "It will help her communicate," he'd said. "Watch her try to talk to that doll. She'll identify with it." But sometimes she loved the doll, and other times she hated it, as though she instinctively knew that it, too, was "different." Contrarily, she seemed to sense that her own hearing aids were her link to the world. Every morning, Bridie reported, as soon as she awoke, Katie toddled to the bureau and pointed to the devices, which she wore uncomplainingly and without interruption until bedtime. Five mornings a week Susan took her to Edith Chambers, a speech therapist, a vivacious, enthusiastic young teacher. And in the afternoons, following instructions from the Tracy Clinic and others, Susan spent hours with the child. Crouching down to Katie's level, Susan repeated one word over and over, a hundred times, a thousand times, keeping her face in a strong light so Katie could see her mother's lips clearly and hopefully begin to imitate the words she saw forming there. When Susan tired, Bridie took over for hour after hour of this endless task, exhausting for "teacher" and "pupil," seemingly fruitless as Katie neared her third birthday.

Worse still, as Katie's need for Susan increased, Richard had begun slowly and not unexpectedly to withdraw. He took no part in the training. Not that Susan asked him to. She'd vowed, when he'd reluctantly acquiesced to Katie's return, that she'd not ask of him something he'd be unwilling, probably unable, to do. Still she hoped he might want to participate, that his paternal love might be stronger than his inherent distaste for this slow, seemingly futile process. Once she coaxed him into the nursery to watch as she went through the patient repetition of one word. After fifteen minutes, he left.

"I'm sorry. I could never do that. I haven't the patience."

Forgetting the agreement she'd made with herself, Susan flared with anger. "Why not? You can do the same stupid scale a thousand times with pleasure. Isn't your daughter as important as your damned piano?"

"That's unworthy of you," he said.

"Unworthy! Richard, this is your child!"

"Yes, and you're my wife. I haven't forgotten either thing. Have you?"

She'd turned back to Katie, no longer angry but miserably unhappy. It was true. She hadn't shared her time and attention as she'd promised herself and him. She couldn't. Katie needed these hours of training now. She'd still need her mother for many years, no matter how well she progressed. Susan thought of the lecture she'd attended at the Parents Group of the New York League for the Hard of Hearing. She remembered the pathetic account of one mother who told how her twelve-year-old daughter had come home one day, thrown her hearing aid on the floor and screamed, "I don't want this! It's your fault! What are you going to do about it?" What would *she* do if, after all the effort and training, Katie blamed her? I wouldn't care, Susan told herself. If she could speak those words, I wouldn't care, as long as she was talking. But it frightened her, all of it. The present and the future. She felt trapped between husband and child. She loved them both and they loved her, possessively, jealously, demanding she make a choice. There could be only one choice, she realized sadly. She had to stay with the helpless one, the little one, even at the risk of losing the other.

Desperately, in the late hours of the night, she tried to make up to Richard for her preoccupation with Katie the rest of the day. She made love to him as expertly and passionately as she knew how. There was a kind of wildness in her when they were together, as though she knew she had only one way to hold him, as though she had to make her body indispensable while her mind was elsewhere. It was tearing her apart and she thought of going back to Dr. Marcus for help. But there was no time. Just as there was no time to travel with her husband, or spend leisurely mornings in bed with him as she used to, or even to go to those hated weekends in Pound Ridge which meant so much to him. Not that she wanted to visit Maria, nor was she even welcome, except insofar as Richard's wife was dutifully welcome, but his parents and brothers and sister were important to him and she knew he resented Katie for interfering with the old order of things.

Sometimes she thought again of leaving him, of setting him free, and the irony of it was exquisite. She hadn't left him when he sent Katie away, nor when she'd discovered he'd been sleeping with Gerry. Now she was considering it in a spirit of kindness rather than revenge. But she didn't want to leave him. She prayed for some kind of miracle that would save her marriage. Perhaps when Katie began to talk, when she went to school, when her constant need for her mother's presence diminished, perhaps then things would be serene again and she'd lose this awful feeling of failing Richard.

And it was not all hopelessness. Edith Chambers was encouraging, full of accounts of successful "case histories," and Bridie was endlessly devoted and optimistic. Bea and Jacqueline spurred her on when her courage failed, and even Kate Fenton, though she disapproved of Susan's limited horizons, was generous in her admiration for her young friend's tenacity. But the staunchest ally of all was Paul. Richard's manager dropped in almost every afternoon, sitting quietly in a corner of the nursery, watching as Susan went through the teaching routine, often with an inattentive, bored and restless child. Sometimes he even took over the job, scrunching his long, lanky frame down next to Katie, his gentle mouth saying, over and over, one simple word. Observing him, Susan sometimes wondered whether Katie thought this was her father. Certainly she saw more of him than she did of Richard. Susan was grateful to Paul, yet a little worried about her husband's reaction to this devotion which was not only for Katie. Paul said nothing to her that could be construed as a hint of love. Still, she knew he was in love with her. Sometimes she half-returned the feeling. He was so kind, so tender with the baby. I wish I'd met him first, Susan thought at difficult moments. Life would have been so much easier if I'd married him. But she knew this was only tired, discouraged thinking. She was in love with Richard. She loved Paul. It was quite different.

"You and Richard are off to Houston next week," she said one afternoon. "I'll miss you both."

He smiled. "Can't you come along, Susie? It's only for ten days. It would do you good, and Bridie can handle this little minx."

She shook her head regretfully. "I'd love to, but I can't. Next week is the big moment. Katie's starting nursery school."

Even he seemed suddenly uncertain. He frowned. "Are you sure that's the thing to do? I mean, can she manage with ... with the others?"

"Edith thinks she can. So do I. It's only two days a week. I've talked with the teachers there. They say it will be good for her to be with other children." Susan smiled. "Kids don't need words to communicate. They have a language all their own. Besides, Paul, I think she's about ready to break through. I honestly do. She's beginning to imitate sounds. Of course, only Edith and I understand them, but it's a start. I'm so encouraged!"

She was breaking his heart with her bravery. Thank God she doesn't know why I really want her with us, Paul thought. Richard was back to his old ways again. There'd been that affair with the socialite in Philadelphia which had quickly ended when her husband found out. But the movie actress on the Coast was promising (threatening?) to meet Richard in Houston. It was insane. They were both too well known to carry off a clandestine affair. Somebody was bound to pick it up—a friend, or a gossip columnist. Susan doesn't need that again, Paul thought angrily. Goddamn Richard! Why does he have to salve his wounded ego with other women just because he can't have a hundred per cent of his wife?

"I'm sorry about the timing. For your sake, I mean."

She looked at him penetratingly. "Is there something special about this trip?"

"No. Of course not. I just thought you could use a change."

Susan smiled. "I could. You're right about that. But I wouldn't miss the sight of Katie in a real school. I've dreamed of this day, Paul." She paused. "I know what you're thinking. I should be with Richard more. I know it, all too well. Maybe I can be, soon. When Katie's mind is on finger-painting and block-building, and her new little friends. Then I'll be able to leave her. To set her free."

I'm using the same words I've thought about in relation to Richard, she realized. Setting *her* free! Setting *him* free. I'm such a hypocrite! I don't want either of them not to need me.

"You're the boss," Paul said.

The film star was sleeping quietly beside him at the Warwick Hotel in Houston when the phone rang in the middle of the night. For a moment, Richard didn't know where he was. Then he remembered the evening. Glamorous Sylvia Sloan had flown in from Hollywood, her blond hair jammed under a disreputable-looking hat, her recognizable face half-obscured by oversized dark glasses. She'd registered as "Mrs. Charles Robinson" and taken a single room which she left immediately for the comfort of Richard's suite. They'd had dinner sent up, had drunk quantities of champagne and laughed over the art on the hotel walls, discovering it really was true that if you removed a painting it left a big space with letters that announced an expensive oil had been taken away. It was an ingenious way to protect good art in a world of light-fingered travelers, and they'd found it hilariously funny. Later there'd been some pretty wild sex, and now Sylvia slept like dead while the phone rang on and on.

Richard switched on the bedside light and looked at his watch. Four A.M. Good God, who'd call at this unearthly hour? He lifted the receiver and said, fuzzily, "Yes?"

Sergio's words came through without preamble. "Richard? Cancel the concert and come home immediately. Mother's had a stroke. We think she's dying."

Chapter Fifteen

Nobody in the family believed it, but Maria Antonini had absolutely no intention of dying. She lay in New York Hospital, in a private room overlooking the East River, paralyzed on her left side, unable to speak and furious about it. It was insupportable, this business of being unable to move or talk when your mind was so clear. Her bright little eyes glittered with anger as the doctors and nurses fussed over her and Giovanni and the children crept in reverentially, as though she were already dead. When Richard appeared, she was outraged. They'd called him back from Houston, obviously made him cancel an important concert! And to make it worse, he'd shown up with Susan. Susan, who must take a fiendish delight in seeing her mother-in-law as mute as her child! Except that *I* can hear and I'll speak again, Maria thought. Katherine is a cripple, which I refuse to be. Her frustration was enormous. Why didn't they all stop hovering? Didn't they know her? Didn't they know she wasn't going to go until her children had reached the heights she planned for them? They're idiots, all of them, she fumed. Without me, they'd be nothing. That's why I have to get well.

"What are her chances, Doctor?" Giovanni had asked the specialist as they stood in the hospital corridor.

"To survive? Good. She's a strong woman, despite her age. For full recovery? I can't answer that, Mr. Antonini. The stroke was relatively mild, but recovery will depend on her determination as much as the therapy we'll begin as soon as she's able. The will to return to a normal life is as important as anything we in the medical profession can do."

Giovanni smiled. "In that case, my wife will fully recover. She has an indomitable spirit."

The doctor nodded, pleased. "Fine. Our job will be easier."

Returning to his wife's room, the maestro permitted himself a rare moment of introspection. Yes, Maria's will to survive was good. For *her*. Even for him, he supposed. He'd learned to depend completely on her in all things personal and professional. It used to irritate him in the early days, having her take over his life. But for many years, since he'd resigned himself to it, his wife's decisiveness and efficiency had made everything easier. In a way, it was pleasant to make no decisions, to be spared the annoyance of dealing with details, to have, face it, his life run for him. Even when he'd strayed, Maria had taken it in stride, waiting out his "romances," knowing he'd always come home.

But Giovanni wasn't certain that Maria was the best

thing for their children. She'd turned Sergio into a ruth-lessly ambitious egomaniac who cared nothing for his wife or children and who saw his brothers only as opponents to be bested. Walter had retreated into a non-performing world, knowing he could not measure up to the flamboyant brothers on either side. Poor Walter. He'd never really wanted to be a composer. Everyone but Maria realized that. Yet he'd be a great one. Walter's and Jacqueline's "marriage of convenience" turned up in Giovanni's thoughts. His daughter-in-law was too strong for such a weak husband. For a long time they'd lived separate lives, but one day Jacqueline might leave him. And for all his pretended sophistication, Walter would come apart under that final admission of inadequacy.

As for Gloria, hers was the saddest example of Maria's obsession with achievement. In her mother's eyes, the girl had nothing. No talent, no looks, not even social graces. How she must loathe Maria! Giovanni thought. How she must have always longed for a mother like Susan's—adoring, uncritical, companionable. Gloria had made the best of it. Even marrying a man who couldn't possibly be in love with her, just to prove to Maria she could get a husband. But she was bitter as, underneath, the others also were bitter. Strange that Maria never recognized her daughter's anger. Or did she? If so, she'd not admit it.

Giovanni's eyes went to Richard and Susan standing quietly at Maria's bedside. Maria was right to put her faith in her youngest as her hope for immortality. He was the most gifted of them all. But she'd made him self-centered and narcissistic. She'd schooled out of him the ability to give of himself in any deep and lasting way. He could only use people. He couldn't return the healthy love of that nice girl he'd married. Perhaps, in fairness, he wanted to. There'd been fleeting signs of it. But as long as Maria lived, her influence would keep Richard from loving. And from facing his own flaws. She'd taught him to look into an altered mirror and see nothing but a perfect, irreproachable image.

Giovanni stared at the motionless figure of his wife and sighed deeply. He wanted her to live. He, alone, was most confident she would. And yet, God forgive his terrible thought, most of her family would be better off if she left them alone at last.

Hearing his sigh, Susan left her husband and came to his side.

"Are you all right, Papa-Joe? Can I do anything for you?"

He smiled gratefully. Susan was the only one who'd shown any concern for him. "No, my dear. Thank you. I'm all right."

"Why don't you come home with Richard and me? You don't want to be alone in that big house. We have plenty of room."

He shook his head. "That's kind of you, Susan, but I'm better off in my own bed. The servants are there. I'll manage." He looked at her affectionately. "How are you? I haven't seen you in a long while. How's my little Katie?"

"She's doing so well! She started nursery school this week."

"And?"

"So far, so good. The other children have accepted her beautifully. They're very kind to her, as though they know, young as they are, that she needs special protection. I'll never again believe that children are basically cruel to each other, the way I've always heard. It just isn't true."

"I'm happy for her. And for you. I know it hasn't been easy, Susan. You've done a wonderful job."

She actually blushed. "Thousands of other mothers have done the same and more. And most of them don't have the financial advantages I have. It must be terrible to have an afflicted child and no money for the best doctors and therapists and private nursing schools, and no one like Bridie to help."

But they have husbands to help in an even more important way, Giovanni wanted to say. They get the

188

kind of moral support and physical assistance Richard is unable to give you.

"If you need anything, Susan . . . anything at all." Giovanni seemed suddenly embarrassed. "I'm afraid the family hasn't been very attentive." His voice trailed off and involuntarily he looked over at Maria. Thank God she couldn't hear this conversation spoken in whispers.

Susan followed his eyes. "It's all right," she said. "It's understandable. I'm sorry about Mrs. Antonini. She's the last person in the world I'd have imagined this happening to. How she must hate being helpless! But she'll be all right, won't she?"

"I think so." What an extraordinary young woman you are, Giovanni thought. You really are sorry, after all she's done to you. Most people would see it as retribution, God's punishment for Maria's arrogant impersonation of Him. Funny. He'd never thought of it quite that way before, but Maria had always acted as though she were the Almighty, directing people's lives, ordaining their futures, almost presuming the power of life or death over them. Her frequent anger was like a thunderbolt from heaven, her rare approval like the warmth of a June day. God must hate that. He made us in His own image, but He didn't intend us to usurp His infinite wisdom. Giovanni was surprised by his musings about God. He'd never been a formally religious man. He left the churchgoing to Maria, but he wondered whether the Lord was so irritated by Maria's righteousness that He'd struck out at this cheeky daughter of His, "smote her with His wrath," as they said in the Bible. The idea was so ridiculous he laughed aloud. Richard looked over at him.

"Father? What is it?"

"Nothing," Giovanni lied, knowing Maria could hear him. "I was just thinking what hell your mother will give us when she gets around to it. We're behaving as though this is more than what she'd call 'a temporary inconvenience.' She'd want you to fly back to Houston today, Richard. She's probably furious that you came

189

at all. I'm sure you can still keep the concert date. They probably haven't even had time to announce the cancellation."

They looked at Maria, who was trying to tell them that for once in his life her husband was absolutely right.

"I agree with your father," Susan said. "That's what your mother would want most. We'll all be here with her every minute, Richard. You should go back for the concert."

He hesitated. Sylvia would have returned to Hollywood, and just as well. When she'd suggested joining him, he'd known it was a mistake. A one-night stand was one thing, but having a nymphomaniac around for days before he performed was too distracting. He wouldn't make that mistake again. He wondered what drove him to these women he really didn't give a damn about. The urge for variety? Monogamy was not man's natural state, after all. Or was it pure pique because Susan chose to stay with the child rather than be with him? He was jealous. He admitted it. He almost hated her for all her bloody, uncomplaining self-sacrifice. Like now. Self-sacrifice, hell! She probably would be relieved if he'd go away again so she could devote herself to Katie.

"All right," he said finally. "If you think that's what Mother would like." He stroked Maria's cheek tenderly. Did he imagine a look of satisfaction in those amazingly alert eyes?

When word of Maria Antonini's illness got out, the press had a field day. For forty-eight hours after the first story, the family could hardly get in and out of the hospital for the crowd of reporters camped at the entrance. It was not so much the matriarch's condition that interested them as it was the chance to report on the suffering of the lofty Antoninis, to put the agony of the famous under a microscope for the "little people"

190

to examine and enjoy for the price of a newspaper or the flick of a television dial.

In the beginning, the stories were more or less routine coverage: photos of a gray-faced Giovanni entering his limousine without comment; quotes from a willing-to-talk Sergio, saying their faith was sustaining them and asking for the public's prayers; daily bulletins from the hospital and live TV interviews with the big-name specialists who'd been called in for special consultation. Though they were not allowed into the hospital, the reporters pestered nurses and orderlies for details of Mrs. Antonini's daily routine. Had she spoken or moved? Was it true she'd had her own furniture moved in? Who was allowed to visit? What famous names had sent flowers? The President and the First Lady? Mr. and Mrs. Vladimir Horowitz? Beverly Sills? Terrific!

But in a couple of days, interest in the subject waned and the Antoninis would have been left in relative peace except for the doggedness of one woman reporter who worked for a weekly "scandal sheet." Her name was Carlyn MacKenzie, and her nationally distributed paper, which outsold *Time* and *Newsweek* combined, was a gossipy sheet called *Open Secrets,* specializing in rumors, speculation and sometimes outright misrepresentation of the private lives of well-known personalities.

Carlyn was a tough reporter who could "smell a scandal a mile away." She knew the Antoninis' closets rattled with skeletons. She'd been doing a lot of quiet digging and her sources were numerous and reliable.

"I'd like your okay to do a series on America's number-one musical family," she told her city editor. "There's a lot of juicy stuff the Antoninis have managed to hush up."

"Such as?"

"Such as the fact that big brother Sergio has a fifteen-year-old retarded daughter hidden in a mental home. And young Richard and his wife tucked away a deaf-mute kid in a ritzy school upstate. And get this.

Susan Antonini had a nervous breakdown when Richard put the child there. She went to a psychiatrist. And she also went up and took the baby out of the school without her husband's permission. I have a contact who works in the place. She says there was hell to pay when Pomeranz, the owner, had to explain to Richard and his mama how that happened."

The editor was getting interested. "Keep going, MacKenzie. Anything else?"

"Plenty. That caper damned near broke up the marriage. They've stayed together, but Richard's been consoling himself elsewhere ever since." She paused dramatically. "Sylvia Sloan was with him in Houston when Maria Antonini had her stroke. He left her in the bed while he flew home to mother."

"Sylvia Sloan the movie actress?"

"None other. And there's more. I can't prove it yet, but I hear the other brother, Walter, is AC-DC. How about that? Him and his supposedly sexy jet-set wife!"

"I'm sold. Go to it. Just try to avoid libel suits."

"No problem. The facts are there. Some of them have even been hinted at, but nobody's done the full exposé."

Three days later the series began. The first article was headlined "Antonini's Baby Will Never Hear Father Play." Carlyn wrote luridly of Katie's affliction and the repercussions, including a mawkish account of the day Richard and Bridie brought the infant to the school.

"The young pianist's handsome face was ravaged with grief as he carried his deaf-mute baby into the silent, secret world to which he'd doomed her. For a moment he seemed to hesitate, as though he couldn't do it. He held little Katherine tightly while Bridie Grey, the baby's nurse, looked pleadingly at him, her eyes begging him not to give her tiny charge to these strangers. But he did not relent, even though those nearby saw tears in his eyes when he handed his daughter to a waiting attendant. 'Goodbye, Katie,' he said. 'We love you,' and then he walked away, not looking back."

It went on to describe Susan's breakdown and therapy and her eventual headstrong decision to retrieve her child. "What the future holds for the Richard Antoninis, for their marriage and their handicapped child, acquaintances refuse to speculate. Those close to them believe, however, that the clash of wills between the glamorous couple has done irreparable harm to the storybook union of the charming prince of the concert hall and his Cinderella bride."

At the end of the story there was a "teaser" for the next one. "How is Richard consoling himself? And with whom? Next week: The continuing tragedy of the Antonini family."

"Good piece, MacKenzie," the editor said.

"Thanks. Wait till you see the follow-ups."

Kate Fenton rang up Susan. "You see this week's *Open Secrets?*"

"You know I never read that rag! It was bad enough when I had to, in case there was something *Vogue* should know. Now that I'm a free woman I don't waste time on that drivel."

"You'd better read this issue, Susan. You and Richard and Katie are the first of a continuing series on the Antoninis." Kate's voice trembled with rage. "Those bastards! They're a disgrace to journalism! Not that you could call this journalism. More like writing on the walls of a public toilet."

Susan tried to stay calm. "What did they say?"

"Everything. The commitment, the 'kidnaping,' your psychiatric care, difficulties between you and Richard. The works. And frankly, even *that* isn't as gruesome as what I suspect is going to follow." She read the "sign off" paragraph. "Sounds like they've got plenty on Richard. I hope there isn't too much, for his sake and

193

yours." Kate probed gently. "Is he still acting up, Susie?"

Her friend's long silence was confirmation. "You know there've been things. You remember about Gerry. But that's over. It happened when I was so depressed and unresponsive. In a way, I couldn't blame Richard. There was nothing for him at home. But things are fine now. They really are."

Kate knew better. She, too, had her sources. There was no point in worrying Susan with the things she'd heard. Kate only hoped that terrible bitch who was writing the series didn't know about all the others, including Sylvia Sloan.

"They've probably shot their bolt," Kate lied. "You know how these sensation-seekers operate. Lots of snide suggestions but no substance. I just thought you ought to know before your phone starts ringing. By the way, how's Maria?"

Susan guessed how Kate's mind was working. "She's making great progress. Improved a thousand per cent in the past few weeks. Now that Richard's home he sees her every day, but she's still not allowed many visitors. And of course no newspapers."

"Good. Keep it that way."

They'd barely hung up when Jacqueline called to discuss the same subject.

"Nasty stuff," Jacqueline said. "You'd think they could find something better to write about than our family secrets! Don't let it get to you, Susan. It's ugly but it's no disgrace."

"Kate's worried about what's to come. She read me the announcement of the next article."

"Yes," Jacqueline said slowly. "The series could be sticky for all of us. I wonder how much they know about things we'd rather not air. I don't give a damn myself, but I'd hate to have my boys disillusioned about their father."

It was Susan's turn to comfort. "It may just die down after they get through speculating about Richard and Katie and me."

"I hope so, but I'll admit I'm worried. Once those bloodhounds pick up the scent, there's no stopping them until they've advertised every stupid mistake any of us has ever made. Maria won't know. But I feel sorry for Joe." *I feel even sorrier for you,* she added silently. *God knows what will happen when you read this lurid, lip-smacking account of yourself and your husband and child. And if they really start detailing Richard's sexual exploits it'll be devastating. Who knows what they've got on* all *of us? Probably plenty.* She tried to sound unconcerned once again. "Oh hell, we're probably getting wrought up over nothing! Let's be nonchalant when our 'dear friends' call. Don't react to this garbage, Susan. That's the wrong thing to do."

"All right."

"Maybe it won't be too bad," Jacqueline added feebly.

"I hope it won't. I'm going to run over to Lexington Avenue now and pick up the paper." She gave a troubled sigh. "I can guess what it says. I've read enough of their stuff to know how piously vicious they can be."

Chapter Sixteen

"I think we'd better have a family conference, Richard." Gloria's voice was business-like. This was her third call. She'd already reached Sergio and Walter and made arrangements for all of them to meet at their parents' house that afternoon.

"What for? Mother isn't worse, is she?"

"It isn't about Mother. That is, not directly. I take it you haven't read the story in this week's *Open Secrets*."

"Story? What story?" Richard was getting impatient. "Get to the point, Gloria? What's in that yellow sheet that necessitates a summit meeting?"

She told him. "Serge and Walter agree with me that we have to plan a strategy. God knows what those people are going to come up with about any of us! This Katie thing is only the beginning. They've already promised to discuss your extracurricular romantic activities next week." Gloria's voice was sarcastic. "*That* should endear you to all those proper Bible Belt dowagers who think you're Little Lord Fauntleroy. And you can bet you're only the *first* target. Wait till they take off on Sergio's life and his idiot child, and Walter and Jacqueline's peculiar marital arrangements! My God, do you think they'll dare say he's gay? We'd better damned well get some good counterpublicity in the works before the Antoninis sound like a family of degenerates! They'll probably drag out those hundred-year-old stories about Father and his 'conquests.' I doubt that even *I'll* be spared, though they can't compare my life with any of yours."

Several thoughts crashed headlong into each other in Richard's mind as he listened to his sister. The first, almost irrelevantly, was how much she sounded at this moment like Maria. No doubt she saw herself in the role of "family commander" now that the real one was wordless and immobile. In spite of his distress, he felt a grudging admiration for Gloria. She might hate Maria but she also envied her. She really wants to be like her, Richard thought. And she foolishly thinks this is her chance.

The idea of a story about his child angered and upset him. He tried to love her, but he couldn't get over the feeling that Katie's handicap was somehow a "disgrace," a reflection on him, and he'd hoped that it would go forever unnoticed by the world. It would have, damn it, if Susan had left well enough alone. If she hadn't sneaked up there and taken the child out of school, nobody would ever have known he had a daughter who wasn't like other children.

Susan. He still loved her, but she was so little his these days. Everything had changed. They barely communicated, each feeling wronged by the other. How much did *Open Secrets* really know about what he did when he was away? He dreaded next week's revelations. Dreaded them for what they'd do to his image as well as his marriage. Sergio and Walter must be just as nervous, Richard thought. Gloria was right. "Idols" as they were, the public would accept only so much before, feeling ill-used, they turned the wrath of their moral indignation on the Antoninis. He wondered what plans his sister had. If only Maria were functioning!

"All right," he said finally, "I suppose we should put our heads together. This afternoon? At the family's? Okay. Shall I bring Susan?"

"God, no! None of the wives is coming. Just the four of us, Richard. Father will be at the hospital. I haven't told him a word of this. Not even about the newspaper article. Oh, I did think I'd ask Paul Carmichael to be here. He's like one of the family and he has good ideas. Lord knows we can use some!"

Richard hung up and wandered disconsolately through the apartment. It was Saturday and Susan had left an hour before to take Katie to the Children's Zoo in Central Park. She'd poked her head into the library to say they were leaving. Not even a question as to whether he'd like to join them. She knew better.

"We'll be back by lunchtime," she'd said, "but if you get hungry Lily can fix you something."

He'd nodded and smiled at Katie, who smiled and waved back automatically. He couldn't reach her as Susan could. Mother and daughter seemed to have an understanding that did not involve words or gestures, but he was an outsider, a strange man whom he supposed Katie thought of as an occasional visitor. Or did four-year-old Katie think at all? How could one think or dream without sounds to relate to? Today the world

197

knew all about his lost child and he felt ashamed. He wondered, suddenly, whether Susan had heard about the article. She hadn't mentioned it. He hadn't told her of Gloria's call or of the afternoon meeting. Perhaps she didn't even know the secret was out. No, she couldn't. She'd have said something.

But when his aimless roaming took him into the library he saw that Susan did know. A copy of *Open Secrets* lay on a table. He picked it up and read the purple prose. God, it was even more disgusting than he'd imagined! He sounded like a monster and Susan sounded crazy. And those last couple of lines. Jesus! He'd like to get his hands on that MacKenzie bitch and on whoever had given her that inside information! Who could it be? Who knew that much about all of them? It was no one in his family, that was for sure. Susan's parents wouldn't have discussed any part of this. Besides, they didn't know about his "consolations." Paul knew everything, but Paul wouldn't talk. It must have been Gerry. Yes, it had to have been Gerry. Hell hath no fury ...

Angrily he tossed the paper aside and went to dress for "the meeting."

Like Richard, Sergio did not discuss the planned conference with Mary Lou. Whatever his wife's part in Gloria's "counterplot," Mary Lou would go along as long as he made it worth her while. He supposed they'd get around to Frances, those devils at the paper, damn their souls, and probably find out about some of his women, too. Well, what the hell. They couldn't destroy the Antoninis. They were artists and every artist since the beginning of time had been offbeat, even scandalous. The public would soon forget. He didn't worry about these things the way his mother and Gloria did.

Jacqueline answered the phone when Gloria called to ask for Walter. She knew instantly what was on her sister-in-law's mind, and she couldn't resist baiting her.

"Looks like we're all going to get quite a going-over in the press, doesn't it, Gloria? I assume you've seen *Open Secrets*."

"Yes. It's disgusting."

"Poor Susan. She doesn't need this."

"Poor *Susan!*" Gloria's tone was shrill. "What about the rest of us? Do you imagine for one moment your husband's peculiar life-style won't be subject to the same ugly scrutiny? Or Sergio's? Or Father's? They have something to lose by bad publicity. What does Susan have to lose? Thank God Mother doesn't know about this! After all she's done to build the Antonini name!"

"Your concern for your mother is touching," Jacqueline said acidly. "Still, you must be relieved that *your* name is Taffin. They may overlook you and Raoul when the rest of us are rolling around in the mud."

Gloria was almost speechless. She loathed this cool, superior wife of Walter's. With effort she restrained herself from taking the bait. Jacqueline always knew how to get at her: by reminding her subtly that she was the "unknown Antonini."

"May I speak with Walter, please?"

"Of course. I'm sure he's around somewhere."

When Walter came back from the phone, Jacqueline looked at him with amusement. "Gloria must be in seventh heaven taking Maria's place during this family crisis. Does she have a master plan? Or should I say a master *key* to keep Pandora's box securely locked?"

Walter couldn't help smiling. Though they had nothing together any more, he liked and admired Jacqueline more now than he had in the days he'd made himself believe he could love her or any woman. They were really friends. She was worldly and sensible and he could always talk to her, knowing she liked him, too, in spite of his late-blooming homosexuality.

199

"My dear sister has called a conference," he said, "to decide how we should combat this bad publicity and worse that's bound to follow."

"It figures. That's what Maria would have done. Except Maria would already have the answers, and I doubt Gloria has. Who's sitting in?"

"Serge and Richard and I. And Paul Carmichael." Jacqueline nodded. "No Giovanni. And no wives."

"Correct."

"And typical. Maria would have done it the same way." Jacqueline laughed. "Isn't it incredible? Gloria detests her mother, but she's even more jealous of her. She's going to prove she's as smart and strong as the old lady, and that none of you really needs Maria as long as her daughter is around. Gloria's finally gotten her chance to shine. Well, God bless! But wouldn't the Signora be in a rage if she knew her bumbling daughter was making a power play while Maria is flat on her back?"

Walter frowned. "I don't think it's quite like that, Jacqueline. Not a power play, I mean. Gloria's really worried. And she's right. Stories like this can do terrible harm. Somebody has to organize a defense."

His wife shook her head. "You're all such a bunch of babes in the woods, poor darlings. What defense, for God's sake? So far they haven't printed anything they'd have to retract and I'll bet they won't, no matter how far they go. The only thing that surprises me is that we've all escaped as long as we have. Well, have fun at your meeting, old boy. Put your little heads together. Me, I'm going to hand mine over for a restyling at Mr. Kenneth's, which I daresay will be infinitely more productive."

The family gathering, as might have been expected, developed into a shouting match, with brother accusing brother of "crimes" more heinous than his own. It was all going nowhere until Paul, who'd been sitting quietly by, cleared his throat and said, "As an outsider, may I make a couple of suggestions?"

"Please do," Gloria said with undisguised relief. This

meeting, which she'd imagined would be as calm and orderly as one Maria might have called, had disintegrated into a series of personal defenses and unproductive outbursts of anger. "Shut up, everybody, and let's hear what Paul has to say."

He'd smiled at her easily from the big chair, his feet propped on an ottoman, his glasses pushed up onto his forehead. "Let's review where we are. First, *Open Secrets* has printed a very unpleasant but true story about Richard and Susan and Katie. Unfortunate, but it had to come out sooner or later, and it's no crime to have a deaf-mute child, no matter how embarrassing some of you may find it."

Richard interrupted. "I suppose *you* wouldn't be embarrassed to be pictured as a man who cried over a baby, nor one whose wife had to go to a psychiatrist?"

"No, frankly, I wouldn't. And I don't think people are going to feel anything but sympathy for you and Susan and your child. It's sad and human. And thousands, maybe millions of people who could never identify with the untouchable genius at the keyboard will now feel a kinship with the man who's been struck by such an understandable tragedy."

There was silence as they tried to absorb this new way of looking at the problem. Paul went on.

"We don't know what they're going to say next. About Richard's 'amourous adventures.' Or any of the rest of you. Let's don't kid ourselves, there's plenty to say, but we don't know how much they have or what they can prove. Seems to me, the biggest problem will not be with Richard's public, but with his wife. If a lot of things Susan isn't aware of suddenly come to light, we can't predict how she'll react. We can only hope she'll stand by and give a lie to the rumors by her presence and her seemingly unbelieving response to 'a pack of vicious lies.' "

Paul sounded calm, but he hated himself for suggesting that Susan play the role of loyal, loving wife. He wasn't sure she would. In his heart, he felt she shouldn't. Or was that part of the old wishful thinking?

201

In any case, it would be the only way to take some of the curse off Richard's philandering.

"You'll have to make a clean breast of things with Susan," he said, "before she reads about it. And then, friend, you'll have to shape up. No more fooling around. You'll have to be living proof of that nice lady's faith in you."

Gloria snorted. Paul ignored her.

"I imagine they'll go after you next, Serge. Same thing applies in both cases, really. Properly handled, your retarded child will create sympathy. And Mary Lou will come on strong as the devoted wife and mother. Maybe both you fellows will have to buy the silence of a few ladies with whom you've been indiscreet. Let's hope that can be done in secrecy." Paul took a deep breath. "Strangely enough, you're in the best spot, Walter, if there is one. You're not literally 'onstage,' but even more importantly, you and Jacqueline are already known as a couple of the 'beautiful people' and your freewheeling life-style is pretty well accepted for the unconventional thing it is. Still, it won't hurt for you to cool it with your 'friends.' Be seen more with your wife and children. Create a 'chic family' impression. Make it all look modern but 'normal.' "

They were subdued now, impressed by Paul's clinical analysis.

"What about Father?" Gloria sounded almost meek. "Will they drag him in?"

"Maybe, but not likely. He's The Maestro and he's untouchable. A living legend with a gravely ill wife. Nobody will have the bad taste to drag up his indiscretions." Paul smiled. "Past or, for all we know, present."

He felt the tension in the room easing. Goddamn these egomaniacs! Show them how they can save their skins and they suddenly get happy and secure again. What do they care how their wives and children will suffer, as long as they come out with their adulation intact and their bloody careers undamaged.

202

"You're terrific," Richard said. "My God, Paul, you're the best friend anybody ever had! You've solved it all, just like that! Why couldn't we see it ourselves? Hell, we've been in an uproar over nothing! Talk about making lemonade out of lemons! This damned ugly series may end up making us all look better than ever—humble and human. It's genius!"

"Hold it," Paul said. "It's not that easy. Your wives will have to go along with all this, and they're not without pride themselves. Do you think Susan is going to easily forgive you when she knows the facts, Richard? Will she submit to interviews about her 'happy married life?' Will she let Katie be photographed and seen for the happy child she is? Those things will be necessary. And what about Mary Lou? Will she start doing active work for retarded children? That should be part of it, too. Part," he said bitterly, "of this sympathy-creating act the Antoninis will have to work like hell at."

"She'll do it," Sergio said. "For a new sable coat Mary Lou will do anything."

Richard was quiet. "I think Susan will go along," he said finally. "She cares about my career."

"Mother will be wild," Gloria said. "She's always been vehement about not publicizing Frances and Katherine."

"I'm afraid Mrs. Antonini doesn't have a choice," Paul said politely. "Unfortunately, even if she has a better solution she's in no position to give it to us."

As they left the house, Richard put his arm around his manager's shoulders. "Thanks again, Paul. In a pinch this family behaves like a bunch of Italian tenors. You really saved the day."

"That remains to be seen. All I did was make some cheap, self-serving suggestions. Whether they work, or what *Open Secrets* has up its sleeve, none of us knows."

Richard was full of confidence. "If we all follow your advice, things will turn out fine."

Will they? Paul wondered as they parted. How could Richard be so blithe about confessing his sins to

Susan? Would she consent to his dishonest game-playing which involved not only herself but the exploitation of her child? Was Richard's career worth that? Paul shook his head. I've never been as disgusted with anybody in my life as I am with myself right this minute, he thought. But I had to try to help them. It's part of my job. What a lousy job! I should chuck *it* and *them* and this whole degrading mess. I would if I had a shred of self-respect. No. I wouldn't if I weren't so hopelessly in love with Richard Antonini's wife.

As he walked down Park Avenue, Richard's momentary vision of an easy salvation began to fade. Paul was right. Nobody knew what *Open Secrets* actually was going to print. Just as no one could predict Susan's response when he told her some ugly truths and asked her to stand by him. Maybe, he thought for a moment, I shouldn't jump the gun. All the paper may know about is the thing with Gerry, and Susan already knows about that. It would be ironic if he ran through a list of his misdoings only to find out later that they need never have been exposed to her at all! Still, he couldn't take a chance. Paul was right. He'd have to tell Susan everything so there'd be no surprises for her in next week's paper. He'd have to throw himself on her mercy and if necessary beg for her support. Beg, hell! He was entitled to that! Even the wives of common criminals were always shown at their accused husbands' sides, vowing belief in their men's innocence. Susan can do no less for me, Richard told himself virtuously. I've done plenty for her.

But he felt less confident when he let himself into the apartment that late afternoon. Susan was reading in the library and she looked up from her book, smiling quizzically when he came into the room.

"You're so late, Richard! I was beginning to worry about you. You haven't even touched the piano today! Where were you, dear? Visiting your mother?"

He shook his head. "I was at the house with Serge and Walter and Gloria and Paul. We thought we should discuss that article in *Open Secrets*. I know you saw it. Where is it now?"

"In the trash where it belongs." Susan's voice was bitter. "I didn't want to discuss it. How dare they, Richard? How dare they say those things about us?"

"You can't keep the press from printing the truth, Susan. You should know that." He hesitated. "And as you read, there's more to come. I think we should talk about that before it appears in the paper. That's what we were meeting about today. We all have to level with each other now and stand together. We're a family, Susie. Families have to protect themselves and make sacrifices so the world will continue to admire them."

She saw what he was getting at: a united defense against next week's promised disclosures about his extramarital sex life. She didn't really delude herself about what had been going on in recent months. She didn't honestly believe, no matter what she said to Jacqueline, that Gerry had been Richard's only mistress since their marriage. She simply preferred not to think about his lack of control. Or she made excuses for it when she did. It was a kind of desperate self-protection. Her concern for Katie was so intense that she couldn't handle another area of distress. She'd avoided speculating about Richard's behavior, hoping, foolishly, that that problem would go away by itself. It hadn't, of course. And now it was all going to come out. Richard had some kind of plan, worked out with his family, in which she undoubtedly was expected to participate. She waited, quietly, for him to explain all this talk about "families standing together." What "sacrifices" was she to be asked to make?

Gently, remorsefully, he told her what he presumed *Open Secrets* knew. The affair with the Philadelphia socialite. The liaison with the film star. "I didn't want you to know, ever," Richard said. "They've all been meaningless, impulsive physical acts that have nothing to do with our marriage or my love for you. But I

205

couldn't let you be shocked by finding out about them in that filthy paper."

"I see," Susan said. She was surprised by how unmoved she was. "So now I know. What am I supposed to do? Forgive you? Pat you on the head and say, 'There, there, little boy. Don't be upset. You couldn't help it?'" Awareness suddenly dawned. "Oh, no. I see what's wanted. You and the family want me to stand by, bravely refusing, in public, to believe a word of this. You need me to be the loving, trusting wife. To help squash scandal by my unswerving faith in you. That's it, isn't it? You probably want me to give interviews denying you are anything but the perfect husband. We'll be seen together more in public, right? I'll suddenly emerge as the only woman you adore. That's the name of the game, isn't it? I suppose Mary Lou will do the same for Sergio when *his* time comes. And Jacqueline will make an extra effort to be portrayed as the blissful wife. It's all you can do, isn't it? All any of you Antonini men can do now is depend on the women you married. If it wasn't so dreadful, it would be funny!"

He didn't answer right away. Then he said, "There's more, Susie. Even more I need of you."

"What more? Shall I get pregnant again to prove how devoted we are?"

"No. But I hope you'll let the other papers and magazines take pictures and do stories about Katie. Maybe you could take part in some fund-raising endeavor for deaf-mute children. In any case, please speak out as often as possible about the love and devotion we've given this child."

She stared at him, momentarily speechless. "Have you gone mad or have I?" she finally asked. "*You,* who always wanted to hide Katie as though she were some terrible disgrace, now want to push her into the foreground? You want me to talk about her disability and the love and devotion 'we' have given her?" Again she saw the answer. "Of course. It's out in the open now. So we might as well capitalize on it. Let's use our daughter's handicap to create sympathy for her father, to make the world judge him less harshly. My God, Richard, is there no end to your selfishness?"

He didn't fight back. It would have been easier if he had. "I can't argue with anything you say, Susan. I only ask you to help. I don't think you really want to see this filthy gossip sheet destroy everything my brothers and I have worked for. I've been wrong about a lot of things. I'm not as strong as you. Not as honest. I don't blame you for being disgusted, but I've never known you to lack compassion for the weak."

The surprising humility disarmed her, but she was not yet ready to agree. "Whose expedient little plan is this?" she asked. "It sounds like something Maria would have thought of. It can't be your father's idea. He has too much self-respect. And your brothers and sister wouldn't have reasoned this through so systematically. None of you has been allowed an original thought since the day you were born!"

He took her scorn without flinching. "It was Paul. Gloria realized we needed counterpublicity, but it was Paul who outlined how to proceed. He's also advised Sergio to have Mary Lou become active in some kind of work for the retarded, talking about Frances the way I hope you will about Katie."

Susan gasped. "Paul! I don't believe it! It's monstrous! Paul wouldn't use people this way! You're lying, Richard!"

"Ask him yourself. Susan, try to understand. As a family, we haven't been a very admirable lot. We thought we could get away with anything. Hiding our affairs and our imperfect children. We believed we were beyond reproach. Above the power of the press. All our lives it's been drilled into our heads that we're special, privileged. That anything we did was okay because we are Antoninis. We never dreamed that one spiteful, ambitious reporter could bring our world down around us. Paul understands that. Still, rotten as we may be, we have something precious to give the world: our music. If we lose the respect and affection

207

of the public, we lose the right to share our talent with them. And in the long run their loss might be greater than ours."

Susan was suddenly deflated. She didn't believe what Richard was saying, but she believed in Paul Carmichael. If he felt these lies and pretenses were worthwhile, then they must not be as shameful as they seemed to her. Paul had integrity. He would abandon it only in a good cause. But this! To ask her to counteract the sordid stories by putting herself and her child on display as proof of Richard's goodness! No, she couldn't. Not to save her husband's career or the Antonini name. Not even if it took Richard years to live down his offensive behavior, his unfeeling attitude toward his child and his unfaithfulness toward his wife. Besides, she doubted the articles would do that much harm. People were used to "celebrity sex scandals." They did not affect the guilty one's career as they might have even twenty years before. Richard would survive. They all would. In a few months the series would be forgotten but the damage she could do to Katie would be irreparable. Even if Paul thought it was the thing to do, she'd have no part of it.

"I'm sorry, Richard. I can't go along with any of this." Her voice was quiet. "I care about your career. Strangely enough, I even still care about you. But I won't have Katie's life turned into a circus to divert attention from your mistakes."

He tried once more. "Will you talk to Paul? He can explain the reasoning better than I."

"No. I won't talk to Paul. I'll go on as we are for now, if you like. Living in the same house, I mean. But that's all. No interviews, no pictures, no speeches or joining causes. Let Mary Lou do that if she can stomach it. I can't."

Abruptly he was enraged. "It must be wonderful to be so pure, so holier-than-thou! I've made concessions for you, Susan. One of them is right there in that nursery instead of in an institution where she belongs. If it hadn't been for your damned willful act of getting her

208

out, none of this probably would have been stirred up! All right. Take your goddamn principles and your righteous indignation and get the hell out of my life! I don't want you here, accusing me with every look! You won't help? Okay. Then move out. Add a little more fuel to the fire. Prove everything they say is true by leaving me. Who cares? I'm a lousy father and a lecher and a fool. That's what you believe. Why not let the world believe it, too?"

He stormed out of the apartment and Susan suddenly knew, helplessly, that she couldn't leave him. He was her husband and she loved him. For all the agony he'd brought her, she was still his wife and he needed her. I must talk to someone, Susan thought. Someone who knows Richard as well as I do. Paul? No. She was hurt and disillusioned by his uncharacteristic expedience. Her mother? Bea would be too emotional. And Kate would be too cynical and Jacqueline too involved. Whom can I turn to who has gentleness and wisdom and knowledge? There was only one. Slowly she dialed a number.

"Papa-Joe, it's Susan. Are you alone? May I come and talk with you?"

Chapter Seventeen

He didn't feel like talking to anyone. Not even to Susan, whom he infinitely preferred over his other daughters-in-law and certainly over his own daughter. Gloria, in fact, was the most tiresome of all. She'd just left, after reporting, in boring detail, the family plan to counteract some stupid publicity in a paper he'd never heard of. He'd half-listened to her agitated talk. How momentous everything is when one is young, Giovanni thought. Not that Gloria was *that* young. But compared with him, she was a child. He smiled. And compared to Arthur Rubinstein, he thought wryly, *I'm* a child. It's all a matter of degree.

His mind came back to Richard's wife. She'd never, in all the years of her marriage, sought out her father-in-law. He knew what prompted this unexpected call, asking if she could come to see him. He welcomed her, of course. He truly liked Susan. It was just that spending hours at the hospital every day was such a strain and he was so tired from sitting beside a Maria who silently but unmistakably resented her illness. He was weary of conducting bedside monologues, full of false heartiness for her benefit. Damn, he thought, why couldn't it have been me who had the stroke? Maria would be much better able to cope with my illness than I am with hers. She'd probably be better able to cope with Susan's problem too.

He was shocked to see how white and drawn Susan looked, almost ill. Giovanni kissed her on both cheeks and motioned her to the chair facing his.

"Drink?" he asked. "I'm going to have one."

"No, thank you. I won't stay long, Papa-Joe. I know you must be tired. How is Mrs. Antonini today?"

"Coming along remarkably. You've been very sweet about visiting so often, Susan." He cleared his throat as though the words were difficult to say. "I know she hasn't always been kind to you. She's not an easy woman. But I'm sure she's grateful for all the thoughtful things you do."

Susan shrugged off the compliment. "She's been very sick. One doesn't hold grudges at a time like this."

"No." Giovanni took a sip of his scotch. "Well, now. What brings you here, dear Susan? I daresay it's not to discuss Maria." The piercing brown eyes seemed to bore into her. "It's Richard, I suppose." Vague

210

snatches of Gloria's conversation came back into his mind. "Yes, of course. That nonsense about a series of articles. Gloria told me about it a little while ago. Can't say I pay too much attention to such things. People love to gossip but they quickly forget. Can't think why the children are making such a fuss over nothing."

"It isn't exactly nothing," Susan said. "That is, I agree with you. The best thing to do would be to ignore it, but the others don't think so." She took a deep breath. "Richard and I just had a terrible fight over it. I don't know what to do. I'm sorry to burden you, Papa-Joe, but I don't know where to turn for advice."

In spite of his impatience, Giovanni felt pleased. It was the first time any of them had come to him for advice. Even Gloria, telling him what they planned, hadn't been asking his opinion; she'd simply been informing him of a decision, the way Maria would have done. For that matter, if Maria were around they'd have left it up to her to inform him, if she thought it necessary for him to know. I should have listened more carefully to Gloria, he thought. I would have, if I'd had any idea my views would matter.

"Let me hear your version of all this, Susan," he said gently. This time he'd listen, knowing it was important.

She told him, straightforwardly, about the first article and the one already announced. She spoke of what was bound to follow. She recounted Richard's "confession" to her about the women he'd been with. "I hate it," Susan said, "but, crazy as it sounds, it's not his faithlessness that makes me so miserable. I have to take part of the blame for that. A contented married man has no impulse to cheat." She forced a smile. "At least not on so regular a basis." Then the sad look returned. "What I can't accept is Richard's asking me to publicize our 'happy marriage' and use Katie as the device. He wants me to expose her not as his beloved daughter but as a cross we've had to bear together. He's begging me to make speeches and join groups devoted to helping the parents of deaf-mute children.

211

He wants to generate sympathy to overshadow the things that will be written about us. Mary Lou's going to do that with Frances, but I'm not able to. I told him so tonight, and he told me to get out. He says I owe him this, Papa-Joe. Do I? He's your son. You must understand him. What shall I do?" Susan wiped her eyes. "I don't want to leave him. I still love him. But how can I endure this exploitation of our child?"

Giovanni searched desperately for the right words. It was a new role for him, this business of being approached as an oracle. How would Maria handle it? he wondered. She'd probably remind Susan of her duty to her husband, tell her to stop being so unworldly and do what she was told. But she'd be wrong. Susan wouldn't obey orders. She'd proved that before. She had to be reasoned with, approached like the intelligent woman she was. In any case, Giovanni thought with satisfaction, she'd never come to Maria with this problem. She'd know Richard's mother would automatically take his side. He felt ridiculously proud that Susan had brought her troubles to him. Such a little triumph, and so late in life. Yet it made him feel more a man than he had in years. He hoped he could be as wise as this young woman believed him to be.

"Susan, my dear, let's look at this as objectively as we can. You always wanted Richard to openly acknowledge Katie, not be ashamed of her. You took it hard, rightly so, when he sent her off to be, let's face it, hidden away. You defied him by bringing her home, getting help for her, sending her to nursery school with hearing children. You've never made a secret of a handicap she can't help. On the contrary, you've wanted, more than anything, for her to be part of the world. Am I correct?"

"Yes, but . . ."

"Let me finish. Now he *is* anxious to acknowledge her. Granted, for the wrong reasons. But is that not less important than the fact that he is coming forward, with you, to tell people that he has a deaf-mute child and considers it no disgrace? This is what you've al-

212

ways hoped for, Susan. It's not the *way* you hoped for it, I admit, but what difference if the end result is good? Is it asking too much for you to make a few little talks, pose for a few photographs in exchange for having your husband at your side, helping you raise your child instead of your trying to do it alone? And you'll have your own identity. The world will applaud you. You've *won,* Susan. In a strange way you've won. And the irony is that Richard doesn't realize it."

She stared at him. Won? If so, it was a hollow victory, achieved not through Richard's compassion or fatherly love but through his fear, his weakness. It didn't make him love Katie. It didn't make him want her. Giovanni didn't understand. What on earth had possessed her to come to this sweet, ineffectual man whose world was as limited as his son's? For the first time, she almost sympathized with Maria. They'd both married children who were unwilling or unable to assess the true value of things.

Giovanni took her silence for agreement. "I knew you'd see it sensibly, Susan dear. A little role-playing, some humane forgiveness for Richard's past mistakes, that's all that's involved here. Now that everything's out in the open, your marriage will be better than ever. When you've been married as long as I have, you come to learn that life's path is full of tiresome little detours. This is one of them, child. And the road will be all the smoother for it, I promise you."

She wanted to cry out that he hadn't understood anything of her problem. He couldn't comprehend that the strain of publicly pretending to be delighted with her life was an unbearable prospect. This wasn't the kind of "identity" she wanted. And he couldn't envision what the sudden thrust into the limelight might do to Katie, who was only beginning to find her way. Lord knows I'm not looking for applause! He grasped none of it. None of the dishonesty, the deliberate use of innocent people. He was not an evil man. Simply an incredibly sheltered one. Susan stood up.

"Thank you for talking with me, Papa-Joe. It

helped. It really did." She gave him a soft kiss on the cheek.

"You're a bright young woman, Susan. You won't find this as hard as you imagine. Besides, consider how much you'll be helping other parents with handicapped children! By speaking out, you may save more marriages than just your own."

Save my marriage, Susan thought as she walked slowly home. That's what it comes back to, always. Is it just foolish pride that makes me unwilling to admit I was wrong in marrying Richard? Was I? Did I go into it too quickly, as Mother and Dad said? I still can't believe that. But how much can I swallow while I look for the happiness I thought this life would bring?

But maybe, in a crazy, contorted way, Giovanni was right. She had always wanted Richard to share her pride in Katie, to let the world know that there was nothing "disgraceful" in having a handicapped child. Maybe this was the way, distasteful as it was. Maybe it would let some light into the dark corners of their marriage. To be able to talk about Katie freely would release some of her own long-suppressed frustration and make her feel a better person. Perhaps it was fate. This publicity that was being forced on her could be the very tool she needed to convince Richard that they were not unique in their problem, that hundreds of thousands of others lived with it and were strengthened by their resolve to give an extraordinary child an ordinary life. Maybe this would, as his father said, bring Richard to her side. Maybe the end did justify the means. She didn't know the answers. She simply knew that her choice was to go along with the scheme or refuse and risk losing everything she cared about. If this disaster produced a constructive change in Richard, then it would be worth it, no matter how vulgar or difficult the role. And was it all that difficult, really? A few pictures, some interviews and speeches. They probably wouldn't hurt Katie. They might even, in the long run, help her.

By the time Richard came home she'd come to

terms with the situation. She'd play the game as carefully as possible, protecting Katie as best she could. She even rationalized that, as his wife, she owed him something. But it was the kind of indulgence a woman owed a little boy who looked to his mother to get him out of a nasty scrape. That's what I really am, Susan thought sadly. I'm really the mother he has to have. He never needed a wife. Maria always reached him. In this case, she can't. So it's up to me.

"I'm here," she called from the library, where she'd been sitting for hours in the dark.

He came in, switched on the light, looking at her warily. The anger had left him and he seemed uncertain.

"I thought you'd be gone."

"I'm not going. We'll get through this together. I'll do what all of you want. We'll work it out."

He seemed to crumble with relief. "I'm sorry-I said those things, Susan. I didn't mean them. I know how you hate . . ."

"Never mind," she said.

It was as grotesque as she'd imagined. More so. The second article in *Open Secrets* pulled no punches about Richard Antonini's success with women. Apparently MacKenzie had well-documented proof of his affairs, those he'd told Susan about and a few others he'd neglected to mention. Susan read the story with a feeling of nausea and it took every ounce of strength she could muster to sound unconcerned when Bea Langdon called, almost weeping with pity for her child.

"Darling, what are you going to do?" Bea wailed. "It was terrible enough when they wrote about Katie. But this! Is it true, Susan? Is this how Richard has been behaving? Why didn't you tell me? How *could* he? No wonder you had to go to Dr. Marcus."

"Mother, stop it! You're getting everything wrong. It's not true. None of it. Do you think I'd put up with it if it were? This is simply a bunch of lies. They run stories like this all the time about famous people! And for heaven's sake, you know I saw Dr. Marcus when Katie was taken to that school, not because Richard was being unfaithful to me!"

Apparently she sounded convincing. Or Bea was simply anxious to believe her. Whichever, she calmed down. "I know what your father will say: Demand a retraction. If they won't give it, sue them! They shouldn't be allowed to get away with such mudslinging. I'm sure Richard and his family agree with us."

"No, they don't. Neither do I. Mother dear, people don't pay attention to retractions buried on page forty-two after the damage has been done on page one. The best thing to do is simply ignore it. In fact," Susan continued to lie, "it's an odd coincidence, but Richard's new press agent made arrangements only yesterday for *House and Garden* to photograph Katie and Richard and me here in the apartment. They've been wanting to do it for a long while, but I've been too busy. It's good timing now, to show how secure and happy we are as a family. I'm going to do more of that, I think. It's the best way to put these revolting rumors to rest."

Beatrice Langdon was not a stupid woman. The "odd coincidence" was, she realized, part of a hastily constructed plan based on the Antoninis' nervousness about this projected series. She felt hurt that Susan chose to pretend with her, as though she were a stranger, but she kept quiet. All she said was, "I'm sure you know best. What else are you planning to do?"

Susan tried to sound enthusiastic.

"Richard and I are going to join the Parents' Group of the New York League for the Hard of Hearing. You remember. I investigated it when we first found out about Katie."

"I also remember that Richard wanted no part of any of that."

"Yes, I know. I still don't think he'll have time to be very active, but *I* will. They'd even like me to speak.

216

It's really worthwhile, Mother. I'll probably start doing a lot of speaking on the subject of handicapped children. I'm excited about it. You know how much I've wanted to do something, make some kind of contribution."

"You always said you hated public speaking, Susan. You said it scared you to death. Remember when you were on *Vogue* and the Fashion Group asked you to speak at a meeting? You wouldn't do it. Said you'd be too nervous."

Why doesn't she stop? Susan thought. She knows this is a game I have to play, so why can't she make it easier for me? "That was different. I was just a kid and terrified of all those lady executives. Now I have something valuable to say. Something really meaningful. And I'm going to do more tours with Richard. We hate being apart so much. Besides, it's good for his image as a serious musician to have his wife with him, giving interviews to the women's pages in the cities where he appears."

Bea couldn't contain her sarcasm. "What a sudden change of heart we've had! Extraordinary! And to think it just 'accidentally' happened at the same time as this bad publicity."

Susan gave in. "All right, Mother. I'm sorry. I shouldn't insult your intelligence this way. You know we have to do everything we can to lessen the effect of this bad press. I can do much more for Richard than he can do for himself." It was a relief to speak the truth. "I hate it. I wanted to do something on my own, but I've never wanted to be a 'celebrity.' Certainly not this way. It's so phony. But it has to be done."

"What about Katie?"

"She'll be all right. I'll draw the line at certain things. She won't be personally involved in appearances and things like that. And she's well and happy at school and content and safe with Bridie at home. Even the speech therapy has gone faster than we dared hope. I can leave her more often now without worrying about it."

Bea sighed. "Are you sure you know what you're doing, darling? You're going to put yourself under a terrible nervous strain, traveling and speaking and doing all these things you hate. Is it really necessary, Susan? Do you love Richard so much you can let him do this to you?"

She didn't answer the last question. She merely repeated, "It's necessary, Mother, or I wouldn't do it."

❁

"You're becoming a household word," Kate Fenton said. "Every time I pick up a paper or a magazine, there you are. You and Richard in *Town and Country*, looking unutterably silly at the Swan Ball in Nashville. You and Katie posing for a mother-daughter fashion spread in the Sunday *Times Magazine* section. You giving interviews to *Cosmopolitan* about the 'joys' of being married to a genius, and sounding off on handicapped children in *Good Housekeeping*. I know this was the deal you made a year ago, but aren't you overdoing it? What are you bucking for—sainthood?"

Susan unsmilingly finished her third martini.

"And that's another thing." Kate scowled. "When did you corner the world market on vodka? Three drinks at lunch? My God, Susie!"

"It keeps me going. You can't imagine how tired I am."

"Then why the hell don't you slow down? You've done everything possible to counteract that *Open Secrets* series, so how about relaxing? The damage is done and you can't undo it. None of it. Not even including the windup on that Hollywood tart. I know, Richard confessed everything before it got into print so the gory details didn't come as a shock to you. You took it. All this time you've been making wifely noises to disprove the whole mess. MacKenzie had her day, but it's *over*. The whole damned Antonini family survived. Including, to my surprise, you. Except you're not

218

going to survive much longer if you don't stop killing yourself with booze."

"It never lets up, Kate. Once Maria found out about it—and I could kill Gloria for telling her—she saw how she could use the Antonini wives to build up the eternal flame in front of the family shrine. She pushes us all the time. It's too damned bad, God forgive me, that she recovered." Susan's speech was a little slurred. "I think I'll have another vodka martini."

"You don't need one. You didn't need the last two."

"My! Haven't we gotten moral!"

"My!" Kate mimicked. "Haven't we become a jackass!"

The sharp words momentarily sobered Susan. She looked around, half dazed. Everything was strange these days. Even this out-of-the-way restaurant. A year ago, they'd have been lunching where they'd see and be seen. Now Susan wanted to hide whenever she could. So they faced each other across a checkered tablecloth at a tiny table in the rear of Billy's, a First Avenue neighborhood saloon-turned-restaurant where well-known people came for late-night hamburgers and steaks but almost never for lunch. The turn-of-the-century place had a certain studied charm, having retained its long oak bar with the brass footrail, its shirt-sleeved bartenders and aproned waiters, its original gaslight fixtures, now electrified, and its simple menu posted on the wall. I came here often before I knew Richard, Susan remembered. It was fun then, noisy and informal in the evenings. Evie and I used to have dinner here alone or with dates when we roomed together. It seems a hundred years ago. Such an exciting, carefree time. Now I come because I don't want to be stared at, because I can't bear to pick up another copy of *Women's Wear Daily* and read about myself in "The Eye."

"Nothing's turned out the way I expected," Susan said.

"Things seldom do. Is that any excuse for getting sloshed in the middle of the day?"

Susan didn't answer. She *was* drinking too much.

She didn't need Kate to tell her that. Of course she was unhappy. Who wouldn't be? She was so weary of pretending. No one seemed to understand how she hated being a "prominent person," how displaced she felt, how continually, totally inadequate under an exterior that seemed so poised and "sophisticated." How could they understand? Hadn't she always maintained she had to have an "identity" of her own? Hadn't she even tried for it, early on, with the short-lived column? They couldn't see how different this identity was, how "tolerated" she felt by Richard and Richard's family, how fragile the structure of her life really was. All the appearances as Mrs. Richard Antonini, all the graceful speeches and tasteful interviews she gave were like well-rehearsed lines from a play on which the curtain never mercifully descended so the leading lady could relax and "be herself." She was never herself any more. She was what Richard wanted—a suitable wife and a willing bed partner. What Maria wanted—an available spokeswoman for "the best of the Antoninis." She supposed she was even what Paul Carmichael wanted, since it was he who'd cynically cast her and the other wives into their prominent roles as social, civic and charitable leaders.

Mary Lou and Jacqueline didn't seem disturbed by it all. They'd easily adjusted to the new and greater demands on them. Jacqueline and Walter had made it a point to tone down their separate lives, had become more discreet than ever about their continuing affairs. Mary Lou had plunged wholeheartedly into her work for the retarded. Incredibly she seemed to enjoy talking about Frances after nearly fifteen years of shamed silence. The image of "wonderful people" that Maria had tried so long to project to her family was now coming true. Her sons had achieved new respect, greater fame through the campaign launched in retaliation for the scandal-sheet series. Maria herself was as physically whole as she'd been before her stroke and even more demanding. She'd been toughened by an experience that would have humbled weaker women. Her ambition for her "boys" was now insatiable and her standards more rigid than ever. The slightest sour note in a critique of Richard's performance sent her into a rage, not at the critic but at the man who'd played with something short of perfection. A damning written word about Sergio's conducting brought a tirade of accusations about her eldest son's sloppiness. And just as a poor composition by Walter evoked her scorn, so now did any lapse of activity by Susan or one of the others provoke her anger. A dynasty, powerful and impregnable, was what Maria wanted, and her obsession to see it created before she died was reaching manic proportions. She was increasingly into every facet of their lives, from the highly publicized public appearances they made to the theoretically private way they raised their children.

Why am I the only one who finds this so shattering? Susan wondered. She's only more of what she's always been. The difference is that she used to ignore me. Now she's involving me, and I haven't had years of getting used to it, the way the others have. If only Richard would stand up to her. If only he'd say we have the right to our own lives. But he won't. None of them will.

Richard. On the surface their marriage seemed firm. There'd been no more affairs after Sylvia Sloan. At least none she knew of. That had been the most sordid of all somehow, cheap and ugly. Whether Richard was now faithful by choice or because she was so seldom out of his sight, Susan didn't know. She traveled almost constantly with him now, hating it more than ever, loathing the pat conversations with reporters, the earnest little speeches at luncheons for parents of the deaf-mute where she sounded off on the needs of other handicapped children while she neglected her own.

That, above all, was the source of her greatest unhappiness, her most deep-seated guilt. She had so little time with Katie these days. The beautiful little six-year-old was closer to her nurse and her speech teacher than she was to her own mother. Even when Susan was in New York, she sometimes could spend no more than an hour with her daughter each day, for the mother's time was filled with "do good" duties and social, cultural events that enhanced the father's professional image.

Sometimes Susan felt as though she was in the eye of a tornado, dead-center in a whirling funnel of ceaseless activity, spinning like a giant cone toward some awful eventuality. Why didn't she, as Kate sanely suggested, slow down? What could they do to her—kill her if she stopped doing all these torturous things? They're not pushing me, Susan suddenly realized. I'm pushing myself. I'm trying so hard to believe this is the only way my marriage can survive. I'm too proud to admit I'm not cut out for this pattern of overachievement. I'm a pygmy among giants, a dumb marigold in a hothouse of orchids. I'm not even good at what I'm trying to be. Why can't I face that?"

"I feel as though I'm lunching alone," Kate said. "You haven't said a word in five minutes."

Susan was apologetic. "I'm sorry. I got off on a whole stream-of-consciousness thing inside my head. It's your fault, really, for asking me why I didn't slow down. I was trying to figure out why I didn't."

"And . . . ?"

"The jury is still out on that one."

"Susan, I'm worried about you. Look at you. Your hand is shaking. You're skinny as a rail. Not just chic-skinny, more sick-skinny. How long since you've seen a doctor?"

"I'm fine, Kate. Nothing wrong with me that a week at Maine Chance couldn't cure."

"Then why don't you have one?"

"Sitting around with all those overweight ladies would drive me mad. I'm not the spa type, sinfully luxurious as it would be to do nothing but sleep, get massaged, facialed and whipped into shape. I don't really want to go to a health farm, not even Elizabeth Arden's," Susan said slowly, "but I could use a little time to myself. If I could just get away for a few days alone to think things out. No, it's out of the question. My damned schedule is too full."

"What are you, the indispensable woman?"

"On the contrary, everything really important would go on just fine without me."

"Then for God's sake take a vacation! You must! And do something completely different, something no Antonini would ever do."

Susan smiled, but she was intrigued. "Like what?"

Kate thought for a minute. "I don't know. Have you ever been to Las Vegas?"

Susan burst out laughing. "Las Vegas! No, and I don't think I want to go. I hear it's terrible! Honky-tonk. Men in short-sleeved shirts and white socks and dumpy women with curlers in their hair playing the nickel slot machines! You really are crazy, Kate. Las Vegas!" she said again. "Can't you just see Richard's face if I told him I was going there?"

Kate shrugged. "Okay, then how about Palm Springs or Palm Beach? They're in the Antonini tradition—rich, exclusive and more of the same."

"You're serious about Las Vegas, aren't you?"

"Sure I am. I think more than anything you need to forget the world you know, and the one that knows you. I'd even use a different name. Just be sure it matches the initials on your luggage. Let's see. 'A'. How about 'Armstrong?' By the way, do you gamble?"

Susan shook her head. "Never even tried."

"It's fun. I remember the Casino in Monte Carlo. Not that Vegas is anything like that, I'm sure. Still, there's a kind of Never-Never-Land feeling about rooms full of people staking everything on the roll of the dice or the turn of a card. Hell, you might become a roulette addict! Or have an affair with a blackjack dealer. Who knows? Where's your spirit of adventure?"

"It's the wildest suggestion I've ever heard! Of course, I would love to see it. They say it's indescribable." Susan was beginning to toy with the idea. "I could go to Palm Springs for a few days and then maybe nip over to Nevada without telling anybody."

223

Her eyes suddenly began to sparkle. "Kate, do you really think I could?"

"I think it would be the best thing in the world for you."

Susan continued to plan. "I wouldn't have to tell anybody where I was going. Only Bridie, in case Katie needed me. Richard would understand Palm Springs. He knows I'm tired. If he found out about Vegas, I could always say I just had the idea on the spur of the moment when I was out there. How would he find out anyway? I could call him every night." She was getting excited now, more like the old, enthusiastic Susan. "Oh, Kate, it's an insane, marvelous idea! Only you would have thought of it! I do need to hide out in some place just like that. Some place where they've never heard of Stravinsky or Tchaikovsky or Liszt's *Transcendental Études!*"

Kate nodded approvingly. "Better still, some place they think Antonini is the name of an Italian shoemaker or the owner of a pizza parlor."

Susan threw back her head and roared with laughter. It felt absolutely marvelous.

Chapter Eighteen

"Going away next month for a week? By yourself?" Bea Langdon looked hard at her daughter. "*Why,* Susan?"

"No special reason, Mom. I suddenly realized I desperately need a holiday and Richard's too busy to take any time. Even when he's home, he works six or seven hours every day. Much more than he ever did before."

"I should think as he got more famous he'd need to practice less."

Susan smiled. "It doesn't work that way."

"What about Katie?"

"Bridie's better with her than I am. Do you know she's reading? Isn't that incredible? Six years old and she's picking whole sentences out of her picture books. What's even more amazing, she's learning to say words! God bless Edith Chambers! What a marvelous teacher she is. She must be to Katie what Anne Sullivan was to Helen Keller."

Involuntarily, Bea cringed. She hated being reminded of her only grandchild's tragedy. It broke her heart every time she saw that dear little thing with her hearing aids and listened to the strange speech that was incomprehensible to Bea. She adored Katie, but she wished Susan would have another baby, a healthy, bouncing one. Susan loved children. What was more, a pregnancy could release her from all her exhausting activities, the way Katie's conception had gotten Susan and Richard out of Maria's house. But there'd be no more grandchildren for the Langdons. Susan had already made that clear.

"I wouldn't risk something going wrong again," she'd said before, when Katie was taken away.

You wouldn't. Bea had wondered then. Or is it Richard who wouldn't? She still wondered about it, just as she fretted secretly over the whole status of her daughter's marriage. Now this trip alone. Was she running away? Had something else happened between Susan and Richard?

"Don't look at me like that, Mother. I can read your mind. Nothing's wrong. Richard's on his good behavior and perfectly happy for me to get a rest. I'm going to Palm Springs, not to Reno for a divorce." Susan smiled. "Now that I think of it, does anybody go to Reno for a divorce these days? I suppose not. Not with Mexico offering 'quickies.' Don't look so serious! Lots

225

of couples take separate vacations. They say it strengthens the marriage."

Does yours need strengthening? Bea wanted to ask. Strange. Close as they were, Susan didn't talk much about her private feelings. Perhaps she confides in Kate, Bea thought with a twinge of jealousy. Maybe she thinks I wouldn't understand, being so blessed in my own marriage. All that awful scandal last year. And all the things they were still doing to present a "united front." It wasn't natural. Susan was showing the strain. Probably a week to herself was a good idea at that.

"Well, it sounds like fun, dear."

"I'm not looking for fun. Just peace."

There it was again. That little hint of unhappiness.

"When do you leave?" Bea asked.

"In about three weeks. Richard's playing in Washington week after next. When he comes back, I'll take off."

"You're not going with him to Washington?"

"Not this trip. It's just a short one. Only three days. I need to get a few new clothes, and with him away I'll be free to organize myself and spend some time with Kit-Kat." She smiled as she used the child's nickname. She was Kit-Kat only to Susan. To everyone else, she was Katie. Except to Maria, who, when she referred to her at all, called her Katherine. "I wish I could take her with me. She'd have fun in the desert. But I can't let her miss school."

She really meant it. She'd happily have taken Katie to Palm Springs and stayed there, forgetting that nonsense about Vegas and assumed names. But it would be selfish to uproot her, even for a week, when she was doing so well in school. She mustn't miss her classes. Or her lessons with the speech therapist. Or any of the other things I can't do for her, Susan thought, feeling a little pang of self-pity. I'm not nearly as important any more as the company of her peers and the help of her teachers. I've lost touch with her since I've been on this merry-go-round. She doesn't need me so much any

226

more. But I need her. She's the only tangible thing in my life.

Damn that MacKenzie woman and what she'd done to them with her stories! Even after a year the gossip went on. About Richard and his women. And Sergio and his. And Walter and his young men. And the poor children, Frances and Katie. Just when we think everything's quiet, somebody rehashes it all in a magazine article or on a talk show. Sometimes she suspected Sylvia Sloan kept the whole thing alive for her own purposes. Richard hadn't seen her again. Susan was positive of that. But who'd believe it?

Who'd believe any of this? Susan thought cynically. Who'd believe I go on, week after week, trying to make sense of my life? I *must* change. When I come back, I will.

Richard watched his mother in complete fascination. Looking at her, listening to her, even he found it hard to believe that a year ago she'd lain mute and helpless in a hospital bed. Most people would be left with some sort of difficulty after a seizure such as hers, but not even those who knew her best could detect the slightest trace of an aftermath. She walked erectly and had regained full use of her hands. God knows she'd sweated to accomplish that. She'd worked harder than the doctors recommended, exercised furiously, doubled, tripled the amount of therapy they'd suggested for a woman of her age. She'd been fanatic about it. "I won't be p . . . p . . . itied," she'd said the first moment her speech returned. "I'll g . . . get well. Make a f . . . full . . ." She seemed to be groping for a word that eluded her. The patrician brow wrinkled in frustration for a few seconds before she completed the sentence. "I'll make a f . . . full recovery!"

And to their admiration and amazement, she had. True, the stroke had not been as severe as it first seemed, but Richard knew that was not the reason she

227

was now facing him in full command of her movements and her speech. She'd simply refused to let this defeat her. At the beginning of her recovery she'd had trouble speaking without hesitation, had sometimes seemed unable to find a word she wished to use. Even this limitation outraged her. She would not have it. She would not go through life stuttering and stammering like an idiot.

She'd gotten a speech therapist immediately, adding those lessons to the physical exercise, working day and night on every part of her afflicted body. And it had turned out as she was determined it would.

Most women, most men for that matter, would not have come out of this so totally intact. Some, Richard thought, might even have used a handicap as an added weapon in their arsenal of power, wielding a cane to make a point, or demanding even more service, using as an excuse a hand or leg that never came back to full strength. But not Mother. She didn't need these devices to reinforce her domination. Indeed, she would have none of them, lest they be construed as weakness. She'd fooled them all, and she presented a smug expression of condescension as the doctors congratulated her on an extraordinary rehabilitation.

"You had me counted out, didn't you?"

"It *is* a remarkable recovery, Mrs. Antonini."

"Not for me, it isn't."

Richard smiled, remembering the sight of the big specialists being reduced to silence by this tiny, indomitable woman. They'd been like embarrassed schoolboys proved wrong by the teacher. He felt a little like a schoolboy himself right now, as Maria raised her eyebrows and said, "Susan's going to Palm Springs alone in February? How very odd, Richard."

"Not really, Mother. She deserves a holiday. She's worked her tail off for the family this past year. She's tired."

"I see." She didn't at all, of course. "Would she like to look up some of my friends there? I know a number of people with charming houses."

228

"I don't think so, thanks. She says she plans to sleep twenty hours a day."

Maria shrugged. "Well, it's your business . . ."

"Yes, it is, dear. Susan's and mine."

Maria ignored that impertinence and changed the subject. "Richard, how do you think your father looks?"

"All right. Why?"

"I don't think he's well. That awful flu. It took him two weeks to get over it!"

"Darling, everybody takes time to get over flu. And Father's getting along. People don't bounce back so fast as they get older." He looked at her pointedly. "Most people, that is. Thank God you're made of iron."

She smiled, pleased.

"Susan's going away alone for a week," Jacqueline said.

"Good for her." Walter kept on reading the morning mail. "Where's she going?"

"Palm Springs."

"She could get a divorce in Mexico in twenty-four hours."

Jacqueline laughed. "Haven't you heard? Antoninis don't get divorces. It makes for messy publicity. You really don't like Richard very much, do you?"

"Nope. Not very much." Walter looked up. "Mostly because he's not honest. At least we know where we stand, but he keeps trying to fool himself and Susan."

"I thought he was behaving."

"You obviously haven't heard the gossip about the Senator's daughter."

"Oh no! Not again!"

229

"Susan's going to Palm Springs. Without Richard," Mary Lou said.

Sergio looked mildly interested. "Really? I didn't think she had the guts."

❀

"You didn't tell me Susan was going away by herself for a week," Raoul said. "I ran into Richard and *he* told me."

"Who cares?" Gloria replied.

❀

On Friday afternoon as the plane came in low over the Jefferson Memorial, Richard nudged Paul. "You can see Kennedy Center. Ugly damned thing, isn't it?"

"But the fee they're paying makes it beautiful."

"Christ, Paul, don't you ever think about anything but money?"

"Sometimes. I'd think of it less if I were as rich as you."

Richard looked at him sharply. Even after all the years together, he was never quite sure when his manager was serious or when he was subtly making a joke at Richard's expense. For that matter, close as they were, Richard often felt he really didn't know Paul Carmichael. He spent more time with him than he did with his brothers or even, for that matter, with Susan. Paul knew all about his employer's continuing activities, but he kept his mouth shut. And in the past year he always somehow managed to disappear when Richard suggested a night of "innocent fun" with the out-of-town ladies. Paul never voiced outright his disapproval of Richard's affairs, but it was clear that he did not wish to participate, even remotely, in the unfaithfulness to Susan. He cares more about her feelings than he does about me, Richard thought jealously. He's turned into a damned prig. Sometimes I think he's in love with my wife. But that doesn't make sense. If Paul wanted Susan, he'd encourage me to get into trouble, hoping the marriage would blow up and he could have her for himself. Instead, he always tries to smooth things over, though lately he's made it a point not to know what I'm doing. Like tonight. I'll bet he won't have any part of the evening's plans. He'll pretend he doesn't know Dolly Johnson exists.

The airplane touched down with a series of gentle bumps at Washington's National Airport. Involuntarily, Richard gave a sigh of relief. He was not an "easy flier," just as he was not a relaxed passenger in a car. It made him nervous to know that his life was in someone else's hands. The tenseness went out of him as they rolled safely along the ground. Even the crazy ideas he'd had about Paul in the past few minutes disappeared. He's totally loyal, Richard thought. God knows he's proved himself time and again. I'm more than his meal ticket; I'm his best friend. And he's mine.

Walking toward the exit, Richard genially approached the subject of this evening. "What are your plans for dinner?"

Paul shrugged. "Nothing special. I'll probably hit the sack early. I have to be at the Center early in the morning to check out things before your rehearsal."

"You still have to eat."

"I'll probably have something sent up from room service." Paul hesitated. "What about you?"

"I promised to take Dolly Johnson to dinner. You remember her. The Senator's daughter. The one who's divorced. She's picking me up at the hotel at seven. She knows some nice little place in Virginia where the food and drinks are good. We'll probably go back to her apartment at the Watergate for a nightcap." Richard sounded offhand. "Just a quiet evening. I'm sure she could get a friend for you."

"No, thanks. I'll take a rain check."

The feeling of annoyance returned. "You think I'd be smarter to dine upstairs too, don't you?"

"You're a big boy. Do what you like."

"Goddammit, Paul, you're a pain in the ass lately! You never used to be so pious about my having a few laughs with a beautiful woman."

"You never used to be married."

Richard exploded. They were in the rented limousine waiting for the driver to return from the claim area with their bags. In the privacy of the car, Richard raised his voice. "What the hell do you want from me? What do you *all* want from me? Have I ever missed a concert? Given a bad performance? Flubbed an interview? Jesus, don't I deserve something more than eight hours a day of practice, a martyred wife who hates being a public figure and a mother who's never let up on me since I was old enough to reach the keyboard? Am I not entitled to *any* relaxation, *any* freedom? I'm no ribbon clerk who works from nine to five and forgets the job at the end of the day! I'm always under pressure of one kind or another! You used to understand that. All of a sudden you've turned into a disapproving watchdog!"

Paul turned an equally angry face toward him. "I'm not a watchdog, Richard. Nor a lapdog. If you want to justify your stupid behavior by saying you need 'relaxation,' be my guest! But goddammit don't expect me to keep on getting you out of trouble with your public *or* your wife! I don't need that. I don't want any part of it. What the hell is it you're trying to prove? 'Martyred wife,' for Christ's sake! If there was ever anybody who isn't a martyr, it's Susan! She's been a damned good sport about what we've asked her to do. And she's been a thousand times more forgiving than any ordinary woman would be. But that's not enough, is it? You're starting all over again with the broads, showing yourself and the rest of us that you can make your own rules because you're an artist, a genius or whatever you've come to believe from reading your own publicity. Well, the hell with you and your needs or your freedom or whatever you choose to call it! I think we've come to the end of the road, Richard. You don't need a manager, you need a pimp! I've had all I care to put up with. Find yourself a new boy. After this tour I'm through."

Richard was stunned. "You're quitting me? You can't do that!"

"Why not? I don't have a contract. Just a 'gentleman's handshake' agreement. The fact is, Richard, I can't stand you lately. I hate what you're doing to Susan. I even hate what you're doing to yourself. And God knows I hate what you've done to me and what I've done to a lot of other people as a result."

The chauffeur returned and they started toward the city. Richard lowered his voice.

"All right, you sonofabitch. You don't know the meaning of loyalty or gratitude. That's fine with me. Any manager will be glad to handle me, but how many artists will want you when they hear I've gotten rid of you?"

Paul smiled grimly. "That's exactly how you'll release the news, isn't it? True to form. Nobody ever rejects Richard Antonini. He proposes and disposes, whether it's a woman, a manager or a child he'd like never to see."

"You no-good bastard!"

Paul looked out the window. He'd said everything that had been bottled up inside. Richard might be right. He might have a hard time finding someone as famous and lucrative to represent. But to hell with all the Antoninis and their willful, selfish ways! He'd not miss any of them. Except Susan. For her sake, he hoped she wouldn't guess the real reasons for his sudden departure.

❖

Susan was still up, puttering around the bedroom, getting clothes organized for her trip, when the telephone rang at eleven o'clock that night.

"Mrs. Richard Antonini? This is Harry Penza of the Washington *Post*. We'd like to know when you're arriving in Washington and what your reaction is to the ac-

233

cident. Is Dolly Johnson a friend of yours? Did you know your husband was with her this evening? Do you think he'd been drinking?"

Susan stared stupidly at the receiver. No sound came from her.

"Mrs. Antonini? Are you there? May we have a comment from you, please?"

"I don't know what you're talking about." Susan began to stammer. "What . . . what accident? Has something happened to my husband? Where is he? Where's Paul . . . Paul Carmichael?"

Penza sounded sympathetic. "I'm sorry. I was sure you'd been informed. Your husband was in a car crash on the road from Alexandria this evening. He's apparently not hurt, but his passenger Mrs. Dolly Johnson, is pretty badly banged up. They're both in Washington Hospital Center out on Irving Street. The police won't say anything except that Mr. Antonini was driving and apparently lost control and hit another car head-on." The reporter paused. "Unfortunately, the other car was driven by a man who had his wife and two children with him. The woman and a little girl were killed."

Susan closed her eyes. "Oh, my God!" She began to shake violently. "Was my husband's manager, Mr. Carmichael, with him?"

"No, ma'am. Just Mrs. Johnson. Mr. Carmichael's at the hospital, but he's not giving out any statements. About Mrs. Johnson, the Senator's daughter," the man said again. "Is she a friend of yours *and* your husband's? Will you be coming down tonight? Do you know whether Mr. Antonini's mother and father will come with you?"

"I . . . I don't know anything. That is, I have nothing to say. Please get off the phone, Mr. . . . ."

"Penza. With a P as in Post."

"Please hang up, Mr. Penza. I'm sure Mr. Carmichael is trying to reach me."

"What about the concert? I suppose it will be canceled."

234

"I don't know. I suppose so. Please excuse me but I'm going to hang up now."

She turned away in a daze. Why hadn't Paul called her? What was this all about? Thank God Richard wasn't hurt, but those other people, those poor, unfortunate people in the other car. She thought of calling someone. Her parents. Richard's. Perhaps she could find Paul at the hospital. Yes, that was best. She'd get more facts before she spoke to anyone else. Just as she was about to pick up the phone it rang.

"Susan, I have some bad news. Richard's been in an accident, but he's all right," Paul said hurriedly. "Hardly a scratch on him. Just shook up. They're keeping him in the hospital overnight for observation. This is the first chance I've had to call."

"I know. A reporter from the Washington *Post* phoned. He told me. Paul, he told me about the people in the other car, too. It's terrible! How did it happen?"

"I'm not sure of the facts yet, Susan. It only happened about an hour ago. Richard had them call me at once."

"I'm coming right down."

"No point in starting out tonight. It would be practically impossible at this hour anyway. You can come tomorrow. Listen, Susan. Call the Antoninis and tell them. Be sure to say Richard's perfectly okay, but warn them not to talk to any reporters. And don't you talk to any either. What did you tell the *Post* guy?"

"Nothing. I was too shocked. He wanted to know about somebody named Mrs. Johnson. Whether she was a friend of mine."

There was a small pause. "What did you say?"

"I told you: nothing. Who is she, Paul?" She stopped. "Never mind. I'm sure I can guess."

If Carlyn MacKenzie's editorial pursuit of the Antoninis had been agony, the press coverage of Richard's accident was a crucifixion. The story had all the ingredients of sensational reporting and unlimited innuendoes: the famous, married concert artist in the company of a rich divorcée whose father was a United

States senator and whose reputation, on her own, was none too savory; the late-night drive; the mysterious "loss of control" of the car; the death of two innocent people, leaving a working-class widower and one motherless child. Once again, the recklessness of the country's number-one musical family was rehashed as "background material" for this latest escapade of its youngest member. Nothing and no one would be spared in the weeks ahead. Not only would the investigation of the accident and the consequent hearing be reported in minute detail, but the nation's diligent reporters would dig back into the morgues of their newspapers for photographs of Susan and (God, how Susan regretted having permitted them!) Katie, who, ironically, was the same age as Jenny, the little girl who died in the crash.

Frank Olmstead, the press agent who'd replaced Gerry, accompanied Susan to Washington the morning after the accident. They took a 7:00 A.M. Eastern shuttle, hoping to arrive unnoticed. It was a futile hope. The press had stationed itself at the airport at dawn to meet every incoming New York flight, and when Susan emerged they set upon her, still cameras flashing, TV cameras grinding, reporters shouting questions as she and Frank tried to make their way to a waiting car.

"Look this way, Mrs. Antonini!"

"Are you and Dolly Johnson friends?"

"Was your husband drinking?"

"Will you and Richard attend the Armstrong funeral?"

"Just one more, Susan! Look this way!"

Susan kept walking toward the entrance, not answering the shouted questions, looking straight ahead, her face expressionless. Frank acted as a shield, elbowing them through the crowd, saying over and over, "Mrs. Antonini has no comment. She's anxious to get to her husband. Please let us through. We'll have a statement later."

Only when they were in the car on their way to town

did Susan bury her face in her hands for a moment. Then she looked up, her eyes full of tears.

"I can't bear it, Frank. It's like a zoo!"

"I'm afraid it's only the beginning."

Or the end, Susan thought. I really thought Richard had learned his lesson. All we've done to project the image of a solid, loving family has gone down the drain in the dirty water of another of his escapades. She'd heard about Dolly Johnson. Her name was constantly in the columns, always linked with some glamorous escort, in Washington or Acapulco or St. Tropez. In an earlier age they'd have called her a "madcap heiress," the thrice-divorced, ungovernable only child of a millionaire Oklahoma senator. It didn't take a vivid imagination to see how Richard would appeal to her. And vice versa. Or why they'd been together on that highway in Virginia.

They pushed their way through more reporters in the lobby of the hospital and made their way up to the room where Richard, fully dressed, was sitting in a chair at the window. Paul Carmichael straddled a straight chair on the other side of the room. Both of them got to their feet when Susan came in. She looked at Richard but didn't go to him.

"Are you all right?" she asked.

"Yes. They just kept me here overnight for observation."

"He's been signed out," Paul said, "but I thought it would look better if we waited for you to arrive so you and Richard can go to the hotel together."

"And how is Dolly Johnson?" It was a clipped, pointed question.

There was an uneasy pause. "She has a broken arm," Richard said. "Nothing serious. We were lucky."

Susan stared at him.

"I mean, I could have had my hands smashed up, Susie! Hell, I could have been killed! Look, I know it's awful about that Armstrong woman and the child. But it was an accident! My God, I didn't mean to do it! You don't have to look at me as though I'm a murderer! I'll make some kind of settlement on the husband. I'm sorry. I'm terribly sorry. But it was unavoidable. Something went crazy with the steering mechanism. I couldn't control the car. It wasn't my fault."

She looked at Paul, who was staring at the floor, avoiding her eyes. Even Frank Olmstead, who didn't know them as well, shifted his feet restlessly as Richard poured out his defensive story. In your mind, nothing's ever your fault, Susan thought. And there's nothing that can't be solved with influence and money. Nevertheless, she felt half sorry for him. He was frightened under the bravado. He'd never been involved in anything as serious as this. But he'd get away with it. The Antoninis would provide the best legal talent to defend him against a charge of reckless driving or involuntary manslaughter or whatever they accused him of. The Antoninis would pay off to avoid a damage suit, buy off the widower, who might accuse their darling boy of killing the man's wife and child. Everybody would pitch in again to protect Richard. They'd expect her to stand by him, to give still another performance as the loving, trusting wife. I can't do it, Susan thought. I won't do it any more.

"Shall we go?" Paul finally broke the silence.

A sudden question crossed Susan's mind. Weren't people taken to the police station and booked when they were involved in fatal accidents? Wouldn't charges be preferred?

"Are we free to?" she asked. "Can Richard just go back to the hotel?"

"Yes. He's released on his own recognizance, pending a hearing. He's already given a full statement to the police. He'll have to appear later, but he's free to come and go as he pleases until then." Paul cleared his throat. "In fact, we're not canceling the concert. The lawyers advised us it would look much better if everything appeared as nearly routine as possible. We'll have the full rehearsal today and the performance Sunday afternoon as planned."

"We'd better schedule a press conference," Frank said. "Richard and Susan together. Later this morning, I think. When's the funeral, Paul?"

"I don't know. Tuesday, probably."

"They'll have to show up for that, of course."

Susan couldn't believe what she was hearing. They were expected to talk to the press, look lovingly into each other's eyes, holding hands, no doubt. Richard would go onstage, a modest and saddened figure, while she sat bravely in the first row. They were to go together to the funeral of the woman and her child, appearing pained but innocent. The machinery was rolling, set in motion by the family and run by the people who were well paid to operate it. She felt sick, repulsed by the cold-blooded step-by-step plan in which it was assumed she would co-operate. It was grotesque.

She said nothing until she and Richard were alone in the suite at the Hay-Adams. Paul had gone to Kennedy Center to see about the afternoon rehearsal. It was a final gesture. He'd leave no loose ends and Richard knew it. Frank was setting up the press conference for noon. There'd been another mob of reporters in the hotel lobby, but they'd gotten through in a repetition of the scenes at the airport and the hospital. The telephone operators had been instructed to put no calls through. Susan sank into a chair and said, dully, "You'd better call your parents. Your mother was very upset when I talked to her last night."

"In a minute. Susan, I want to explain about Dolly Johnson."

"You don't have to. I don't care."

"But it isn't what you think! We just went out for dinner. Paul was in a snit and wouldn't go with us, otherwise I wouldn't have been alone in the car with her. I know it looks suspicious, but I swear to God there was nothing to it!"

Susan looked at him wearily. "Don't think I'm an idiot, Richard. You took her out to dinner a couple of

239

hours after you arrived in Washington. Do you really expect me to believe that wasn't preplanned?"

"All right. it was planned. But it was still innocent. You know how I hate eating alone in strange towns. Yes, I called her from New York and asked her to have dinner. Is that a crime? She's an amusing woman. You'd like her."

Susan began to laugh, almost hysterically. "Like I liked Gerry? Like I probably would like Sylvia Sloan and all the others? You're absurd, Richard! You don't fool me. You did once. I loved you. I made myself believe in you. I excused your behavior because I thought you couldn't help yourself. I blamed Maria for spoiling you rotten, giving you your phony values. But it's you who are hopelessly egocentric and thoroughly satisfied to be that way. I can't live with it. I'm coming to pieces under the strain. I won't go through this latest farce nor any that come after it. I'm not going to be at the press conference or the concert or the funeral of that poor woman and her child. You do it. You and your press agent and your whole damned arrogant family! Let *them* come down here and be at your side. I'm catching the next flight back to New York."

"You don't know what you're saying!" There was panic in his voice. "You've got to stand by me through this! How will it look if you run back to New York? My God, that's all I need! People will be sure there was something going on with Dolly Johnson and me."

"Then people will be right, won't they?" Susan went over to the bar and poured a stiff scotch. Her hands were shaking as she added a little water. "Richard, I'm not just leaving you now. I'm leaving you forever. I'm taking Katie and moving out. I've had it up to here with everything. I guess I've known it for a long time. Since the day you took Katie away. But I loved you so. I thought I was always failing you somehow. I tried to be everything I thought you wanted and needed, but no woman could be. When they made Maria, they broke the mold. She's the only woman you respect. And you don't even love her, because you can't love anyone except yourself."

Unexpectedly, uncharacteristically, he began to cry. Deep, painful sobs he tried to muffle with his handkerchief as he turned his back to her.

Don't! Susan thought. Don't play on my sympathy again. I don't believe your tears. She walked to the window and stood looking down at Sixteenth Street, watching the slow Saturday morning traffic move by, trying desperately not to hear him. In a few minutes he became quiet and she turned to see him sitting on the sofa, his eyes on her.

"You're right," he said. "I'm a façade. Nothing happens underneath. Except when it comes to you. That's the one place you're wrong. I do love you. Don't walk out on me, I beg you. I'll give you anything you want, any amount of freedom. I won't let everyone make demands on you, the way they have this past year. I'll change. I swear it. Please. One more chance. I'm on my knees to you. I've never been on my knees to anyone."

"I can't. Don't ask me to." She held up the glass in her trembling hand. "Look at me. I'm turning into a drunk! I need liquor to get me through every day. A few drinks, no, a *lot* of drinks for courage to live a life I hate with a man I don't understand. I'm lost, Richard. I'm frightened and lost and bone-tired. I'm going on nervous energy and booze. The next step will be a real nervous breakdown, not the one I was on the brink of when you took Katie away. Your life, your world is killing me! God help me, I wish I could be like Jacqueline. I wish I didn't care so deeply for you. I'd like to match you affair for affair, hurt for hurt. I wish I could playact and be content. But that's not my style. I'm not a sophisticate like Jacqueline, nor mercenary like Mary Lou. I'm wrong for you, Richard. As wrong as you are for me. The sooner we end it, the better."

He sounded defeated. "If that's what you really want. Just see me through this. One last favor. Then you can get a divorce. I won't fight it. You deserve more than I can ever give you, and I love you enough to want you to have it."

How could she refuse? She knew she was being used again, but he'd been her lover, the father of her child and he was in deep trouble. It wasn't his fault if she wasn't tough enough to protect herself from his selfishness or the highhandedness of his family.

Wearily, she nodded. "All right. I'll go through the motions one more time. But when this is over, I'm through."

"Thank you," Richard said humbly. "I'm grateful." He hesitated. "I suppose you'd like to take the second bedroom? Paul can bunk in with me."

"Yes." She felt a wrench. He'd accepted defeat, but she didn't feel victorious. She felt empty and miserable and confused. It was like before. Like abandoning a child who needed you. But this time I must, Susan thought. This time I must save myself. He's not a little boy for whom I'm responsible. He's a man who could drive me insane. "I'm sorry," she said from force of habit.

"You have nothing to be sorry about. You're doing the right thing."

Chapter Nineteen

She called New York and canceled her Palm Springs and Las Vegas trip, thinking ruefully of her conversation with her mother, wondering whether the nonsense she'd spouted about a Reno divorce might have been some kind of omen. Where *would* she get her divorce, and how soon would she be able to leave without stirring up another cloud of notoriety? She told no one of her plans to leave Richard. Paul recognized the significance of the bedroom arrangements, but the announcement, even within the family, would have to wait until this dreadful period following the accident was over. Just as the announcement of Paul's defection would.

It was a nightmare. It took every ounce of her strength to get through the press conference, to look subdued but calm, to answer the questions with lies and evasions. Yes, of course she knew Dolly Johnson, she said. She's an old and dear friend of my husband's and mine. Certainly I knew they were dining together. No, of course Richard wasn't intoxicated. My husband is a moderate drinker.

A sharp-eyed young woman reporter brashly picked up this subject. "What about you, Mrs. Antonini? There've been reports that you've had some problems in that area."

Richard, under control, answered. "My wife and I enjoy an occasional cocktail, if that's what you mean. I have no idea where you could have heard such a silly rumor."

"From some of the best headwaiters in New York," the girl answered brazenly.

"I assure you they're as misinformed as you."

Throughout the exchange, Susan tried not to look stricken. There is no privacy, she thought. None at all. Even when I have a few drinks at lunch the whole world knows it.

"Shall we get back to the point of this conference?" Frank Olmstead interjected.

"Will you tell us exactly how the accident happened, Mr. Antonini? Just as you told it to the police." The questioner was a local television commentator.

"Certainly. Mrs. Johnson and I were on the way back from dinner. I was driving her car. Something apparently went wrong with the steering mechanism and I lost control. Tragically, Mr. Armstrong's car was approaching from the other direction and we hit head-on."

"Have the police checked the steering mechanism in Mrs. Johnson's car?"

"I couldn't say," Richard answered coldly, "but when they do they'll find it exactly as I've described."

"Will you attend Mrs. Armstrong's funeral?"

Richard looked at Susan. "Yes, my wife and I will be there, if Mr. Armstrong wishes us to be. We don't know the family, of course, but any moral support we can give at this terrible time is the least we can do."

"Is it true that Armstrong is suing you for five million dollars?"

"I have no knowledge of that."

The reporter who'd asked Susan about her drinking put another question. "Mrs. Antonini, don't you find it sad that the child who died is the same age as your own daughter?"

This time Susan looked her in the eye. "As a mother, I find it unbearable."

There were a few final questions about the concert.

"Over the phone last night, Mrs. Antonini, you said the concert would be canceled," Harry Penza said. "What changed the plans?"

"You're Mr. Penza?"

"Yes."

"Then you know you were the one who first told me of the accident. Obviously, I had no idea of the plans."

"Well, why *is* your husband playing? Doesn't it strike you as rather disrespectful?"

Frank spoke again. "On the contrary, it's very courageous of Mr. Antonini to perform. He is doing so against his doctor's advice, but he's an artist who believes his first obligation is to the people who stood in line all night before the tickets went on sale, waiting to buy a seat. Mr. Antonini never has and never will disappoint his public. He comes from a family steeped in that tradition."

"Speaking of your family, Mr. Antonini, how are they taking this?"

"They are saddened as my wife and I. We all want

244

to do everything we can for Mr. Armstrong in his loss."

"Does that mean you'll make a settlement out of court?"

"I told you," Richard said evenly, "I've heard nothing of claims in this matter."

"I think that's about it," Frank said. "I'm sure you have everything you need."

"Just one more question," a voice in the back row called out. "Mrs. Johnson told friends before the accident that you were planning to get a divorce and marry her. Any truth to that?"

Richard reddened. "You heard my wife. Mrs. Johnson is a close friend of both of ours."

"That's not exactly a denial, sir."

Richard lost his temper. "What filth is this? My marriage is happy and secure, and always will be!"

"Okay," Frank said hurriedly. "That's it, people. Thanks very much."

They filed out of the suite, comparing notes among themselves.

"Jesus!" Richard said. "What a pack of vultures!"

"Dolly Johnson is news in this town," Frank said. "Don't worry. It was rough, but you did fine. The worst is over."

But it wasn't. The critical reviews of Richard's performance were generally poor, though the reservations about certain faulty passages were explained in the notices by the fact that "the pianist was obviously under unusual strain, due to his accident less than forty-eight hours before." There were photographers waiting as Susan entered the hall, and she felt as though every eye in the house was on her as she sat through the concert, trying to look composed and absorbed in the music.

Worse still was the double funeral of Mrs. Armstrong and Jenny.

"I don't understand why we're going," Susan said. "We're invading their privacy! Surely Mr. Armstrong can't want us there!"

"He's a little man," Frank said. "A bricklayer. People like that are sometimes strange, Susan. This one is. Even while he blames Richard for his loss, it gives

245

him some kind of weird stature to have the celebrity appear in a secondary role. Besides, from our angle, it shows how stricken you and Richard are, how much you care. A vase of flowers would seem impersonal. People would think Richard was brushing off the whole thing."

"I don't believe it. I think it's indecent for us to show up." She appealed to Paul, who stood by silently through this exchange. "You agree with me, don't you?"

"My instincts are yours, Susan, but I think we'd better defer to Frank. He knows more about public relations than we do."

She said no more. Silently, she endured the drive to the little church in Maryland, suffered the stares and the flashbulbs that went off in her face as they went in and out, stood respectfully in the second row at the cemetery as the big and little coffins were positioned at the modest Armstrong plot. Neither she nor Richard spoke to the reporters, but after it was all over she impulsively approached the widower and his remaining child, Richard behind her. She put her hand gently on eight-year-old Christopher's head, and her eyes brimming with tears, looked at his father.

"I am so sorry, Mr. Armstrong," Susan said. "It's hard to accept God's will."

The man stared at her stonily. "Harder still to know that some folks have everything and others have nothing."

"We want to help you," Richard said. "We'll do everything we can. My attorneys are going to be in touch."

The man didn't answer, but Susan thought she'd never seen such contempt on any face.

The hearing was the following day. Richard told his story and a deputized statement given by Dolly Johnson from her hospital bed corroborated his account. The police confirmed that the steering wheel was defective and the inquiry was closed.

"Cut and dried," the Antoninis' lawyer said as they

left the courthouse. "Let's just hope Armstrong lets it go at that."

"What do you mean?" Richard asked. "I'm not legally responsible. I was cleared. It was an unavoidable accident."

"You never know what some shyster will advise him to do. You being who you are, they might just threaten to bring a multimillion-dollar damage suit, knowing you'll settle out of court to avoid the publicity."

Susan couldn't resist. "Richard, you did tell him you'd do everything to help. You even said your lawyers would be in touch."

The attorney looked surprised. "Did you? Did you say that to Armstrong?"

"Well, hell, yes I did. I thought we'd have to. Listen, I wouldn't mind giving the poor guy a few dollars to help him out right now. Even though I wasn't at fault, I feel rotten about it."

"Let's see what happens." The lawyer frowned. "That steering wheel really *was* defective, wasn't it?"

"Things were just as I said," Richard repeated, "but wouldn't it be smart to give him some money anyway and get rid of him once and for all? If he takes a settlement, he can't come back at us ever, can he?"

The lawyer hid his disgust. He was paid for this, but he hated it. He'd bet the overprivileged bastard was lying. He probably rammed the car because he was drunk. But Antonini was afraid of that kind of publicity. That's why he was so anxious to pay off. It wasn't conscience money. It was self-protection.

"I'll go out and see Armstrong tomorrow and tell him of your generosity. How generous are you feeling?"

"I don't know. About twenty-five thousand dollars' worth, you think?"

Sonofabitch. "I'd say more like fifty."

"Okay," Richard said. "Give him fifty."

✸

Paul Carmichael returned to New York right after the funeral. There was no need for him to hang around Washington for the inquiry. Better he didn't. Better he get as far away as possible from all of them. Thank God it was over. All the years of playing nursemaid were behind him. He and Richard had spoken only once about Paul's resignation. That was on Sunday afternoon.

"You've changed your mind, Paul, haven't you? I mean, all that crap you said in the car Friday about quitting. Hell, buddy, you don't want to leave me any more than I want you to leave! We both lost our tempers."

"I meant it. I'm through, Richard, as of now."

Richard's face darkened. "You're a bloody fool."

"Possibly. But better that than some of the other things I've been."

Back in his own apartment in the brownstone on East Sixty-third Street, Paul relived the past few years, relieved they were over. His only regret was leaving Susan. She'd been so distressed when he said goodbye. He felt pain at the thought of her. He loved her so deeply, so futilely. He wondered how much of his decision to quit Richard had been based on an almost subconscious hope that it would free him to tell her how he felt. He'd felt joyful when she took the second bedroom in the suite. It was an unmistakable sign that things were seriously wrong between her and her husband. Just as the planned vacation alone had been a danger signal he understood, even if no one else seemed to. Maybe now that he owed no loyalty to the man who paid him, he could say what had been in his heart since the beginning. He wanted Susan and her child. He loved Katie, too. She grew more endearing every day, a wide-eyed, always-smiling cherub who didn't need words to communicate affection. She was like her mother, outgoing, full of warmth and trust. How could Richard push her away from him? How could the man help but adore this brave little thing who seemed determined, even at this early age, to be like other children?

Paul knew that Susan worried about spending less time than she should with Katie. Damn it, that was his doing! If only he hadn't suggested she and the others become "more visible" when that *Open Secrets* mess started! The whole family had become involved in the plan just as he'd outlined it. It didn't bother the others, but it was destroying the very one he wanted most to protect.

Angrily, he threw himself down on his couch. He'd been on the verge of suggesting to Susan that she could ease up on all the "image making" activities now that the series was long over. And then Richard pulled the Washington stunt and started the tongues wagging again. He wondered if she'd stand by this time. She'd canceled her Western trip, but she'd said nothing about the future, at least not to him.

He'd been in his apartment barely ten minutes when the phone rang and Maria Antonini's voice, strong as ever, came over the wire.

"I just spoke to Richard and he told me you'd returned," she said without preliminaries. "How is everything down there? Will there be trouble from the authorities or that Armstrong man?"

For the hundredth time he marveled at her quick mind.

"Everything's going to be all right," Paul said. "There's nothing to worry about, Mrs. Antonini."

She snorted. "In this family there's always something to worry about." Then her tone became almost plaintive. "Why can't they lead more orderly lives; all of them? Bad marriages, scandalous affairs, ridiculous scrapes like this latest thing with Richard? How can they expect to be taken seriously as artists when they have so little regard for their personal obligations? I don't know, Paul. I want so much for them. I've tried so hard . . ." As abruptly as she let down her guard, it went up again. "Well," Maria said briskly, "I hope everything was properly taken care of in Washington. I should have gone down, I suppose. Richard is so helpless, and heaven knows Susan is no good at this kind of thing! I'm glad you were there. The publicity was terrible, but it probably would have been worse if you hadn't been around to advise Richard. I don't have much use for that Olmstead man. Gerry was much better. I'll never know why Richard let her go."

There are a lot of things you'll never know, Paul thought.

"This Johnson woman," Maria continued. "Dreadful type. Pushy. Trying to cash in on Richard's prestige, no doubt. I know the family. Vulgar, *nouveau riche*. Oil money, I believe. Let's hope we've heard the last of her!"

Why is she going on like this with me? Paul wondered. It wasn't like Maria to be so open with anyone, particularly with someone "outside the family." There's something more on her mind. When will she get to it?

"Paul, I'd like to ask a favor of you," she said at last. "You're Richard's closest friend, as well as his manager, and Susan seems to trust you more than she does any of us."

He wanted to tell her that he was no longer either of those things to Richard, but he waited, curious to hear what was on her mind.

"I'm troubled about that marriage. It's all the things I feared—distracting to Richard's work, demanding of his time and interest. It was a mistake to bring that child home. I know she's always a worry to him, whether he admits it or not. As for Susan, she's really quite unstable. So emotional! I hear things. Hear she's drinking too much. Hear she's restless. And that solitary trip she planned! Such nonsense! You know very well there'd be all kinds of talk if she went off by herself!"

He waited. What was she going to ask of him? To talk to them about their marriage? To save it or break it up? To convince them that Katie belonged in a special school? What did she think he was, a marriage counselor? But it turned out to be quite different.

"I'd like you to arrange an extended tour for Richard," Maria said. "Right away. To Japan, perhaps. I hear they pay astronomically for the appearance of American artists. Or if not there, at least to

250

Europe. Something that will get him away for three or four months."

Paul was surprised. "I don't quite understand, Mrs. Antonini. There's nothing wrong with the idea of such a tour, from a career standpoint, but what's the urgency?"

"I should think it's obvious," she said tartly. "This past year has been most distressing. Actresses, divorcées. Rumors about my son's irresponsible behavior and his wife's peculiarities. It would be wise to remove them from the scene for a prolonged period. My dear Paul, you read those notices of Richard's concert in Washington. He's *never* gotten such poor reviews! Perhaps he deserved them, but more likely they were colored by his behavior, just as everything that will be written about him in this country for the next few months will also have some sly reference to his personal life. I want all this speculation to die down. It is having a serious effect on his professional reputation. No matter how brilliantly he performs in American cities, the press will find some reason to link his sloppy private life with his work. Fortunately, people forget. In a few months they'll have forgotten this unpleasantness in Washington. But we can't let him be badly and unfairly reviewed in the interim. It could damage his entire future."

So that was it! She didn't give a damn about Richard's personal happiness or Susan's. It was those unexpectedly bad reviews. She was only concerned that a snide press would confuse the man with the artist. She saw her life's work being destroyed by the critics. But why come to me? Paul wondered. Why doesn't she simply tell Richard that he has to disappear for the time being? God knows she's never been reticent before about directing his career.

As though she read his mind, Maria said, "You're probably wondering why I don't just go straight to Richard with this solution. I'll tell you frankly, Paul. Richard's always been the most difficult of all my children, and he's worse since his marriage. He's defensive and stubborn. If the suggestion came from me, he

251

might be just mulish enough to reject it so he could try to prove me wrong. Susan has too much influence over him. I told him long ago what complications marriage brought. Look at that business with Katherine! He should never have permitted that child to be taken out of the school. He even thinks Susan has done more for him than he has for her. He told me so himself. I'm having a very hard time getting through to him lately and I don't wish to engage in an argument with him about this. Coming from you, he'll accept it. From me, he'll think it's overreaction."

Paul couldn't have been more surprised. It was totally out of character for Maria to admit she might fail in some demand on her children. I can't imagine her accepting the idea that someone else could be more influential! How angry she must be that Richard's work could be questioned. But how much more she hates Susan. She's never gotten over that marriage. In the end, everything comes back to that. She doesn't really blame Richard for anything. She honestly thinks that Susan and Katie have caused all his troubles. How extraordinary that people see only what they wish to see, believe only what reinforces their own convictions.

"Mrs. Antonini, I'm sorry I can't do what you want. I gather Richard hasn't told you that I've resigned. The trip to Washington was my last one."

There was a moment of stunned silence. "Resigned? Paul, you can't mean that! Richard needs you!"

"Thank you, but he'll get along. There are any number of good managers who'd be delighted to handle him."

"But you've been much more than a manager. You're like family."

God forbid, Paul thought. "I'll be sorry to leave him, Mrs. Antonini, but it's really for the best."

"But why? Is it money? If so, we surely can set that straight."

"No, it's not money."

"Then what? You never had problems all the years you worked together. It's Susan, isn't it? She's interfer-

252

ing, is that it? We can put a stop to that, Paul. I've suspected all along she's had too much say in Richard's business decisions. That's not a wife's job. She'll have to be made to understand that."

He was glad this was a telephone conversation so she couldn't see his face. Of all people to talk of a wife staying out of her husband's career, Maria was the last one to criticize. She'd manipulated Giovanni through most of his life. But we don't see ourselves, Paul thought again. Not as we really are. No imperfections show. Interfere? Susan? It was laughable. All she wanted was anonymity, especially where Richard's career was concerned. Everything had been forced on her. By them. By me.

"Susan isn't the problem. In fact," he lied, "neither is Richard. It's simply that I need a change. I've only had one job in my whole life, Mrs. Antonini. It's time I moved on."

"Is there nothing I can do to change your mind?"

"I'm afraid not. It's flattering of you to ask."

"Richard must be terribly upset."

"No," Paul said. "He took it quite well. In the long run, he knows it will be the best for all concerned."

He heard anger creep into her voice. "I must say, Paul, I think you might have told me this before I confided so trustingly in you! It wasn't very honorable to let me expose my anxieties and my plans, knowing you were going to leave."

"You needn't worry, Mrs. Antonini. I've had a great deal of experience in being discreet these past years. Your secrets are quite safe with me."

"Goodbye, Paul," she said, and hung up before he could answer.

He slowly hung up the receiver on his end. Poor Susan, he thought. I've added another burden to those she already has. Now she'll be blamed for still another inconvenience: my leaving. There'll be one more black mark against her in Maria's book. Goddammit, why does everything I do end up backfiring against the only woman I've ever cared for? He wondered again what Susan would do. If only she'd leave that bastard! If only she'd give me a chance. He wondered how Maria would sell Richard on the idea of an extended tour. She'd find a way. He had to admit it was a good idea for Richard to keep a low profile for a while and this was a neat solution. Let the smoke die down. Let the Dolly Johnsons and Sylvia Sloans be forgotten. Let the beautiful couple travel together around the world. Paul shook his head. What was the point? It would be only a temporary reprieve. Richard had been on his good behavior before, but he was incapable of staying on it. They could send him to Outer Mongolia and he'd get into trouble. He must enjoy the danger and defiance. He was a complex, quixotic human being, this talented creature called Richard Antonini. In his own crazy way, Paul grudgingly admitted, the damned fool probably loved his wife even while he was being unfaithful to her. The other women had no real meaning. He supposed Susan knew that. He supposed it was why she stayed with him in spite of all the terrible things he'd done to her.

Or maybe, Paul forced himself to admit, she was so much in love with Richard that she couldn't do anything about it. He tortured himself with visions of her moving back into the bedroom with her husband, fantasized her passionate response to sex, seeing himself in Richard's place. He knew how she would feel in his arms, how soft and fragrant her skin would be, how gentle but eager her touch. They would come together slowly, rapturously . . .

"Susan!" he said aloud in the empty apartment. The sound of his own voice startled him. God help me, they've got me talking to myself! I'm right to make the break now, before it gets worse. I hope I never see the Antoninis again. *None* of them.

Chapter Twenty

"The Washington affair," as many of those involved came to think of it, had unexpectedly far-reaching effects. It reinforced the bitterness of some, saddened others, forced at least one to do some deep and painful soul-searching.

Paul Carmichael and Leon Armstrong, in different ways, viewed the circumstances of the accident with heightened cynicism. To Paul, it was confirmation of the rightness of his decision to resign. After he'd blurted out the angry words in the car, he'd been almost sorry. During the evening, before the frantic message from Richard, he'd thought seriously of reconsidering. Maybe he was a fool to throw away this good life in which he'd invested so many years. But after the Dolly Johnson business, he knew he had to get away from the man.

To Leon Armstrong, the discreet payment of fifty thousand dollars by Antonini's lawyers was proof of the pianist's guilt, proof it would otherwise have been almost impossible for the widower to substantiate. He was sure Richard was drunk, but there was no way to prove it. The man and woman in the other car had been whisked away by ambulance while Armstrong was in shock. At the inquiry, Leon could not honestly testify to anything that disputed Richard's story. But he knew. He knew people like that got away with things the average man could not. Money could not replace the loss of his wife and child, but it could ensure the remaining boy's education and ease some of the financial pressure Leon had labored under all his life. He knew it was "hush money" but it was a windfall of undreamed-of proportions and he took satisfaction in knowing that it was motivated by fear of disclosure. He took the payoff sullenly, realistically, smiling inwardly at the idiocy of the man who paid it.

Susan found it all painful and sad. She only guessed at the truth. She didn't ask, didn't want to know for certain. Strangely, she was not angry about Dolly Johnson, not even hurt as she'd been when she learned of Richard's other women. She supposed she'd reached the point where nothing surprised her. A kind of numbness had set in. All she felt was this heavy despair, this utter weariness as she contemplated the future. She'd meant it when she told Richard she was through. How much humiliation 'and unhappiness was she expected to endure? And yet it was as though she was incapable of making a move, too drained to go forward with her plan to divorce him, too exhausted to figure out where she and Katie would live afterward, how she alone would set up a household that revolved around a child who needed so much special care. For the next few weeks she did nothing. Wordlessly, she moved into the guest room in the apartment, spoke politely and almost impersonally to her husband when the need arose. She moved like one in a dream and she drank more than ever, recognizing the need to escape, welcoming the oblivion, not particularly caring who knew. Paul's departure added to her unhappiness. She realized how much she depended on him, how much she liked him and would miss his comfort and understanding. She thought of going to see him and decided against it. What would she say to him? That he shouldn't leave Richard when that was precisely what she, herself, planned to do? She knew how Paul still felt about her. It was the kind of thing a woman sensed. She didn't know how she felt about him. She found him enormously appealing, but that wasn't love.

256

God help me, Susan thought, I'm still in love with Richard, even knowing what a faithless, self-involved, thick-skinned creature he is. In the strict moral sense of the word he is even—she flinched from the idea—guilty of murder. Accidentally or not, he's responsible for the death of a woman and a child the same age as his own. Why do I go on living with such a man? Why can't I stir myself to leave him? What am I waiting for? A miracle? Richard seemed so subdued these days, so chastened. But I mustn't be deceived by that. It's only temporary, as his other periods of "repentance" have been. He won't change. He can't.

She would have been heartened if she'd known the self-examination Richard had been going through since the accident. Instead of fading from his mind, as other scrapes had, he lived with a steady recollection of that dreadful night. He relived the horror in his dreams, thought about it even when he was awake. It was more terrible than anything that had ever happened to him. The affairs he'd had since his marriage had been wrong, of course. They'd hurt Susan and he was sorry about that. But never before had he been responsible for taking the lives of innocent people, and never before had he stopped to take a harshly critical look at himself. He didn't like what he saw: a playboy pianist who was no longer a boy and who had no right to play games with the lives of others. It's time you grew up, Richard, he told himself. Time to be a man and a serious artist. Time to assume your responsibilities as a husband and a father. You've been the "little prince" too long. It was unbecoming, at thirty-five, to go on being carefree and thoughtless. He was no longer the "debutantes' delight," as he'd still unconsciously thought himself to be until the Washington affair. I deserve to lose Susan, he thought. I don't know why she's put up with everything as long as she has. But he prayed she wouldn't leave him. She was the only woman who mattered to him, the only one who ever had or ever would. Maybe he could convince her that he was determined to change, if only she'd stay. Maybe she'd give him and their marriage one more chance if he could somehow prove to her that he could be dependable and considerate, that he was more her husband than Maria's son.

It was strange. He felt awkward in his wife's presence these days, unable to tell her what was on his mind. Her remoteness did not help. Neither did her drinking. He understood both and blamed himself, yet he was incapable of revealing his thoughts, of asking anything more of her. He wished there were someone in whom he could confide, someone who could even speak for him before it was too late. To whom would Susan listen? Her mother? Possibly. But more likely she'd pay attention to Kate Fenton, knowing her friend would be more dispassionate in her understanding. I don't know whether I dare approach her, Richard thought. I've never felt she liked me. Why would she come to my rescue now? No. It can't be Kate. Who then? Jacqueline? Of course. Susan was close to her sister-in-law and Jacqueline was more likely to believe in Richard's change of heart.

He went to see her the next day. It was the first time they'd met since the accident, and Jacqueline was surprised to see how unhappy her brother-in-law looked. She found herself feeling sorry for him, an unusual emotion where Richard was concerned. More surprising still, she was touched as he told her his thoughts about himself and Susan, and almost humbly asked her help in saving his marriage. Nonetheless, she had reservations.

"I don't think anyone can talk to Susan for you," she said dubiously. "I believe you. I really do. It took something drastic to snap you out of your adolescent behavior, but I'm sure this kind of thing would bring anyone to his senses. It was a terrible piece of carelessness, Richard. You'll live with that guilt forever. But some good came out of it. It forced you to take a hard look at yourself. I'm sure it wasn't an admirable view. I don't know whether people will believe it's changed you. I'm not certain Susan will. But you're the only one who can convince her. Nobody can be your proxy. If

Susan wants to talk to me after you've told her the same things you've said here, then I'll back you all the way. But I won't plead your case. People have been shouldering your responsibilities far too long. This problem is of your creation and if you're serious about changing you'll see that the solution is also up to you."

"Yes, it is. You're right. I've always let other people bail me out of tight spots, whether it was Susan or Paul or Mother. I can't think that way any more."

Jacqueline nodded. "You'll make it. By the way, speaking of Maria, she tells me you're not going to play in the States for a while. Says you're going to do a long tour out of the country. Will Susan go with you?"

Richard shook his head. "Mother's wrong. She wants me to make a long trip, but I've already told her I won't. I'm through with running away. That's what it amounts to: lying low until people forget the gossip. I've done enough of that to last me a lifetime. No. I'm going to play the concerts already booked in this country. If the critics are influenced by my personal difficulties, I'll have to live with that. I'll just have to try to be so damned good at my work that they'll have nothing to harp on, at least about my performance."

"Good! About time you stopped acting like a windup toy that Maria can send in any direction she chooses! Does Susan know? I'd think that would be good evidence that you intend to be your own man."

"I haven't discussed it with Susan. I haven't had courage to talk to her about anything." He gave an almost embarrassed little laugh. "I guess I'm afraid that if we have a serious conversation she'll tell me when she's leaving. It's the one thing I can't bear to hear."

"You have to face it sometime," Jacqueline said gently. "You can't live in suspense forever. Neither can she."

"I know. It's postponing the inevitable."

"Maybe not. Wasn't Susan going to take a little holiday alone just before that mess in Washington?"

Richard nodded. "She was going to Palm Springs for a rest."

259

"Why don't you encourage her to go now? Put her on a long leash, Richard. Let her get away from you and everything for a few days. I believe she'll think things out in the desert. Tell her what you feel. Ask her to take time to be alone and gather her thoughts. I have a hunch she'll come back to you."

He was almost pathetically eager to believe her. "Do you really think so, Jacqueline? Do you think she'll give us another chance?"

"She's hungry for honesty from you. God knows it's worth a try." She hoped she sounded more convinced than she felt. She wasn't at all sure Susan would try again. She'd had so many disappointments, suffered so many wounds. She's not as tough as I, Jacqueline thought. The only kind of marriage for her is an old-fashioned one. I don't know whether she'll believe Richard capable of that. Hell, I'm not sure I believe it. I want to, but deep down I'm wondering if he's sincere. He thinks he is, but can a man like that really repent? Maybe the Antoninis are all alike: constitutionally incapable of being good husbands. What makes me think this one is different from his father or his brothers? Just because he's momentarily humbled, maybe a little scared, doesn't mean he's undergone a permanent transformation. I'm afraid that's what Susan will think, too. Can't blame her if she does. It would all be so easy if they could live as Walter and I do, separate but equal. But they can't. At least Susan can't.

Richard was getting ready to leave.

"Thanks, Jacqueline, for the good advice. I'll talk to Susan tonight, and I hope she'll come to see you after."

"Call me Ann Landers," she said flippantly. And then she sobered. "Good luck, Richard. I hope everything works out for you and Susan. If it does, you'll be the one who makes it happen. You'll have to do all the changing." She looked at him sharply. "It won't be easy."

"I know. But I want this."

We all want things we can't have, Jacqueline

thought. You're finding that out for the first time, late in life. It must be a shattering experience.

❀

"Can we talk?"

Susan looked at him over the rim of her after-dinner brandy glass. She was a little high, but not drunk. "Of course. What do you want to talk about?"

"Us," Richard said. "You and me and Katie. Our future together."

"Do we have one?"

"I hope so. I want us to very much, Susan."

"Really? That comes as news."

He began to pace the living room nervously. "I've given you a rotten time, right up to and including that business in Washington. I've been a lousy husband, a failure as a father. I told you that you were right to leave me. I guess you still are, but I'm hoping you'll change your mind. I've been doing a lot of thinking, a lot of growing up. I haven't slept much, going over my whole life, realizing how impossibly selfish I've been, thinking how much damage I've done. Susan, I want to be different. I intend to be. If you'll let me, I'll show you I can change, that I can be the kind of husband you deserve. I love you and I love Katie. I've come close, more than once, to blowing everything that matters. Maybe I've already blown it, but I'm asking you, begging you for another chance. Things have become clear to me. Things I never even thought about before. Sure, I've been influenced. By Mother. By a worldful of fawning idiots who made me feel like Superman. But I know now how I've wallowed in self-delusion. I see how impossible to live with I've been. I don't know how you've stood it this long, but I give you my solemn oath that I won't fail you again." He came and knelt down beside her. "Please. Please say we can try to make it work. Please believe I mean every word."

There's nothing I'd rather believe, Susan thought,

but how can I? How do I know this isn't just another act you're putting on to get your own way as usual? I want to believe you so much, my darling, but I'm afraid you've destroyed my faith forever. Like that other little boy, you've cried "wolf" too often.

"I think you mean what you're saying," she answered. "At least right now. At this moment I know you're utterly sincere. But you speak of self-delusion. How do I know this isn't more self-delusion, Richard? You have the ability to convince yourself of anything you want to believe. Anything expedient to your own comfort. Where will all the lofty resolutions be a year from now? A month from now? When your remorse has faded, your remorse about me and, I'm sure, about those poor people who died, will you still feel the way you do right now? How can I believe that? Why should I feel so sure you've changed?"

He took her hand, looking at her pleadingly. "Because I have. I swear it."

Susan pulled back. "You've sworn so many things." Her voice was harsh. "What is your oath worth when you can put your hand on a Bible in court and swear to a pack of lies?" She felt him cringe. "I'm sorry," she said. "That was cruel. I didn't mean to say that."

"It's all right. It's only the truth. It was one of the things that made me stop and think. I was still saving my hide, Susan. I admit it. But no more. Even Mother can't make me crawl back into that protected, unreal life." He told her of Maria's plan for the tour and his rejection of it and the reasons for his rejection. "It isn't much," he said, "but it's something. A start. A few months ago I'd have jumped at the chance to avoid a lot of unpleasantness with the gossipmongers across the country. It was a big step for me, not to take the easy way out. It would be routine for most people to face the music, but it's never been routine for me. I'm not bragging about such a little accomplishment. I'm only telling you because you know the old Richard couldn't have done it. I'm hoping it proves something to you."

262

She was surprised. He was quite right. The "old Richard" would have been obedient to his mother, would have been all too eager to run from hostility, public disapproval or criticism. It *was* something, she admitted. But was one gesture enough to erase the doubts in her heart and mind? Yes, said her emotions, No, said her reason. "I'm glad you made that decision," Susan said slowly. "It is a hopeful sign. But again, how long will this new strength last? How can I expect a metamorphosis in you? Can I repledge my life on the basis of one brave, manly move? I don't see how that's possible. Even as gullible as I am, I've been disappointed too often to believe in your rebirth."

"Give me time to prove it. Just say you won't get a divorce, at least for a while. Let me show you it's true. If I go back to my old ways, I swear I'll never ask for another chance. You can leave me and have anything you want. But you won't darling. I'm betting my life on it. Because I'm going to earn your respect. I've never had that. Love, yes. But not respect. I've never been dependable, strong and protective. I'm going to be, if you'll let me."

Susan wavered. It was almost impossible to think he didn't truly mean what he said. "I don't know . . ."

Richard leaped at this first sign of hope. "Darling, at least think about it. Go on a little holiday alone as you planned. Rest and relax. Bridie will take good care of Katie while you're away. I'll even have a chance to get to know her. I want that, too. A week or so in Palm Springs will do you a world of good. And I'll be here waiting for you."

Some impulse made her say, "I didn't plan to go to Palm Springs. I was going to Las Vegas."

He looked startled. "Las Vegas? Why would you pick that place?"

"It was Kate's idea. She thought I should do something absolutely out of character for an Antonini. I agreed with her. I wasn't going to tell you where I'd be. I don't know why I have now. Maybe it's because I

263

can't bear the idea of any more lies between us, not even over something as trivial as that."

"Las Vegas, Palm Springs, Los Angeles, who cares? Go where you want, any place, any time. I want your happiness, Susan. I want you back, dearest, so I can make up for some of the pain I've caused."

She'd never been able to refuse him anything when he was like this. "All right. I'll go for a week and make a decision. But I really want to be left alone, Richard. I'm not even going to use my real name. In fact, Kate and I decided I'd call myself . . ." She stopped, horrified by the coincidence.

He was in good spirits again. "Call yourself what? Or am I not allowed to know?"

"You have to know," Susan said slowly. "You might need to reach me in an emergency. I was going to call myself Mrs. Armstrong."

There was a moment of heavy silence. How strange Kate had picked out of thin air the name of the woman who, so soon after, was to die because of Richard. Susan was first to speak again.

"Kate said I should choose an initial that matched my luggage." She sounded dazed. "How horrible. Like an omen." I can't call myself that, she thought, shuddering. My husband took her life and, God help me, I was going to take her name as well!

Richard understood. "I'm sorry, darling." He was very gentle. "How about another 'A' like Anderson or Allen?"

She shook her head. Dr. Marcus would probably say she was punishing herself. Maybe it was masochistic, but she didn't want to forget the real Mrs. Armstrong. She mustn't forget. It was important that she remember. "No," Susan said unexpectedly, "I'll stay with the first choice. Maybe if she'd lived, Mrs. Armstrong would have enjoyed going to Vegas in style." Her voice was bitter. "After all, what's in a name? *She* has no use for it any more."

The stewardess, pencil poised over clipboard, leaned over their seats in the first-class section of the plane. "Your name, please?"

Susan looked up from her book. "Armstrong," she said firmly.

"First initial?"

"S."

"Thank you, Mrs. Armstrong." The young woman with the polished, practiced smile (did she rehearse it every morning in front of the bathroom mirror?) turned to the man in the aisle seat.

"Tanner," he said. "Martin."

"Of course, Mr. Tanner. Nice to have you with us again. We'll be airborne in a few minutes. Would you care for a cocktail before lunch?"

Tanner silently deferred to his seatmate. Good-looking woman, he thought. Classy. It wasn't just the trappings that spelled money, the Hermes handbag, the Vuitton tote at her feet, the well-tailored, obviously expensive suit. Any rich broad could acquire those things with the help of *Harper's Bazaar* and a charge account at Saks Fifth Avenue. No, he'd drawn a real lady to sit next to on the flight to Vegas. She hadn't spoken a word since they boarded at Kennedy, had studiously applied herself to her reading, hadn't even looked up when he slipped into the place beside her. He was glad she wasn't one of the chatty traveling companions he sometimes cursed the airlines for pairing him with on the trip he took so often. He sometimes had to be downright rude to those talkative types. Not this one, Martin thought. I'd like to talk to *her*, but she's making it very obvious that the feeling isn't mutual. He noticed the diamond band on her left hand. Where is Mr. Armstrong? Maybe there wasn't one. Maybe she was widowed or divorced. He rather hoped so. It would be pleasant to have a companion like Mrs. Armstrong for a change. He was fed up with Vegas show girls. Hell, what was he thinking of? He was going to gamble and probably lay some gum-chewing, bare-breasted, mindless dame who worked in one of the clubs. He had no time for this cool customer, even if she was available.

"I'll have a double vodka on the rocks," Susan said.

Well, well. Eleven o'clock in the morning. Maybe the lady drank a little, Martin thought. Maybe she drank a lot.

"Scotch and water," he said, sitting tensely in his seat. The new issue of *Time* lay in his lap, but he didn't open it. He never really relaxed until the plane got off the ground. He'd heard that the first two minutes of any flight were the most dangerous. He only felt easy when the "No Smoking" sign went off. That meant the pilot felt they were up there to stay. Unobtrusively he crossed his fingers. He was superstitious. All gamblers were, and Martin Tanner made his living as a professional gambler. A good, if somewhat erratic, living.

His companion had returned to her reading. She obviously was not a "white knuckle flier" as he was. Relaxed, withdrawn, composed. Not a care in the world, he supposed. But why did she have those faint circles under her eyes? Maybe the lady was not as content as she seemed. He felt the plane gather speed, tensed as it left the ground, took a deep breath as it gained altitude and slowly unclenched his fists as it headed west and the warning signs were turned off. Almost immediately the stewardess brought their drinks, and as Susan reached over to accept hers, she looked directly for the first time into the eyes of Martin Tanner.

As he had appraised her as "classy," she now involuntarily thought of him as "dangerous." He was almost too good-looking, too expensively, casually dressed, too sure of himself, as he courteously took her vodka from the tray and handed it over with a faint, knowing smile. She smiled politely in return, coolly, uninvitingly. She had no wish to start a conversation with this attractive man. For that matter, she wanted to talk to no one. She was seeking anonymity. She'd even used that spine-chilling alias to avoid recognition by anyone who might have heard of her or Richard or any of the Antoninis. She yearned only to be alone, to live an uncomplicated existence for the next week while she made up her mind about the rest of her life.

It was ridiculous to think her traveling companion could intrude on that plan. What was the matter with her? He hadn't spoken a word to her. Probably couldn't care less whether she talked or not. Certainly their paths would never cross when they left the airplane. Yet there was something in his eyes, in that half-smile that contradicted her rational thoughts. She felt, oddly, that he could see through her. Not just into her mind but right through her clothes. How crazy! She had the sensation of sitting naked next to a stranger! Sipping her drink, she went back to her book, but her mind was no longer on the printed page. She was aware that he was watching her and she felt an unwilling thrill of excitement. Automatically, she turned the unread pages, looking up only when the stewardess reappeared with menus.

"I don't care for lunch," Susan said, "but I would like another drink, please."

"You, too, Mr. Tanner?" the stewardess asked.

"No, thanks. I'll have the beef. Very rare." As she left, he turned to Susan. "Don't blame you for hating airplane food," he said companionably. "Pure cardboard. Even at these prices."

Susan smiled politely, not raising her eyes.

The hell with her, Martin thought. Who does she think she is? Some damned society bitch, going slumming in Vegas. Probably going where she can stay drunk without anybody knowing or caring. He was so annoyed with her that perversely he refused to be rebuffed.

"Been to Vegas often?" he asked.

Susan looked up. "No. My first trip."

"Is that so? Where do you usually do your gambling?"

Her impulse was to end the conversation with a pleasant smile and a return to her book, but good manners prevailed. "I don't gamble. I'm going simply for a rest."

He gave a good-natured laugh. "A rest? Now that's what I call a switch! It's a twenty-four-hour marathon, don't you know that? Nobody sleeps there. There literally isn't a clock in the whole damned town! Forgive me. I know it's none of my business, but why in God's name would you pick Vegas for a *rest?*"

You're right, Susan thought. It's none of your business. She took her second drink, noticing he'd barely gotten through half of his first one. Why am I bothering to talk to you? I don't want to speak to anyone. She was surprised to hear herself answering pleasantly. "I've heard it's one place where nobody pays any attention to other people. That can be more restful than going to a health spa where one is constantly being fussed over, or a smart resort where you're bound to run into friends-of-friends. The fact is, Mr. . . ."

"Tanner. Martin Tanner."

"The fact is, Mr. Tanner, I don't intend to talk to anyone except waiters for the next week. I probably won't leave my hotel room. I won't even have to answer the phone because I don't know a soul in Las Vegas."

"I see. Sorry. Didn't mean to intrude." He picked up his magazine and began riffling through the pages.

God, how boorish I sound! Susan thought. The man is only trying to be pleasant. I'm so damned touchy these days. He just wants to pass the time in a little innocent conversation and I've come on like an utter snob. Or was there something more? There was something magnetic about Tanner, something excitingly different. It was the first time in years she'd met someone who exerted such physical appeal, who was so unmistakably sexy. She'd not felt like this since she met Richard. It was insane, but she knew why she was being so reserved. Martin Tanner had an animal-like quality to which she responded. It frightened her. As

268

she had before, she thought, He's dangerous. But now she silently added, And I'm vulnerable.

"Forgive me," Susan said, "I know that sounded terribly rude." She held out her hand. "I'm Susan . . . Armstrong."

He took her hand. His was strong, warm as he held hers briefly. "Nothing to forgive," he said. "You've paid for your seat and your privacy. To tell you the truth, I don't even know why I imposed. Usually I hate talking to people on airplanes. Bloody bores, most of them. Traveling alone has its disadvantages that way, don't you agree?"

"I wouldn't know. I seldom travel alone. I'm usually with my husband."

"Oh. I see."

No, you don't, Susan thought. You don't see at all. "Actually, this is the first time I've been anywhere without him in more than six years. I needed a holiday and he . . . he couldn't get away just now." She gave a nervous little laugh. "They say separations are sometimes good for a marriage. Brief ones, I mean. Do you think that's true?"

You're in trouble, lady, Martin thought. You're running away, probably from a marriage you can't decide whether or not to continue. You're a sitting duck for a big adventure, whether you realize it or not. But when he spoke, his tone was deliberately offhand.

"I don't know. My only marital separation was permanent. Ended in divorce four years ago. Maybe my wife and I should have tried vacations alone first, if you believe that 'absence makes the heart grow fonder.' Personally, I've always leaned more toward the theory of 'out of sight, out of mind.' Who knows? Every case is different."

"Yes. I suppose it is." She felt more relaxed now. The second double vodka was beginning to take effect. "Do you have children?"

"No. Just a niece I'm crazy about. You have kids?"

"A little girl. Katie. Six last November. She's beautiful."

269

"Of course. She'd have to be."

Susan actually blushed. "She's in New York with her father and her nurse. She's being well taken care of while I'm away."

Martin looked at her carefully. Why was she feeling so guilty that she had to explain the child was in good hands? What was it with this beautiful woman who'd seemed so remote at first and now was almost over-eager to talk? The drinks, he supposed. The infallible tongue-looseners. She was sipping the dregs of her vodka when the stewardess put his unappetizing lunch tray in front of him.

"You're right to turn down this food," Martin said again. "I should have done the same." He looked at Susan's empty glass. "Would you like another drink?"

"I really would, but isn't two all they'll serve?"

"You can have my second one. Besides, no problem. I'm a regular on this flight. The girls will bend the rules for me."

He watched as she downed her third cocktail. Three double belts before lunch! Jesus! It was enough booze to put a strong man under the table, but aside from making her less formal, all that alcohol didn't seem to have much effect. She was still clear-eyed and she spoke distinctly. She was used to plenty of booze, no doubt about that. The lady is a lush, Martin told himself. Too bad. What would make a woman like that drink so heavily? What was she trying to forget? She intrigued him. Maybe, he thought, she doesn't want to be alone quite as much as she says. Maybe this could turn out to be an interesting week after all.

Chapter Twenty-one

Martin's world was as totally alien to Susan as Richard's had once been: two spheres in which she'd suddenly set foot, knowing little about either. First the snobbish, inbred world of the arts, and now the wide-open, slightly unsavory milieu of the professional gambler. She'd always assumed she'd live an orderly life, economically comfortable and intellectually middle-of-the-road. Instead, marriage had catapulted her into the realm of the rich and famous, an arena in which she was ill-equipped to do battle and one which had driven her to despair and, literally, to drink. She'd never fitted into Richard's world. It was as though everything conspired to keep her from becoming an accepted part of it. She did not have Maria's iron will, Jacqueline's worldliness, Mary Lou's self-absorption. She hadn't been able to cope with the demands, understand the eccentricities, adjust to the prerogatives of money and status as they were bestowed on the Antoninis.

Nor, she thought, would she ever feel at ease in Martin's atmosphere, as foreign to her in a totally different way as the one she'd left behind. She'd never seen anything like Las Vegas. The whole city seemed to be one huge playground, a tacky, tawdry, vulgar amusement park devoted to pleasure yet underlined with the grim and serious business of flirting with luck.

By the time they landed. Martin took it for granted

she'd spend her trip with him, and she did not disabuse him of that idea. Why not? she'd thought defiantly, a little drunk. He's attractive and he knows his way around. Why should I sit moping in a hotel room, chewing over problems I'll never know how to solve? I don't know why I came here. In retrospect, Kate Fenton's idea of an "unlikely vacation" seemed stupid in the light of all that had happened since her friend originally suggested it. I could come to this decision as easily on Park Avenue as I could in a room at the Flamingo Hilton, Susan told herself. So, what the hell? As long as I'm here I may as well find out what this place is all about. And if anybody can show me, Martin Tanner can.

And what did Martin Tanner want in return? Three guesses, she thought. This was not the kind of man who'd settle for a platonic friendship. He wasn't desperate for companionship. He seemed to know everybody, from the croupiers and pit bosses in the gambling casinos to the maître d's in the special hotel dining rooms set aside for the convenience of the "big spenders." He'll expect me to go to bed with him. Will I? Can I? Do I want to? She didn't know. It had been easy enough to avoid it the night of their arrival. She'd been able to laugh off his suggestion that he come in for a nightcap as he took her to her room at three in the morning.

"Be a good boy," she'd said. "I have jet lag and I'm already drunker than I should be! See you tomorrow."

He hadn't made a fuss. He was quite sober, though he'd had a great many drinks during the evening, and he kissed her hand with exaggerated politeness.

"I'll accept that," he'd said. But then he'd given her his little smile and added, "For tonight." There was no misunderstanding the words. Tomorrow night there'd be no acceptable excuses.

And "tomorrow night" is here, Susan thought as she ran a tub and prepared to dress for dinner. Decision time.

She made a drink and took it into the bath with her,

thinking irrelevantly how convenient it was that the oversized marble tub was shaped with armrests on which she could put the glass of vodka. She tried to relax, stretching full length in the warm water, slowly sipping the liquor and reviewing the past twenty-four hours.

Las Vegas, she mused, looked and sounded like a giant pinball machine, all bells and gongs and flashing lights. From the time the cab drove up "The Strip," flanked by garish hotels with their huge signs announcing the appearance of big-name entertainers, to the moment they'd entered her hotel lobby (which was barely a lobby as she knew one, but more an anteroom to the huge casino straight ahead), Susan had been openmouthed. She'd never seen so many people, heard such a constant buzz of voices and a current of strange noises. As far as she could see, there were blackjack and crap tables, roulette wheels, rooms for keno and rows of slot machines greedily awaiting anything from a nickel to a silver dollar. The loudspeaker never stopped paging someone. Grandmothers clutching paper cups full of dimes and quarters went through a bizarre ballet: drop in a coin, pull the lever, wait impassively for a winning combination, start over if it did not appear. Ordinary-looking men and women sat motionless on high stools at the blackjack tables, conducting their serious play with few words. The big spenders threw dice and placed bets at the roulette wheels, sometimes, Martin told her, winning or losing thousands of dollars in an hour. Tired-looking young girls in short skirts made change for the slot-machine addicts and brought free drinks to the other players who accepted them without looking up from their "work." It was all intense and rather frightening and compulsive.

Martin was staying at Caesars Palace, but he had brought her to the Hilton and had taken her for a quick tour before she checked in. He watched, amused, as she surveyed the scene.

"It's incredible!" Susan said. "It's the middle of the afternoon!"

"Same at any hour. I told you. There are no clocks. Time doesn't mean anything here. Gamble when you can, eat when you must, sleep only when you're ready to drop. That's life in Vegas."

"But the people! Most of them look as though they can't afford to gamble."

"Most of them probably can't. They're dumb amateurs. Always sure they're going to make a killing. They don't know the odds. Or don't want to. Poor slobs. They save all year to come here and get rich. They refuse to believe it won't happen. Still," Martin said, "they love it. It's a helluva vacation. They gamble, see entertainment they'd never be able to see anywhere else for the price of a dinner, go home and tell the neighbors they really lived it up in Vegas! In their minds they've rubbed elbows with Frank Sinatra and Sammy Davis. They probably think they'll run into Howard Hughes playing roulette at The Sands." Martin laughed. "It's the Great American Dream Machine and even suckers are entitled to a go at it."

"Is it honest?"

"If you mean are the games rigged, they're not. No need to be. The odds are all with the House. Nobody gets cheated here, Susan. Nevada's damned sticky about protecting the greatest ongoing gold mine in the U.S.A."

She shook her head. "I can't get over it. It's unreal."

"Not for me," Martin said. "It's my living."

She stared at him.

"I gamble, lady. It's my profession. Do you mind?"

"No. Of course not. I mean, what business is it of mine how you earn your money? It's just that . . ."

"You've never known an underworld character before." Martin finished the sentence for her. "That's what you're thinking, isn't it? That I'm some kind of Legs Diamond or Bugsy Siegel? That I'm a mobster and you're my moll, like in the old movies?" Martin laughed again. "Don't worry. I'm so bloody respectable

274

you can't stand it. I don't know what Mr. Armstrong does for *his* daily bread, but if he uses computers I use cards. It's just another kind of business and I'm damned good at it." He patted her cheek lightly. "Come on. You'd better check in and unpack. Take a little nap. I'll pick you up about eight-thirty and give you another look at life in Las Vegas."

He'd done just that. They'd dined quietly and elegantly in the reserved area at his hotel. "No tourist traps for us," Martin had said as they passed long lines of people waiting to get into the big showroom. "The peasants queue up for hours waiting to sit at long tables with thirty or forty strangers from Mule Shoe, Nebraska, and eat indifferent food while they gawk at the overpriced talent." He shuddered. "No way! If there's some special show you must see, we'll go at midnight. I have a special pass that will get us right in, not that I use it much. I prefer a quiet meal in a civilized room before I settle down at the tables. Will it bore you to watch me play?"

"No. I'll be fascinated."

"Maybe you'll bring me luck."

Susan sighed wistfully. "Don't count on it."

During the evening while Martin gambled, she wandered off from time to time, drink in hand, watching the people, inspecting the shops that sold everything from ugly souvenirs to expensive jewels and furs. She felt removed, almost disembodied. For fun she put five dollars' worth of quarters in a slot machine, won a few times, eventually put the whole lot back. That's what Martin means about the odds, she thought. If you stay at it long enough, you're bound to return whatever you win.

At three in the morning, he got up from the roulette table.

"That's it," he announced. She saw him hand some money to the croupier. The man nodded his thanks.

Martin casually put his arm around Susan, steering her out of the casino.

"Sure you weren't too bored? It must be dull when you don't gamble."

"I wasn't bored. Did you win?"

He nodded. "A couple of thousand."

She gasped. "A couple of thousand! Do you always do so well?"

"No. Sometimes I lose. Particularly if I get careless."

"You must make a lot of money every year." She stopped. "I'm sorry. That's rude of me."

"It's never rude to talk about money," Martin said. "It can buy you anything you want." He smiled. "Where would you like to go now?"

"I think I'll call it a night, if you don't mind. It's been a long day."

That's when they'd had the little exchange at the door of her room. It had been graceful, lighthearted. But it won't be again, Susan thought, as she lay in her tub. Tonight when he's through gambling Martin will have other ideas. I wish I knew whether I have courage for an affair. It would be so easy. One week. I'll never see him again. Jacqueline would think it a good idea. Therapeutic. And God knows I owe Richard no fidelity after all he's done! I'm a grown woman. It could hurt no one. Maybe it could even make me feel something again. It's been so long since I've thought of myself as anything except Richard's wife, the mother of his child. Martin Tanner doesn't even know who I am. For all he knows, I could be an expensive whore. The thought amused her. In a way, she supposed, that's what she was to her husband: a sexy body he'd bought with his charm. Certainly he'd never really shared a life with her. On the surface, yes. But she didn't know the meteoric man she'd married. She didn't really comprehend his motivations or understand his constantly changing attitudes. She'd seen him in so many incarnations in a few short years. How real is this latest one? Susan wondered. Has he really "reformed?" Is there any chance for us at all?

I still love him, Susan thought hopelessly. I still want to believe in him, in spite of his lies. But something inside me also wants to hurt him, to pay him back for hurting me.

She climbed out of the tub and dried herself with a thick towel, looking critically at the image reflected in the big bathroom mirror. Hers was a young body, slim and firm, not even showing signs that she'd given birth. As though she were inspecting a nude in an art gallery, she took in every detail of the rounded breasts, the flat stomach, the well-shaped thighs. Naked, she walked into the bedroom and poured another drink. Maybe if she had enough vodka she'd lose her stupid inhibitions. Out of nowhere the thought crossed her mind that she wished it were Paul Carmichael with whom she probably was going to be unfaithful. Paul loved her, had always loved her. Gentle, patient, understanding Paul should be taking advantage of this moment of defiance or weakness or desperation—whatever it was. It should be Paul who would be the instrument of revenge; not some stranger Richard would never know about.

I must be losing my mind, Susan thought.

"What do you hear from your wife?"

Richard looked at his mother from his place on her right at his parents' dining table. "She's only been gone three days," he said patiently.

"Hasn't she telephoned?"

"Yes, she called when she arrived to say she'd gotten there safely."

"And she hasn't been in touch since? Isn't she concerned about that child of hers?"

"*Ours*, Mother. Katie is *our* child, not just Susan's." Her needling annoyed him. "Damn it, can't you use their names? Must you always refer to them as impersonal objects?"

Maria arched her eyebrows. "Really, Richard, you're frightfully testy. I've never seen you so on edge. I'm afraid to open my mouth to you!"

From the other end of the table, Giovanni chuckled.

His wife shot him an angry look but Richard smiled grimly. He knew all too well what his father was thinking. When Maria said she was afraid to "open her mouth" it was the prelude to a sermon delivered "for your own good." He followed the long-established format.

"I'm sorry, Mother."

"I should think you would be!" But she was mollified, ready to launch into a discussion of Susan's "abandonment" of him. "I can't think what's gotten into that young woman, running off to that dreadful place, leaving you to cope with her responsibilities! For that matter, Richard, I can't understand your permitting it! And she doesn't even care enough to find out what is happening in her own home while she's gallivanting about, doing God knows what shocking things!"

He kept his temper. "I wanted her to have this little holiday, Mother. I told you that. I know Susan. She's much too good to do anything 'shocking' as you put it. I could have called her last night, but I don't want her to feel I'm checking up. She's earned a little peace and privacy, and she knows very well that between Bridie and me things are under control. She needed to get away. It's been hard for her these past years, and that mess in Washington was the last straw." In spite of his best efforts he felt himself getting angry. "My God, she hasn't *left* me! She's taking one lousy little week for herself. Is that so terrible? I suppose you'd like me to divorce her for desertion and have her declared an unfit mother!"

Maria was quiet for a moment. Then she said, "You said it Richard; I didn't."

Her son and husband stared at her in disbelief. Giovanni was the first to recover.

"My dear, I'm sure you don't mean that the way it sounded. You may not be overly fond of Susan, but you must admit she's been a loyal wife to Richard and a devoted mother to little Katherine."

"I also admit she's a troublemaker," Maria retorted. "She's connived to alienate her husband from his family, to embarrass us all by requiring psychiatric care. She's insisted upon this ridiculous burden of keeping a deaf-mute child at home. She's courting some ugly publicity by running off to Las Vegas alone. And," Maria went on bitterly, "as if all that weren't enough, the whole world knows she's become an alcoholic and God knows what she'll do next! I've tried to get along with her, but she makes it impossible. She's brought Richard nothing but unhappiness. She's the one who's forced him into some of those impetuous, ill-advised acts. If he had a suitable wife and healthy children, things like that unpleasantness in Washington never would have occurred. I knew the first minute Richard brought her up to the country that she was all wrong for him. But he wouldn't listen. She had him hypnotized, even then. Just as I'm sure she's influenced him in this unwise decision to continue with his concerts here instead of taking a long tour out of the country. I believe she gets a fiendish pleasure out of making people gossip and laugh at us behind our backs!"

Richard abruptly pushed his chair back from the table and stood up, trembling with rage. "Stop it!" he shouted. "Stop it right now, Mother! I won't listen to any more of this! You're talking about my wife. The mother of my child. You hate her because she wants us to have a life of our own. You can't stand anyone trying to wriggle out from under your thumb. You're furious that I won't run away from criticism. That's what this is all about, isn't it? You're offended by anyone who has the guts to go against your wishes!"

"Richard!" Giovanni interrupted. "Calm down! I won't permit you to talk to your mother that way! She's devoted her life to her family. She wants what's best for you."

"No, Father, she wants what she *thinks* is best for me. For all of us. She didn't want me to marry, or leave home or be anything but her little boy. She'd like to turn me into you, Father—dependent on her for every thought and action. She knows she's met her match

279

in Susan and it's driven her wild. It's also damn near destroyed us. She made me believe that I wasn't subject to the rules other people live by. Susan won't stand for that. It's taken me a long time to see that she's right."

Maria slowly rose from her place. The color drained from her face and her voice cut like a knife. "This is the thanks I get for bearing you," she said slowly. "This is the reward for all the years of devotion. I think you'd better go home, Richard. I don't think I want to see you again for a long, long time."

The ingrained habit of submission took over; the implanted guilts returned as Richard heard the quiet words. My God, he thought, I must be a monster! How could I talk to her like that after all she's done for me! She meant well. She still does. What kind of ingrate am I? I forget she's getting old, that she's been desperately ill, that she loves me so much she refuses to believe, even now, that anything rotten I do is my own fault. He went to her side, penitent as a small boy.

"Forgive me," he apologized. "I didn't mean to hurt you. I'm going to straighten things out, Mother. You're right: Susan should come home. I'll call her tonight. And I'll think about scheduling that tour. It's probably wise."

"Don't do things to please me, Richard. It's not my future I'm concerned with. I have very little left."

"Don't say that. Look at the recovery you made. Besides, I'm not doing this for you. I'm doing it because I want to. I'll work it out," he said again. "I promise."

She turned away without answering. Neither her son nor her husband saw the tiny flicker of a triumphant smile on her face.

It was eleven o'clock New York time when Richard entered his apartment. Eight in the evening in Las Vegas. He placed a call to Susan Armstrong. Her voice sounded strange when she answered, as though she were expecting someone else.

"Susan? Darling? How are you?"

280

There was a pause as though she were gathering her thoughts, and then she said, "Richard? Why are you calling? Is something wrong? Is Katie all right?"

"Everything's fine, except I miss you. Are you having fun?"

No, she thought, I'm not having fun. I'm hating myself. I loathe what I did last night. Loathe the memory of Martin Tanner's body on mine. Loathe the fact that it was glorious and I loved it. At the moment. Today I'm ashamed and disgusted with myself. And yet I'm dressing to meet him again. He was an expert lover, Martin Tanner. For a little while he'd made her forget everything—Richard, Katie, all the things that mattered. For a while she'd been primitive, an animal and very drunk. But not so drunk she didn't know what she was doing. Not so drunk she couldn't remember every sensuous gesture, every tempting, tingling motion, every second of the ultimate fulfillment. And, shamed as she was, she wanted more. She supposed she knew now how Richard felt when he went to bed with a woman. It had no deep meaning. There was no love. It was blatantly physical, exquisite in its variety, tantalizingly dangerous. She saw how an act could be regretted and repeated. Weirdly, her unfaithfulness to Richard made her understand him for the first time. Made her, in a strange way, love him more. A sob rose in her throat.

"Susan? Are you there?"

"Yes. I'm here." Her voice was blurred. Even these few words come out with difficulty.

She's drunk, Richard thought unhappily. God help us, she's probably been locked in that hotel room all this time, drinking herself senseless.

"I asked whether you were having fun."

"No. Not fun. Have you been having fun?"

"No, sweetheart. Anything but. Susan, come home tomorrow, won't you? I know it's selfish, but I want you here. The apartment is terrible without you." He tried to laugh. "I'm getting a taste of what it's like for you when I go away. No good, love. I'm rattling around in all this space."

"How is Katie?" she asked again.

"I told you. She's fine. Bridie took her to the Children's Zoo in Central Park. She had a wonderful time."

"Why didn't *you* take her? *I* always take her. I wish you'd spend more time with her, Richard. She needs you."

"I know. I will, darling. I'm going to do a lot of things differently. We're going to have a different life. Please believe that. Don't take any more time to think about it. Just come home to me. Forgive me for all the awful things I've done. I know you can, sweetheart."

Yes, I can, Susan thought. But can I forgive myself?

"All right," she said slowly. "I'll come home tomorrow."

He was jubilant. "Wonderful! Call me when you've booked your flight. I'll meet you."

"That will be nice."

"Have a good evening, darling, and get to bed early."

It was so unconsciously ironic she nearly laughed aloud.

❖

Martin looked baffled when she told him at dinner that she was leaving in the morning.

"Has something happened? Why are you cutting your trip short?"

Susan smiled. "Yes, something happened, Martin. *We* happened."

He took her hand. She looked so beautiful in this low-cut beige chiffon dress. She was a desirable, sensuous woman and she'd been wild in bed. He didn't want her to go. Not that he had any long-range plans. He was adept at extricating himself from sticky situations with women who fell in love with him. He'd never marry again. But Susan Armstrong was someone he'd planned to see more of, not only here but in New York. He hoped she hadn't read any romantic meaning

282

into last night. He assumed this was not her first affair. Mr. Armstrong, whoever he was, must have had other rivals for his wife's affection. Still, why was she running away? He returned her smile.

"We 'happened' very good, as I remember."

She was straightforward. "It *was* good. You're a marvelous lover, by my limited ability to judge. You're only the fourth man I've ever slept with, Martin. Two boys before I was married. And since then, no one but my husband." She withdrew her hand. "Don't look so upset. You didn't seduce me. I wanted to be with you. I still do. But I won't be again. I can't handle this kind of thing. God knows I'd love to be modern and 'sensible' about it! I'd love to enjoy sex for its own sake. My husband always has. I never understood before how he could want to be with anyone but me, because I know he loves me. I can understand it now, but that doesn't wipe away my guilt. And it probably won't make it any easier for me to forgive him if he does it again. Maybe you've made me a little more 'liberated' in my thinking, and I thank you for it, but I don't *want* to get used to this new freedom. It confuses me. And I don't need that. I'm mixed up enough. I had to see you and say 'thank you.' It's been wonderful. If I were unattached I'd follow you from Las Vegas to San Juan. But that's not the way it is, or ever will be. Goodbye, Martin. Take care of yourself."

"Wait!" he said as he stood up. "Where do I find you in New York. I want to see you again, Susan. You want to see me, too."

"I may want to, but I won't. And you can't find me."

She left the restaurant abruptly, before he could answer, and went back to her room. The telephone rang half a dozen times during the evening but she didn't answer. She couldn't trust herself not to let him come up for one last forbidden night. Methodically, she drank her way through half a fifth of vodka and finally, sometime after midnight, fell into a deep sleep, looking forward to tomorrow and half-welcoming, half-dread-

283

ing it. She dreamed she confessed her adultery to Richard and when he answered he'd turned into Maria, who grabbed Katie and vanished with her into the night, the child screaming her mother's name. She woke in a cold sweat, turned on the bedside light and looked at the clock. Four A.M. She already had a terrible hangover. She tried to forget the nightmare. How insane that she should have dreamed of Katie screaming her name. Little Katie, who could barely make a coherent sound! She considered taking a sleeping pill and decided against it. She had to be up early to catch the plane to New York. Richard was waiting. They were all waiting.

Chapter Twenty-two

She saw both of them the minute she came through the doorway from the plane. Richard was searching for her in the crush of people racing toward the baggage area as though they actually expected their luggage to get there ahead of them. She waved at him and he returned the signal, then pointed down to a tiny figure beside him, almost invisible in the crowd. He'd brought Katie to the airport. Susan was unreasonably delighted. It seemed a good omen, as though his willingness to appear in public with his child indicated a change of attitude about many things.

Susan rushed to them, kissed Richard swiftly and then picked up Katie, holding her so their faces almost touched.

"Hello, my love," she said clearly. "Remember me?"

There was a big smile. "Muh-muh."

"Yes, Kit-Kat. Yes, darling. Mama. Mama is home. Did you have a good time with Daddy?"

"Day-de," Katie said confidently. "Purg."

Susan looked inquiringly at Richard. "Park? She's saying park."

"Right. We went this morning."

"You and Katie?"

He laughed. "Don't look so amazed. You told me we should. As a matter of fact it was fun. That brat of ours is absolutely fearless. She led me a merry chase, up and down rocks and around trees. Damned if I know how you and Bridie keep up with her!"

She was touched. "Thank you for doing that."

"Don't thank me. I should have done it long ago. I must confess, though, I was afraid to face it alone. I took Bridie along for moral support."

Susan wondered why she felt relieved. Didn't she trust the child with her own father? What nonsense! She had to start thinking of them as a threesome. If they were to start over, Katie would have to be a shared project. She understood that now. Just as she felt she understood a great many other things that had eluded her. When she'd heard Richard's voice on the phone she'd known that she wanted to come back to him, no matter what. She deeply regretted the night with Martin Tanner. No. She didn't. I learned something from that, she thought. I learned that unfaithfulness can happen from boredom or disappointment or hostility. That it's a means of blotting out other things. Like liquor is. I also learned it isn't for me, but the experience has made me less self-righteous.

A long, long time ago, her roommate had tried to tell her that female sexual attitudes had to change, along with other demands for equality. Evie was right, she supposed. Yet I won't do it again, Susan vowed. I can't handle it. Right now I feel terribly guilty. I wish I could confess to Richard, but he'd never understand. He's still a double-standard man.

She could see why married people so often felt compelled to admit their affairs. It was a selfish thing, as though by telling the injured party it became his problem, shifting the weight of guilt from the wrongdoer to the wronged.

Whether he intended to or not, that's how Richard had made her feel when he told her about his infidelities. She'd been angry and hurt, but her primary emotion had been a sense of failure, as though she weren't enough of a woman to keep him satisfied. I've always felt inadequate, Susan thought as the three of them walked through the airport, Richard chatting easily about trivial things. Perhaps I've even blamed myself for Katie, for giving Richard a flawed child. Her grip tightened on Katie's small fingers contentedly entwined in her own. That's stupid. I'm not at fault. No one is. Why have I been punishing myself and punishing Richard? We're both simply human. I can thank Martin Tanner for teaching me that. I knew I wasn't tackling an easy project when I married this man. Did I really think I could change him? How young and foolish I was! He's been bad, but why did I expect him to be good?

"I got a lot of things straightened out in my head on this little trip," Susan said suddenly.

He didn't ask what they were. Her tone told him she was home to stay. That was enough.

In a way, it was as though they turned back the clock to the early days. Susan recognized her potential drinking problem and took pains to control it so that her senses, no longer dulled, responded to Richard's heightened affection. She almost put the Martin Tanner episode out of her mind and devoted herself contentedly to her husband and child. She would not dwell on the past—not Richard's or her own.

These were good days, the best ever. Together, they took Katie to the park, enjoyed prebedtime romps with her. One day, Susan even talked Richard into going to the nursery school to see how well Katie fitted into this environment. Another day, they had had a long talk with Edith Chambers, who was highly encouraging.

"Katie's doing remarkably well," the speech therapist said. "I know it seems slow to you, but believe me she's making exceptional progress."

"Will she ever speak normally?" Richard asked.

"Probably not, Mr. Antonini. Not in the way you mean. But she'll become more and more intelligible. She'll manage nicely. Her lip-reading is extraordinary. You've done a great job on that with the home training. I think she understands as much, maybe more, than most hearing children her age."

"But she'll never hear." Richard sounded resigned.

"No. At least very little." The teacher hesitated. "I know what you're thinking. Music is your life."

"Music is my career," Richard said. "My wife and child are my life."

He seemed depressed after that visit. "I let that woman give me credit for something I don't deserve. I haven't helped Katie at all. I try, Susie. But I don't do well at it. I don't think I ever can. It just doesn't come naturally to me."

"It doesn't come naturally to any of us. We expect people to react and respond in the way Katie can't. But you're doing so much better. I know how you're trying."

He shook his head. "It's no good. I'll never be a good father to a child who requires so much patience and understanding." He tried to smile. "Well, it could be worse. At least we get A for effort, even if we struck out at our first and only time at bat."

He wasn't talking about the failure he considered they'd had with Katie. He was saying there'd never be another baby. I didn't want another one either at first, Susan thought. But I do now. I want to give Richard a child he can relate to. It must be terrible for him to realize that the best he has to offer literally falls on deaf ears . . . that the one he most wants to be proud of him can never hear his music.

She was about to discuss the idea of a second baby, but she stopped. He'd never consent to it, even though the doctors had assured her the odds were good that she'd have a normal child next time. Do I dare, Susan wondered? He seemed so happy about Katie in the beginning. A whole, healthy child would bring us such joy. He might be upset at first, but later he'd be delighted to have that "little musician" they'd hoped for.

Six weeks later the doctor confirmed she was pregnant. She was delighted and simultaneously worried about how to tell Richard. She chose a quiet moment in bed after love-making, knowing he was deliciously weary and full of tenderness for her.

"Darling, I have some good news."

He lay still, eyes closed. "What?" He was half-asleep.

"I'm pregnant."

He sat bolt upright. "Pregnant! Susan, you can't!"

"Why not? There's no medical reason why we shouldn't have another child. The odds are all in our favor. It will be wonderful for us and for Katie, too. She should have brothers and sisters. I'm so happy about it. Please, you be happy too."

He stared at her in the dim light. "You didn't even discuss it with me. You know how I feel about that risk!"

"I know. I should have discussed it with you, but I was sure you'd never agree. Have faith in me, Richard. I'm so certain this child will be perfect. I want to do this for you more than any other reason. I want to give you someone who perhaps will carry your genius as well as your name. We're really getting our life together after so many disappointments. Things are going to be good for us, better when we have another baby."

He sank back on his pillow, half-disturbed, half-happy. It was true he'd like to have a child he was proud of. But how could Susan be so sure they'd not have another like Katie? They couldn't stand that, ei-

288

ther of them. It was foolhardy. Even the slightest chance of a repetition was too much. He imagined what Maria would say when she heard, especially since he'd half-promised to make the tour she was so dead-set on. That idea would have to be canceled now. He couldn't leave a pregnant wife and he couldn't drag one halfway around the world. Damn!

"Richard?" Her voice was almost timid.

He turned and looked at her. "I wish you hadn't done it, Susan."

A tear rolled down her face and it was like a reproach. He took her in his arms. "All right, baby," he said. "I trust you. Scared as I am, I'm glad, too. Just keep injecting me with doses of your faith. God knows I need 'em!"

She clung to him, feeling relieved and confident. There was no medical reason for him to resist another child, but he had every right to be angry that she hadn't consulted him. He'd been upset about that. It was only natural. Or was it? Was there something more, something she didn't know? Was there something in his family he hadn't told her? Some history of this kind of thing that he'd kept secret? Was that why he was so afraid?

"I do not believe it," Maria said flatly.

"It's true, Mother. Susan and I are going to have another child. And we're delighted."

"You're insane. Both of you."

They were alone in her drawing room. Richard tried to placate her. "The doctors assure us there's only the remotest possibility this baby will be impaired."

"Doctors are asses. So, it seems, are concert pianists."

Irritated, he blurted out the truth. "As a matter of fact, I didn't know Susan planned to get pregnant again. It came as a total surprise to me."

Maria raised her eyebrows. "I might have guessed.

289

So you've been tricked again, have you? Just as I was. Like mother, like son. Your wife is as devious as your father. Incredible how you refuse to recognize that, Richard! The first pregnancy was deliberately done to get you out of this house. Now I suppose this one is to keep you from going on that long tour. Very clever of her. Very stupid of you to allow it."

"Susan doesn't even know I was reconsidering the tour. Anyway, I didn't promise. I only said I'd think about it."

"Don't quibble over terms. You were going to go before this happened."

"Maybe so. What difference? I can't go now."

"No," Maria said, "obviously not. Unless, of course, you come to your senses and insist Susan terminate this selfish pregnancy. I don't quite know why she's done this to you. Perhaps she was afraid of losing you."

"That's not true, Mother. We've been closer than ever since I convinced her to come home for good. It was I who was afraid of losing her when she went to Las Vegas."

"Don't be a fool, Richard. She never had any intention of divorcing you, not any of the times she pretended she did. Pity she didn't, instead of putting one impediment after another in your way. She doesn't want you out of her reach. Any moderately intelligent person could see how she operates. Unplanned pregnancies, psychotic behavior, alcoholism. My God! How much can you put up with?"

Richard's face darkened. "How much can I put up with? How much has *she*? Susan didn't wish for Katie's condition! What woman wouldn't have been on the verge of a breakdown when we took her child from her? What woman wouldn't have turned to drink or drugs or anything she could find to give her courage when we asked her to mouth a lot of embarrassing statements to protect the family name? Tell me, Mother, what woman wouldn't have long ago given up on a husband who couldn't keep his hands off of anything in skirts?"

Maria's voice was scornful. "I'll tell you one woman who wouldn't. *This* one." She let the words sink in. "You know some of the things I've gone through. But I had discipline and intestinal fortitude. I was willing to make sacrifices for your father and for all of you. I didn't think about my own precious 'happiness.' There were bigger things at stake. I knew that. Susan refuses to learn it and you refuse to hear what I've been saying for years. If you permit her to saddle you with another child, handicapped or not, you're a blind, spineless, unintelligent caricature of a man. You deserve to be tricked into fatherhood over and over again. You deserve to be bogged down with a domineering wife and a houseful of demanding children. Go ahead. Play father. Play devoted husband. But don't also expect to play genius. Those things don't go together."

As always, she could outtalk him, muddy his mind with reminders of the past and dire predictions of the future. She could make him feel small and foolish and inarticulate in the face of her strong opinions and facile phrases. He was so torn. Who was right? Who was wrong? Music was everything to him, he told himself. Far more than babies who were begun without his knowledge or consent. Babies who didn't hear or speak. He didn't need them. Why was he giving in so easily to Susan's idea of a "perfect marriage?" Damn her, anyway! Why was he talking himself into something he didn't want? He didn't have to. He was Richard Antonini.

Troubled, he walked slowly home, considering the things Maria had said. It was true. Susan hadn't consulted him on either conception. His children were as unwanted as he had been. And his wife had been a problem in so many ways. Defying him by bringing Katie home when she should have been left where she was, in a safe and secure atmosphere. That was wrong. It had always been wrong. Just as it had been wrong of her to constantly threaten to leave him, making him nervous. In his mind, she was responsible for those bad notices in Washington after the accident. Susan with

291

her accusations and her damned injured pride! He wouldn't be surprised if Paul knew what a bad influence she was on Richard's work. He'd probably seen the handwriting on the wall and left before he found himself handling a failure.

It was all irrational and meteoric, but disquieting thoughts grew from the seeds Maria had planted over the years. Hell, even yesterday's recording session had been a near-disaster. It had taken frustrating hours to complete, something that never used to happen. Normally, he would have sailed through it easily and confidently. But he'd faltered time and again, made errors a first-year student wouldn't have. And all because his mind was on what he'd learned the night before. He was full of fears about another child, full of resentment at Susan for doing this to him. He saw that now. Goddammit, the personal side of his life *was* interfering with the artistic one. That had to stop. His mother was right. The wife of an artist had to bear up under inconveniences and eccentricities. It was her job to nurture a special talent, not go to pieces under every damned little pressure, the way Susan had all their married life. Jacqueline and Mary Lou never gave Walter and Sergio the problems Susan gave him. His brothers hadn't chosen neurotic, unmanageable wives. Why had he? Why did he have to fall in love with a woman who wouldn't conform? No longer afraid of rejection, he felt suddenly determined. No more babies. No more giving in to Susan on things he didn't agree with. No more being used. If anyone did the using, it would be he.

The innocent victim of his rage was lying contentedly on a chaise, reading, when Richard barged into the bedroom. Susan looked up at him lovingly.

"Have a good visit, darling?"

He didn't answer. He was looking at her as though he hated her. The familiar knot in her stomach told her there was a storm brewing. She pretended not to notice his expression.

"How are your parents? Did you tell them our news?"

His voice came out as a vicious accusation. "Why do you always start a baby without asking me? I've been thinking about it. My first instinct was right. We can't have another child."

For a moment she was speechless. These past weeks had been so good. Even two nights ago he'd seemed reconciled to her pregnancy. True, he'd had doubts. But she'd thought they were momentary. Of course. Maria. She of the powerful influence, the insatiable jealousy. Maria had put her son into this new and terrible mood. She tried to answer quietly.

"What happened? I thought you were happy about the baby."

"You haven't answered my question. Why didn't you consult me?"

"You know why. I was afraid you'd say no. And I wanted to give you another child. One you could be close to. One who'd appreciate your artistry. It's as simple as that."

"Simple? Nothing with you is simple! You make decisions for both of us. You must have your own way, no matter how it affects me. You must raise a handicapped child yourself. You must be free of my family. You must make demands on me that destroy my concentration, drive me out of my mind with worry about your drinking and your mental state and your threats of divorce! And now this! Another 'simple pregnancy' you knew I wouldn't want. One that could produce another misfit!"

Angry counteraccusations rushed into her mind. What of his selfishness, his unfaithfulness, his lack of sensitivity to her needs? What of his weakness in the face of Maria's sick domination? She got up and closed the bedroom door. No need for the servants to hear this ugly quarrel. No need to broadcast their unhappiness. She stood quite still, looking at his flushed face, his wild, tormented eyes. How could he be so manipulated? And yet Maria could only light the fires of discontent. It was Richard who willingly warmed himself at the flames.

"Well?" he shouted. "Are you just going to stand there? Aren't you going to say anything?"

Her voice was almost a whisper. "What do you want me to say? That you're right? That everything wrong with our marriage is my fault?" She shook her head. "No. I take the blame for my share of our troubles, but I don't accept the picture you've painted. Any more than I accept your convenient forgetfulness of your part in our problems."

"Whatever I've done, you've made me crazy enough to do!"

She flinched. It was unreal. Perhaps he was a little crazy. Certainly he needed help. But he'd never understand that. Never admit such a need. God knows what Maria had said to get him worked up that way. No doubt she'd goaded him about losing his "manhood," allowing another child, implanting fears that all this "permissiveness" was somehow affecting his work and that he was letting his wife run his life. As though his mother didn't, Susan thought cynically. As though she hasn't always called the shots and still does.

"What is this all about?" Susan asked. "The baby will be all right. I know it will. Please, Richard, don't let your fears distort your thinking about us. We were doing so well. I was truly happy. I thought you were. I don't know what's been said to turn you so against me, but I don't believe you mean those things. I *can't* believe it. Darling, only you and I count in this. You and I and Katie and the new baby."

"No! You can't have this child. We can't risk it. I can't work with this worry in my mind. I knew that from the first, and when I talked to Mother . . ." He suddenly stopped. His voice faltered and he seemed to crumple. "All right, I know you think she has too much influence over me, but in this case she's right, Susan. You must have an abortion. Now, while it's still safe."

"An abortion?" she was incredulous.

"It's our only hope. You said it yourself: We were happy. But we'll never make it with this hanging over

294

our heads. Don't worry. We'll find a good man. There are plenty of them as long as you can afford the best. And we'll get the best."

"No."

He was genuinely amazed. "But you must! Haven't you heard anything I've said?"

"I heard *everything* you said, and the answer is still no. Because it doesn't make sense. I won't give up this child to pamper you, Richard. To free your mind and leave your concentration undisturbed. A human life means more than that to me. I'm not some poor, forsaken kid who has to get rid of a baby. I want this child and I'm going to have it. If you can't cope with that, then you're not the person with whom I choose to spend my life."

His anger turned to pleading. "Please, Susan. I know what you believe, but I can't feel the same. I want you, but not the terror of another seven months of wondering and fearing. I didn't mean those things I said about you. I know you've tried hard to make things work. You've been wonderful."

She laughed. "Wonderful? Hardly. I've been a damned fool, self-deceiving and masochistic. I'm sorry, Richard. Sorry for you. Sorry for myself. Sorry that we failed at something that could have been wonderful."

He was furious again. "Failed? I haven't failed! I'm not responsible!"

"No," Susan said. "That's just it. You never have been."

Chapter Twenty-three

Giovanni had not been present the day before when his wife and youngest son had the discussion that brought Richard and Susan close to the breaking point. He frowned when Maria reported the gist of it to him next morning over the breakfast table.

"Imagine!" she said. "That young woman deliberately getting pregnant again! And without letting Richard know what she planned! Unthinkable for them to have another child! So like her to use Richard's infatuation to make sure she holds him. It's the last straw among all the destructive things she's done! Never mind. I think I finally made him see her for what she is. There'll be no more unwanted babies in that household!"

He knew her so well. Without having heard the words he could imagine how she'd worked on Richard, played on his fears, made him feel the injured party, the innocent victim. She would have pulled out all the stops. And Richard, poor, weak Richard, probably went home full of righteous indignation and raised hell with that nice, patient girl. For all anyone knew, Maria's clever manipulation might have worked this time. She'd been hell-bent on destroying that marriage from the start, and from the satisfied look of her this morning, she may well have finally made it. There must be a limit to what Susan would take, Giovanni thought. He pretended to be oblivious of the "minor crises" within his family, but the maestro was more aware than he seemed. He knew the strain Susan had been under, was sure she'd thought more than once about chucking the whole thing. She wasn't like his other daughters-in-law, any more than his sons were like him. He felt uneasy, listening to Maria rattle on about how she'd "straightened out" Richard. The sensitivity that was so much a part of his nature told him that this was something to seriously worry about.

There was something else to worry about, too. Something he'd not told anyone, not even his wife. The "routine" prostate operation he'd had six months before had turned out not to be routine at all. He'd made the surgeon promise to tell him, and only him, if there was a malignancy. Giovanni felt there was. And he was right.

"But at your age," the doctor said, "it won't kill you. Try to forget about it. It's a slow process and, frankly, a man of your years probably will succumb to natural causes before this takes over. I don't mean to sound heartless, Mr. Antonini, but you are seventy-six years old, and at your time of life this kind of carcinoma is less dangerous than the inevitable passing of time. We think we have your problem under control, in any case. The side effects of your treatments should be minimal."

And they were. So minimal that he was able to keep the results of the biopsy from everyone. But Giovanni knew he did not have long to live. The knowledge did not particularly distress him. He had had his "glamour." Standing ovations from his audiences, slavish devotion from the men and women to whom his name was second only to God's. He'd had his share of beautiful women, good food and wine, satin sheets for his bed and silken words for his ego. He'd missed very little. He'd even had the outward appearance of a "perfect" family—a supportive wife, talented children, a gracious home in which they'd fostered the Antonini "dynasty."

He knew his dying would scarcely disrupt that home life. To call Maria "self-sufficient" was a gross under-

297

statement. And his children were self-confident and not, for that matter, so close to him that his passing would cause any deep and lasting grief. He had no need to worry about them. None except Richard, the only vulnerable one of the four. For all his selfishness, his outrageous conceit, this youngest son was the one for whom Giovanni felt most concern, as Maria did, but in a different way. She expressed her love by dominating, almost consuming, the late, unwanted child. Giovanni appeared unconcerned and remote, yet he recognized that Richard was not strong enough to make it alone. While Maria was alive, he could cling to her, defer to her, as he was doing now. But Maria would not live forever. Richard had instinctively chosen the right wife, the one he could depend on always, the one he needed now, even while his mother lived. Giovanni could not stand by silently and let his wife destroy Richard's future happiness and security. And there was so little time to save the boy from her.

Maria scarcely noticed the uneasy silence with which Giovanni received her account of this latest development in Richard's life. She was used to him, too. To his lack of response, his "ivory-tower disinterest" in the day-by-day emergencies. She knew him less well, though, than he knew her—a fact which would have surprised her considerably. She did not dream he cared deeply for his family, that he regretted nothing except having been a withdrawn and apparently unreachable "father figure" to his children. It was the only thing in his life he wished he'd done differently. But Maria's strength and, he admitted, his own selfishness had made it easier to abdicate parental responsibilities. He'd been the poorer for it. And so, he feared, had his sons and daughter.

It was too late to do anything about Sergio and Walter or Gloria. But there was still time to help Richard and Susan. Or at least still time to try.

He finished the last of his coffee and looked over at Maria, who was going through her mail.

"You don't think you might be meddling in Susan and Richard's lives with all this well-meant advice?"

She raised her eyes, surprised. "Meddling? What a peculiar word to use, Joe. Of course I'm not meddling. Richard always talks things over with me. He needs a sounding board. You don't think he'd have come here yesterday if he hadn't been concerned about his marriage, do you?"

"From what you said originally, I thought he came to tell you he was pleased about the baby."

"Nonsense! He was never pleased. That was simply an excuse to see me. He knows the trouble he's in. He needed reinforcement."

"Reinforcement for what?"

"For what he had to do about that headstrong girl, of course! To stop her from complicating their lives further with another child."

"That's true? You weren't making one last stab at breaking up that marriage?"

Maria's mouth tightened. "That's a stupid suggestion and you know it. I've never tried to destroy the marriage. I've only tried to make it acceptable for Richard."

"And what about Susan? Doesn't she matter?"

His wife sighed. "I can't think what's gotten into you this morning. What does Susan mean to you?"

"Quite a lot," Giovanni said mildly. "I think she's the best thing that ever happened to Richard."

Maria stared. "You must be getting senile! She's been unsuitable from the start!"

"To whom? To Richard or to you?"

Before she could answer, the maid announced that Mrs. Antonini was wanted on the telephone.

"It's Mr. Richard, madame."

Maria nodded and gave Giovanni a smug little smile of vindication. "I daresay he's going to tell me he asserted himself."

She was back in a few minutes, looking complacent. "I was right. Richard laid down the law to her and she's threatened to leave him. *Again.* She won't, of course, even though he's foolish enough to believe her.

299

He told her he didn't want the baby and she flatly refuses to have an abortion. Naturally, she will have one. She's not going to let go of a good thing like Richard."

"Isn't he terribly upset?"

Maria shrugged. "For the moment. But he'll get over it. He's a child himself. He can't see she's simply going through one of her acts."

"Are you sure she is?"

"Of course I'm sure. Joe, you don't understand devious people. You never have. You haven't a clue to how to handle things like this. I don't even know why I tell you about them. Leave this to me."

"When does Susan say she's going to leave?"

Maria shrugged. "I have no idea. Richard said something about their discussing it today. Presumably she expects him to make some financial arrangements for herself and Katherine. But what difference does it make? It's academic. She won't leave. She's played this same scene before. She was going to leave him after that business in Washington, and she didn't. She won't now. Not that I'd care, to tell you the truth. I've tried very hard to help Richard make his marriage work, but she's a stumbling block. The proverbial millstone. He could move better and faster without her and in his heart he knows it. But he's stubborn. Like all the Antoninis. He won't admit he's made a mistake, so the only thing he can do is make her see that he won't put up with all her nonsense. I think I got that across to him yesterday." She gave a self-satisfied little nod. "Yes, I think Miss Susan has finally realized that Richard won't knuckle under to her demands any longer."

Giovanni pushed his chair. "I'm going for my walk," he said. It was his habit to walk two carefully counted miles every morning after breakfast. It was his "thinking time," an hour when he could escape from everything, from the boredom of Maria's overorganized household, even from the work he loved. He enjoyed these solitary strolls. Sometimes he walked down Lexington Avenue, past rows of tacky boutiques and cut-rate drugstores, losing himself in the crowds of harried shoppers who didn't recognize him. He found the hustle and bustle somehow restful, liked the idea that he appeared to be just another elderly gentleman window-shopping in front of Alexander's. Sometimes he walked home by way of Third Avenue, passing the elbow-to-elbow movie houses where the "Ticket Holders Only" lines were forming for the noon performance. Who on earth went to the films at this hour? he wondered. Bored housewives? Salesmen who should have been making calls on customers? Out-of-work men who had nothing to do between job interviews? He was curious about a world that was not his, speculating on the people who stood at open-air counters eating hot dogs and pizzas, wondering who bought the ugly clothes and bad art and fake antiques in the shops that lined these avenues. Maria thought he was quite mad.

"How can you bear to be shoved around in the middle of that mess?" she'd ask when he told her the sights he'd seen. "It's become Coney Island! Hippies and freaks! For heaven's sake, Joe, can't you walk up Fifth Avenue and look at Central Park? Or Madison where at least the shops are chic?"

Sometimes he did take those more "respectable" routes. Once in a while he ambled along Park Avenue where there was nothing more interesting to look at than high-rent apartment houses and expressionless doormen, and where, unfortunately, well-dressed matrons sometimes stopped him to gush over his latest triumph at Philharmonic. He was always polite, but the "smarter areas" bored him. Trashy as they were, First, Second, Third and Lexington Avenues pulsed with life. Fifth, Madison and Park were sterile and "suitable."

As "suitable," he thought this morning, as Maria would like Susan to be. She'd like to see all the life taken out of that young woman. He winced at the unintentionally literal comparison. Maria wanted Susan to give up her unborn child, to be docile and proper in her role as Richard's wife. He wasn't surprised that

301

Susan would agree to none of that. She was not selfish, but she was proud and, in her own way, stubborn, too. As stubborn as Maria, really, and as strong. But with much more heart and much less arrogance.

I must help her, Giovanni thought again. For her sake and Richard's. I must get to them before Richard destroys everything by playing the ventriloquist's dummy, with Maria mouthing the words. But how? I can't openly tell Richard not to listen to his mother. I can't suddenly become a concerned father after all these years of tacit acceptance of Maria's child-rearing rules. Richard would never understand. But Susan would, if only I could get her alone.

As though something or someone was guiding his steps he found himself on East Sixty-third Street between Park and Lexington. Someone he knew lived on this block, but who? He stood for several moments gazing sightlessly at the Miró and Picasso prints in the window of Pocker's Picture Framing Store until it came to him. Paul Carmichael lived somewhere around here. He'd never been to Richard's former manager's apartment, didn't even know the exact address, but he was sure it was Sixty-third. Paul. Maybe Paul was the way to reach Susan. He'd always liked her, Giovanni knew. Sometimes he suspected that Paul was even a little in love with her. Perhaps that forbidden attraction was the reason he'd left Richard. In any case, Paul was a gentleman and he was Richard's friend, his *only* friend as far as Giovanni knew.

He found a public telephone booth on the corner and looked up Paul Carmichael in the directory. He was only three houses away. Not knowing what he was going to say, Giovanni dropped a dime in the slot and dialed the number.

Kate Fenton listened attentively as Paul told her the involved, incredible story. Every now and then she shifted the telephone to her other ear, holding it with her shoulder as she lit a cigarette. She said almost nothing as Paul talked for ten minutes, telling her what was happening to Susan and Richard, reporting Giovanni's surprising visit to him that morning, and now asking her help.

"The old man wants to get to Susan without Richard knowing it," Paul said. "He's determined not to let Maria wreck that marriage and he thinks he can help if he can talk to Susan alone. I don't know what his plan is, Kate. I'm not sure *he* knows. But he cares about Susan, as you and I do."

Kate heard the pain in his voice. Yes, you care, she thought. You always have.

"So Papa-Joe came to ask you to get Susan out of the apartment so he could talk to her."

"Yes," Paul said, "that was his original thought. But I explained that I wasn't the right one. If I called there, Richard might pick up the phone. Even Susan would wonder why I'd turned up after all these months. It seemed to me you were the logical person to get hold of her for Mr. Antonini. You're her dearest friend. You could tell her you wanted to see her right away and she'd come."

"Maybe she's already left," Kate said. "Maybe she's gone to her parents'. He could try getting hold of her there. Her mother might be a better go-between. I've been out of town on an assignment. Just got back this morning. I haven't spoken to Susan in weeks. My God, I didn't even know she was pregnant!"

"I don't think she could have left yet, from what Mr. Antonini tells me. I'm sure she means to, but she's sensible enough not to walk out until she knows Katie and the new baby will be provided for. And that will take some wrangling with Richard. She probably will try to pin down the arrangements quickly, but Richard will stall. I don't know if the maestro can save the day, but he thinks he can, and he's damned determined to try! Surprising old bastard, isn't he? We always had the idea he never thought of anyone but himself."

"Surprising is hardly the word. Stunning is more like

303

it. But I wonder if he's right. I wonder if that rocky marriage *should* be saved. Susan might be better off without it." Kate paused. "Seems to me you're being pretty unselfish about all this, Paul."

He knew what she meant. It must have been obvious to everybody how he felt about Susan. How he still felt. And he'd thought no one suspected. Kate did. So did Giovanni. He supposed Susan knew. I must be a lousy actor, he thought. Evidently I don't have a sleeve big enough for the heart I carry on it.

"I care about Susan. *And* Richard," he said carefully. "But I'm something of a fatalist, Kate. If things are to be, they'll be."

She snorted. "If you really believed that, you'd stay the hell out of this, as you should. As *I* should. But we won't, of course. I don't have any more sense than you. All right, I'll call her. What's the plot?"

"Ask her to meet you for lunch today. Your apartment. Mr. Antonini will be there. He's calling me back in thirty minutes to see if that works out."

"I think we've all gone crazy," Kate said. "Do you really think a woman who's about to move out bag and baggage is going to stop in the middle of everything to keep a lunch date?"

"I think Susan will. Especially with you. She probably is desperate to talk to someone, and you're the only candidate. I'm sure she needs you a lot right now. She'll come. I'd bet my life on it."

Kate sighed. "Okay. I'll get back to you." She lit another cigarette, swiveled around in her desk chair and stared pensively out the window at the New York skyline. What a mess! That bloody Richard and his rotten, scheming mother. Poor Susie. What will happen to her next? The last time they talked was just after her return from Vegas, just before Kate left on assignment. Susan had confessed about what's-his-name, Tanner. She'd been remorseful, unnecessarily swearing Kate to secrecy, terribly ashamed of what she'd done. And yet she'd seemed more relaxed. Purged, somehow. She'd said she was determined to make a go of it with

Richard, that she honestly felt they'd both changed. She'd seemed more in control of herself, more optimistic than she'd been in a long while. But, Kate thought ruefully, she must have carried that euphoria too far. Pregnant! Dear Lord, how did she dare? For a moment, she had the sinking fear that this child might be the product of that fling in Vegas. No. Susan was such an honest little idiot she'd have stupidly told Richard if that were the case. And from what Paul said, that was not the reason Susan was being pressed to have an abortion. It was simply Richard's "normal fears." And Maria's, of course. Kate was the only one who knew about Tanner.

With a heavy heart, she made her phone call. A subdued but grateful-sounding Susan said yes, she'd love to come for lunch. She had a lot to tell her. Kate didn't say she already knew.

Fortunately for Giovanni, Maria had left the house when he returned from his walk. He breathed a sigh of relief. He never went out for lunch. How would he have explained this mysterious appointment? He told the servants he wasn't hungry and wouldn't take his usual one o'clock meal. He'd be working in his study and didn't wish to be disturbed. He closed himself into the quiet room and thought of what he'd say to Susan. What would convince her not to leave Richard? He was not an eloquent man, but he'd have to find the words. They were there, in his heart, if only he could use them to reach Susan's own.

The subject of all their thoughts sipped vodka and tonic as she dressed to meet Kate. It had been a terrible morning. First thing, she'd been sick to her stomach. Odd. She'd never had morning sickness with Katie. Nerves, of course. She'd hardly slept all night.

She lay awake on the "emergency bed" in Katie's room, the one kept there in case Bridie needed to be near her charge. She'd been afraid to move for fear of waking the child, not realizing at the time how absurd that was. Katie without her hearing aids could not have been disturbed by a herd of elephants. Sometimes I forget, Susan thought. She seems so complete to me that I forget.

She wondered if the new baby would be all right. It worried her more now, knowing she'd be having it alone, knowing she'd have the sole responsibility of raising and educating two children. She'd tried to talk to Richard about that this morning, but he'd brushed her off and left the house. She couldn't go until they decided the financial things. She wanted nothing for herself, but Katie's care was frighteningly expensive. She'd never been able to earn enough to support the private schools and the therapist and all the things the little girl had to have. And what if, God forbid, the second one needed the same help? She could stay with her parents until she had her baby, but then she'd have to get a job. Could she go back to *Vogue?* Could she afford to? Realistically, she had little choice. She was trained for nothing but magazine work and it would be hard to make ends meet on the salary she'd probably earn, but she'd have to. Even if she had to ask Bea and Wil to let the three of them and Bridie stay in Bronxville indefinitely. Her parents would be more than willing, of course, but it would be a tight squeeze, taking four more people into the house. It would be hard on everybody, getting Katie into town for her lessons, caring for the infant, to say nothing of paying Bridie's salary. Richard would *have* to help. She'd force him to, even if it took "blackmail" in the form of threatened sordid publicity.

She shuddered. It could all be so easily solved. She could agree to the abortion, forget the terrible things Richard had said, try for a marriage as loveless and "sensible" as Jacqueline's and Walter's. But it would be total prostitution of everything she believed in. An empty, let's-pretend life.

She fixed another drink, even while she was thinking she should take it easy. If anyone had dared suggest she was an alcoholic, she would have vehemently denied it. She wouldn't admit her drinking was a form of escape, a necessary buffer against life's rough edges. She was convinced she could give it up completely. Hadn't she drunk practically nothing for the few weeks when she thought everything was all right between her and Richard? Didn't that prove she wasn't hooked? Anyone in her present situation would need something to bolster them. She was about to end her marriage, to start over with Katie and a baby whose father didn't want it. And incredibly, no matter what he did, she was in love with her husband. There seemed to be no way she could stop loving him. It was a sickness for which she had no cure.

Thank God Kate had called. There was ESP between them. Kate was the one person she could talk openly to; the friend who understood and invariably sensed when she was needed. She hadn't been appalled or disapproving when Susan told her about Martin Tanner. Not as Bea Langdon would have been. Mother would have forgiven me and tried to understand, Susan thought, but she couldn't be analytical and unemotional about her own child. No mother could be. I'm not. Not about the one I have or the one I'm going to have.

Kate had been matter-of-fact about the Tanner affair. All she'd said was, "You had to get it out of your system, kiddo. It was a way of paying Richard back. You realize that, don't you? Put it out of your mind. I assume you're never going to see Tanner again."

"Of course not. He doesn't even know my real name."

Kate had nodded. "Leave it that way. It was immoral, sure. Wrong, probably. But maybe it will help you understand how these things can happen to the best of wives. *And* husbands."

She'd felt better after their talk, more loving toward Richard. Too loving, she thought bitterly, thinking of the child she'd meant to be a special gift. What will Kate say when I tell her what's happened? What do I expect her to say?

She was a little drunk when she arrived at Kate's duplex penthouse on East Fifty-second Street. She'd always loved this crazy little "upside-down" apartment with its big, fabric-draped bedroom on the lower floor and its small, chic living room at the top of the curving staircase. She smiled, remembering her amazement the first time she saw it. "It's topsy-turvy!" she'd said. "Bedrooms are supposed to be upstairs and living rooms *down!*"

"I know. Whimsical, isn't it? But there's a valid point. The big terrace with the view is upstairs. That's why the living room is there, for the view."

It was a spectacular view. The apartment faced the East River on one side, the United Nations building on another and the jagged outlines of the Empire State and Chrysler buildings on the third. It was designed to make guests gasp with pleasure.

The friends hugged as Kate opened the door.

"I'm *so* glad to see you!" Susan said.

"Me too. There's someone else who's anxious to see you. Come on upstairs."

"Someone else?" Susan was disappointed. "Who?"

"A friend of yours."

Giovanni was waiting at the top of the stairs, his handsome face serious but his eyes full of sympathy.

"Papa-Joe?" Susan was incredulous. "What are *you* doing here?"

"I'm afraid we tricked you, but I had to talk to you, away from the family. Miss Fenton was kind enough to arrange it."

"With Paul Carmichael's help," Kate said.

Susan looked from one to the other. "What is this all about? You and Kate plotting? And Paul? I don't understand."

308

"Come and sit down and I'll try to explain," Giovanni said.

Kate gave her a little shove. "I'll be downstairs if you need me." She patted Susan's arm. "We'll talk later. Right now, Mr. Antonini has a few things to say to you."

Obediently, Susan took one of the big chairs at the fireplace. Giovanni faced her in its twin.

"There are things you should know, Susan," he began. "Things that I hope will make you reconsider your decision to leave Richard."

"Papa-Joe!" Susan was incredulous. "What are *you* doing here?"

"Hush, please, dear Susan. Hear me out before you make up your mind. I love you very much, you know. As much as I love my son. That's why we must talk together. Like loving people."

And so he began.

Chapter Twenty-four

Susan was never to forget that afternoon in Kate's apartment, an hour that ultimately started a whole new chain of events.

She'd always been fond of her father-in-law. For all his fame, he was a lonely man, taken for granted and virtually ignored by his family. At first, his lack of involvement in their activities puzzled her, but eventually she decided he was above competition, that he didn't care to be part of the plots and counterplots that swirled around him. The only conversational area in which he showed any animation was that of music. Here, his was the voice of authority and he enjoyed holding forth. In other areas he seemed to be a man of intellectual narrowness, with no interest in worldly affairs and little insight into the behavior of others.

That day she learned how wrong she'd been. Giovanni was attuned to the complexities of people, surprisingly tolerant and analytical. He proved to be a clever man and, as he'd said, a loving one.

"I've come here to beg you not to leave Richard," he said bluntly. "I know something of what's been going on and I can guess at the rest. His mother wants only what she honestly believes is best for him but sometimes her judgment works against the boy. Unfortunately, he's easily influenced by her. Always has been. You know that better than anyone, of course. But perhaps you don't know the basis of her extraordinary hold on him, the simple thing that motivates some of his reactions and makes him so pathetically insecure."

Susan looked at him curiously. "Richard insecure? Immature, perhaps, but insecure?" She smiled sadly. "I'd hardly call him that."

"I know. But it's true. As it's true of anyone who discovers he was an unwanted child."

The words came slowly from Giovanni's tightly set lips. Susan stared at him for a long moment.

"Unwanted? You didn't want him? I can't believe that. But even if it's so, how did he find out?"

"His mother told him long ago." Giovanni's voice was bitter as he related the events of that long-ago New Year's Eve. "Maria and I had not lived as husband and wife for years until that night. She was repelled, and I suppose rightly, by my infidelities. But that night there was champagne and sentiment and perhaps a kind of anger in me. In any case, Maria acquiesced, but in her memory of it, she was raped. Or, at least, tricked. So, Richard was conceived, twelve years after Maria thought she'd had her last child. It's a

310

paradox. She loves Richard more than any of her children, yet she's never forgiven me for siring him. What she really hates, of course, is herself, for having been vulnerable enough to forget her 'principles' for one passionate moment. It was the first, and probably the last, time she was not completely in control of her own feelings."

"But I don't understand why she would tell Richard such a thing." Susan was horrified. "Who'd tell a child he wasn't wanted? Who'd be so cruel, and for what purpose?" In her agitation she went to the bar and poured another drink. "Make something for you?" Giovanni shook his head, waiting until she sat down again. Then he answered her question.

"I've wondered that same thing over all these years. I'm not a student of psychology, but I've thought a great deal about it. I believe telling him was my wife's way of getting back at me for that night. Letting Richard know he was an 'accident' has somehow made him feel apologetic about being alive. It's kept him from loving me as I love him. When a child knows his father was unfaithful for years and then 'seduced' his mother and conceived him out of lust, what could he feel except resentment? He's felt, all his life, the need to please Maria as though he owed her something. His anger at me has been her revenge, and his 'guilt' her weapon. She uses it to this day to make Richard do anything she wants."

"That's insane!" Susan said. "I could understand a child feeling irrational guilt if his mother died giving birth to him. I could even see how he might hate his father. But to feel those things because he was conceived in a careless moment? No. I can't believe it. Richard's too bright for that."

"The brightest people get caught in emotional traps, especially when they're up against a clever woman like Maria, who knows how to subtly play on a feeling of 'obligation.' Of course, it's insane! Logically, Richard knows his mother is a strong woman who doesn't need protection. He also knows that if it hadn't been for my

311

'selfishness' that particular night he wouldn't even be here! But he isn't logical where this matter is concerned. He's always been more bound to her than the other children. His brothers and sister defer to her, but in the end they are independent. Only Richard feels obliged to make up for something that was done years ago, as though he needed to justify his existence by pleasing her in every way. He's never been allowed to forget the infidelities that were a prelude to the circumstances of his birth. There's that, too. He's outraged by the attraction women have always had for me." Giovanni smiled. "And, of course, vice versa."

Susan's head began to reel from the several drinks she'd had and from the strange story her father-in-law told. She had a sudden sharp pain in her stomach. She winced and ignored it. "But in many ways he's imitated you," she said. "He's been unfaithful over and over, as you admit you were. He once even forced himself on me, and much more literally than you did on Mrs. Antonini. He attracts women and responds to them. Papa-Joe, he's more like you than any of your children!"

"Exactly. But he doesn't see that. Or doesn't wish to. He can't admit he shares my craving for admiration, a need that leads us into meaningless outside relationships. He won't face the fact that we're both easily influenced by others, or that we have the same God-awful feeling that we don't deserve our success." The old man sighed. "Yes, he's very like me, Susan, except that I don't carry his burden. I was not an unwanted child. At least, if I was I never knew it."

"I still don't understand." Susan's words were a little slurred. The pains were worse now. They were coming steadily. "Why is he so angry with me because I'm going to have a baby? He seemed happy at first. As he was with Katie. Now he wants me to have an abortion. And he isn't really close to Katie. He's tried, but he can't accept her because she isn't perfect, and he doesn't want this one because he's afraid it won't be perfect either. I've told him there's practically no risk. I only want to give him a child he can love."

Giovanni realized she was quite drunk. If she hadn't been, she'd have seen the point of his story. Slowly, patiently, he tried to sum it up.

"Susan, my dear, listen carefully. Richard was happy about both children until Maria pointed out to him that he had no part in planning either of them. To him, they represent the same kind of unwanted child he was. He blames you for 'forcing' them on him, just as I 'forced' him on Maria. He sees it as her life in reverse. He's unconsciously identifying with his mother. She's made him feel that in the conception of your children he was used—that he was not in control, as my wife was not in control years ago. She's told you are conniving, selfish, and devious, and reminded him that once again you took a major step without his permission. She has practically insulted his manhood, making him feel tricked, as she felt tricked. It's sad. He was just at the point of learning to love his first 'unplanned child' when you presented him with the fact of another."

"But why does Mrs. Antonini do this? Why does she hate me so?"

"She doesn't hate you. No more than she'd hate any woman Richard loved. She simply refuses to give up her hold on him."

Susan refilled her empty glass. Maybe another drink would help the pains go away. "It's hopeless, isn't it? I'm right in knowing I have to leave him."

"No," Giovanni said, "it isn't hopeless. There's time to make it right. Richard loves you. He loves you so much he took his first defiant steps because of you. He married you in spite of everything Maria tried to do. He left home because you wanted it. He's managed more independence of action in the past eight years than he's ever shown in his life. You've won most of your battles, whether you realize it or not. But you can't win when you strike at the very thing that has always eaten at Richard. You cannot have this child or

313

any other you don't plan with him. It comes down to that."

Her eyes widened. "You, too? You think I should have an abortion?"

He answered reluctantly. "Yes. I hate the thought of it. Even more, I hate the irrational reason for it. But it's there, and it won't go away. You're young. You can have more children. Babies you *and* Richard decide to have. But not this one. This one will destroy your marriage." He paused. "And, selfishly, I know that will destroy my son."

"But he doesn't want me! All the cruel things he said . . ."

Giovanni shook his head. "You didn't hear Richard. You heard his mother. He's the product of the last person he talks to. Especially if that person is my wife. Didn't he apologize? Didn't he swear he didn't mean the accusations he must have made?"

She nodded miserably.

"I'm sure he regretted his outburst. He always regrets them. He's telling the truth. He doesn't see you as Maria does. He loves you, Susan, and I beg you to help him."

"I can't. I can't get rid of my baby." Suddenly she was angry. "Why should I? What about me? Haven't I some rights?"

"Of course you have. But you and Richard have time to set things straight. Unfortunately, I haven't." He hesitated. "I didn't want to use emotional blackmail, Susan. I hoped I could convince you without asking a personal favor, but I'm reduced to anything that will save my boy. I'm dying. And I can't die knowing my son's life has been ruined by this madness of his mother's. I can't abandon him to her. When you came along, I thanked God. I thought, He's all right now. He won't be a lifelong penitent with no will of his own. But if you leave him, Susan, his mother will own him again, body and soul, as she did before. He'll be a great man but a lonely, useless one."

Susan heard the words, but everything was overshadowed by the hideous knowledge that Giovanni was dying. The shock momentarily sobered her.

"You can't! You can't die! What do you mean you're dying?"

"Hush! Miss Fenton will hear. I don't want anyone to know. I've known for some months that I have cancer, but I've told no one. I don't plan to tell anyone. I wouldn't have told you, except that I'm a desperate, bumbling old man trying to do one last, good thing." He sighed. "It's too bad you're not a different sort of woman. This would have been so easy if I could just have offered you a million dollars to stay with Richard. But you can't be bought. I know that. And still I'm not above trying to buy you by appealing to your compassion. It's the only thing I want: to die in peace knowing the children I love are safe. I'll go to any lengths for that."

She stared at him. "But you won't tell them? You won't let them be close to you for whatever time is left? That's selfishness, not love. You must tell them. They deserve to know."

"For what? So they can pity me? So they can pretend at long last to love me? I haven't earned their love. Why should I expect the obligatory gentleness and concern one shows a dying man? No. You must keep my secret. That kind of dutiful devotion is ugly. As ugly as disease. More ugly than death itself."

She wanted to cry for this lonely man, trying to put things in order before the cancer killed him. Too proud to seek comfort. Too frightened, perhaps to talk about it.

"You must tell the family," Susan repeated. "You think they don't love you, but they do. It's only that you're so withdrawn. You've made yourself unapproachable. Give them a chance to show how much you mean to them, how important you are to all their lives. Please. I beg you. Don't be unfair."

"Unfair?" Giovanni managed a smile. "When have I been known for my fairness? What good would it do

315

for them to know? It would only be a burden and it wouldn't help me."

"I think it *would* help you. I think you'd see you have the affection you've always wanted."

He wavered. "I'm not sure. I suppose I really don't know my own children very well. I've always been too busy or too preoccupied to think much about them since they've been grown. Only Richard. Because he was the baby. And at home." He looked at her with pathetic eagerness. "You think they care? You honestly think they love me?"

"I know it."

"Well, we'll see. Right now I'm more concerned with you and Richard."

She looked away from him. "I'll stay with Richard. I'll have the abortion."

"I'm grateful," he said slowly, "and ashamed. You're a fine young woman. A good person. Maybe too good. It's wrong of me to ask this of you, knowing you wouldn't refuse."

It was she who was ashamed. She wasn't good in her own eyes. She was difficult. She drank too much. She'd never been the kind of "professional wife" a performer needed. She'd even broken her marriage vows. Oh, she could make excuses for all those things. She could blame them on the shabby treatment she'd had from Richard and most of his family. On the fact that she'd never felt needed. But that wouldn't wash. What she'd done she'd done out of weakness or willfulness or both. She had reacted like a human who'd been hurt. But that didn't excuse her. And it certainly didn't deserve praise.

"I'm not staying because of you, Papa-Joe. I'm staying because I love my husband."

Giovanni accepted the half-truth. "Thank you for that, Susan. Thank you for everything. I know the sacrifices you're making. I'm sorry."

There was a lump in her throat. Why you? Why does it have to be you who's going to die?

He kissed her hand and turned to slowly descend the

316

stairs. He seemed old and fragile, a man who felt himself a failure despite all his success. For a moment, Susan wondered whether it was all a clever ploy. Could Giovanni have made up this extraordinary tale just to keep her from leaving Richard? No. It was too bizarre to have been invented. She suspected even Richard did not know how deep his guilts and resentments went. Her husband was not an introspective person. She felt sure he'd never come to grips with the obsession Maria had instilled and nurtured over the years. In this area he was, as his father said, a "penitent," a robot programmed for remorse. Why does Giovanni think I can save him? she wondered. Why do I even try? Is Richard's future worth trading for the life I'm going to destroy? Why did I agree to an abortion and another try at this marriage? Because a pitiful, dying man asked it of me? Or because, deep down, I know I shouldn't bring an unwanted child into the world? Am I punishing myself for my own mistakes?

She was so mixed up. So utterly lost in a world that was more than she could cope with. The Antoninis are selfish and heartless, she thought. Even Giovanni, using the sentimental, vulnerable side of her nature. Damn them all! Damn Richard for ever coming into her life. Damn the conscience and, yes, the love and pity that kept her from walking away from him. Damn her own stupidity!

She heard Kate bidding Giovanni goodbye at the front door, heard her friend climb the stairs to where Susan stood looking at the afternoon sun coloring the tips of the spires of St. Patrick's Cathedral. I wish I were a religious person, Susan thought. I wish I could ask God for help and believe I'd receive guidance and absolution. The pains were more intense now. She clutched her stomach, almost bent double with each spasm. She straightened up. What were these violent cramps that came and went with the ferocity of labor pains? She turned and saw Kate staring at her.

"You knew, didn't you?" Susan asked. "You knew the whole story before I got here."

317

"Some of it. Paul told me everything Giovanni told him." She explained how the meeting had been arranged. "So where do you go from here?"

"Back to square one." Susan laughed mirthlessly. "Back to Richard and his family and Katie. Back to a life that's totally pointless." It was her turn to explain. She told Kate everything. How she'd been touched by Richard's nervous efforts to be a father to Katie. How she'd believed she could make him happy with another child. How hideously it had all backfired because of Richard's twisted, unshakable beliefs. "And now Giovanni's dying," she said. "Dying in anguish over his son's future if I leave him. I promised him I wouldn't." Her voice was flat and hopeless. "I told him I'd get rid of the baby. That I wouldn't have another one unless Richard and I planned it together." She was quite drunk now. "Richard thinks I used him!" She giggled. "Isn't that insane? My God! I only wish I were smart enough to!"

Kate watched her carefully. Susan was on the verge of hysterics. Drunken hysterics. She literally staggered as she started toward the bar.

"I hate to be a nag," Kate said quietly, "but don't you think you ought to lay off that stuff? You look terrible. Are you all right?"

Susan unsteadily poured a stiff drink. "Not to worry. I can handle it."

"I wouldn't say so. Susan, that isn't going to do any good. Booze won't solve your problems. You've got to keep a clear head. Sit down. Let's talk. I don't know whether you want to leave Richard, but I'm damned sure you don't want an abortion. It's your body. You have a right to do with it what you want; not give in to Richard's wishes or even let a clever old man twist you around his finger. Has it occurred to you that Giovanni may be using you? Maybe he'd like you to stay with Richard just to spite Maria. Who knows how these people think? He's got to harbor a lot of resentment toward her, Susan. Maybe he's the opposing force, try-

318

ing to keep the marriage together because he knows she wants it to come apart."

Another searing pain shot through Susan and this time she cried out. She wanted to tell Kate she'd rejected that idea. Richard's father was good. He loved his son. But she couldn't speak for the hot, grinding agony in her stomach.

"Susan! What is it?" Kate sounded frightened.

"I . . . I don't know. Terr . . . terrible pain." She held onto the edge of the bar. The room spun around. And then it was all black.

She awoke wondering where she was. It was an unfamiliar room, a hard, narrow bed. She remembered the spasmodic cramps and a feeling of something warm and sticky between her legs. She supposed she'd fainted. She opened her eyes wider and saw the gentle, concerned face of her mother.

"Hello, darling," Bea said. "How do you feel?"

"Awful."

"I'm sure. You had a dreadful experience, but you're all right."

"What happened?"

"A miscarriage, sweetheart. Kate got an ambulance and brought you to Doctors Hospital. I'm sorry, Susie." Bea looked as though she'd been weeping. "It's terrible to lose a baby, but thank God you're all right."

"God takes care of drunks and fools."

"Don't talk like that." Bea hesitated. "Maybe it was a bad seed. Maybe it wasn't meant to be born."

Susan turned her head away wearily. "No, I'm sure it wasn't."

"It happens that way sometimes, you know. It's nature's way of solving a problem, making sure you couldn't go full term with a . . ."

Susan interrupted her. "Don't, Mother! Please. It's gone and I'm glad. I don't want to talk about it. Where's Dad?"

319

"Just down the hall, with Richard and Kate. We've been waiting for you to wake up." She tried to smile. "You took long enough, I must say. Shall I send Richard in now?"

"No. Kate first."

Bea didn't understand any of this. How could Susan be glad about the miscarriage? Why didn't she want to see her husband at this sad moment? But apparently it wasn't sad. Bea didn't know what was happening, but she didn't question her child. She did say, "All right. As you like. But Richard's been so worried . . ."

"Kate, please, Mother." Richard worried? Hardly. He must be delighted. Everything always works out for him, Susan thought. Even this. I wonder if it's possible to subconsciously will a miscarriage? Maybe I did, to avoid the abortion. What would Dr. Marcus say about such a neat solution? As she waited for Kate, Susan decided the whole thing was an analyst's delight: Richard's brainwashing by his mother; Giovanni's "dying request"; the miscarriage of a fetus nobody except herself had ever wanted. How much of our destinies do we control? she wondered. How much can we make happen?

"Susie?" Kate's voice was anxious. "You okay?"

She turned. "I'm fine."

"Well, I feel like killing myself! I shouldn't have been so rough on you. I didn't know you were in agony."

"You couldn't know, Kate. I didn't know, myself, what was happening when it started, long before you began giving me hell. I had pains while I was talking to Papa-Joe, but I thought it was nothing serious." She half-smiled. "It could easily have been the beginning of an ulcer. Seems to me I'm ripe for one between the aggravation and the drinking." Susan turned serious. "You were wrong about Papa-Joe, though. He wasn't using me. He really cares."

"I'm sure. You know me. Given to half-baked theories. Anyway, my dear, sad as it is, you no longer have the problem of an unwanted child. I suppose it's for the best. You can have others. The doctor told us so."

There was no humor in Susan's voice. "That must have thrilled Richard."

Kate didn't answer.

"I've been lying here wondering whether I could have willed it. Do you suppose I actually provoked an act of God?"

"No. It was nobody's fault, Susan."

"I suppose not. Nothing ever is. Thank you for taking care of me, Kate. I'm grateful to you. I'm always grateful to you."

Richard took her home two days later. In the hospital they spoke only briefly of the miscarriage and, as though by tacit agreement, they did not discuss the implications of the loss of the child. At least, Susan thought, he's not hypocritical enough to say he's sorry. I don't think I could forgive him that.

Her husband was gentle and affectionate, seeing that she was tucked safely into their big bed, bringing Katie in to hug her mother, making Susan promise that she'd take it easy. There was no talk of the ugly quarrel that preceded all this. No discussion of her leaving. It was as though Richard took it for granted they'd pick up their life together in the way he wanted it.

She told him nothing of her conversation with Giovanni. It was obvious he didn't know his father had been at Kate's, just as it was apparent he knew nothing of the man's illness. Susan wondered when, or if, Giovanni would do as she asked. Maybe he won't tell them, she thought. He hadn't really said he would; only that he'd think it over. What difference did it make? What difference did anything make these days? She felt as empty and as fragile as a shell, emotionally drained, too defeated by the circumstances of her life to do more than go through the motions of living.

It was strange. She tried not to think about the baby she'd lost. Most of the time it seemed as though it had never happened, and yet there were moments when she wondered what it would have been. A handsome, gifted boy like Richard? A happy, carefree little girl like Susan had been? Or would it have been another Katie—mute and pathetic, another "bad seed?"

When such thoughts came to her, she reached almost automatically for a drink. But she was drinking less these days. Only at the really bad moments did she escape into the blessed fog of liquor, for though she had no real will to assume her old life, she knew she would. She'd promised Giovanni she'd stay with Richard and she meant to keep that promise as long as the old man lived. In truth, she wanted to stay. Crazily, she still hoped they could recapture the happiness they'd once had. And there was Katie. Katie was her real reason for being.

Despite the emptiness inside her, she forced herself back to something near normalcy. Her sexual relationship with Richard resumed in a more stable, even a more meaningful way. For now she knew his secret and she was able to be tender with him, understanding, though he did not know she did, the awful demon that plagued him. She was glad Giovanni had told her. It made many things that were once strange and infuriating explainable. She felt sorry for Richard, driven by his guilt. She could even halfway pity Maria for her twisted outlook, though she could never forgive her for what that warped vengeance had done to her son and her husband, nor what the woman's scheming mind still wished to do to her son's marriage.

As Susan regained her strength, she resumed her role as wife, hostess, mother. She made the proper appearances, gave the little dinner parties attended by the "right people," shared Richard's pleasure when such events produced favorable newspaper publicity. And all the while, she waited for Giovanni to keep his part of the "bargain."

It was two more months before they were summoned to the Senior Antoninis', all the children and those they'd married. It was a 'no excuses accepted' invitation for 9 P.M. issued that morning on the phone by a strangely subdued-sounding but very firm Maria.

322

"Mother, we can't make it," Sergio had said. "We're going to a sitdown dinner at the Leonard Bernsteins'."

"Cancel," Maria said tersely. "And don't ask questions."

"I'm leading the Hunt at the crack of dawn tomorrow," Gloria protested. "We can't come all the way in town tonight!"

"You can and you will."

"What's this all about?" Walter asked. "Sounds like a command performance."

"That's exactly what it is," Maria answered.

"Darling, if it's about Susan and me, everything's fine," Richard said.

"It's not about you, except indirectly. I don't wish to explain, Richard, but all the family will be here."

He'd hung up puzzled. "What the hell do you think that's all about? Mother's demanding a tribal powwow. No notice at all. I wonder what's up."

Susan didn't answer; she knew. He's finally told Maria and now he's going to tell them all, just as he promised. She felt heartsick, knowing what lay ahead. How would Papa-Joe handle it? With calm and dignity, she answered herself. Please let them respond as I assured him they would. Please let them come out of their selfish shells to be loving children. Don't make him wish he hadn't told them.

It had been a long while since she'd been in the house on East Seventieth Street, but nothing had changed. It was exactly the way it had always been, the way it was the first day Susan ever saw it as a quite nervous magazine writer come to interview the famous young pianist. More than seven years ago, she thought. What dramas we've lived through since those rose-colored days!

They were all prompt. Maria insisted upon that. Always had. "To keep others waiting is an insult, as though you think their time is less precious than yours." Susan had heard her say it more than once in the course of "schooling" her grandchildren in the conduct of "ladies and gentlemen." It was one of the few things she and Maria agreed on. Susan hated to be kept waiting, too. She knew enough psychiatry to know tardiness was a sign of hostility. At two minutes past nine, the eight adults were seated in the drawing room. One minute later, Giovanni and Maria came in.

She looks more ill than he does! Susan thought. For the first time she honestly felt that this cool, distant woman loved her husband, within the bounds of her capability to love. She must be devastated, knowing she's going to lose him. Theirs was a strange marriage by ordinary standards, but there were more than fifty years of shared memories, good and bad, mutually enjoyed or endured. It must be like losing part of yourself. Even a part you unthinkingly accepted on a day-by-day basis. Maria was not weeping, but she looked infinitely sad, and in the only clinging gesture they'd ever seen her make, she held tightly to Giovanni's hand. There was not a sound in the room as they entered, a far cry from the usual babble.

Giovanni seemed unusually tender toward his wife, seating her courteously in a chair before he turned his face to his silent "audience."

"You're very sensitive people," he said without preamble. "You know your mother and I have something serious to say, so I will be quick to say it." He cleared his throat. "I've known for some time that I have cancer."

There was an almost simultaneous intake of breath from his children, a shocked, horrified response to the bald words. Susan saw Jacqueline's eyes fill with tears, Mary Lou's mouth fall open in surprise, Gloria wince as though she'd been struck. "The boys" made no motion, but terror was written on their faces. Terror and a kind of stunned disbelief.

"I hadn't planned to tell anyone," Giovanni went on. "Not even your mother. I'm the product of a generation that was almost ashamed of having cancer. In my

324

day, we didn't speak of it. Perhaps we superstitiously hoped that by not talking about it it would cease to exist. But mostly it was a kind of disgrace." He smiled. "I guess you'd say it wasn't an 'elegant' disease. Anyway, that's the way I was brought up and that's the way I'd intended to handle it. But something happened to make me see how wrong and selfish of me that was." He carefully did not look at Susan. "Someone made me realize that you, my dearest ones, had a right to know. And that I had an obligation to tell you.

"I haven't been a 'model father' and because of that you've not been 'model children.' I wish we'd been closer, more outgoing toward one another. I wish we'd been able to share things. I wish I could have helped you more. My fault. My choice, really. But I've loved each and every one of you—my children since the days of your happily awaited births, my children-by-marriage since you honored us by becoming part of the family. You make me proud, as your mother makes me proud. I respect you as I do her. Life owes me nothing. All I've hoped for and dreamed of has come true in you—in your talents, your grace and your beauty."

He looked slowly, tenderly at each of them in turn. "Don't be sad," he said. "God has been good to me. Exceptionally good. Possibly better than I deserve."

The silence that followed seemed interminable. Susan closed her eyes. Why doesn't someone say something? Don't his children realize how hard this is for him, how much courage it took to even discuss it? What are they thinking? That he should have told each of them privately? Are they being competitive even at a time like this? Or are they reacting as he was afraid they would: repelled by disease, denying their father's death because it brought them one step closer to the inevitability of their own? How would I feel if it were my own father standing there telling me he was going to die?

In the end, it was not "one of his own" who spoke first. Jacqueline finally asked softly, "How long do we have, Joe?"

"We," she'd said. Susan blessed her for that. Not "How long do *you* have?" Jacqueline was doing what her sister-in-law hoped; telling this almost diffident-sounding man that they wanted to share every moment that was left.

Giovanni shrugged. "The doctors think it could be quite a while. They think old age will get me before the cancer does. That seems highly possible." It was said lightly, but his tone told them he didn't believe it. "In any case, the odds are in my favor. I'm playing on the Lord's money, so to speak. I passed my limit long ago. From here on, it's poverty poker in this game."

Susan looked up, startled. Why on earth was Joe using the jargon of gamblers, a manner of speaking totally foreign to him? For a crazy moment he sounded like Martin Tanner, using the slang of the casino. She realized he was looking directly at her, a little smile on his face. Is he telling me that he knows about Vegas? Did he know about it when we talked, but wouldn't use that as a weapon any more than he'd have tried to bribe me with money? If he knew, what must he think of my moral tone, discussing his infidelities and Richard's and never confessing my own! She reddened. But did he really know, or was it pure coincidence that he'd chosen to discuss his life expectancy in gambling terms? She'd never be sure. Giovanni went on, looking now at the others.

"Life's a gamble from the day we're born. Some of us play out the game until the end, trying to bluff our way through it. And some of us go through our days holding nothing but winning hands. I've been one of those lucky ones. I intend to go on being lucky. I'm not depressed. In fact, I'm declaring a holiday. Your mother and I are going to take a real vacation. We haven't had one in years and it's high time we traveled for fun."

"A vacation!" Sergio was incredulous. "Is that wise, Father? Shouldn't you be near your doctors?"

"No need. They've done all they can."

"But we don't want you to go away from us now!"

326

This from Gloria, the one who'd always seemed the least caring. "We should all stay close, Papa, for as long as we can."

"She's right," Walter said. "Don't deprive us of the time we have."

He looked as though they'd given him a gift. "We won't stay away too long," he said. "I want to be with all of you, too. But I also want some time with your mother. She's been so busy with my career and yours that we've not had much time alone. I have many things to tell her, most of them long overdue."

Susan was aware that of all the children, Richard was the only one who'd not spoken. Was he going to say nothing? Until that day at Kate's, she'd had no idea he bore a grudge against his father. There'd always been the outward appearance of "normalcy" between them, as "normal" as Giovanni's relationship with any of his family, but now Richard's silence struck her as significant. She wondered what he was feeling, whether he regretted what he'd always secretly felt. He simply sat there, expressionless, as the others began to chatter nervously, crowding around Giovanni and Maria, trying to pretend nothing had changed as they spoke of mundane things.

Maria, for once, was as quiet as her youngest son. Susan had never seen her like this—answering in monosyllables, obviously distracted, her eyes rarely leaving her husband's face and her hand once again in his. Susan felt an involuntary flicker of pity for her. Ruthless, ambitious and cold as she was, Maria had once known ecstasy with this man, and even through all the time beyond those early, passionate days she had been loyal and faithful to him. In many ways, she'd made him happy, Susan supposed, happier perhaps, than he'd made her. Happier than I've been able to make Richard. Maria was not a woman who inspired pity but at this moment Susan felt sorry for her. She'd go on, as dominant and opinionated a widow as she'd been a wife. But she was losing the one person who'd always depended upon her strength. Susan knew it. She might have nothing else in common with Maria, but she could identify with the need to be needed.

Chapter Twenty-five

It was quite a joke, Giovanni thought as he opened his eyes that last morning in the spring of 1972. Doctors! They always figured out a way to be right. Last fall when they told him old age would get him before the cancer did, he should have realized there was no way they could be wrong. In another month he'd be seventy-eight years old. Who could say at that age what they'd list as "cause of death?"

He didn't know how he knew this was the final day. He felt no worse than usual. He'd been lucky. There'd been no hideous suffering, not even much disability beyond the normal slowing down of a man who'd lived hard for nearly eighty years. And yet he sensed there'd be no tomorrow. Odd. He wasn't frightened. Almost curious and quite satisfied.

In these past months he'd behaved normally. That is, he'd kept several already-scheduled engagements, conducting the New York, Boston and Philadelphia symphonies, telling no one outside the family of his illness and showing no signs of it at the performances. He was proud of that.

He was also proud of his sudden ability to communicate with his wife. He and Maria had gone off for their holiday alone, and though it was no rapturous thing, it had been a peaceful two weeks in Jamaica. They kept to themselves, sunned on the beach and talked long hours into the night. Giovanni could hardly remember their ever talking so much before. Not since the first days of their marriage. Terrible how people drifted apart. He mourned for how much they'd missed and he told her so.

She'd nodded as if to say, "I know," when he said he'd always loved her, in spite of his unfaithfulness and the distance it had put between them. He told her that he was grateful for the wife and mother she'd been, and aware of what she'd contributed to his success. It felt good to say these things, and better still to mean them. She was far from perfect, and he said that, too. But she was a strong and determined woman and he knew that any "shortcomings" she had were brought about by the need to survive with him.

"And your warts aren't a patch on mine," Giovanni had said, smiling. "For every flaw in you, my dear, there are twenty in me. How could you have put up with me all these years?"

She'd looked young then, soft, like the girl he'd married almost fifty-five years before.

"I loved you," Maria said. "I still do." She'd smiled back at him. "I've done some selfish things, too, Joe. Other kinds. But we can't help how we're made, either of us."

He wondered whether she was thinking of Richard, whether he should ask her to let go of the boy. Boy, indeed! Incredibly, Richard was thirty-eight years old. Too late now to change his thinking. Or Maria's. At least, Richard seemed content these days. Susan was doing a good job. She was more than keeping her word about standing by. Richard would be a great man and, thank God, not an empty one.

They'll be all right, Giovanni thought as he rose that morning and went about his meticulous grooming routine. All my headstrong, difficult children will be. As he shaved and showered he thought of them. Sergio was a fine conductor, but he'd never achieve Richard's stature. And Richard would never achieve Walter's. That was another curious circumstance. Walter, the most "different" of his sons, would undoubtedly be the immortal. Performers and conductors, the best of them, were eventually almost forgotten. But Walter's music would live on for other artists to interpret. In generations to come, as in the past, the names of composers were eternal, while those who conducted their works or gave them expression faded into dim memory. Walter, the least competitive, the least publicity-conscious, the least aggressive of the boys, would be the Antonini future generations would revere and remember. Fate did have its way of being whimsical.

As he put on his clothes, Giovanni thought of Gloria, the frustrated, "untalented" child who produced nothing. But that wasn't true, of course. She produced a complete, well-organized life for a husband and four beautiful children. Giovanni hoped it was also happy. He wished they'd had a more usual father-daughter relationship. In most families, the girl was "Daddy's favorite," especially when she was the only girl. But Gloria had always been too fierce, somehow. Too unfeminine. He supposed she felt she had to fight to be noticed among her glittering brothers. But she'd never allowed herself to be loved for her own qualities. And, in fairness to her, neither he nor Maria had spent much time looking for the qualities in Gloria that were unique.

Too late for that, Giovanni sighed. He was grateful to have glimpsed Gloria's tenderness the night he told them he had cancer. He was glad to know some love was there, regretting he hadn't realized earlier how much she'd wanted to reach out to him.

He walked slowly downstairs to the big room dominated by the concert grand. He settled himself in his favorite chair and picked up the new score Walter had left the night before. It was a piano concerto, incredibly difficult, nearly impossible but thrilling and unbearably beautiful. Walter hoped Richard would perform it,

330

but before giving it to his brother, he wanted his father's opinion.

I'll be able to tell him it's more than good, Giovanni thought. It's genius. A challenge no pianist could resist. Richard will perform it brilliantly. The family will be proud.

He let the sheets of paper fall into his lap. He was so tired. His last thought was that he must tell Richard this was his brother's most important work. He could hear it in his head, soaring, torrential, carrying him with it. He rushed along with the passages and felt a strong surge of power within himself that matched the music—a great outpouring of hope and triumph that reached a final, crashing crescendo.

And it was over.

Where was the constrained, pathetic woman who had clung to her husband's hand a few months before, when he told his family of his illness? Watching Maria organize Giovanni's final tribute, Susan felt she must have imagined that soft, clinging creature. Certainly she bore no resemblance to the dry-eyed, straight-backed, calm widow who directed every phase of the elaborate procedure. It was Maria who found him that morning. Maria who called the children and announced, with no show of emotion, "Your father is dead." And it was Maria who supervised every detail from there on in, giving directions for the kind of spectacular "farewell appearance" Giovanni Antonini deserved.

Observing Maria in action, seeing her children jump to do her bidding, Susan marveled again at the strength of this petite martinet. And listening to her give crisp concise orders, Susan realized, uncomfortably, that Maria must have been planning this since the day she learned her husband was dying. The efficiency of it gave Susan cold chills. It was only practical, she supposed, to plan for the inevitable, especially where a man as famous as Giovanni was concerned, but it seemed so impersonal, so cold-blooded.

"Your mother is incredible," she said to Richard at one point. "What strength she has! She looks so frail, but she's more composed than any of us. I haven't even seen her cry."

"And you never will. She's a lady to her fingertips."

Intentional or not, Susan felt the terse comment was a slap at her own emotional nature. She looked at Richard, trying to read his thoughts, but his face was impassive. She mustn't be so thin-skinned. They were so controlled, all of them. Not just Maria, but her children and those they'd married. Why couldn't she be like that? But she couldn't. My God, have they no feelings? Don't they grieve for him at all? Was it "unlady-like" to shed a tear for the loss of a dear one?

She watched and listened, fascinated, as the business of the moment went on, orchestrated by Maria. There would be a private funeral service and a public tribute. Giovanni's closed casket would lie on the bare stage of Carnegie Hall and the greats of the music world would come to hear Sergio deliver the eulogy.

"Sergio is the one to do it," Maria said. "If we asked someone outside the family there'd be no end of hurt feelings. They'll all be there, of course. Giovanni's peers. Ormandy, Stern, Heifetz, Horowitz, Menuhin, Iturbi . . . all of them. Best to let Serge do it. He's the oldest son. I wonder if Beverly Sills is in town. I'd like her to sing something. Walter, try to reach her, will you? And Jacqueline, my dear, call Bergdorf and have them send over three or four black dresses for me to choose from. Gloria, be sure the invitations are *hand-delivered.* And Richard, you'd better arrange for the flowers. There'll be millions, of course, but the family will want a blanket. Red roses, I think. They'll look best against the black velvet curtain. Mary Lou, you take care of the seating in the hall. A ticklish bit of protocol, but you've had some experience at that with Sergio's concerts."

Susan, aghast at the performance of a woman who'd

332

been widowed only a few hours, could also not help noticing that she and Raoul Taffin were the only ones to whom Maria did not assign duties. She's always found Raoul hopelessly weak, Susan thought. As for me, it's a calculated way of showing I'll never belong. Damn her. I won't let her exclude me.

"What may I do to help, Mrs. Antonini?"

Maria looked at her as though she was surprised to find her there. Then she frowned. "I think everything's in order, thank you. The papers have the obituary up to date in their files, of course. I don't know, Susan. Perhaps you could help with the children. They're all pretty well grown up, except for Gloria's little ones. You might keep on eye on them at Carnegie Hall. I don't suppose you'll want Katherine to attend."

"Why not? She's going on seven. Only a year younger than the twins."

"Well, yes. But I don't think it would be meaningful to her, my dear. She'd find it very disturbing, I'd imagine, not being able to hear."

Susan set her lips firmly. "Katie is deaf but she's mentally alert. I want her to remember what a great man her paternal grandfather was."

Maria shrugged. "As you like."

It went exactly as planned—the gathering at Carnegie Hall attended by every important figure in the arts. The crowds on West Fifty-seventh Street, held back by police barricades, strained to see the celebrities enter and leave, nudged each other and clicked their cameras as they recognized composers and conductors, violinists, pianists and opera stars. When Maria stepped out of her limousine, escorted by her three tall sons, a murmur ran through the crowd and a few sentimental women wiped tears from their eyes. "How brave she is," they told each other. "Isn't she dignified! She's up in her seventies, you know, but look at that figure! I

333

bet she doesn't wear more than a size six. What a marvelous woman."

The "marvelous woman" looked neither right nor left as she mounted the steps, head high, showing just the right amount of awareness of those who came to gawk and comment. She was, in fact, loving every minute of it. She was sorry Joe was dead, but she'd had time to get used to the idea of his dying. We all have to go sometime, she reasoned, and how many of us leave this world so universally mourned? Joe would like being surrounded by his adoring fans. He always had. Just as she liked being the center of public attention and seldom was. For once, the spotlight was hers alone. She was the symbol of the family, widow and mother of great men, the keeper of the faith. She intended to play that role to the hilt.

Sergio spoke movingly (Thank God Richard's publicity man had been able to write a eulogy that was neither too impersonal nor too mawkish!) and Beverly Sills's glorious voice singing the *Ave Maria* filled the hall and was amplified to the hushed crowd outside. As prearranged, one by one the musical greats came forward at the end of the ceremony. Slowly, the living legends crossed the stage in silence, paused a moment before Giovanni's casket, then moved on, heads bowed, faces showing their genuine grief. Joe would have liked that, Maria thought, watching from her front row seat. He always cared about the recognition of his peers. He always appreciated a good piece of showmanship.

"That was quite a production Maria put on." Kate Fenton's voice was matter of fact. "You have to hand it to her. She's a born impresario. I'm surprised she didn't walk behind the hearse from Campbell's Funeral Chapel to Carnegie Hall."

Susan, seated beside her friend on a banquette in the art-deco atmosphere of Maxwell's Plum, looked slightly shocked. Sometimes Kate could be so callous. Not that it wasn't true. Maria had turned her husband's funeral into an event the world would not soon forget. And yet it managed to be more impressive than tasteless, more tribute than three-ring circus. What it lacked, Susan knew, was heart. They'd all been so well bred, so composed. Oddly, the only one who wept uncontrollably was Gloria. She'd been pathetic, this big, athletic woman crying like a child for a father she must have loved more than she ever dared show.

"Your silence is stunning," Kate said. "What's the matter? Did I speak out of turn or are your eggs Benedict covered with curdled hollandaise?"

Susan smiled. "Sorry. I was just thinking about Gloria. Of everyone at the funeral, she was the only one who showed any honest emotion. I guess it surprised me, seeing how deeply she felt. She's always been so . . . I don't know, I guess 'formidable' is the word."

Kate nodded. "It would be helpful if we all had X-ray eyes. Then we'd know what was really going on inside people. Or maybe it wouldn't. We're probably better off not knowing." She deliberately changed the subject. "You know, I like this restaurant. All the marvelous stained-glass décor and *art nouveau*. We should come here more often. I keep forgetting about it. It's kind of off the beaten path over here on First Avenue."

"Not off the beaten path for half the world," Susan said. "It's packed."

"Yes, but not with the same old faces from *Women's Wear Daily*, thank God! I get awfully bored with so-called socialites who have nothing better to do with their lives than decide between sole amandine and beef Wellington. And speaking of people who don't know what to do with themselves, where do you go from here?"

"Bloomingdale's, I think. I need curtains for the kitchen."

"Very funny. That's not what I mean and you know it. I'm talking about what you're doing with your life. Joe's gone and your promise to him is canceled. My goddaughter is at the stage where she doesn't need you

335

every minute. Here you are, kiddo, light years married and no prospects, I assume, of a bigger family. You're at a kind of crossroad, aren't you? Are you ever again to do something on your own? Or are you always going to be a shadow of Richard? Whither the hell are you drifting? Are you content to abandon all your potential? Can you really sublimate the need to accomplish something more satisfying than a well-planned dinner? You can't just mark time, Susan. That's not enough for you. You're a giver, a doer, a bright lady. Kitchen curtains, for God's sake!" Kate impatiently lit a cigarette. "I'm sorry. It's probably none of my damned business, but you've been in limbo too long. Isn't there anything you'd really like to do?"

"Yes," Susan said slowly. "I'd like to be needed. I know that sounds insane, but it's true. Katie's doing so well, I can't really contribute much more to her life than a mother can to any bright, busy little girl. Not that I'm not happy about it! It's what I've prayed for. Edith Chambers and Katie's teachers at school assure me she can go to college when she's ready. They say she'll be able to drive a car and engage in sports and get married and be like her friends in every way. Think of it, Kate! Isn't it a miracle what these people have done?"

"You were the one who always believed it could happen. Never forget that."

"I know. I'm glad for that. Glad I made that decision." She sounded wistful. "Even though it really was the beginning of the end for Richard and me."

Kate was silent for a moment. Then she said, gently, "What about Richard?"

"I love him," Susan repeated. "And in a strange way he loves me. But we don't share anything, Kate. He doesn't need me. He has his work, his success, more family obligations now that his father's gone."

Kate snuffed out her cigarette angrily. "You mean Maria is more demanding of his time than ever. Naturally! The widow's clinging to her baby boy. God! It's obscene! It's really sick! If you tell me you've

336

agreed to spend the summer with her, I swear I'll kill you!"

Susan smiled. "No. Fortunately, she hasn't asked us. She'd love to have Richard there, I'm sure, but that would mean Katie and me, as well. She still wants no part of that. As a matter of fact, we're going to take a house in East Hampton. I've seen a lovely one, right on the beach, and Richard's agreeable."

"So you *are* going to stay with him, even though Joe's gone. You still think you can make it work."

Susan looked away. "I want it to work. Maybe I'm looking for another miracle, but I can't get away from the fact that he's the only man I've ever loved."

"Or you still have the guilts about the Vegas episode."

"No. I've almost forgotten that. That had nothing to do with love. That was part of my insane period. Like the heavy drinking. I hope you notice I'm not doing that any more, either. Something good will happen this summer, Kate. I just feel it will. Maybe Richard and I can get really close again. Maybe it will be like our honeymoon on the Cape. He needed me then. Not just physically. It was a spiritual thing. We were one person. Maybe we can recapture some of that when we're alone."

Her friend didn't answer. No need to tell Susan she was still dreaming dreams, trying to believe that everything that happened in the past could be wiped out by one idyllic summer that had no chance of coming true. True romantic that she was, Susan always kept coming back for more. It was such a waste. Especially when there was someone who cared so much for her, someone who'd devote his life to making her happy. Why couldn't she face the fact that Richard would *never* need her? Why did she cling to this impossible hope?

"Paul keeps calling me to ask how you are."

Susan looked at her curiously. "How is Paul? I saw him for a minute at Carnegie Hall."

"He's fine. Has his own flourishing business. Represents half a dozen artists."

337

"I'm glad. I was always so sorry he left Richard."

"You know why he did, of course."

"Yes. That dreadful Washington business. I don't blame him. He couldn't be a party to any more of that."

"Oh, come on, Susan! Who the hell do you think you're kidding? Paul left because he was in love with you. He still is. You know that! If you had a grain of sense you'd give up this business with Richard and grab a terrific guy who's mad for you. And, I might add, for Katie!"

"I'm not in love with Paul. I wish I could be."

"Well, maybe you ought to try! Maybe you should stop behaving like a schoolgirl and get wise to the fact that you can have a pretty damned good life with someone who's anxious to give more than he takes! This isn't *True Romances,* Susan. It's life. When are you going to get over being sixteen years old?"

"Is *that* what you think I should do with my life— marry Paul?"

"Not necessarily, but it isn't such a bad idea. I just want you to do something besides chase rainbows! I don't care if you get a job or write a book or take up good works, but for God's sake get off your ass! They've drained all the spirit out of you. They're making you a blob!"

Susan straightened and her eyes flashed fire. "Damn you, Kate, how dare you say such things to me? Who do you think you are? What have you done with *your* life that's so terrific? I don't think being a hotshot editor with no personal life exactly qualifies you for Woman of the Year! Have you ever known what it is to love a man so much you could suffer torture and still want to be with him? Have you ever hated yourself for your weakness in staying and yet be unable to leave? What do you know about spirit? Don't you think it's taken spirit to cope with the whole damned Antonini family—Richard included?" She stopped, aghast at the words that had come pouring out. Why was she attacking her best friend—the only person who

338

cared enough to see that she had become a woman with no will of her own? For Kate was right, of course. She was drifting, purposelessly, waiting for that miracle. It wasn't going to come. Richard would never be faithful or unselfish or truly in need of her. She was such a fool. Why couldn't she face that? She blinked back the tears. "Kate, forgive me. I'm crazy. I know you're right. I don't know what made me say those hateful things to you."

But Kate was grinning. "Well, it's about time! I figured you were still a spunky kid, but I didn't think I'd ever break through that shroud of martyrdom!"

"You're not angry?"

"Angry? I'm delighted to find they haven't removed your spine!"

Susan managed a little laugh. "But I still don't know where I'm going."

"Maybe not. But at least now I have hope that you won't be too blinded with self-pity to follow the road when you do find it!"

Chapter Twenty-six

When they finished lunch and Kate hopped into a cab at Sixty-fourth Street and First Avenue, Susan went off to do her errand at Bloomingdale's. Though it was a few blocks out of her way, she decided to cross town on East Fifty-seventh Street, past the "spit and polish" apartment buildings between First and Second Avenues, past the odd little antique shops and bookstores and the "discount fashion outlet" where "Name Designer Clothes" could sometimes be found for less than the regular price. She glanced at the marquee of the Sutton Theatre, and into the windows of Schrafft's, and ambled west toward Lexington Avenue, admiring the antique crystal chandeliers in Nesle's elegant shop and stopping to inspect the astounding household gadgets displayed by Hammacher Schlemmer. At Lexington, she turned north again, toward her destination. The going was more difficult on this avenue. It literally swarmed with people. Young men and women in jeans and T-shirts; nervous matrons with blue-dyed hair and purses firmly clutched; young housewives in pants-suits and dark glasses; crazy, raggedy old people mumbling to themselves; wild-eyed, raggedy young people peddling ugly homemade jewelry from folding stands illegally set up on the sidewalk. The atmosphere was carnival-like, the smells of food from open-to-the-street lunch counters downright nauseating. And yet there was something fascinating about it all. She thought, as she so often did these days, of Giovanni. He'd adored this part of town, loved to prowl the streets, marveling at a city that was such a study in contrasts. She understood that fascination. In a five-minute walk, one could leave the liveried-doorman-guarded block that housed New York's senior United States senator and his social wife and be in an area that was dirty, shabby and unabashedly commercial. "Bloomie's," as New Yorkers called the department store, was a kaleidoscope of its surroundings. The neighborhood had "grown up around it" in the past fifteen years, with new high-rise apartments and tall office buildings. Bloomie's was the mecca for rich women and couturier clothes. It was also the place for basement bargains and "in" clothes the secretaries loved, and "far-out" fashions that attracted high-school kids and homosexuals and hookers. Susan responded to the electricity of it. Crowded and confusing as it was, she found it a "miniature New York" with all that was beautiful and tawdry and tough and chic and throbbingly alive. No other store offered such infinite variety of selection, nor such disparity of social and financial status among its shoppers. Even finding what you wanted and getting waited on was a challenge only for the stouthearted, strongwinded shopper. Bloomie's was no kinder to models and movie stars than it was to mothers' helpers.

As she pushed her way onto the escalator, Susan felt ridiculously at peace amid the chaos, marvelously self-sufficient as she put up her own battle in the crowds. She even began to smile as she thought of the conversation with Kate. Dear Kate. Deliberately making her defend herself, forcing her to think about the future, daring her to prove she'd not become a nothing of a person. The confrontation had been good for her. She'd been running away from remembrance of the past and stubbornly unwilling to make decisions about the years to come. Kate had made it impossible for her to duck the issues any longer.

What was it she really wanted? "To be needed," she'd said. What a stupid, pat answer! Everybody wanted to be needed. Ridiculous of her to sit back and hope for Richard to suddenly realize he couldn't function without her. He could. All too well. Giovanni had been wrong. It wasn't necessary for her to "save" her husband from a life of emptiness; it was more to the point that she save herself.

As she picked through the rows of kitchen curtains, hardly seeing them, she mentally listed all the things that had plagued her throughout her marriage. In the beginning, it had been unjustified jealousy over the strange women who literally threw themselves at Richard when he was on tour. Later, the jealousy and hurt had been real as she learned about film stars and socialites and senators' daughters and other women in her husband's life. There'd been the great periods of loneliness when she gave up traveling with him because of Katie's need of her. And, indeed, there was Katie herself. No plague this. This was her pride and joy, adorable Katie, whom she'd literally snatched back to her bosom from the exile that Maria had decreed and

341

Richard—with his irrational desire to please her—had imposed. Katie, whom her father simply could not love.

We've survived so many things, Susan thought. The Washington fiasco and its aftermath. Her foolish, well-meant second pregnancy, so "conveniently" terminated. Giovanni's death and Maria's now greater-than-ever hold on her youngest son. Nothing, Susan told herself, has turned out as I thought. A spoiled, sought-after thirty-eight-year-old didn't magically become a paragon. Marriage didn't terminate women's interest in him, or his in them. He wouldn't lose his ego or his love of attention because he had a wife. I should have known he wouldn't have the patience for any part of Katie's upbringing. What an utter dreamer I am! And what am I hoping for now? A magic reconciliation? A metamorphosis in Richard? Kate must think me infantile. Everyone must. How they'd laugh if they knew what I'm secretly hoping: that this summer Richard and I might decide together to have another child. What nonsense! You'll never have a "normal" marriage. So forget it, Susan! Grow up! Kate's right. You've come to a crossroad. Put up or shut up. Live with Richard as he is and stop whining or concentrate on accomplishing something for yourself, with or without him. This time *you've* got to have breathing room. You're suffocating in boredom.

"May I help you, madam?"

Susan came back to reality with a start. She realized she'd been standing with the same pair of curtains in her hand for God knows how long. She smiled and blushed.

"Yes, thank you. I'll have these. Charge and send."

The girl produced her sales book. "You have your charge plate?"

"No. Sorry. The name is Antonini. Mrs. Richard Antonini. That's A-n-t..."

There was the usual wide-eyed reaction.

"You don't have to spell it. I'm a concert buff. I
342

think your husband is simply wonderful, Mrs. Antonini!"

"Yes, he is," Susan echoed automatically. "Simply
wonderful."

❀

"I'm worried about Susan," Bea Langdon said.

Wil reluctantly switched off Walter Cronkite. "Any
special reason?"

"We hardly ever see her. She doesn't even phone often these days."

"Honey, she's been through a bad time. She was
very fond of the maestro. And don't forget she also
had a miscarriage not too long ago."

"That's another thing. She never talks about the
baby."

Wil sighed. If he lived to be a hundred, he'd never
understand women. "Bea, dear, isn't it healthy that
she's not brooding? Besides, it wasn't a real baby. I
mean, she was only two months pregnant."

"You wouldn't understand. Any life inside a woman
is real from the moment she knows it's there. Losing it,
deliberately or accidentally, is traumatic. The normal
reaction would be for Susan to unburden herself, to cry
over her loss, instead of acting as though it never happened."

"So she's a strong girl. Good head on her shoulders."

Bea's glance was withering. "That girl's in trouble.
You mark my word. She's tight as a drum. I know she
just doesn't want to worry us, but there are things she's
bottling up inside. I feel it, Wil. I'm frightened for her.
I want to help and I can't reach her."

He came and sat next to her on the sofa. "She'll be
all right. I know Richard has his faults, but Susie has a
husband to turn to. The marriage has lasted almost
eight years. It must be solid enough, my dear, even
with all its ups and downs. Try to relax. They're
going to have a good summer in East Hampton. In

that atmosphere, problems have a way of disappearing. I suppose the vastness of the sea really does point up the insignificance of our petty little lives." He played his trump card. "Besides, Grandma, think what a swell time your Katie's going to have!"

Bea smiled and stroked his cheek. "What would I do without you, Wil Langdon? You make my world so safe and sane."

"My job, lady. And I love it."

Don't ever leave me, she silently begged him. I'm no Maria Antonini. I couldn't go on without you.

As she opened the apartment door, Richard called out to her from the terrace.

"Susan? Come on out and soak up some spring sunshine."

She found him stretched out on a chaise, Walter's concerto carelessly tossed on a table beside him as though it had been thrown there in disgust or anger. She looked at the messy sheets as she sank gratefully into a chair.

"Lord, I've walked my legs off! It feels good to sit. Have you been home all afternoon? How's it going with the concerto?"

He scowled. "To answer your last question: lousy. I'll never master the damned thing!"

"Of course you will. You said yourself it was brilliant."

"More like diabolical. I swear to God I think Walter set out to write something Horowitz couldn't play! I wouldn't be surprised if he deliberately did it to drive me up the wall!"

Susan smiled. He sounded so like the angry child he was. He'd conquer it, of course. If only to prove that his brother couldn't get the best of him.

"Come on," she said teasingly. "You know you're as good as Horowitz."

Richard relaxed. "Not yet. But I will be. He has a

344

thirty-year head start on me. It'll take another year or so to catch up."

She was pleased to find him in such a good humor. "Be a sport. Give yourself two years."

Richard laughed. "Okay. Two years. So how was Kate? Abrasive as ever?"

Susan refused to be ruffled. It was too nice a day. They were having a rare, "married people" kind of easy conversation. She wouldn't spoil this relaxed moment by getting uptight over the little crack at Kate.

"Of course. That's Kate's personality. Abrasive but interesting. She's fine. As you know, she goes to Europe in July, as usual, to do fashion features for the magazine. She says she's bored with it, but she never will be. After all these years, she still loves that by-line. She'd miss the excitement of dealing with people and the stimulation of feeling important. She'd be lost without applause. Kate needs recognition."

Richard was quiet for a moment, and then he said, "Who are you talking about, Susie? Kate or yourself?"

She looked at him in surprise. It was rare for Richard to be so perceptive. He was right. She hadn't consciously realized it as she spoke, but she was describing herself. That was one thing she missed: the ego-building. She had, in fact, determined that very day to find some form of it again.

"I was talking about both of us," she admitted finally. "I didn't realize I was so transparent. But I've been thinking about it all day. I don't like what I've become. Or what I've *not* become. I'm not sure how to solve the problem, but I've still got to find something that's uniquely mine. Can you understand that?"

"Yes, believe it or not, I think I can. Any idea what you'd like to do?"

"No. Not a clue." She felt very cheerful. "But by the end of the summer I'll come up with an idea."

"I think you should. I've been doing a lot of thinking too, Susie. I've been unfair to you. I took a lively, confident career woman and tried to make her an ambitionless 'second-rate citizen' for my sake. That's

345

wrong. I guess I've always known you shouldn't be expected to change while I went on exactly as I always have." He smiled. "The knowledge has come a little late, but I *can* see you must have something of your own. An 'identity,' I think they call it. I want you to know I'm all for it, and I know it won't hurt our marriage. It might even help it."

She could hardly believe what she was hearing. Richard urging her to find outside interests? Richard admitting he'd been wrong about her role as an "Antonini woman?" Hating herself for her suspicions, she wondered what had produced this sudden insight. She could hear Giovanni's voice. "Richard's the product of the last person he talks to." Whom had he been talking to? That was unfair. Why couldn't he simply have been thinking about her, recognizing that she, too, had needs? He couldn't have been untouched by his father's death. Perhaps he saw in Maria what happened to a woman when a cause to which she'd been devoted for years was taken from her. He must be relating that to us, Susan thought. He must have been thinking, all these weeks, what my status would be if something happened to him. I've given up every outside interest. She felt very close to him. He'd shown so little outward emotion over Giovanni's death, but he must be overwhelmed with sadness for all the resentment-filled past. Death can sometimes bring other truths sharply into focus. Perhaps he's remorseful about depriving me of children. Her thoughts were interrupted by the sound of her husband's voice.

"Maybe you should go back to work for the magazine," he was saying. "At least on a part-time basis. It would put you back in touch with people, give you the activity and self-importance you need." He stopped as though something had just occurred to him. "Why don't you go to Europe with Kate? That's an idea! She's always wanting you to do some writing. And if *Vogue* won't pay for it, you can go anyway. The money's no problem. Especially now. We're very rich, Susie. Father was a multimillionaire and he left it equally to Mother and all of us. She was telling me at lunch . . ." He stopped abruptly. "Anyway, darling, why not discuss it with Kate? Maybe you don't have to search for something to do. Maybe you can go back to doing what you loved when we met."

In that instant it was all blindingly clear. Maria. Always Maria. She knew about *Vogue* covering the collections. She wanted Richard with her for this first summer she didn't wish to face alone. It was *her* idea to get rid of Susan temporarily so she could have her "baby" for six weeks in Pound Ridge. She could hear Maria subtly making Richard think this was his own brainstorm. Anger welled up in Susan. All that talk about "understanding her need for identity" was just so much convenient hogwash! Richard didn't give a damn. This time she wouldn't fall into the trap. She wouldn't let Maria have her way.

Pretending surprise, Susan looked at him innocently. "Go to Europe? Give up a wonderful summer with you and Katie in East Hampton? Darling, I wouldn't dream of it! That's so dear of you. So generous! But nothing could make me sacrifice those weeks we've been looking forward to. No. Don't you worry. I'm just so thrilled you understand that I have to get busy again! But *Vogue*'s not the answer. In the fall, I'll find the right thing to do. You'll see. You'll be proud of me, Richard. Just as I'm so proud of you for your unselfishness."

He looked confused. "Well, of course," he said finally. "It was only a suggestion."

"And a wonderful one, darling. Thank you for thinking of it." She rose casually. "I'll go check on Katie. She must be home from school by now. Oh, by the way, I ran into one of your fans today. She sells curtains at Bloomingdale's. I didn't even have to spell my name for her. She knew it well." She gave him a bright smile. "You see, sweetheart, there are compensations, being married to a celebrity!"

Inside the living room, out of his sight, she felt as though she were going to be actively ill. Would this cat-and-mouse game never end? She straightened up and the moment of disgust gave way to determination. Damn you, Maria. It's really come to a pitched battle now, hasn't it? With Giovanni gone, you want more of Richard than ever. Well, you won't have him. You're quite an actress, but I can be an actress too. I just proved that.

She felt very different from the indecisive young woman who'd sat on the banquette at Maxwell's Plum a few hours earlier. Kate was right. She still had spine. She was still Susan Langdon, no matter what. And a dozen Maria Antoninis weren't going to destroy her. How could I ever have felt sorry for her? Susan wondered. There's never a moment when she isn't scheming or playing a part. I don't believe she was even deeply touched by her husband's illness or his death. She simply portrayed what was expected—a shocked and saddened wife and a brave, grief-stricken widow. I don't think she can feel much of anything. People see her as strong and courageous, but all she is is totally self-involved. I made the mistake of thinking of her in terms of my own mother, who knows how to love deeply and unselfishly. I imagined what Mother would feel if something happened to Dad. Susan shuddered. It was an idea she refused to entertain. A morbid, unacceptable thought. Both her parents were in good health, thank God. And of course they were years younger than Richard's.

Still, I shouldn't neglect them as I have lately, Susan told herself. Except for each other, I'm all they have. I've been so deep in my own problems, I've hardly given a thought to them. Not that they've complained. They never would. All my life they've been understanding, easy to talk to. She felt an urge to talk with them now. Bea, especially. It was a need, she realized, to be part of a happy, giving, unselfish family, a childish wish, perhaps, to go back even for a little while to an atmosphere that was safe and undemanding. I really trust Mother more than anyone, Susan thought, somewhat surprised by her discovery. She's not as worldly as Kate nor as cynically realistic as Jacqueline. They're wonderful but I'm Mother's flesh and blood. I could tell her anything and she'd accept and forgive me because she loves me without reservation.

I'll call tomorrow and make a date to go to Bronxville for dinner. If Richard doesn't want to come along, he doesn't have to. She faced her feelings squarely. In fact, Susan thought, I hope he won't.

She made her way toward Katie's room. I hope my daughter always feels as much need for her mother as I do for mine. I hope we never lose the precious emotional reaction that's more sustaining than any amount of logical dissection. With Kate I can be honest and know I'll get a sensible, analytical appraisal and good advice. But with Mother I can be comforted even when I'm wrong.

He'd never debated so long over anything. For days Martin Tanner had tried to decide whether to call the woman he knew as Susan Armstrong, the woman who had, for God's sake, turned out to be Susan Antonini. Mrs. Richard Antonini. Socialite, patron of the arts, wife of one of the world's most famous concert pianists! The discovery had rocked him. He'd known she was hiding something. He'd suspected she was using a phony name. But he hadn't expected her to be a celebrity, vulnerable to publicity, even blackmail, if she'd been unlucky enough to run into the wrong guy.

What was she? A nymphomaniac? A nut? Or didn't she give a damn? Running off to Vegas, staying stoned out of her mind most of the time, going to bed with a stranger she picked up on a plane. What kind of madness was that? Other women, ordinary women, might do those things, but the wife of a public figure was insane to run such risks with her husband's reputation, even if she didn't care about her own.

And obviously she didn't, Martin reasoned. It was ridiculous to think he was her only affair since her marriage, no matter what she said. And yet he wasn't sure. There was something about her half-fright, half-bravado that had gotten to him. She wasn't your usual bored wife out for a good time. He'd felt it then. He'd been almost surprised when she let him make love to her. For that's what it had been. She'd responded, but initiated nothing, as though she was holding back, out of guilt or fear or shame.

He had to admit she piqued his curiosity. Even after she left Vegas so precipitously, he hadn't been able to get her out of his mind. There weren't many women who left such a deep impression. He'd looked up Armstrongs in the New York phone book when he returned, but there were dozens who could have been possible. It was a silly idea. He didn't even know her husband's first name. And it was clear she didn't want to see him again, even though she'd told him, with a disarming lack of coyness, how much he attracted her, how she'd pursue him if she were free to. But she wasn't free and she obviously wasn't the kind of married woman who had the stomach for the sordid little hidden affair. He'd almost dismissed her until he saw the pictures of Giovanni Antonini's funeral service at Carnegie Hall. There, on the steps, was Susan, holding the hands of two little girls while a small boy about the same age stood nearby. Three children? He remembered her mentioning only one. No matter. It was Susan, all right. Unmistakably. His heart unexpectedly leaped at the sight of her and he remembered the soft, supple body, the deep, intelligent eyes, the voice that was so gentle, so full of suppressed wishes and a certain sweet sadness.

The caption under the picture identified her as Mrs. Richard Antonini, daughter-in-law, leaving the hall with her own daughter, Katherine, and her niece and nephew, Claudette and Pierre Taffin. He'd dropped the paper and gone back to the telephone directory. No Richard Antonini there, of course. They were too well known to be listed. But that was easy. It was his business to know where the rich and famous were at all times, especially the ones who had a weakness for no-limit poker games or dollar-a-point gin rummy. "Celebrity Service," to which he subscribed, wouldn't give out a private phone number, but his friend in the sports department of the *News* probably could wangle it out of one of the society columnists. His friend could indeed. In ten minutes, Martin had Susan's telephone number. For days he looked at it, once dialed half of it and then replaced the receiver. What the hell was the point? No reason to think she'd feel any differently now than she had in Vegas.

And yet on this beautiful late spring morning, he suddenly was overcome with a longing to see her. She had liked him. Very much. Maybe things had changed. She was unhappy enough when he met her. She could be even more in need of comfort now. It was chancy to call her house. Concert pianists, like gamblers, obviously didn't leave for the office in the morning. Suppose her husband answered? Well, what if he did? Martin would give odds that Richard Antonini had never heard the name Martin Tanner. Susan was not the kind of hysterical female who'd come home and confess all.

A soft voice he recognized answered the phone.

"Hello, Mrs. Armstrong. Martin Tanner. I called to say I'm sorry about your father-in-law."

He heard a quick intake of breath, and then with a remarkable composure, Susan said, "Well, hello! What a surprise to hear from you."

"Is it?"

"Yes, of course. When did you get into town?"

"I'm always in town, remember? I live here. I'm even in the phone book under my own name, which is more than I can say for you." He paused. "Susan, I'd like to see you. Would you like to see me?"

"That would be pleasant, to catch up, but I'm not sure I could manage it. We're going away for the summer and I have a million things to do."

She sounded so determinedly casual he realized she

351

wasn't alone. The husband must be in the room. Or a servant. Or maybe the child.

"I gather you can't talk."

"That's right. It would have been fun. I'm so sorry. Ring up again when you're in New York. Richard and I would love to see you."

"I'll be having lunch at La Croisette tomorrow at one o'clock," Martin said. "It's a nice restaurant but nobody seems to know about it. Fifty-eighth Street and First Avenue. I like it because you never see anybody you know. I'll be the guy in the back room at the corner table. Goodbye, Susan."

"Thanks for calling. Goodbye."

He wondered if she'd come. Yes, she'd be there. But for what reason he couldn't be sure. She knew very little about him, in spite of their fleeting intimacy. She might come out of fear. She might be afraid he planned to blackmail her or put pressure on her to be with him. If so, she'd try to appeal to his "better nature." She might come because she was attracted to him and was excited by the prospect of seeing him again. Or she might still be as reckless and unhappy as she was in Vegas, still running away from something. He hoped that was not the case. He didn't need a complicated, screwed-up female in his life. Not even one he was as drawn to as he was to Susan.

Why did I bother? Why didn't I leave well enough alone? He was almost sorry he'd called her. Maybe he wouldn't show up at Croisette himself. That would be the end of it. She'd never call him. He remembered something his Jewish grandmother used to say. "He who has no trouble makes himself trouble." Martin laughed aloud. That was him, all right. Risk-taking was his business. It was in his blood. He couldn't resist. He'd be there tomorrow.

And so, ninety-nine chances to one, would Susan.

352

"Who was that on the phone?" Richard asked.

"An old beau," Susan said lightly.

"Oh?"

"I haven't seen him for a long while. He just found out I was married to you."

"*How* old a beau?"

She laughed. "I think you're jealous!"

"Don't be ridiculous," Richard said.

Chapter Twenty-seven

As she paused inside the doorway of the restaurant, Susan wondered why she'd never noticed the place before. She'd actually walked past it only two days before, after she left Kate. It was attractively done, with a tiny bar, comfortably spaced tables and walls covered with murals of the South of France, in particular that stretch known as La Croisette. She'd never seen the Côte d'Azur, but she recognized the Riviera from photographs of the "playground of the rich"—Cannes, Nice, Cap Ferrat, Juan les Pins, all the expensive, exciting locales she associated with F. Scott Fitzgerald and the "Reckless Twenties."

I could see those places this summer, she thought suddenly. All I'd have to do is tell Richard I'd decided to go to Europe with Kate. I could hop down there from Paris. The exotic names were like music. Cap d'Antibes, Beaulieu, St. Tropez, Villefranche, Monte Carlo . . .

"May I help you, madam?" The smiling captain gave a little bow.

"Yes. I'm meeting Mr. Tanner. Martin Tanner."

"But of course. Monsieur Tanner is already here. This way, if you please."

Martin was right. There were only three other tables occupied. She felt sorry for the proprietors but relieved that it apparently was as he'd said, an "undiscovered" restaurant. She followed the captain down the length of the room, past a large fish tank where several mournful trout swam aimlessly back and forth, waiting to be chosen for someone's lunch or dinner, and into the square "back room," which was totally empty except for the man who waited for her.

He's even more attractive than I remembered, Susan unwillingly thought. She felt awkward and self-conscious as he greeted her with one of those meaningless little kisses on the cheek that are as usual to sophisticated New Yorkers as handshakes are to casual acquaintances in other cities.

"I'm glad you came. I was afraid you wouldn't."

She took a deep breath and tried to relax. "But you knew I would, didn't you?"

Martin grinned. That dangerous, exciting, sure-of-himself expression. "There's no such thing as a 'sure thing.' That much I've learned in my business. But yes, I would have given odds you'd come, Susan. I saw no reason why you shouldn't."

"That's right. No reason at all. This isn't the Victorian age. Even a married woman is entitled to have lunch with an old friend, isn't she?" God, she sounded so inane! In her nervousness she was prattling like a frightened virgin. Martin pretended not to notice.

"What will you drink? Vodka?"

"Nothing, thank you."

His raised-eyebrow surprise was comical. For the first time since she arrived, Susan smiled. "I don't blame you for being startled, but I'm hardly drinking at all these days. You go ahead, though. Please don't let me stop you. I'll have tomato juice, if I may."

354

He ordered scotch for himself, tomato juice for her, told the waiter they'd look at the menu later. Then he sat back and stared at her, shaking his head in pretended amazement.

"Mrs. Richard Antonini," he said. "My, my! Who would have thought it? My lovely little companion from Vegas turns out to be part of the most publicized family since the Kennedys. Little did I know I was rubbing, uh, elbows with such a famous lady."

Susan ignored the innuendo. "I'm not famous," she said. "Not at all. My husband is, and his family. But not me."

"I think you're overly modest. Antonini is a name every shopgirl knows. Even uneducated, culturally underprivileged gamblers read about all of you in the columns. We may not read concert reviews, but we're very big on gossip sheets like *Open Secrets*. Or even reputable papers like the Washington *Post*. Funny, I must have seen your picture dozens of times in the past few years and I didn't recognize you in Vegas. It didn't click until that photo of you leaving Carnegie Hall. Then I realized who your husband is. The Don Juan of the symphony set. The bad boy of good music. No wonder you have to break loose once in a while."

She should have been angry, but she wasn't. He was too close to the truth. Or what used to be the truth. It's different now, Susan thought. At least that part of it. I'm quite sure Richard's been faithful since I went to Vegas. That in itself is ironic, she thought, looking across the table at the man who for one night had been her lover.

"I'm not sure what you're driving at, Martin. I suppose you're saying that because Richard's affairs have been so flagrantly publicized, I have every right to go around leaping into beds. Is that it?"

"Not exactly, darling. You're not the type for the promiscuous stuff, but you're sure as hell entitled to some kicks of your own when your famous husband is so well known for his extramarital activities. All I'm saying is that I understand what happened in Vegas a little better now. I couldn't quite figure it before. You were too classy, I thought, for that pushover scene."

"And now you think I'm not."

"Let's just say I still think you have class, and I find you more interesting than ever."

"So you'd like to pick up where we left off."

He reached for her hand. "Wouldn't you? Why shouldn't you?"

She let her hand stay in his, but there was no thrill to his touch. *Now that he knows about Richard, he's sure I'm available. He could never understand that the Vegas thing was unique; that I don't want anyone but my husband. Why shouldn't he think as he does? I did go to bed with him. I did tell him he attracted me and I wished I were free to follow him. It was true at that unhappy, confused point in my life, right after that terrible Washington episode. He can't know that in spite of Richard's behavior and mine, I cherish fidelity more than I seek diversion.*

"Martin," she said quietly, "listen to me. I don't blame you for what you think I am. You have every reason to assume I'd be the most likely woman in the world to embrace a single standard. But I'm not. You met me in a strange period. I liked our love-making. Even more than I wanted to. But I'm working at my marriage. So is Richard. We lost a baby a few months ago." She swallowed hard. "I'm not drinking much these days because I don't need liquor to get me through. I still have problems. Lots of them. But you or someone like you isn't the answer. I can't blot things out any more. I have to stay sober and fight for my life. My life with my husband and my child. I didn't lie to you when I told you that you were the only man I'd been with since my marriage. You are. I think you always will be." She smiled. "You're great in bed. It's a pity I'm so hopelessly old-fashioned. I can't 'take my fun where I find it' as the cliché goes."

"Not even when your husband can?"

"Not even then."

He shook his head. "Why did you come today?
356

Were you afraid I'd make trouble for you if you didn't?"

"No. You like to picture yourself as a rough diamond but I know you're a gentleman. I wasn't afraid of what you'd do or say. You'd never hurt me. I came because I wanted you to know that my life is better now, partly, I think, because of you. You made me feel alive and wonderful, Martin. It was what I needed—to feel wanted that way. But I can't handle the price. I realized that when I came home and looked at my husband and my child." He started to interrupt but she stopped him. "You're going to remind me again of Richard's ability to have a marriage and sex outside of it. But that's the male mentality, my dear, I know. These days women are supposed to be just as free and guiltless and independent of the institution of marriage as their husbands are. I know we're supposed to take sex as men always have—as something apart from love and emotion. God bless the women who can be so 'sensible.' They're probably absolutely right. I think I envy them. I just can't emulate them. I was born a little too early to think it doesn't matter who knows me intimately or that coupling isn't really all that big a deal. To me, it is."

"You don't make sense. You even told me you could understand your husband's flings better, after ours."

"I know I did. And it's true. Even though, strangely enough, he seems to have settled down in that department."

He was impatient. "For how long, Susan? Christ, everybody knows his reputation!"

"That still has nothing to do with the way I handle my own. Perhaps it should, but it doesn't."

"You're worried about your kid, aren't you? You're afraid she'll hear some gossip about you. That must be a big part of this."

"Not really. I'd never want her to be ashamed of me, but my child doesn't hear. She barely speaks. She's a deaf-mute, Martin."

357

He was stunned into silence. Then he said, "I'm sorry. My God, that's terrible!"

"It's hard for her and sad for us, but it's not terrible. She's being brought up like any other little girl. She'll have a nearly normal life. She already wants everything her nonhandicapped friends have. She's a spunky kid," Susan said, echoing Kate's words, "and she's going to be a happy woman."

"But the burden of that on you! And that guy you married who's given you nothing but trouble! What kind of life can you have? Even those supercharged in-laws I've read about!"

She looked at him gratefully. He'd virtually forgotten himself and his own desires in this real concern for her.

"My life's okay," she said. "I'm no object of pity, but thank you for caring, Martin. You're a nice man." She hesitated. "I don't think we should see each other again. I wish we could be friends, but we can't. The attraction is much too strong."

He managed to smile. "Well, thanks for that much, anyway. All right. Do it your way. Don't let me or any other guy make you miserable. And I would. Because I couldn't see you without wanting you. You're one hell of a lady."

It was her turn to thank him. And then she said, almost in embarrassment, "By the way, did you by any chance ever run into my father-in-law?"

"Are you kidding? Where would I have met a man like him? What makes you ask?"

"It's not important. Just a crazy idea. Once I thought he was trying to tell me indirectly that he knew about us. It was just a wild notion. My guilty conscience plaguing me, I suppose. Pure coincidence. Forget it."

"Come on, you can't leave it at that! Don't you think I have any curiosity?"

"You're right. It's not fair." She told him about the night Giovanni had disclosed his illness, the night so soon after she'd come home. "He used expressions I'd never heard from him. Gambling terms I didn't even think he knew." Telling it now made it seem all the more ridiculous. "You can see how silly I was to think it was deliberate. He was simply equating his life with the odds. Perfectly natural. I'd never have noticed it if you hadn't been so fresh in my mind." She looked thoughtful. "Funny. I'm almost sorry he didn't know. I think in a way he'd have been glad to know I had that much spirit. Even if it meant I was cheating on his own son."

"They say he had his share of fun," Martin said. "I've heard he was quite a ladies' man in his day. Didn't *his* wife ever try to get back at him?"

"She got back at him every day of his life," Susan said, "but not by being unfaithful. Not the way I tried to punish Richard. Her way was more insidious, more evil, really."

"Sounds like a rough broad."

It was such an unlikely description of the well-bred Maria that Susan laughed.

"I guess that's just what she is, in a very smooth way."

Martin looked uncomfortable. "What you said a minute ago, about being unfaithful to punish your husband. Was that all it meant to you, Susan?"

"That's the way it started," she said honestly. "But my feelings changed very quickly. You know that. I'm glad I decided to leave while I still could. We'd never be right for each other, Martin."

"Speak for yourself," he said roughly.

Richard Antonini felt very put-upon these days. He was always bored and restless at this time of year, facing a summer in which he played no concerts and heard no applause. But this period was worse than any he could remember. He felt trapped by Susan, realizing she'd somehow outwitted him, that she was no longer worshipful. He loved her, he supposed, but this sudden feeling that she saw through him and was laughing at

359

him disconcerted him and made him angry. Damn it, what did she want? What was all this constant crap about "something of her own?" She had plenty of her own! A big apartment, all the money she could spend, the opportunity to be as social as Jacqueline, as acquisitive as Mary Lou, even as prominent as Maria, if she wanted to. But she didn't want to. What she wanted was to possess him, to build some kind of stupid "togetherness" probably involving more children and a regimented, predictable existence like the one her parents had.

Well, she couldn't have it. God knows she should have realized that by now. She was married to an artist, and artists didn't make middle-class commitments to a stiff, structured life. He'd tried, after Washington, to change. But he chafed under domestic demands. Responsibility wasn't for him.

Even Maria was driving him crazy, always wanting him near her, nagging him about his work, implying he "owed it to her" to be great. What the hell *did* he owe her? Was it his fault she'd gotten knocked up damned near forty years ago? Obviously, he was glad she had, even if she'd been stupid about it. How had she managed all these years to make him feel so apologetic about his birth? The others weren't made to feel they'd been unwelcome. She didn't make *them* feel guilty. And he'd bet they weren't "planned," either. For that matter, aside from occasional meddling in the upbringing of their children, Maria didn't interfere much with Serge and Walter and Gloria. Only me, Richard thought. I couldn't feel more responsible for her if I were an only child.

He was so edgy. If only there were someone to talk to. He missed Paul. His new manager, George Reagan (Richard still thought of him as "new" even after all this time), was capable enough, but there was no personal closeness there, the way there'd been with Paul. He thought wistfully of the good times they'd had, the road tours, the women, the laughs. Since Paul had left, the tours were all work and little play. Oh, there was always a girl if he wanted one, and sometimes he did. But George had no part in that side of his life. He wasn't the type. And Richard wouldn't have trusted him to keep his mouth shut anyway.

He paced the apartment, stopping now and then to pick up Walter's blasted concerto and throw it down again. He couldn't concentrate, he was so bored. And it would be worse in a few weeks when they moved to East Hampton. There'd be hours of nothingness, endless practice interspersed with a few dumb parties at the big houses on Lily Pond Lane and a lot of hokey socializing at the Maidstone Club. Susan was looking forward to the summer. She still thought they'd rediscover something. That "one-happy-little-family" dream again. *Susan's* dream. *His* nightmare. He'd be running back and forth to Pound Ridge, pacifying Maria, trying to keep Susan happy and hating himself, always hating himself, for his inability to love a child with whom he couldn't communicate.

What damned rotten luck to have a daughter who was like a reproach. Another yoke around my neck, he thought. My life seems to be full of them. In no time I'll be forty. Forty! It seemed like the end of the line. The beginning of middle age with nothing to look forward to. He thought of all the times Susan had been ready to leave him. He almost wished he'd let her go, so he'd be free and desirable again. But his vanity wouldn't permit him to admit he'd failed at his marriage. He wanted it both ways: a wife and a series of sexual adventures. The way his father had had it. If the old man had been able to get away with it for years, why couldn't he? Because Maria never really gave a damn, as Susan does, Richard realized. She never really loved Giovanni. And she was right. Romantic love was a pain. What had somebody once called it? "A sweet folly." That just about summed it up.

The apartment was so bloody quiet it unnerved him. Susan was out somewhere, probably doing one of those endless housewifely chores of hers. He wondered whom he could call. Not the family. He was in no mood for any of them. He'd liked to have called Paul, but that was impossible. He'd never make the first move toward that ungrateful bastard. I haven't any friends, Richard realized. Not male or female. I only have an ex-friend and a lot of ex-lovers, like Dolly Johnson. The memory of Washington and the accident was still bitter, but the thought of the Senator's "mad-cap daughter" brought a smile to Richard's lips. She'd been a good sport, Dolly. Ready for anything. A girl of the moment who didn't thumb her nose at the future but simply pretended it didn't exist. He needed some-one like that now. A Dolly Johnson. Or a Gerry Carter. Or even that dizzy little Hollywood actress who'd been with him in Texas when Maria had her stroke. What was her name? Sylvia. Sylvia Sloan. He hadn't thought about her in a long time, hadn't even heard her mentioned. She'd dropped from sight. He supposed the career had gone sour, the way careers often do with not-too-talented actresses.

It would be fun to see Sylvia again. He hadn't been in touch with her since that morning so long ago when they'd called him and he'd torn out of the hotel in Houston, hardly saying goodbye to her.

He went to his desk and fished out the little address book he kept buried in the back of the middle drawer. There it was. Sylvia Sloan. Impulsively, with nothing special in mind, he dialed the number. A sleepy voice answered.

"Sylvia?"

"Yeah. Who's this?"

"Richard Antonini."

She became instantly alert. "For Christ's sake! Richard! Where are you?"

"In New York. I was just thinking of you and won-dered how you were."

"Well, if that's not the damnedest thing! After all this time! Last I saw of you, you were streaking out of the Warwick with your shirttail practically flapping out of your pants!"

Richard laughed. She made him feel young and carefree.

"I read your mother got over her stroke okay. I was sorry to hear about your father."

"Thanks."

"How's everything else?"

"I've been working hard."

"*That* I know, dummy! You're not exactly an obscure figure. That was some mess you got yourself into in Washington a while back. Really juicy! But you're still married. I have to hand it to you, pal. You do keep your women."

"Do I? I haven't kept you."

"You haven't exactly knocked yourself out trying."

"What about your life, Sylvia?"

"The acting career went down the toilet. I didn't really care. I got married to a rich old jerk from Oklahoma, mostly so I wouldn't have to get up for those studio calls at five in the morning. We were divorced three months ago and the settlement is just fine. I'm living it up in a big house in Beverly Hills."

"Oh? I thought you were in the same apartment. The phone number's the same."

"That's *all* that's the same, buddy. I'm a loaded divorcée now. Why don't you come out and see how the idle rich do it in California?"

"I wish I could," Richard said, "but I don't see how I could work it. Maybe I'll see you in the fall. I'm scheduled for an appearance at your Music Center."

"We may all be dead by fall. Or I may have found another sucker to marry. Oh well. It was a good idea, but you've obviously become a solid, settled citizen. Too bad. I always had a big thing for you. You used to be the sexiest kid on the block."

She couldn't have said anything more challenging.

"I don't know why I couldn't run out there for the long Memorial Day weekend," Richard said suddenly. "Might be a good idea. I could check out the fall concert."

"Terrific! That's next weekend. I'll plan a bash!"

363

"Don't do that, Sylvia. I'll want to keep my visit reasonably quiet. You can understand why."

"Oh, sure. Just a few discreet friends, okay?"

"Sounds good. I'll see you Thursday. Oh, by the way, you'd better give me your new address."

She gave him a number on Rodeo Drive. "It's close to the Beverly Wilshire. I assume you'll check in there, though I don't expect you to spend much time in your suite. The room service here is much better, if you know what I mean."

He hung up, laughing. She was really terrible. Brash and vulgar. But she'd make no long-term demands on him. She never had. He wasn't sure why he'd suddenly decided to go. It was sophomoric, as though he couldn't resist a dare. No, it was more. He needed it, this kind of unplanned, spur-of-the moment adventure. It was a good idea. One of those "why-not" inspirations. The kind he'd often had when he was a bachelor. Just pick up and go. He was *entitled*, Richard told himself, before the long, dutiful damned summer descended upon him.

Susan accepted, without question, his evasive announcement that he had to run out to the West Coast on business the following weekend. She was almost too understanding these days, Richard thought uncomfortably. As though she knew he was up to something and didn't really give a damn. He found himself giving a much too elaborate explanation for his trip, a dead giveaway that there was something out of the ordinary about it. He realized, to his amazement, that he felt guilty. The awareness only angered him. Damn them! They really were turning him into a solid, settled citizen. He wasn't ready for that. Not for a long, long time. Maybe not ever.

"You don't seem to mind my leaving." His tone was almost petulant.

"Of course I mind! But I know you wouldn't go, especially over a holiday, unless you had to." Susan seemed absolutely serene. "Richard dear, it isn't the first time we've been separated, for heaven's sake! Why would you think I'd be upset about a short trip?"

Maria was another matter. "I don't understand," she said. "Why on earth do you have to go to California in May for a concert scheduled in October? For that matter, why do you have to go at all? That's what your manager is for. To check into details." She tapped her foot impatiently. "Really, Richard, it's most inconvenient! You know I planned to have all the family in Pound Ridge for the Memorial Day weekend. Even your wife and child."

"They can come without me. I'm sure Walter and Jacqueline will bring them if Susan doesn't want to drive."

Maria looked at him as though he were crazy. "Are you being funny? You know very well your wife will be thrilled to have an excuse to avoid the family. I was surprised she agreed to come in the first place. I suppose she felt she had to do it for your sake. This gives her a marvelous out. I'll bet *she* wasn't a bit perturbed about your going away."

Why didn't I see that? Richard wondered. Of course. Susan wasn't upset about his sudden trip because it meant she didn't have to spend the weekend with Maria. It had been a pitched battle to get her reluctant agreement. She didn't suspect anything. No wonder she was so cool. She'd gotten a reprieve.

"That's not it at all, Mother. She was looking forward to it." He hoped he sounded convincing.

"Oh, please, Richard! It's bad enough to disappoint me. Don't play me for a fool as well!"

"I'm sorry. About the weekend, I mean. I wouldn't go if I could avoid it."

She tried another tactic. "It's all right, dear. I shouldn't be upset. It's just that it's the first holiday we won't all be together. It will seem strange, not having your father there. And now you won't be there, either.

365

Never mind. It really isn't important. I'm just being a foolish, sentimental old woman."

For a moment he considered canceling. It was rotten selfish of him, he supposed. Maria watched him carefully.

"Please forget what I said, Richard. Of course you must go if it's necessary. Your work comes first. It's the most important thing in your life. And mine."

He felt like a heel, but the mental picture of a wild weekend with Sylvia and her friends was too tempting. To hell with it. Maria had her other children and all the grandchildren. Susan had already said she'd take Katie to Bronxville for a long-overdue visit with her parents.

"You're a darling," Richard said. "I can always count on you to understand. I'll make it up to you. We'll have plenty of other weekends. Maybe you'll come spend some time with us in East Hampton."

"Of course," Maria said, making it perfectly clear in two words that she had no intention of doing anything of the sort.

"Richard and Susan won't be coming to Pound Ridge for the weekend," Mary Lou said. "He's going to California."

Sergio looked surprised. "California? What the hell for?"

"Your mother says it's business. Something to do with his appearance there next fall."

Her husband laughed. "If she buys that, I've got a great piece of underwater land in Florida I'd like to discuss with her."

"You mean he's lying?"

"When did you ever hear of a pianist going five months ahead of time to set up arrangements for a concert in a hall he's played a dozen times?"

"Well, what's he doing?"

"I have no idea. But I'll bet if it's business, it's monkey, not music."

Jacqueline turned around so Walter could zip up the back of her evening dress. "Lucky Susan," she said. "Richard's going to California Thursday, so she doesn't have to go up to the Antonini Olympics."

"California? What's out there?"

"*He* says the Dorothy Chandler Pavilion."

"And what do *you* say?"

"A woman. Or a weekend party. Or both."

"Now why would you think that? Richard's been on his good behavior for a long time."

"That's exactly why I think that. Too good. Too long."

"Come on, Jacqueline. That's pretty farfetched. Hell, if he wanted to fool around he wouldn't have to go all the way to the West Coast."

She shrugged. "Maybe you're right. But who does business on a holiday?"

"Your brother-in-law Richard and his darling wife won't be with us at Mother's next weekend," Gloria said.

"How come?"

"He has to go to California."

"That's too bad."

"Don't be stupid, Raoul. It's great. She's the world's worst party poop. And Richard's not a barrel of laughs these days, either. Personally, I think it's a break."

"You and Katie coming for the weekend? Oh, darling, I'm delighted! I'm sorry Richard can't come, though."

367

"He's sorry, too, Mother. Something came up unexpectedly about his appearance in Los Angeles next fall. But we'll have a chance for a really good gossip."

"Would you like me to plan anything? Anyone you'd like to see?"

"Just you and Dad. No festivities, please. I want to fall apart. It's been a hectic period."

"Yes, I know," Bea said. "Your father and I were discussing that just the other evening. Are you all right, Susie?"

"Never better. I think I've really gotten my act together again. But I need a sounding board. And you and Dad are the best ones I know."

Susan hung up, frowning. It was true. She had been feeling more optimistic lately. Even slightly victorious that she'd won out about her "banishment" to Europe. And she'd handled the situation with Martin Tanner like an adult. Things seemed to be going well with her and Richard. Despite Maria's best efforts, she thought they were finally settling into a reasonably contented, harmonious life, beginning, at long last, to understand and accept each other's frailties.

And now this.

He was patently up to something. It had to be another woman. The story about business would have been laughable if it hadn't been so upsetting. He's cooked up something, Susan thought. I feel it in my bones. God knows what he's up to. The only thing I do know is that he's lying. And the only satisfaction is *he* knows *I* know he's lying. Methinks you do protest too much, dear husband. If you're bored and restless, why couldn't you just say you need a few days alone, the way I did when I went to Vegas? No, that would be too easy.

Not that she thought for a moment he simply intended to be alone. Not Richard, who'd always been only fleetingly faithful.

Why am I so suspicious of him? Well, why shouldn't I be? I can love him, desire him, respect his genius. But I can never trust him. Why don't I accept him for

what he is—an unpredictable, self-centered, hyp-
notically attractive man who needs injections of outside
adulation? He'll be immature and insecure as long as
he lives. And still I want to live with him. I mustn't let
foolish pride make me so possessive. I've got to give
him a long lead, knowing, no matter whom he meets,
he'll always come back. The way I did.

Chapter Twenty-eight

There were a few frightening days following his return
from California, days threatening enough to subdue
even Richard. But by mid-June he dared relax and put
thoughts of Beverly Hills and Sylvia Sloan out of his
mind.

He'd agreed with Susan that the big, weather-beaten
old house in East Hampton really was more than they
needed for themselves and Katie, Bridie and two other
servants. It was a huge establishment with nine bedrooms, a pool and tennis court. But it was luxurious
and lovely, set high on the dunes, with stairs leading
down to a private beach, and it had a sweeping view of
the ocean. The deciding factor, though, was the vast,
air-conditioned living room, which could be kept at the
carefully controlled temperature necessary for his piano. Not too many houses at the beach provided such
an important feature for his precious possession, which
was trucked out from New York by the local "Home
Sweet Home" moving company. It was this room that
sold him. Rapid changes of heat and cold or moisture

and dryness were a constant threat to the fine instrument. Changing climatic conditions called for endless tuning, and on humid days the felts of the piano could stick annoyingly. The room's controlled temperature, in which he could practice and refine the works for his upcoming fall concert, was the deciding factor in their choice of this house.

He sat there now, running his fingers lovingly over the keys as he thought about the future. He intended to be more brilliant than ever in his upcoming concerts and he spent hour after hour appraising his own work, perfecting an already near-perfect technique. Some of the unfriendly criticism of the recent past still rankled. One reviewer had dared call his performance "a bland, superficial display, unworthy of the artist who used to make audiences feel he was afire." He'd show them. He'd give them the old, dazzling Richard Antonini. And later he'd play that damned concerto of Walter's, which he still hadn't mastered to his satisfaction. But he would, by God, if it killed him.

His old confidence had returned. He'd really come to terms with his life with Susan. He glanced out of the window and saw her on the beach with Bridie and the child. They presented a peaceful picture on this hot July afternoon. He'd been unfair to them, he supposed. It had taken that horrifying weekend with Sylvia to make him appreciate the sanity and security he had at home.

God, what a scary experience that had turned out to be! Lucky Susan had not asked much about the trip or its aftermath. Experienced liar that he was, he really wasn't very good at it.

His thoughts wandered back to those few days. He'd checked into the Beverly Wilshire Hotel, feeling adventurous and free, and been greeted by the assistant manager, an old friend, Bud Porter.

"Keep the press off my back, will you, Bud?" he'd asked. "I just want to relax. It's a quiet, personal visit. Sorry to disappoint your publicity lady, but I'll make up for it when I come back in a few months."

"Of course. Anything we can do for you?"

"Not a thing. I'll be out most of the time with friends."

What an understatement that had been! Sylvia had almost devoured him, never wanting him out of her sight, sexually demanding when they were alone, embarrassingly possessive when she allowed a few intimates to join them in her big, vulgar, over-decorated mansion in Beverly Hills. For the first twenty-four hours, Richard had enjoyed the attention and the intense passion of a woman whose bizarre sexual practices were titillating but almost shocking, even to him. At first, he hadn't even minded the high-handed way she behaved when her few friends were around, as though he was her personal possession. But by Saturday, he began to feel uncomfortable, uneasy. Sylvia was not the carefree, amusing "sex symbol" he'd known in Houston. He was sure she was heavily into drugs. She'd even lost the lush blond beauty that had first attracted him. In fact, she was haggard, dissipated-looking. She seemed desperate, somehow, pressing too hard. On Sunday night, physically exhausted and troubled by her state of mind, he tried, diplomatically, to talk to her about her behavior.

"Let's keep things in perspective, Syl," he said. "You know I'm fond of you, but there's never been anything long-term between us. I don't think you should give friends the idea that this is a serious affair. I don't even know when I'll see you again. This trip was a spur-of-the-moment thing and I've enjoyed it. You're really terrific, but I'm married, you know. There can't be anything for us except some laughs once in a while."

She didn't seem to understand what he was saying.

"Then why did you come back to me? Why did you leave your wife to fly out here and be with me? You love me. I know you do."

"No," Richard said kindly, "I don't love you. You sounded gay and amusing on the phone, and I remembered what good times we had in the past. No strings

371

attached. I was anxious to see you again and it's been great. But I didn't 'come back to you,' Sylvia, because in spite of Houston, you and I know there was never anything to come back *to*. You're a beautiful woman," (what harm in a compassionate lie?) "and right now you're feeling a little displaced after your divorce. But you'll meet another man. You're young and marvelously sexy and you're a famous name." He tried to sound relaxed and casual. "You don't need a married piano player who lives three thousand miles away, for God's sake! All you have to do is crook your finger and half the studs in Southern California will come running! Come on, where's your sense of humor? It isn't like you to turn a simple, sexy weekend into a heavy commitment. You know better than that. You're the glamorous Sylvia Sloan, the beautiful lady of Beverly Hills!"

Her response was a mirthless laugh. "More like the whore of the Hollywood Hills," she said. "I thought you were going to make me come alive again, Richard. I thought you were the answer after all the months and years of screwing around with guys who didn't give a damn. I have nothing. Don't try to be kind. It's all gone. My looks. My career. The marriage I thought was 'safe.' Even what you call my 'glamour.' Nobody gives a damn for me. Nobody ever has. Until you. I thought you did, coming back in spite of that scandal. I wanted to believe you could give me something to live for." The despondent, droning voice suddenly turned loud and accusatory. "Who the hell asked you to start this up again? What was I supposed to think, after all this time, when you called? You sonofabitch! You're like all the rest! All you want is the only thing I have left: a body. The only difference between you and the rest is that you're willing to fly three thousand miles for a good lay while the others are only willing to drive twenty minutes!"

Richard was stunned and shaken. "My God, I didn't mean to mislead you! I thought you knew where we stood. Where we've *always* stood. I didn't realize how unhappy you are. Or how lonely."

She screamed at him. "I'm not lonely! I'm surrounded by people who eat my food and drink my booze and share my bed! The public still adores me! You're right. Who needs *you?* Get the hell out of my house and don't come back until you have something more to offer than one of your 'simple, sexy weekends!' Get out! Now!"

He'd gone back to the hotel, puzzled and faintly disgusted. He felt sorry for her, but the woman was a lunatic. He'd never given her a hint that he wanted her as permanent fixture in his life. Jesus, he thought, if I'd known what I was getting into! Poor Sylvia. He hadn't realized how unloved she felt, how hopelessly she clutched at any ridiculous dream. But he couldn't save her. He had no wish to. She had no reason to think he could.

He called American Airlines and booked a 1 P.M. flight to New York next day. Before I leave, I'll send her something expensive, he decided. A good piece of jewelry, maybe. She'd like that. It occurred to him that she'd probably tell the world it had been a present from her "adoring lover" Richard Antonini. He frowned. So what? Let her, if it gave her any comfort. Besides, who'd believe her? By this time all of Los Angeles must know she's out of her head, living on pills and liquor. Pathetic. What a waste. She'd sure gone downhill since the days in Houston.

At three in the morning, his phone rang. He answered groggily. It was Sylvia and she was crying.

"I'm sorry," she stammered. "I don't know what got into me. I know you don't love me, Richard. It's just that I need someone. So much. So very much."

He tried to shake himself awake. "It's all right," he said. "Don't worry about it. I understand. You had a little too much to drink."

"No, you don't understand. I love you. I always have. I never thought I could have you, but when you called and came out, I thought . . ."

"I know. It was foolish of me. I didn't think how it would seem to you. Stay well, Sylvie. Take care of yourself. And, I don't mean to sound heartless, but try to forget about me, will you?"

"Yes. Thank you. Goodbye, Richard."

"Good night, my dear. Get some sleep."

"I will. I promise."

"Good girl. And let me know how you are."

"Yes," she said again. "I will."

He was thankful to be safely back in the apartment Monday evening, deserted as it was. He called Susan at her mother's.

"I'm home and glad to be here! How are you, darling? How's Katie? When are you coming back?"

"We're fine. We'll be in tomorrow morning. Have a good trip?"

Was there a coolness in her voice? Richard wasn't sure.

"It was okay. Pretty uneventful. I got a lot of details firmed up for the fall."

"Good." There was a pause. "Sad about that actress, wasn't it?"

"What actress?"

"The one you used to know. The one *Open Secrets* made so much of. Sylvia Sloan. She took her life sometime early this morning. It was on the six-o'clock news. Sleeping pills, they said."

He was near panic. Susan had put two and two together, adding up Houston, and his quick trip, and this. But she couldn't prove anything. Nobody could unless, God forbid, that insane woman had left a note! He made himself sound deliberately remote though sorry.

"Good God, that's terrible! Sylvia Sloan! I haven't thought of her in years!"

There was silence at the other end of the line.

"You know what I mean," Richard said. "Not since that foolishness in Texas. I always regretted that, Susie. You know I did."

"Of course." The voice was calm. "That's one of the things we've put behind us, isn't it? I certainly had no

374

love for her, but it's sad when such a beautiful, talented young woman wants nothing more than to go to sleep forever."

The words were chilling. The last thing he'd said to Sylvia early that morning was "Get some sleep and let me know how you are." She'd agreed so meekly. She must have known exactly how she was going to keep both those promises.

"Well," Richard said, "those things are beyond understanding. You're right, it's sad, but some people are beyond help. Okay, dear, I'm going to turn in. See you tomorrow. Sleep well." He paused. "I love you."

"Good night."

He raced to the television set and turned on the ABC eleven-o'clock news in time to hear the commentator say, "Friends of Sylvia Sloan, the former Hollywood star, were shocked to learn of her death early this morning in her Beverly Hills home. Cause of death was an overdose of sleeping pills accidentally or deliberately administered. Miss Sloan, recently divorced from millionaire Harley Custin, was discovered by her maid, who went in to awaken her at noon, Los Angeles time. Police say no note was left by the actress, who starred in such films as . . ."

Richard switched off the set. No note. Thank God. Thank God, too, that Monday was a legal holiday. The good jewelers were closed, and he hadn't been able to send her the gift he planned. Sweat poured over his body at the thought of a delivery turned over to the police. They couldn't involve him in this sordid story now. Not unless some of those creepy friends of her chose to tell the world he'd been with them over the weekend. And they might. They were all publicity-mad. He'd deny it, of course, but much good that would do! Susan would be certain and the world would be suspicious. Those bloody reporters who caused him so much trouble would be on his tail again. Goddammit! What a stupid idea the whole weekend had been!

But surprisingly, nothing more happened. Sylvia Sloan was no longer important enough to rate more

375

than a TV glimpse of the simple funeral service for the actress, who, it was officially decided, accidentally ended her life. The millionaire, probably a conservative pillar of his community and loath to have the details of his ex-wife's lurid life exposed, must have hushed up the "hangers-on," Richard concluded. The man sensibly wanted no sensational publicity. Thanks, Harley Custin, whoever you are, Richard thought as the days went by and there was no mention of the old scandal. You not only saved your reputation and Sylvia's, you also rescued mine.

On the surface, Susan seemed as calm and contented as Richard did, but inwardly she agonized over her husband's latest escapade. It didn't take a genius to figure out that Richard had been off to some adventure when he left so precipitously for California. Her comment about Sylvia Sloan had been a shot in the dark, but the moment she heard his tone of voice she knew that Richard's trip and Sylvia's overdose were no coincidence. She tried hard not to think that the young woman's death had anything to do with Richard, but with a wife's instinct she felt he was directly involved. It was such an intolerable suspicion that she could discuss it with no one, least of all with him. I don't want to hear another of his confessions, she thought. I couldn't bear having this terrible certainty confirmed. If it's true, if he somehow drove that pathetic creature to her grave, how in God's name can he live with it? For that matter, how can he be so extraordinarily serene, so enthusiastic about his work, so loving and tender toward me? He even seemed slightly less subservient to Maria these days. It was incredible, as though a new Richard had returned from California, a more appreciative and contented Richard, at peace with himself.

She tried to put it out of her mind, rationalizing that no one isolated incident drove a person to suicide. If the actress had taken her life, it couldn't have been because of one weekend with Richard. Such things were the result of a long buildup of despair and loneliness and fear, the final act of a mind that had been sick for a long, long time. But it was a mental state that Susan, for all her moments of terribly personal tragedies, could not fully comprehend. Even at her lowest point, when her child was taken away, she had not wished to die. Oh, she might have said so, but she'd never reached the point of not wanting to live. Life was often hard, sometimes nearly insupportable, but it was precious and never totally devoid of hope. She wondered, heartsick, how it felt to be so utterly despondent that death could be the only release. She'd retreated after her own sorrows, withdrawn, turned to drink, even sought solace in infidelity, but she'd never considered ending her life. It chilled her to know that such misery was possible. I'm lucky, she thought. In spite of everything, I'm much luckier than that golden girl who seemed to have everything—beauty, success, public adoration. And yet she had nothing because, obviously, she lacked something to live for, someone to love her.

Had Sylvia loved Richard? Did she die for impossible love of him? Susan could not accept that. Sylvia Sloan died because she was mentally ill. Too many other women had survived their dismissals by Richard Antonini. She was sure they'd wept, probably pleaded or threatened. But they did not destroy themselves at the dapper clay feet of the idol.

As the weeks wore on, the memory of a woman she'd never even met dimmed, and, like Richard, Susan was more tranquil than she'd been in a long time. Another scandal, if there was one, never surfaced. Richard seemed happy. He was working hard and well, enjoying the beautiful summer days, even making fewer and fewer "duty trips" to his mother's country house. They lived quietly, accepted few invitations. Walter and Jacqueline came for a weekend and so did Kate and the Langdons, and it was all easy and congenial. Their only argument came over Susan's stubborn refusal to go to a big party with him. Richard didn't really enjoy most of them, but this was one he wanted to attend. Susan begged off.

"Why?" Richard asked. "It's *the* big party of the year. There'll be lots of people we know from the city. I think it'll be amusing. We could do with a little outside stimulation."

"I'm sorry. I just don't feel like it. I hope you don't mind."

"Well, I *do* mind! How will it look, my showing up without my wife?"

"It won't be the first time." Susan's voice was icy.

He glared at her. "Are we starting that all over again?"

"No. Sorry. I lost my temper. I just meant I saw no reason for you to stay home because I know I wouldn't have a good time." She knew she was making an issue over nothing. She was simply tired of doing what he wanted. The party and the people giving it bored her. For once, she would please herself. It was one of those small gestures that every now and then she felt compelled to make . . . a pathetically insignificant rebellion that somehow made her feel independent of Richard. She was being foolish, but she stuck to her decision, though she softened her attitude.

"Darling, *do* go to the party! It'll be fun for you. And honestly, I'm dying to do some more work on the book. I want you to go. Please. You can always say I have a cold."

"Well, all right. But I still say it's crazy."

"It probably is, but you know you married a crazy lady."

His thoughts went back to Sylvia and he remembered being thankful that his wife was so sane. "You're the most levelheaded female in the world," he said, smiling, "even if you do go off half-cocked once in a while."

"Then you *will* go?"

"Yes, I'll go and leave you in the company of the Muse. How's the book going, by the way?"

"Agonizingly, but I love doing it."

"The old identity search again, right?"

She smiled at him. "Afraid so. But it's more than that. It's also a labor of love."

Starting the book had been one of the most unexpected and joyful events of her life. It had happened quickly and completely out of the blue. Soon after they arrived in East Hampton, she and Richard had gone to a small dinner party at the home of a famous publisher. At table, Susan was seated next to an attractive young man named Rhett Wilson, one of the host's senior editors.

"You obviously belong in publishing," Susan said lightly, "with a name like yours."

He winced, pretending pain. "Did you have to?" he asked. "You seem so bright and pretty I was hoping you'd be one of the rare ones who wouldn't ask whether my mother was reading *Gone with the Wind* during her pregnancy."

Susan laughed. "Was she?"

"Of course, damn it. I can only give thanks that she hadn't the bad taste to marry a man named Butler."

Susan found him amusing, rather whimsical and yet completely professional. She was so relaxed that, after having told him about her job on *Vogue*, she confessed, with embarrassment, that the ambition of her life was to write a book. "I know that's the cliché of all time," she said. "Every person who's ever written a magazine article or a newspaper piece or an ad thinks he could become an author. It's nonsense, of course. Even *I* know that writing a book is far different from doing a short feature. It must take enormous discipline, not to mention talent."

Wilson seemed suddenly cool. "Yes, it does," he said, and then quite deliberately changed the subject to talk about tennis, which he claimed was his overwhelming passion.

Susan felt foolish and rebuffed. He must think me a typical opportunist, taking advantage of a social situation to get an "in" with an important editor! I'm sure

379

every other person he meets attacks him with a silly idea about writing a book. He must be bored out of his mind with it. She hid her discomfort, and throughout the rest of the dinner chatted about other things, still finding him a delightful companion. He'd rented a small house in Bridgehampton for the summer, he told her, and was there every weekend. He hoped she and her husband would "come slumming" one afternoon.

"We'd love it," Susan said. "And you must visit us." She scribbled the phone number and address on her card. "Please call when you feel like it. I'm a poor tennis player and Richard won't touch a racket because of his hands, but we do have a court and I'm sure we could get a game for you."

Next week in the mail she received a current bestseller and a note from Rhett Wilson saying he'd enjoyed talking with her. The week after, he sent two more books, and that weekend she called him.

"I should write you a proper thank-you note," Susan said, "but I thought I'd make it an invitation instead. You've been so kind to send the books and we'd love to see you again. Can you come for lunch on Saturday? There'll just be Richard and me."

"Be delighted. By the way, how did you enjoy the books?"

She hesitated. "Honest answer?"

"By all means."

"I liked the novels but I was disappointed in the nonfiction account of the woman in the Peace Corps. It's nervy of me to say so, but I didn't think it was awfully well written. She had a chance to turn a moving experience into a meaningful account of the suffering and fears of the lepers in India. How they affected her, I mean. I think she missed the boat. There wasn't enough heart in it."

She could imagine him smiling at her audacity, but instead he said, "My reaction exactly, though I haven't said so because it wasn't my book. I mean, I wasn't the editor, and we don't like to criticize our colleagues'

380

projects. You're right, I think. It should have been great and it was only medium-good."

Susan felt pleased and even more delighted when he said, "You know, I had a hunch. I sent you those books for a purpose. Just to see how astute a critic you are. Now I know you understand writing, so maybe we ought to talk about *your* trying a book. Do you have an idea?"

"No. Not really. I was just fantasizing that night at dinner."

"Well, think about it. And we can talk Saturday."

She was feverishly excited when she reported the conversation to Richard. Surprisingly, he seemed to take to the idea.

"Why not? You're a good writer and this could be the thing you've been searching for ever since we were married. It's something you can do at home or even when we're on tour. Sounds like a good idea to me. What would you write—a novel?"

"I don't know. I'm not sure. Listen, don't let me get carried away, will you? I mean this is a far cry from having a book under contract. I don't want to get all steamed up and be disappointed when nothing happens. It's purely exploratory. Probably won't amount to a damn."

He teased her. "You don't believe that for a moment and you know it. I can see that glint in your eye. You *know* you'll be the next Jacqueline Susann."

Chapter Twenty-nine

Rhett Wilson seemed dubious when Susan told him her idea for a book.

"I don't know," he said. "It's a touching story, this account of your and Richard's determination to bring up Katie in a hearing world and having it all turn out so successfully. It's just that, commercially, it might not sell. People, by and large, don't like to be reminded of the handicapped. Even if I could get you a contract, there'd be a ridiculously small advance. Probably not more than, say, fifteen hundred dollars, based on projected sales. Would you want to waste your time for that?"

"The money isn't important," Susan said. "I know that sounds terribly snobbish, but I really don't care what I'm paid for it. Whatever I get I'm going to donate to one of the organizations that help deaf-mute children and their parents. The thing that matters to me is to tell people that it can be done. That they don't have to hide their children or condemn them to a silent, abnormal existence. And," she admitted, "I guess there's something of an ego trip involved here, too. As I told you the first night we met, anybody who's ever been paid to put pen to paper is secretly hungry to see his name on a book jacket. But the main thing is to give encouragement to others. God knows we received precious little of it ourselves in the beginning!"

"I'm sure of that. Look, Susan, I'll be perfectly frank with you. If I can get the publishing board to accept this idea, one of the reasons will be because you are Mrs. Antonini. That means automatic publicity. Would you be willing to promote at publication time? Would you go on TV talk shows and make personal appearances in book departments around the country and give interviews to the press? It's hard work, but it moves copies. Frankly, I think that's the best way I can sell this idea to my people."

She was quiet for a long moment. This was not at all what she expected. She hadn't thought about trading on her husband's name. She simply wanted to tell her story as a mother, no different from thousands of mothers faced with the same wrenching decision. When the family was frantic for good publicity they'd encouraged her to speak out about Katie, but she was sure their attitude would be quite different now that there was no "crisis." She hadn't even told Richard she planned to write about their child. He still thought she was going to do some kind of novel. He'd be upset even by the idea of this book. And he'd have a fit if she was all over the country selling it, "letting her name be used" so blatantly and commercially. As for Maria's reaction, the temporary truce would end and the war with her mother-in-law would start up again, probably more intense than ever. She remembered how Maria had carried on years before when Susan began to write a relatively impersonal column. She had killed that idea, innocuous as it was. Wait until she heard this one!

Rhett correctly guessed some of what was going through her mind. "Why don't you give it some thought? It's the kind of thing you'll want to discuss with your husband, I'm sure. Let's face it, Susan, we'd be taking advantage of the Antonini name, and Richard may object to that. I think you could do a good and useful book even under a pseudonym, but the commercial facts of life still exist. More people are going to buy a book by Susan Antonini than one by

Susan Nobody. We all have to accept that, right up front. It doesn't downgrade your talent as a writer. It's just the way things are."

Richard had left them alone after lunch while he went into the house to practice. She could hear him now, going over and over the same passage, toying with the phrasing, striving for perfection, seeking his own interpretation of the music, bringing his emotions to the world. That's what I want to do, Susan realized. I really want to tell the world what I believe about the power of love and its miraculous ability to strike down obstacles. These are *my* emotions and my public tribute to a brave little girl. I can't help how Richard and his family feel. I'm proud of Katie, and grateful to those who've helped her. And I damned well am going to say so.

"You're very understanding," she said. "And quite right in assuming that the Antoninis don't like their name exploited. But I still want to do the book, Rhett, if your company will accept it. And I'll do as much promotion as I can without neglecting my husband or my child."

"You're sure? You could try a novel that wouldn't call for such soul-baring. I'm sure you're imaginative and you must have a lot of experience to draw on. Maybe you should consider that, instead of the nonfiction story of Katie."

"No," Susan said firmly. "I want to write a love letter to my daughter. That's what this really is, you know."

He nodded. "I think I can understand that. By the way, that's not a bad title if we can clear it: *Love Letter to My Daughter*. But I'm getting ahead of myself. First we have to get a contract."

He explained the procedure. She'd have to give him a detailed outline of the book and write the first hundred pages of it with no guarantee of acceptance. "I know you've been a magazine writer," Rhett said, "but to us you're an 'unpublished author.' We have to get an idea of your style, see how you organize the first few chapters. When that's done, I'll present the whole package and hope for the best. Let's see. This is the first week of July. Think you could get something to me around mid-August?"

Susan mentally calculated. Six weeks. Forty-two days. Even if she did only three pages a day she should easily be able to meet that deadline. On *Vogue* she'd been used to much more "rush assignments."

"I'll try," she said. "I think I can."

"Good. I'll be looking forward to it." He glanced at his watch. "Good Lord, I've got to run! Say goodbye to Richard for me, will you? And thanks for the lunch."

"Thank *you!* I'm really excited about this, Rhett."

"Believe it or not, so am I. I think you'll write a helluva book that probably would sell without the hoopla. But the promotion will be added insurance. Do a good job, Susan, and call me if you need help along the way. I'm looking forward to being your editor. It's always a vicarious thrill to discover a new talent."

She wandered into the house, smiling, already plotting the outline in her head. Richard came out of the living room when he heard the screen door slam.

"How did it go?"

She was radiant. "Wonderfully! Darling, I have to do an outline and a hundred pages by mid-August and then Rhett will see whether he can get me a contract!"

"Good for you!" He seemed genuinely pleased. "Now that you've talked to 'your editor' are you going to break down and tell me what the novel will be about?"

"It isn't a novel. It's a nonfiction book. About how we're raising Katie."

Richard's expression changed from indulgence to dismay. "A book about Katie! Are you mad, Susan? You can't seriously be thinking of putting the intimate details of our life into the hands of every shopgirl on the subway! I won't hear of it! You led me to believe you were going to write some innocuous little novel. Something to fill your time. And now you propose to

385

go into the sordid story of our deaf-mute child. Absolutely not! I forbid it!"

She went rigid. "You *forbid* it? How dare you say that to me! Don't give me orders, Richard. I've had enough of that! I'm your wife, not an employee!"

"Damned right you're my wife. And I won't permit you to flaunt the sordid story of our unfortunate parenthood!"

"That's the second time you've used that word," Susan said passionately. "You *do* find it sordid, don't you? You always have. Well, I don't. I find it beautiful and inspirational and something to be proud of. Katie is all those things, even if we're not. It's *her* story, Richard, not *ours*. You don't have to worry," she said nastily. "I'd already planned to leave out the part about your rejecting her. I'm going to pretend we chose this course together, worked on it together and rejoiced together in the happy outcome. I won't destroy your precious image, have no fear. I'd never let the world know how you've tried to ignore your child most of her life. You'll come out smelling like a rose, if only because one day Katie will read this book and I want her to be proud of her father as a father, not just as an artist."

He was livid. "How can you be so insensitive? Using your own child! Embarrassing yourself and me! Publicizing the most private part of our life!"

"You seem to forget I did it once before. For your sake and your family's. You've conveniently forgotten that thanks to the gossip about you, I was forced to speak publicly about this problem, to portray the Richard Antoninis as a close, devoted family. It was all right *then*, when you wanted to counteract the filth about your affair and your brothers' lives. But now, when I want to pay a loving compliment to an extraordinary little girl, it's suddenly 'sordid' because *you* don't need it. Well, *I* need it. And I'm going to do it. You can scream and yell all you want, but I'm going to write this book. It's important to me. In a way it's my therapy."

"If you need more therapy, why the hell don't you go back to your precious Dr. Marcus? At least that's privileged information!"

"I'm not the one who needs professional help, Richard. If anyone does, it's you!" She stopped, appalled, sickened by the terrible things they were yelling at one another. Yet she couldn't apologize. Everything she'd said was true. And in spite of Richard's fury she was going to write the book. "I wish you weren't so angry about it," she said slowly. "I wish you understood. This is something I have to do. I've lived with the fear and sadness so long that it just has to come out. I'll try to do it with taste. I promise there'll be nothing in it to offend you. Please, Richard, back me up, even if you don't approve."

Her measured voice calmed him. At least he stopped shouting and tried reasoning with her. "What good will it do to drag all this up again? Katie's doing fine. We're all adjusting. Things are peaceful and good between us at last. Why do you want to stir it up, Susan? There must be other kinds of books you can write."

She felt like a traitor. She couldn't logically refute his arguments. She just knew this was meant to be. It was as though fate had put her beside Rhett Wilson at that dinner table. It was the only legacy she alone could leave Katie. Richard could leave her money and a name that opened any door. But only her mother could bequeath the warm and lasting inheritance of love.

"I could write a different kind of book," Susan said, "but that would be meaningless to me and that child. And it wouldn't help other people with heartaches like our own."

He turned away, shaking his head, recognizing defeat. He knew Susan well enough to recognize that, pliable as she was, when she really made up her mind to do something, nothing could stop her. She'd shown that when she virtually kidnaped Katie from the school. He believed she'd have killed anyone who tried to stop her. It was far different than the times she threatened

387

to leave him and allowed herself to be talked out of it. Even today, Richard thought, she's never tried to find out about Sylvia Sloan, though he was certain she suspected his part in the story. Susan fought for the vital things, the changeable things. Mostly, she fought for her child. But sometimes, as now, she also fought for herself.

Susan left the room. It was an unhappy victory, as all her victories seemed to be, and yet she felt strong and sure. Richard loved her, even when he couldn't control her. A mischievous smile appeared on her lips. How I'd love to be a fly on the wall when he tells Maria about this! Then she frowned. Maybe he won't have to. Maybe they won't accept the book and all this will have been for nothing. She realized she hadn't said a word about the "promotion" that would be involved if her "love letter" were published. God knows it was no time to add *that* fuel to the fire! Time enough later to break that news to Richard if it was necessary. And maybe by then, when he'd read the book and seen how gently she handled it, he'd be less upset. He might even be proud of me, Susan thought. I want him to be proud of me.

From that moment, she religiously spent four hours every morning at her typewriter, struggling with the outline and then beginning the engrossing business of telling what it was like to discover that the beautiful, cheerful baby they adored could neither hear nor speak.

She and Richard had no further discussion about the book. They maintained a reasonably harmonious relationship, conversed, made love, acted as though she was simply answering mail or doing household accounts when she disappeared after breakfast into the little room she'd set up as her "office." From lunchtime on, she tended her domestic duties, overseeing the menus, driving into Southampton to shop for groceries at Herbert's or clothes at Saks or knicknacks at Cal Alexander's. Bridie stayed on the beach with Katie

388

while Richard practiced. And on the surface, everything was normal.

She told no one else what she was doing. Not even her mother or Kate knew. It would be too disappointing if the book were rejected, but a lovely surprise if it were not. She was sure Richard had not confided in anyone either, but for a different reason. He must be secretly wishing hard that the publishers would turn it down and he'd not have to face the "embarrassment" of it or the ordeal of breaking the news to Maria.

At the beginning of August, two weeks ahead of her deadline, she'd finished the material Rhett needed. She was not completely satisfied with it, but she knew from experience that she'd never be thoroughly satisfied with anything she wrote. No use worrying it like a dog with a bone. There was just so much revising and polishing one could do at this point, otherwise a year from August she'd still be rewriting and probably making it worse instead of better. Nervously, she called Rhett at his office and told him that the outline and hundred pages were done.

He was delighted. "Terrific! You're ahead of schedule! My heart leaps with joy at the thought of an author who actually turns in work ahead of deadline! I'll be out this weekend. Shall I drive over and pick it up?"

"Please do. I won't sleep a wink until you've read it and given me your opinion. Can you come Saturday? We'll give you lunch or a drink."

"A drink will be great. About six?"

"Perfect. Thank you, Rhett."

"Save that for the big moment when we notify you you've become a full-fledged author."

"From your mouth to God's ears, as we used to say on Seventh Avenue."

He laughed. "It's going to be good. I feel it in my bones."

He arrived, tanned and handsome, promptly at six on Saturday, accepted a drink and said, "I hope I remembered to tell you to make a carbon copy! Not that I won't guard your manuscript with my life, but it's madness for you not to have a duplicate in case I get killed driving home!"

"I have one." Susan smiled, but she seemed uneasy. "I'm sorry Richard can't join us. He isn't feeling too well."

"Nothing serious, I hope."

"No. Just a bad headache. Too much sun, I guess." She wondered whether Rhett knew it was a lie. The truth was that Richard had flatly refused to see their guest. He hadn't made a scene, he'd simply said, "I don't feel kindly enough toward Mr. Wilson to have a drink with him. Make my apologies."

Rhett seemed to accept the falsehood without question. "Sorry I missed him. Next time." He picked up the Manila envelope with her life's blood in it. "I'll try to read this tomorrow and phone you. I know writers. Nervous wrecks until they hear. Of course, you'll only be getting *my* opinion. And even if it's enthusiastic—which I expect—I still have to let a few other people read it and take it to the meeting. So don't start donating your royalty checks quite yet. It will take a couple of weeks, at least, to get the final decision."

He called the next afternoon. Susan literally held her breath until she heard him say, "It's *really* good, Susan! I cried twice and that's the test. I'm taking it into the office tonight and I'll start circulating it tomorrow. You'll hear from me."

On the fifteenth of August, she received a telegram. "Dear Susan. You are now a full-fledged Doubleday author. *Love Letter* passed publishing committee with flying colors. Congratulations. Rhett."

She read it three times and burst into tears. She wasn't sure whether she was crying with joy or nervousness. She felt something of both as she ran down the long flight of stairs to the beach and picked up Katie, whirling the nearly-naked, bronzed little girl round and round.

"Kit-Kat darling," she said distinctly, "I've written a book and it's about you. All about how I love you."

Katie smiled and stroked Susan's cheek. She read the words on her mother's lips but she wasn't sure she understood exactly what they meant. It didn't matter. Something had happened that made Mummy very happy.

Holding the precious telegram, Susan went silently into the room where her husband was working. She curled up in a chair, waiting for a break in the music before she spoke to him. He seemed unaware of her presence, deep into an intricate Liszt polonaise which would be part of his fall program. It was a good ten minutes before he stopped playing, looked up and saw her sitting there, watching him.

"What do you think?"

She smiled. "It's wonderful. Breathtaking."

"I'm not sure. Maybe the Tchaikovsky concerto in B-flat minor . . ."

"Richard, it's been accepted."

"What has?"

"My book." She held up the telegram. "They're going to publish my book."

She waited, holding her breath. Let him be happy for me. Just for once let him show the bigness of spirit I still believe he has.

Without a word he came over and took the piece of yellow paper from her hand, reading it impassively.

"I was hoping they wouldn't, you know. I was putting out all the negative thought-waves I could."

She didn't answer.

And then with one of those meteoric changes of mood that were part of his nature, he leaned down and kissed her. "I'm glad for you, Susie, I know you want this more than anything. There should be room in the Antonini family for another talent. Will you let me read what you've done, now that it's a *fait accompli?*"

She was going to cry again, damn it. But this time with relief, with gratitude that Richard's generosity was bigger than his ego, stronger than his aversion to anything that might reflect unpleasantly on the image he spent his life building. The tears she couldn't contain

391

fell on his soft silk shirt as she put her arms around him and wept with happiness. He held her tenderly, her face against his chest, glad she couldn't see the annoyance he felt. He hated the vanity that made him unwilling to share glory with anyone, but it was ingrained in him. He was jealous when Sergio was praised for his conducting, angry when his damned faggot brother Walter wrote a piece of music that defied even the enormous talent of Richard Antonini. He knew it was petty, but he'd lied when he said there was room for another talent in the Antonini family. There wasn't. In his mind, history had reserved space only for him.

Not that Susan's little book was likely to make history. Not that it was in any way a threat to his superiority as an artist or a man. As he held her, he knew it was infantile to wish she'd been denied any recognition beyond that of being his wife. Still that was how he felt. Despite the words that made Susan so happy, he damned the day Rhett Wilson had come into their lives. He didn't want Susan independent in thought or deed. He wanted her to need him for her identity as well as her material comforts and her social and sexual satisfaction. Richard could not tolerate less than total ownership of his wife. He hated her self-sufficiency and was frustrated when she exerted it. Had he been wise enough to recognize it, he would have seen that one reason for marrying Susan had been to squelch that quality in her and make her dependent upon him for her happiness. And had he been schooled in the workings of the human mind, he also might have recognized that he sought a wife as totally unlike his mother as any woman could be. He would have seen that, pretending to love women, he really feared them, that the devotion he thought he felt toward Maria was resentment of the knowledge that he needed her. He preferred to believe he needed no one except as a satellite orbiting around the glow of his greatness.

Susan was looking up at him now, the old adoration in her eyes. At last she answered his question.

"Darling, I can't *wait* to have you read what I've done! It isn't really very good, I'm sure. Not great writing, but straight from my heart. From yours, too, I hope." She seemed almost timid. "Richard, I'm so glad you've taken this attitude. I was afraid . . ."

"That I'd fly into another rage when I heard they'd bought the book? No. As I said, I'd have preferred they didn't. I still don't take to the idea of hanging out the wash for public scrutiny. I never will. But I can't be so rotten that I'm not pleased for you. I had my tantrum when this whole thing started and," he said ruefully, "it didn't do me a damned bit of good. So what's the point of my screaming now?" He smiled. "The only thing I *should* do is make *you* break the news to Mother. I'm sure you know how *she's* going to feel."

Susan took him seriously. "I don't mind telling her. Why don't we both go to see her? That is, if I'm welcome."

He shook his head. "You're welcome any time. Don't be silly. But it'll go better if you're not around when I give her the word. I'll do it this weekend. No use postponing the hysterics. But let me read it before I try to sell it to her, will you?"

"Of course. I have a copy. Don't move!"

She ran to her office and brought back the outline and first five chapters.

"I'm sure they'll want me to make changes, but this is the stuff they bought." There was almost a wistful, little-girl tone in her voice as she said, "I hope you like it."

Bea Langdon was ecstatic when Susan phoned to tell her the news.

"Imagine! Selling a book on the first try! Susie darling, it's marvelous! I'm so proud of you. We've always known how talented you are, but *this!* Why, I've heard that writers get a hundred turndowns before anything is ever published! Wait until your father hears. He'll burst!"

"It was luck, Mother. Really. If Rhett Wilson hadn't been at that dinner party . . ."

"Nonsense! I'm not saying it wasn't lucky he was there, but if you hadn't had the talent and the discipline, nothing would have happened. I swear, I don't know how you do it! Managing that enormous place, spending time with Katie, catering to Richard and still finding time to write a book! You're marvelous!"

Susan laughed. "And you're wildly prejudiced. Anyway, it isn't written yet. I have a long way to go."

"When will it be published?"

"Fall, seventy-three, Rhett said when I spoke to him this afternoon. That is, if I can finish it by December."

Bea sounded disappointed. "Fall seventy-three! That's more than a year away. I was hoping it would be sooner."

"These things take time, Mom. I'll try to explain it to you—as much as I understand it—next time we get together."

Kate, when she heard, was equally delighted and even more impressed with the "instant success." "Thank God," she said on the phone. "At last you're doing something more intellectually stimulating than squeezing cantaloupes at the market!"

"Much you know," Susan teased. "At Herbert's you don't squeeze the merchandise. You just accept it reverently and pay through the nose. Seriously, Kate, I *am* excited."

"Why not? I'd be, too. How about the Boy Wonder? Can he cope with the competition?"

"He's been wonderful. Oh, he doesn't really like the idea of my writing about Katie and he raised holy hell when the idea came up, but now he's darling. He's going to Pound Ridge this weekend to inform You-Know-Who."

"*Bonne chance* to him," Kate said. "By the way, I haven't heard you mention the Scourge of East Seventieth Street lately. How is that dear lady?"

"Unsinkable. Going stronger than ever, Richard reports. I don't see her at all in the summer. She won't come here. Says she hates the beach. I also get the feeling she's not exactly bereft that I haven't been to Westchester. We're cordial on the phone when we accidentally speak, but I imagine our little détente will end when she hears about the book."

"Who cares? With a mother-in-law like that, it's too bad you don't belong to one of those tribes that puts a limit on the time anyone can spend with the parent of a spouse. I'm much more interested in the public acceptance of your book, and in the way you'll feel. You're overdue for a little recognition. You've had none of your own for damned near eight years. Which reminds me. You have an anniversary coming up soon."

"Next month. I think I'll plan a party. I feel so good about everything these days. Not just the book. Everything."

"Things are going well."

"Yes," Susan said. "Oh, we fight. But what married couple doesn't? But mostly we're behaving like adults. It's so peaceful here, Kate. Sometimes I think I'd like to stay forever. It's so undemanding. Richard works well in this atmosphere and so do I. And Katie is flourishing. It's a remarkably cloudless horizon."

She didn't mention the nagging doubts about Richard's trip to California and the coincidental death of Sylvia Sloan. She'd said nothing to anyone about that. Apparently, the case was closed. If he'd been involved, no one had suspected. Or at least been able to prove it.

"Is it all right if I tell people about the book?" Kate asked. "Friends, I mean."

"Such as."

"Well, Paul for one. I know he'll be delighted. We keep in touch and he always wants to know how you are."

"By all means tell Paul. I've never stopped being fond of him. I wish he were still Richard's manager. I think Richard wishes so too, though he'd never admit it."

"Funny you should say that. I get the same feeling when I talk to Paul. Pity those two are so stubborn. They were a great team."

"More than that," Susan said. "Paul was the best man-friend Richard ever had."

"The only one, you mean."

"Yes, I'm afraid that's true."

Paul called over the weekend to congratulate her. Susan wondered whether Kate had offered the gratuitous information that Richard would be away, visiting his mother. They spoke briefly but warmly. Susan was tempted to invite him to East Hampton. Maybe she could effect a reconciliation. No, she mustn't meddle in Richard's affairs. That was Maria's kind of thing, not hers.

Chapter Thirty

Richard drove back to East Hampton, Maria's tirade still ringing in his ears. She'd been as angry about Susan's book as he'd expected, and as sarcastic about his ability to control his own wife. I should be used to it by now, he thought wearily. Women. My whole life has been shaped by them in one way or another. Especially the strong ones, like Mother and, yes, Susan. They were more determined, when they put their minds to it, than any man, but their strength was the thing that attracted him. He saw it in different forms in Gloria and Jacqueline and Mary Lou and begrudgingly admired it in Kate Fenton. Even Susan's mother was strong in her seemingly soft way. Spineless women were those who fawned over him or, like Sylvia, killed themselves for "love" of him. He despised them, as he loathed anything or anyone he could dominate. His mind went back to his first interview with Susan and he remembered telling her how passionately he felt about a piano. In this reflective mood he sensed that he adored this object because he could never truly control it. It constantly challenged him. As Maria and Susan did. It was not passive and obedient, as were many of his past bedmates. Nor dependent, as was his handicapped child.

He frowned, thinking of Katie and the years ahead. No matter what Susan believed, Katie never would be self-sufficient. He cared about her, dutifully, because she was part of him, but he also was irrationally angry with her. Every time he saw the healthy children of his brothers and sister, he pitied his own misfortune. He supposed, reluctant as he was to admit it even to himself, he also felt a sense of shame. Not simply because she was "different" or because there was always the lingering doubt that his genes might have contributed to Katie's condition (though the doctors flatly said this disfunction was not inherited) but more because he knew he hadn't carried his share of the burden these past seven years. He left that to Susan, who had long since stopped hoping he'd be a father in anything but name.

He'd felt guilty when he read the first pages of Susan's book. She wrote well and touchingly about the first months of Katie's life. It was not a maudlin, syrupy account, but it had great tenderness. It was factual and yet it was not true, for she'd changed the description of Richard's attitude and had left out any mention of the baby being sent away. The reader would believe that Susan and Richard together had taken on this monumental task of raising Katie as though she were any little girl, and that they shared equally in the slow, tedious process of drawing her into a hearing world. He appreciated that. He wasn't proud of how he'd resisted and finally withdrawn, and God knows his real attitude would make him a villain in people's eyes. He wished that what Susan had written was true: that he really was that kind of father. But he wasn't. The best he could manage was resigned tolerance and an occasional, forced show of affection for his child. At least that was better than the downright revulsion he used to feel.

So let Maria scream, he thought crossly as he pulled into the parking area next to his summer house. I can't stop Susan from doing this book, and when Mother finally reads it she'll see that it's really good publicity for me. He'd tried to tell her that, but she wouldn't listen. All she could see was that a family flaw was to be advertised, unnecessarily, once again.

"I thought we'd reburied those skeletons!" she'd said when he finally told her on Sunday. "You don't see Mary Lou still running around talking about Frances, do you? She was willing to discuss it when it was necessary, but she has better sense than to keep *reminding* everyone that Sergio has a retarded child! One would think your wife would realize that this situation is precisely the same."

"But it isn't," Richard had protested. "There's nothing wrong with Katie's mind. She's bright as any child her age. She's nothing to be ashamed of, Mother!"

"That's your point of view. Some people think there's no shame in having a retarded child, either. I happen to think neither is something one wishes to shout from the housetops." Maria, dressed in golf clothes, rose to end the discussion. "Since there's nothing I can do to stop your wife, I see no point in continuing our talk, Richard. I have a golf date in fifteen

398

minutes, so I'll say goodbye to you and hope you'll come soon again."

He'd kissed the remarkably unlined cheek. As he made the automatic gesture, it came to him that he couldn't remember Maria ever kissing him or any of the others on the mouth. He couldn't recall her ever holding them lovingly, as Susan held Katie. She was always there, a figure of dependability, but a cold one. Some head-doctor would say he'd spent his life looking for the tender mother-love he'd missed. That they *all* had, probably. Bull! What had set him off on that psychiatric hogwash? Mother was Mother. Period, paragraph, full stop. And none of them had turned out badly for lack of sloppy cuddling.

He let himself into the East Hampton house and called Susan. She came out of her "office," eyebrows arched in an unspoken question.

"It went just as I anticipated," Richard said. "Mother would gladly skin you alive."

"I'm sorry she gave you a hard time."

He shrugged. "I expected it. What did you do over the weekend?"

"Nothing much. Took Katie into the village for ice cream. Worked, mostly. Oh, by the way, Paul called."

"Paul? What did he want?"

"Kate told him about the book. He phoned to congratulate me." Susan paused. "Richard, I'd love to ask him here for a weekend before we go back to town. He was always such a good friend to us. It's a pity to lose him."

"I didn't lose him. I kicked him the hell out."

"But you once said it was just because you lost your temper. You even indicated you regretted it."

"Damn it, Susan, get off my back! I don't want to see that ungrateful louse, so let's drop it! I've been through enough this weekend because of the bloody book. Now you're starting a crusade about getting Paul back! Forget it!"

Susan didn't answer. All she said was, "I'll tell Cook you're here. Dinner in about thirty minutes, okay?"

"Sure. Listen, I'm sorry I flew off the handle. It's been a tough couple of days. But I don't want to get involved with Paul again. You can't pick up relationships with people as though nothing ever happened. Paul and I agreed to disagree. You understand that, don't you?"

"Yes, I suppose I do. But I can't really accept it. Not if two people still have some feeling for each other."

"Well, I accept it. So, no more Paul."

You should be glad I don't believe that old ties never can be re-established, Susan thought as he left to shower and change. If I believed that, you and I wouldn't be together. Even with all that's happened to us, I still think it's possible to forgive and forget and pick up a relationship that, by your standards, should have been smashed beyond repair. She wondered exactly what Maria had said about the book. Not that she couldn't guess. Kate said it: Who cares? To hell with her. At least Richard was being more supportive than she'd dared hope. And the writing was really going well. She loved every moment of it.

It was broiling hot that first day of September when Susan drove into the center of East Hampton to pick up a few packages of typing paper and carbon. It was incredible how she seemed to eat up supplies now that she was nearly two hundred pages into the book. She was surprised she did not find it painful to relive the past years. Probably, she thought, it's because I'm making the story what I've always wished it really was. All the things about Katie were true, all the wrenching moments of discovery, the sympathetic but doom-laden pronouncements of the doctors, the hours of endless, painstaking work, even the child's remarkable, blessed progress. But the implication of Richard's unselfish participation was a tissue of lies. And even that was forgivable, Susan told herself. He couldn't help being

400

the way he was, and it would have been unnecessarily spiteful to show him in his true light. People who didn't know the influences that had molded him wouldn't understand his turning away. Even more importantly, for those with similarly afflicted children, it was vital to stress that the co-operation of both parents was imperative if they hoped to succeed. She'd been lucky to have gotten this far without Richard's assistance. From talking to other parents, she knew that few made it alone. For the hundredth time she thanked heaven for the patience of Bridie and the skill of a dedicated Edith Chambers. They'd been the support other women found in their husbands. By the time Katie was old enough to understand the book, she'd have forgotten how withdrawn her father had been for most of these formative years.

Susan had a sense of well-being as she drove down Main Street, passing the local library where she'd recently spent hours checking things in medical books, glancing at Guild Hall, the cultural center of East Hampton with its museum and summer theater and its endless program of art exhibits and other "old-money" sponsored events. As always, she found herself smiling indulgently as she skirted the charming, meticulously maintained Village Green, zealously protected by the Ladies Village Improvement Society. It was a nice town, a different atmosphere from the blatantly expensive environs of Southampton or the determinedly "arty" aura of Bridgehampton with its colony of well-known writers and what were once called "jet setters." East Hampton had a feeling of wealth and permanence. Many of its inhabitants lived there year round, as opposed to the influx, no matter how chic, of the "summer people" who boasted of their modern houses and sixteen-thousand-dollar tennis courts in the other nearby villages. This whole area of Long Island, a hundred miles, give or take, from Manhattan, had a charm of its own, however, and Susan was in love with all of it. She almost dreaded the return to the city right after Labor Day. Not that she didn't love New York, but it was demanding, dirty and supercharged. She already missed this quiet place where she could be more alone with Richard, could write her book in peace and watch her child happily and safely at play.

Thinking now of Katie on the beach with Bridie, she stepped up her pace, eager to get home to them. I have the "end of summer blues," she thought as she made her purchases and got back into the car. No use moping. There's always next year.

Richard's thoughts as he sat at the piano were quite different than Susan's as she hurried through her errands. He was glad the summer was ending. It had gone well enough, but he was getting restless, anxious to plunge back into the pulsing tempo of the city and more anxious still to begin the fall tour. Anonymous living did not suit him for long. He blossomed in the spotlight, grew taller to the sound of applause. Only another ten days, he thought, and we'll be back in the apartment. He was pleased that Susan was planning a big cocktail-buffet party a week after their return, in celebration of their anniversary. It would be fun to see "his kind" of people again, to talk of his upcoming concerts and accept compliments on his becoming tan. He and Susan had been too much alone out here. Her wish more than his. True, most of the people were boring, but he'd have welcomed a little more social activity. Susan seemed to want almost none. All her foolishness about that damned party! It had been amusing. The people were rich and civilized and made a well-bred fuss over him. Still, he hadn't gone out often alone. There were too many pretty young girls, too much temptation. And East Hampton was too small a village not to immediately hear of any "unacceptable behavior."

With ingrained discipline, he put these wandering thoughts out of his mind and went back to his practicing. He was still fighting Walter's concerto, but coming closer now to interpreting it in his own way. He could taste the sweetness of the victory, savor the idea that

402

his big brother wasn't, after all, capable of presenting him with a challenge he couldn't meet.

A persistent tapping at the door broke his concentration. Who'd dare disturb him now? Susan was in the village, and even she rarely interrupted when he was working. Irritably, he called out, "Yes? What is it?"

The door opened a crack and Bridie's timid face appeared. She looked green.

"I'm sorry to disturb you, sir, but may I ask you a favor?"

He answered impatiently, "Come in! Come in!"

The nurse entered, holding Katie by the hand.

"I'm feeling awfully sick," Bridie said. "I tried to wait until Mrs. Antonini got back, but I just can't. I think it's food poisoning. What I came to ask, sir, was would you mind keeping Katie for a little while? Just until Madam returns. I'm sorry to disturb you, but . . ."

She really did look as though she'd be violently ill at any moment.

"Isn't there anyone else who could watch her? Where are the others?"

"It's Thursday. The rest are out for the day."

Richard sighed. "All right. Leave her with me. She can sit in that chair over there and be quiet."

"Thank you, sir." She led Katie to a chair and said slowly and distinctly, "Sit here and be a good girl, darling. Your daddy will take care of you."

Katie nodded as her nurse's lips moved, then she looked at Richard and smiled. The sight of her in her little red swimsuit, sitting with her legs straight out, so small and silent in the big armchair, made Richard uncomfortable. I don't even know how to talk to her, he thought. He smiled back and returned to his music as Bridie left the room, but he couldn't keep his mind on his work. He could hear Katie stirring restlessly, making little crooning sounds to the doll she held in her arms. That damned doll, fitted with hearing aids. He wanted to smash it. He'd never had any faith in the idea that a toy pretending to have her impairment would help her adjust. It was grotesque.

403

He suddenly felt very nervous. It was strange, being alone with his daughter, and the responsibility made him uneasy. Besides, he couldn't concentrate while she was moving and making those undecipherable noises. How in God's name did Susan stand it day after day? He got up from the piano, picked up the sheet music and went over to Katie. Crouching down, as he'd seen Bridie and Susan do, he looked into her face and spoke rapidly in a shout.

"Let's go down to the beach until your mother comes back. I'll study my music and you can play in the sand."

A look of bewilderment crossed the child's face and Richard remembered it did no good to speak loudly. One had to speak in a normal tone, forming every word with care. He tried again.

"We will go to the beach. You and I."

The smile returned and she climbed down out of the chair and trustingly took his hand. It was so small and soft, that little hand, so confidently holding his own. She looked up at him adoringly.

"Du-de. Katie. Beach."

He felt her tearing at his heart. She was his. So brave and so sweet. So proud to be with him.

"That's right. Daddy and Katie will go to the beach."

They carefully descended the steps to the sand where Katie had left her pail and shovel and Bridie her canvas folding chair. Richard settled himself in it and said, "You play."

She nodded and went busily about her lonely, fruitless digging in the sand. Richard watched her for a few minutes, shaken by the unexpected tenderness he'd felt at that first moment of contact. She was a sweet child and well behaved, but he could never be around her for long periods of time. It was too heartbreaking to watch. How terrible life will be for her, Richard thought. What will she ever do? What man will ever want her? Susan was insane with all that talk about college and marriage. Katie was hardly any better off than Frances. Worse, maybe, because Frances would never grow up, and this exquisite little thing would become an unhappy woman, all too aware of the pleasures she never could have. Oh, he knew there'd been cases when children like this turned into functioning adults. Once or twice in the beginning, Susan had tried to tell him what miraculous things were possible, but he'd cut her short.

"That's wishful thinking," he'd said curtly. "Can't you face the truth?"

Watching Katie now, he knew, sadly, he was right. This was reality: a human being who'd never be independent, never truly desired, never a whole person. A cheerful little robot would grow into a bitter adult. He felt an unaccustomed lump in his throat. It was so unfair. So goddamned unfair. To her. To all of them.

To shake such thoughts, he picked up Walter's concerto and let the bliss of total involvement take over. Later, as he went back over and over the scene in his mind, he realized that he was engrossed for only five or six minutes, ten at the most, before he looked up and saw nothing but an empty beach.

When Susan returned thirty minutes later and saw the Fire Rescue Squad truck, a police car and another vehicle parked at her house, her legs turned to water. She could hardly find strength to jam on the brake and throw the gearshift into "park." She flung herself out of the seat and ran frantically to the house. A hysterical Bridie was waiting inside the door.

"Bridie! What is it? What's happened? My God, is it Katie?"

The woman was almost unable to speak. Susan caught snatches of words. "Sick. My fault. Mr. Richard. Undertow." Susan brushed by her and ran into the living room, where she heard the sound of low voices. Richard, his clothes soaking wet, sat in a chair, his head buried in his hands. Nearby, looking miserable, were several members of the fire department and a sad-faced young policeman. And on the big couch, unmoving, lay Katie.

Susan screamed as she ran to her child, holding her, shaking her as though she could shake her back to life.

"Katie! Katie, angel! Mummy's here! Katie!"

She felt strong hands behind her, gently lifting her from her kneeling position beside the sofa. She fought them off, holding onto her baby, but at last the hands forced her to her feet and turned her around. She looked into the sympathetic eyes of the local doctor.

"I'm sorry, Mrs. Antonini. Everybody got here as quickly as possible after your husband pulled her out of the water. We did everything we could. But it was too late."

She stared at him. "No! I don't believe it! It's not true! Not my Katie!"

"I'm sorry," he said again. "It's hideous and it happens too often. That damned undertow out there has taken much stronger swimmers than your child. Your husband made a superhuman effort to get to her, but no one could have helped. When those big waves come in . . ."

"Stop it!" Susan's voice was a scream of pain. She stared at Richard, who'd raised his head. Tears were streaming down his face.

"Susan, I only took my eyes off of her for a minute. She was playing in the sand. I didn't know she'd go in the water. I was studying Walter's concerto and I . . ."

"You killed her! You and your goddamn selfishness! You and your stupid music!" Her own tears came now. She did not ask how he'd happened to be alone with their child on the beach. Those questions would come later. All that possessed her now was a demonic rage intermingled with shock and overwhelming grief. "You let my baby drown! You didn't care! You've never cared!"

"No. It wasn't like that, Susan. I swear. I tried to get to her, but I couldn't reach her in time." His sobs matched her own. "My God, what kind of monster do

406

you think I am that I wouldn't try to save my own child! I'd have given my life! You must believe that!"

The strangers in the room, with the exception of the doctor, went quietly out the door, pitying the bereaved parents, embarrassed by the scene.

"Let me give you something so you can rest, Mrs. Antonini. It's a terrible, tragic accident and you're in shock. Let's go to your room where you can lie down."

"No! I won't leave my baby!"

The doctor was very gentle. "There's nothing more you can do for her. Please. Come with me."

Susan felt as though she were going to faint. There was a terrible weakness in her whole body and she sagged against the doctor. "My mother," she said. "I've got to call . . . to tell her to come."

"We'll call her. Your husband can tell us who should be notified."

"I'll call, Susan." Richard's voice was almost inaudible. "I'll get your mother. Please do what the doctor says. I'll take care of things here."

She turned on him, making a snarling sound like a wounded animal. Like you took care of them when I was away! she wanted to scream. Like you took care of the baby you never wanted! But no words came out. She simply looked at him in terrible accusation, and the eyes that had flashed hatred were now vacant except for unmistakable contempt. And then, because it was too much to bear, her mind mercifully held out the salvation of unconsciousness and she collapsed in the doctor's arms.

She barely remembered the next twenty-four hours. She knew that Bea and Wil Langdon came and that next morning her mother helped her dress for the drive back into the city where Kate Fenton waited at the apartment. She was heavily sedated, only dimly aware of Richard moving like a restless ghost in and out of her room. People spoke to her and she didn't answer. They brought her food and she didn't eat it. Only when Bridie came into the room did Susan hold out her arms to the crushed woman and try to comfort her as others

407

were trying to comfort Susan. They clung together, the two women whom Katie had loved and who had loved her as though she was the child of both. It was from Bridie that Susan finally heard the whole story. Bridie, who blamed herself for leaving her charge, who felt responsible for the whole hideous accident.

"I never should have left her," the nurse sobbed. "If I hadn't left her, she'd be here today."

"Hush," Susan said. "You mustn't blame yourself. You were sick. There was no one else. Why wouldn't you turn a child over to her own father to watch after for a few minutes? Dear Bridie. You're not at fault. It's not you who must live with the guilt. You were everything to Katie. Closer to her than I. She loved you so much. She wouldn't want you to do this to yourself."

"I should have known better. Mr. Richard never took care of her alone before. He didn't know you couldn't take your eyes off her for a minute on the beach. He didn't know how she loved that dangerous water. Don't blame him, madam. He hadn't been around her enough to realize that when she faced the beach she couldn't hear the sound of those big waves coming in behind her, like the one that . . ." The nurse couldn't go on.

"You didn't know he was going to take her to the beach," Susan thought. "You thought she was safe in the living room."

Trying to comfort someone who was as brokenhearted as she gave Susan the strength to face the ordeal ahead. Dry-eyed, superhumanly controlled, she indicated to her mother and Kate what she wanted done. No prolonged period before the burial service, no morbid "viewing" at Campbell's, and as little publicity as possible, though that, of course, was too much to hope for. The accident had already made headlines and the press was all over them once again, trying fruitlessly to get at Richard or Susan or Bridie or anyone even remotely close to them. There was no way to stop the newspaper stories, but at least the family would not

408

reveal the time of the service, in the hope that the curious "celebrity watchers" could be avoided.

Susan remembered the spectacle of Giovanni's "tribute" and shuddered. Perhaps the great man would have wanted it the way Maria had arranged it. As a public figure, it was the proper way for him. But Katie was only a baby. She'd been sheltered from the curious for most of her life. She'd have the same protection in death, as far as her mother could manage it. The service would be quick and private.

"I'd like Edith Chambers to say a few words," Susan told Bea.

"All right, dear, though I thought perhaps Kate might be the one. She was Katie's godmother."

"No. Kate couldn't do it. She was too close. Besides, Edith taught Katie to speak. It seems only right that she should say the last words about her."

Bea marveled at the reserve of strength Susan had found. I couldn't do it if it were my child, she thought. She's more in control now than she was when they took Katie away from her the first time. I don't know how she can handle this. She must be dying inside.

Kate Fenton was less sure that Susan was really in control. True, she did go about the arrangements quietly, did seem almost fatalistic about it after her initial outburst, the details of which Richard unexpectedly confided to Kate. But Kate watched her friend apprehensively. She was too calm, too disciplined. It was unnatural and frightening. Susan spoke to Maria and to the members of Richard's family who appeared at the apartment uttering appropriate condolences, but she did not speak to Richard. She hadn't, he told Kate, since that first afternoon. He was almost crazy with grief and guilt, and it was to Kate, of all people, that he unburdened himself. She supposed he could not face Bea Langdon's natural resentful anguish or, conversely, his own mother's blind defense of him. He didn't want to be "forgiven" by a biased Maria who would assure him that he was not at fault. He knew he was, and he was willing, almost eager, to be punished for it, as

409

though suffering was as necessary as it was natural.

"I don't blame Susan for refusing to talk to me," he told Kate. "Why should she ever talk to me again? My God, Kate, how can I live with this? Is this retribution for all the rotten things I've done? If so, why this way? Why did it have to come through that innocent child?"

"I don't know," Kate said. "I couldn't possibly answer that. No one could." It was impossible not to blame him, but equally impossible not to feel some pity. He'd been stupid and careless. Tragically so. His only defense was, as Bridie had pointed out to Susan, the fact that he had no idea how carefully Katie had to be watched. And even that was his own fault, Kate thought bitterly. If he'd taken the slightest interest in his daughter's upbringing, he'd have realized she was an easy victim of any menace she couldn't hear. Like the sound of an oncoming car or the wail of a speeding ambulance or, Kate shuddered, the booming roar of a huge, enveloping, shore-bound wave. There was no comfort for Richard. The best he could hope for from Susan was pity and the resigned acceptance of his folly. Slim consolation and a thin thread on which to continue a marriage.

"I won't be silly enough to tell you not to blame yourself," Kate said. "You *were* to blame. Only a fool would pretend otherwise. What can I say to you, Richard? That I understand? I don't. I never have. But perhaps, in time, Susan will. She's always been able to understand you better than anyone, and perhaps she'll be able to accept the 'mitigating circumstances.' All you can do is wait and hope. It was a terrible lesson learned at incalculable expense. If there's any good that possibly could come out of this horror it will be a long-overdue awareness of your own selfishness and your disinterest in the problems of other people."

"Do you think Susan will stay with me?" It was a plea for reassurance, a desperate grasp at something to live for.

"I don't know. No one knows what's going on in her head at this moment. I doubt she knows that herself."

410

Chapter Thirty-one

For the second time in one year, the families sat to-gether at the last goodbye for one of their own. Aside from Edith Chambers, the only "outsiders" at the simple service at Campbell's were Kate, Bridie, Evie Maxwell and Paul Carmichael. Susan had told Kate to ask Paul to come.

"He was the only man, aside from Giovanni and my father, who loved Katie," Susan said in the flat, lifeless tone in which she'd spoken since the day of the acci-dent. "In the early days, I believe she thought Paul was her father. I want him there."

"Will Richard . . . ?"

Susan's expression was hard. "I don't care what Richard wants."

Paul was touched by Susan's request and equally certain Richard had played no part in the decision. He sat far back in the funeral chapel, removed from the others, a voluntary outcast from the Antoninis. From his seat he could see only the backs of heads, but he recognized them all. Richard's nieces and nephews were the only ones drastically changed since the days when Paul first was involved with the family. Sergio's and Walter's children were so grown-up. Joseph was twenty-three and playing guitar, to his grandmother's horror, in a rock group in Greenwich Village. His sister Patricia was twenty and in college. Walter's Calhoun had graduated from Harvard in June, and his younger

411

brother was there in his junior year. Even Gloria's children, except for the twins, who were nearly eight, were leaving "babyhood." Raoul, Jr., was thirteen and Maria eleven. It was hard to believe the third generation of Antoninis were all young adults, or nearly so. Where had the years gone? It seemed only yesterday that Richard had introduced "his girl" to his parents and his brothers and sister and their pack of overactive kids. Pierre and Claudette Taffin weren't even born then, and now here they were at "the age of reason." The age, Paul thought despairingly, that Katie had not lived to see. Anger welled inside him. Goddamn Richard! Damn him to hell for this and a thousand other heedless acts!

He could see the faces of Bridie and the closest members of the family as they entered last and took their places in the front pew. Ironic that Maria should be among them, the grandmother who literally had no use for her youngest son's child. The tiny figure, straight and youthful at seventy-three, came in first. Richard, looking destroyed, followed her. Susan moved like a wooden doll, her uncovered face a study in controlled agony. Behind her came Bea and Wil Langdon, Bea veiled to hide the tears she knew she'd not be able to restrain; Wil gray and drawn; Bridie openly weeping.

Paul suffered for the last four. Even for Richard, though part of him wanted to kill the man who'd let this happen. But his heart went out to the woman he loved. He wanted to take Susan in his arms and comfort her, hold her as he'd often seen her hold the one who now lay in the small coffin under a blanket of sweetheart roses and baby's breath. He'd sent the same flowers. A tiny basket of them, suitable for a child. On the card he'd written simply, "To Katie from her friend Paul." Susan would know how much love was in that message.

The service was mercifully brief. A clergyman spoke a few words and said appropriate prayers and then Edith Chambers walked to the podium and began. Her

412

soft voice filled the chapel but her words were for Susan.

"I speak for Katie. For Katie who was learning to speak for herself. For Katie whom God chose to afflict, but whom He also chose to place in the tender, patient hands of those who loved and believed in her.

"Hers was such a brief life. But filled with so many things. In less than seven swift years she knew more suffering and frustration and bewilderment than most of us know in a lifetime. Yet she knew more joy, was more loving, more giving, more instinctively understanding than we who are seven times seven, or ten times that number.

"Katie was a child who did not hear and barely spoke. But she was not a silent child. She did not need speech to communicate happiness. She had no need of words to express her cheerfulness. Man-made sounds were not necessary to convey her generosity of soul and spirit. She was a brave little girl. And we loved her.

"For each of us, she had special gifts. For me, her teacher, it was the delight of touching a responsive chord, of seeing her awaken to the everyday pleasures of life. For her little friends it was the company of a gay, uncomplaining schoolmate who asked no special consideration. And for her family, most of all, she gave the special gifts of unending adoration expressed in the radiant smiles, the small, surprisingly competent hand always outstretched to touch the faces of the ones she loved.

"Young as she was, I think Katherine took nothing for granted. Everything was new and wonderful. To recognize a word in a book, to identify a flower, to utter a first, small, hesitating sound and be understood. She did not know these things were her due. To her, every moment was a discovery, every day a great adventure. She was not handicapped in the sorrowful way we are wont to use the word. For Katie was not deaf to the nuances of love nor speechless in her gratitude for them. She heard and spoke with her heart.

413

"We mourn. And there is cause to mourn the death of one so young. But there is cause to rejoice in her life. She heard her own music, this elfin child. She danced through a storybook world bathed in sunshine that defeated the dark and ugly clouds. She made her own place, a little kingdom, a tiny Camelot filled with shining moments. And we were allowed to enter and fleetingly share the magic with her, to see goodness through her innocent eyes.

"She left us rich in recollections of her enchanted world. She left us strength and hope and serenity through our sadness. She took from us our golden moments of glory. But their blessed memory remains."

Bridie and Bea were sobbing uncontrollably as Edith sat down, and Richard's head was buried in his hands as it had been when Susan saw him that terrible day in East Hampton. Only Maria and Susan were dry-eyed, the former apparently unmoved, the latter so devastated she could not find merciful release in tears.

We've lost the two best ones within months of each other, Paul thought. The oldest and the youngest Antonini. He closed his eyes and sent forth a silent prayer. "Let her survive this, God. Above all, let Susan survive."

Susan and Richard returned from the cemetery to a silent and empty apartment. Only Bridie rode back in the car with them and not a word was uttered on the long trip home. Richard gazed sightlessly out of the window of the limousine and Susan stared at the driver's back. Bridie crouched in a corner, quiet, feeling out of place in this car with her employers. She would not be with them much longer, she supposed. They had no need of her now. The realization brought tears to her eyes once again. It was not finding a job she worried about. Competent baby nurses were always in demand. It was simply that after nearly seven years she couldn't imagine being anywhere else or taking care of any other child. Katie had been almost as much hers as her mother's, just as Mrs. Antonini had said. And no matter how many reassurances she offered, Susan would never convince Bridie that she did not bear the blame for their loss.

It was not until they were entering the apartment that Susan turned to the nurse and took her hand.

"You'll stay with us, Bridie, won't you? At least for a while. Until things are settled."

Bridie knew what she meant. She'd wondered whether this unhappy couple would stay together. If only they could. It was times like these when a man and a woman needed each other. She found that out when her late husband Patrick (May he rest in peace,) saw her through the agony of their stillborn child so many years ago. She could never have another and she was sure she couldn't have survived without Pat to comfort her and share the misery. After he passed on she turned to taking care of other people's children. She loved them all dearly. All her little charges over the years. But she'd felt about none as she had about Katie.

Of course, though they both were nearly crazy with sorrow, Mr. and Mrs. Antonini's problem was different than hers and Pat's had been. Here there was also guilt and bitterness, along with the memories of seven years of a living child. They needed each other but they had other terrible feelings to overcome before either could offer or accept comfort.

"I'll stay as long as you want me," Bridie said.

"Thank you. There's a lot . . . There are things to be done."

Bridie knew what she was trying to say, though Susan couldn't get the words out. Katie's nursery had to be dismantled and Katie's clothes and toys given away. Even in her dazed state in East Hampton, Bridie had had enough presence of mind to hide the doll with the hearing aids. Mrs. Antonini had never seen it since that day, and she never would. It was safely out of sight in the back of Bridie's closet, where it had been since she smuggled it back to New York in her suitcase. But there were all the other reminders to be gotten out of the apartment. Susan couldn't face that. Bridie would do it.

"Yes, madam," she said quietly. "I'll see to them."

"I don't understand why Susan wouldn't let us come with her." Bea's swollen-with-tears face mirrored her distress as Wil drove toward Bronxville. "She shouldn't be alone now."

"She has her husband, dear."

Bea stared at him. "Do you know what you're saying? Her husband! My God, Wil, she can barely look at him, much less speak to him! I'd be less worried if she were really alone than with that man!"

"You're wrong, my love. Yes, this terrible tragedy was Richard's fault. Directly. But indirectly, Susan is to blame, too."

"Wil!"

"I'm sorry, sweetheart, but it's true. If Richard hadn't been permitted to abdicate all responsibility toward his child, things might have been different. Susan let him drop out. Maybe, in a strange way, she was so possessive about Katie that she never really wanted him to participate. I know that's shocking to you, but put yourself in her place. Would you have stood for it if I'd flatly refused to have any part in our daughter's upbringing? Would you have turned a nursemaid into that child's other parent? Damned right you wouldn't! You'd have yelled and screamed and forced me to do my duties as a father. And don't give me all that stuff about Richard being 'different' because he's an artist. He's still a man, a husband and he was a father. Why did Susie permit him to stay aloof from a mutual problem they should have been sharing all these years?"

Bea was indignant. "Have you forgotten how he behaved from the moment he knew Katie was handicapped? How he and that mother of his took the baby away and Susan and I had to kidnap her to bring her

416

home? Have you blocked out all the embarrassment he's caused Susie with his women and his wild escapades? I don't understand you, Wil. It's unthinkable that any of the blame for this could fall, even indirectly, on that girl. She did nothing but try to raise Katie singlehanded, without an iota of interest from Richard!"

"You've just said the viable words. 'She did nothing.' She did everything for Katie, and I admire her for that, but for years she did nothing to make Richard part of it. If she was going to raise Katie as a single parent, then she should have left her husband and really become one. But she wanted it both ways. No, dear. Richard can't be blamed for all of this. Any more than you could blame a child for burning down the house if you hadn't told him what could happen with matches." Wil's voice trembled. "God knows I hold no brief for Richard. He should have had enough common sense to know you have to watch any small child near the water. But most children *can* be ignored for a few minutes. The trouble is, Richard was able to avoid the fact that Katie wasn't 'most children.' "

The stern set of Bea's lips told him that she refused to believe a word of what he said. In her mind, Susan was a saint and Richard a devil. It wasn't as easy as that.

"Look," Wil said, "nobody in this world—including you—loves Susie more than I. Nobody is more heartbroken over what's happened to her. But she hasn't been a hundred per cent right in this. I hate to think of how she's going to go on punishing that poor bastard who's already in hell."

Bea snapped at him. "I honestly think you feel sorry for him! It's incredible! Men really do stick together, even at a time like this! He's responsible for the death of your grandchild and you're worrying about his suffering! What about Susan's suffering?"

"I worry about that, too. Believe me I do. But I also pray she has enough compassion and charity in her to understand her role in this. It was an accident, Bea. It

417

happened so fast! It could have happened to anyone. It could even have happened if Susan had been reading a book on the beach or Bridie had nodded off in her chair. Except that neither of them would have done that because they were well instructed in the care of a nonhearing child. Richard was not. And he's paying heavily for his ignorance."

"It was ignorance he chose."

"Yes," Wil said, "but it was an option he should never have been allowed."

"I suppose Susan really will leave Richard now," Jacqueline said. "I'm sorry. Until this happened, I think they were really beginning to make a go of it."

"I know. And it had to be my damned concerto he was so wrapped up in. It really makes me feel partially responsible."

"Don't be ridiculous. It could have been Mozart."

"Do you think Susan will stay with Richard?"

Sergio looked at his wife. "Would you have left me if I'd let one of our kids drown?"

Mary Lou considered that. "I don't know. I don't know how much any woman can forgive a man she loves."

Gloria and Raoul went back to Maria's house with her. For once, Gloria was sincerely sympathetic.

"I feel so sorry for them," she said. "My God, it must be terrible to lose a child. And especially that way."

"I hope it won't affect Richard's work," Maria said.

"He has a very heavy schedule. An important tour. He'll have to get over this by next month."

❀

"Could I ask you a favor?"

"Of course, Kate," Paul said. "Name it."

"Would you mind spending the rest of the day with me? I have a feeling I'm going to get terribly, terribly drunk and cry a lot."

❀

I wish I could have said it better, Edith Chambers thought as she returned to her office. It was like walking on thin ice. I couldn't mention Susan and ignore Richard. I couldn't mention Richard without reminding everyone of the circumstances. And I loved that child so much. I had such hopes for her. She would have made it. Damn it! She blew her nose hard and wiped her eyes before she sat down at the desk and picked up a folder marked "Katherine Antonini." She supposed she should keep it. It was valuable research. But her emotions were stronger than her professional assessment. Almost in anger, she ripped the file in two and threw it in the wastebasket. Goodbye, Katie. I'll miss you. The buzzer on her desk sounded.

"Your two-o'clock appointment is here, Miss Chambers. George Drue."

Another silent two-year-old with his mother. I can't bear it, Edith thought. How often can they break my heart?

"Thanks, Penny. Send them in."

❀

The silence was everywhere and it was killing Richard. A week after the funeral, and Susan had not spoken to him. Not a single word, though they faced each other at the dining table each night, their only

419

meal together. Susan had moved into the guest room, not even discussing it with him, and had her breakfast sent in there. She was never home for lunch. He did not know where she went, and dared not ask. He waited for her to say what was going to happen to them, and she said nothing. It was eerie. As though she had assumed the role of the deaf-mute child, Susan did not hear or speak.

He spoke to other people, his family and his business associates, but he only half-listened and automatically responded. They assumed he would go on the tour as planned, leaving in three weeks. He did not tell them he couldn't even think about performing, that he had not, in fact, touched the piano in the ten days since he left it to take his child to the beach.

Several times in the past week, alone in the apartment except for the servants, he'd gone into the room where he usually practiced, had sat in front of the keyboard and stared at the music on the rack. But his hands lay quiet in his lap, and after a few minutes he'd gotten up and walked away.

I must get back to work, he told himself fiercely on this clear September morning. It's all I have. I must pick up my life. I must go on with my music. All of them said so. Mother, Serge, Walter, Frank Olmstead, George Reagan. All except Susan, who's as silent as the grave. The rest talk to me, but hers is the only voice I want to hear. I need her, Richard thought, almost in surprise. I need her and I've lost her forever.

The realization was unbearable. He'd given lip-service to his marriage, taking all and giving as it pleased him, certain of Susan's devotion, even when she'd threatened to withdraw it. Now her love had died with the child, and there was none left for him at the moment he could not live without it.

From somewhere in the back of his mind, he remembered some much-quoted lines from Shakespeare. How did they go? "If music be the food of love, play on." What was the rest of it? Compulsively, he went to the library and found the anthology of

Shakespearean quotes. There it was. *Twelfth Night.*
Alone, he read the passage aloud:

> "If music be the food of love, play on;
> Give me excess of it, that, surfeiting,
> The appetite may sicken, and so die."

He closed the book and went back to the piano.
Take the plunge, he told himself. Start with Walter's
concerto. Don't think. Just begin where you left off.
He raised his arms and nothing happened. His fingers
were like ten sticks of marble, inflexible, unmoving.
Frantically, he tried to warm the stony hands, rubbing
them against his chest, placing one stiff set of fingers
over the other. Nothing. He stared at them in disbelief.
Only a moment ago he'd been thumbing through the
pages of a book. Now, in one hideous instant, he had
no use of his hands. The terrible word burned in his
brain. Paralysis. My hands are paralyzed. I can't move
them. Inside he was screaming, but no sound came out.
Susan found him three hours later, still sitting at the piano, staring at the lifeless fingers which lay like accusatory pointers on the black and white keys.

The diagnosis was "hysterical paralysis." The
specialists were cautiously optimistic. The top men in
the country were called in for consultation and they
nodded their heads solemnly and said yes, indeed, it
was psychosomatic. Nothing physical involved. Thoroughly understandable. They felt it would go as quickly
as it came. One day, when Richard had worked out his
grief and guilt, his hands would move again, as swiftly
and magically as ever. But he must go into therapy,
they said. Psychotherapy. Not the kind that got
muscles moving after a stroke, as Maria's therapy had
done, but the healing of a mind that had brought upon
itself the worst kind of punishment, one it unconsciously sought. This was delayed shock, they opined.

There was no organic problem. It was a case for a psychiatrist.

The doctors explained it carefully to them—to a stunned and frightened Richard, a sick-at-heart Susan and an almost belligerent Maria, who called it all "hogwash."

"It's impossible," Maria said firmly. "I will not accept that diagnosis. There must be a physical reason and we'll consult every doctor in the world until we find out what it is. 'Hysterical paralysis,' indeed! Richard has never been hysterical in his life. He has too much control for that. He's a disciplined man. My son has been through a trying time, I'll grant you that, but until now he's functioned well, as he's been trained to do."

The doctors glanced at each other as the feisty little woman spoke. "A trying time," they thought. A man sits by while his child drowns and she calls it a "trying time"! Good God, the woman wasn't stupid, she was simply blind! They hoped Richard and his wife would override this refusal to accept the facts. If not, Antonini had no chance. All the exercise and massage in the world wouldn't help. Somewhere in the dark corners of his mind he didn't want to play again, didn't want to relive the moment when he'd resentfully left the piano to care for his daughter. Couldn't Mrs. Antonini see that? The man was in mental agony. Probably had subconsciously been suffering for years. The tragedy only triggered a breakdown which inevitably would have come sooner or later. Child prodigy. Driving mother. Genius father. Competitive family. Too much fame and adoration all his life. Not a normal existence in any sense. And now this. This terrible guilt that cried out for unspeakable revenge. Lucky he has a sensible wife, the doctors said among themselves. His mother is a raving maniac.

Susan knew what they were thinking. Her own days with Dr. Marcus had given her a layman's insight into Richard's problems, particularly as they related to her own. Because of the psychiatrist she'd survived eight years of this turmoil-filled marriage. Because of the doctor and her own solid background, her quite ordinary and happy childhood, her own undemanding and devoted parents, she'd kept her sanity. Giovanni had helped her understand other things. She'd even kept her love for Richard. Until he let Katie die. Then nothing helped. She couldn't forgive him. Couldn't speak to him. Thought of nothing but how and when she could get away from this self-involved, heedless man.

Yet when she found him dazed and stricken, deprived of all he cared for, she wept for the first time since Katie's death. She'd gone to him, this man she didn't recognize, and thoughts of escape left her mind as she held him and comforted him and saw her own tears drop on the immobile fingers. It was more than pity. It was a sad realization that they lived as strangers, not daring to expose their real feelings, hiding behind arrogance and anger and false pride. It was all such a waste, such a farce.

She saw in him the same withdrawal she'd felt when Katie was taken to the school. She remembered the unwillingness to be part of the world, the retreat, into a shell where no reality could penetrate. He must get help too, she thought.

How many years of resentment and fury and disgust with himself must lie behind this hideous tangible evidence of guilt! How many things must have been pushed far back in his mind, hidden behind the facile smile, the confident air, the consuming self-interest. How much he must have suffered while refusing to face his suffering, hiding his uncertainty from himself, from me, from everyone. Susan tried to speak to him and he didn't answer that first day. Only later, after he'd listened to the doctors and smiled sardonically at Maria's rejection of their diagnosis, did he agree to try psychoanalysis.

"It's a bitter joke, isn't it?" he said to Susan. "I was so scornful of your need for help. I must have tempted fate just a little too far."

If it's a joke, it's a terrible one, she thought. It's heartbreaking self-punishment. Even more than he deserves.

Chapter Thirty-two

"You're not very pleased to be here, Mr. Antonini, are you?"

Richard shifted uneasily in the chair facing Dr. Beekman's desk. "No, not particularly. But nothing else has worked. I've been through all kinds of physical therapy in the past month and it does no good. I still can't move my hands." A bitter expression crossed his face and his voice was suddenly angry. "My mother recovered completely from a stroke. I've had nothing as serious as that and yet I'm more a cripple than she. I have a manservant to dress me, a chauffeur to open car doors, and a wife to cut up my food and feed me. And now I have you, Doctor, to massage my mind. You're my last resort. Not pleased to be here? That's the understatement of the century. I hate being here. I have no hope that you can help."

"I see. That makes things a great deal more difficult for both of us. Most patients come because they no longer can cope with life. They know they're sick, and they're hoping I can help them find their own cure. An unwilling patient is not one I usually accept, Mr. Antonini." The young doctor was kind but very serious. "If Dr. Marcus, whom I respect so highly, had not asked me to take you, I don't think I would have. You see, you're not a genius to me. You're just another human being with all the stresses and rages and guilt of lesser mortals. I hope I can help you help yourself. But I'll need your co-operation." He paused. "Can I count on that?"

"I'm here," Richard said listlessly. "And I'll be here five afternoons a week until I'm cured. Or until we mutually decide that I'm a lost cause. I'll try to co-operate, Doctor."

"Very well, then. Let's start from the beginning."

Susan sat in Paul's apartment, her feet propped up on a big ottoman, a glass of club soda in her hand. She'd been there many afternoons in the past weeks. Since Richard's paralysis, she had most meals with her husband, feeding him as though he were a child, talking quietly to him, gently urging him to get professional help. It had taken a month to get past his stubborn resistance, a resistance abetted by Maria, who shot down every argument the doctors and Susan presented. But finally even Richard could see that the physical therapy was useless, and, over Maria's last, lingering protests, he'd begun to see Dr. Beekman every afternoon. He'd been in therapy only a month, too soon to expect results, yet every day Susan thought she could see him beginning to scratch at the bars of the cage he'd inhabited all his life. He talked a little more freely to her about the doctor, conceding that the man had a way of making him recognize things he hadn't realized were bothering him. Yet even with these small admissions, he remained a disbeliever.

"But what good is it if I still can't move my fingers?"

"Richard, you can't expect an overnight cure! Whatever caused this probably was years in the making. How could it go away so quickly? Give it time."

"I know what caused it. What I did to Katie. Will that go away, Susan?"

425

"No," she said slowly, "it won't go away. Not the fact of it. But you'll come to see why it could have happened; why, perhaps, your whole life had been moving inexorably toward that moment."

"And then I'll be able to forgive myself? You'll be able to forgive me?" The words were a challenge.

Susan felt so weary. "I'm no doctor. I can't answer that."

"You're a woman. You're my wife."

"Yes, I'm both those things, but I still can't answer for you, or for myself."

"Will you ever love me again?" His voice was desperate.

She turned away. She wanted to tell him that she'd always loved him, that she'd spent long hours searching for understanding and forgiveness for them both. But she knew that until he reached the full depths of knowledge about himself, theirs was nothing but the façade of a marriage.

"Susan, I can't live without you."

God, how she once would have sold her soul for those words! How desperately she'd longed to be needed by him. All the single-minded devotion to Katie had been more than mother-love. It had also been compensation for Richard's independence. The dependent child had, in a peculiar way, taken the place of the indifferent partner. They were two different kinds of love, hers for her husband and her daughter, yet at the bottom of both was this crying out for someone on whom to shower love, to indulge her need to be indispensable. I used you, Katie, she thought. I adored you, but I used you for the fulfillment I wouldn't find with your father. What colossal ego I must have! What is this consuming wish to be all-important?

"I won't leave you," she said quietly. "I know you need me. I need you, too."

The relief in his face was evident. But a second later the pleased expression turned to a scowl as he looked at his immobile hands. "Need me?" He almost spat out the words. "Who needs a husband who can't make you

426

feel what you used to feel? Who needs a goddamn wooden Indian who has to be dressed and fed and even taken to the bathroom, for Christ's sake?" He was getting terribly worked up. "Without my hands I don't want to live! Why couldn't it have been my eyes? I'd have been better off blind. At least I could have worked! I could have made love. My God, I wish I were dead!"

She tried to soothe him. "You're going to be all right," she said firmly. "The doctors all say so."

"Doctors! Quacks! What do they know?"

"They know a great deal. Your case is not unique. Hysterical paralysis is not all that uncommon, Richard. They know how to deal with it. Please believe that."

He'd subsided and gone to the big chair by the window, sitting there quietly, looking at nothing, his useless hands hanging motionless at his sides.

Susan sighed, thinking of a dozen other episodes like it in the past weeks. She'd turned to Paul for comfort after Katie's death. Every afternoon that he was free she left her apartment and walked to his, like a lost soul seeking refuge. He was the only person with whom she found true peace these days. Kate, Jacqueline, Bea—all the women she felt close to were ready to offer advice and companionship. But though they talked *to* her, *at* her, trying to help, none had the serenity of this man. Sometimes she and Paul sat for an hour or two, never exchanging a word. Often he worked at his desk while she simply rested nearby, lost in her thoughts. She'd given up drinking entirely. She was confused enough without living in an alcoholic fog.

No one knew of these frequent visits. No one would have believed them platonic. Paul had never done more than give her a kiss on the cheek, or put his arms around her when she unexpectedly burst into tears, as she often did these days. Sometimes she wondered whether she came here subconsciously hoping he'd make love to her. She missed physical satisfaction. She was a sexy woman and there had always been a strong attraction between her and Paul. And yet neither of them made a move, understanding without words that she was not seeking an affair but a haven.

There was in this period no sex with Richard, an unspoken agreement as much for his pride as for her still ambivalent feelings about him. There had been, a week after the funeral, a note from Martin Tanner, a properly written message of condolence. Had she wished to, Susan could have picked up with him. But it was as though she was in limbo. Even her capacity for passion was suspended. If she had been able to seek forgetfulness in a man's arms, Susan knew she would have reproached herself, been ashamed that the grief she morbidly hugged to her could be even momentarily forgotten.

But then why do I keep running to Paul? she asked herself. If I'm not hoping for affection, why am I here? It wasn't fair to him. She knew how he'd felt about her since the day they met. What right did she have to use his devotion when she wasn't ready to return it?

My God, Susan, she thought, you really are loathsome! Here is someone who wants you, needs you in a healthy way, and you play games with him, treating him like a "big brother," expecting him to keep his distance. She could not contain these thoughts. It was dishonest and insulting to someone as kind and generous as Paul Carmichael. Hesitatingly, she cleared her throat and he looked up from the correspondence he was studying.

"You ahem-ed, madam?"

"Afraid I did. Can we talk or are you too busy?"

"Never too busy for you. Glad to take a break, in fact. You all right?" He glanced at her empty glass. "Want a refill?"

"No, nothing." Susan paused. "I was just sitting here wondering why you let me impose on you this way."

He raised an eyebrow. "Impose? It's no imposition. I'm flattered. You know that. I'm glad there's somewhere you want to come. I'm glad I'm the one you want to come to."

"But I sit here afternoon after afternoon, sometimes not even talking. It must be a bore for you—me and my tragic act! I'm feeling guilty about taking so much of your time, Paul. It's life-sustaining for me, but what's in it for you?"

"Does there always have to be 'something in it' when friends help each other?"

"That's just the point. I'm doing all the taking. I draw strength from you, and contentment. For a few hours I'm away from all the unhappiness at home. I can almost forget there are questions without answers; you reassure me that there is still sanity and solidity in this world. But I give back nothing. We're not 'friends helping each other.' It's one friend—*you*—helping a very unsatisfactory me."

He moved away from the desk and perched on the edge of the ottoman. "You give everything back," he said, "just by being here. I know what you're thinking, Susan. You think you should return my hospitality by going to bed with me. You know that's what I've always wanted and you're feeling guilty because you sense how strong that desire is. And it is. Every minute we're in the same room I want to make love to you. But, my dear, you're not ready to make love to me, and you don't have to be sorry about that. I want you, Susan. I damned well do. But I'm not one of those high-school boys you used to know who tried to get to you by telling you how painful it was to suppress a strong sex urge. Don't feel sorry for me. Or worried that you're causing me physical or mental anguish. I've lived with the mental anguish for eight years. As for the physical, I wouldn't let you try to ease that unless you wanted to. If someone goes to bed with me, I sure as hell don't want it to be out of pity. Right now, being near you is enough. I can hope for more, one day, but time will have to resolve that." He leaned over and patted her cheek. "Dearest Susan. Don't you know

429

you're not the only one who finds pleasure in giving? Other people need to be needed, too."

She took his hand and held it tightly. "Oh Paul, I do love you."

"I know you love me, Susan. I'm waiting to see if I'm your *true* love." He disengaged his hand. "Meantime, don't stop coming here. You need it just the way it is. And so do I."

The simple matter-of-fact words had a peculiar aphrodisiacal effect upon her. For a moment she felt the quickening of desire, the urge to kiss him deeply, to touch him and be touched. As though he sensed it, Paul walked away.

"Time for me to kick you out," he said flatly, "before I start giving you a line like your old high-school dates. Go home, friend. And come back tomorrow."

When the door closed, Paul angrily kicked the wastebasket, overturning it, ignoring the trash that fell on the floor. Who the hell do you think you are? he asked an invisible Susan. How much longer can you put me through this? Come to me or stay away forever, but for God's sake don't torment me with your blasted unplanned seductiveness! What do you think I'm made of? And then he laughed at himself. What a pack of lies he'd just told her to relieve her mind. It was agony for him when she was here. Agony to want her and know nothing was going to happen, to be almost afraid to speak, lest one ill-chosen word end her visits forever. I can settle for crumbs, Paul thought. I'd rather have her around this way than not see her at all. And I *am* one of those high-school kids. I physically ache with desire. If it can't be Susan, it'll have to be someone else.

Deliberately, he called and made a dinner date, knowing where he would spend a mindless night.

Three days before Christmas, Kate and Susan had their annual preholiday lunch. In years past, Susan had looked forward to this event. She was childish about

430

Christmas, the gifts, the gaiety, the warm and loving spirit of it that made even grumpy New Yorkers smile at each other on the street. But this year there was no joy in her. She had no heart for any of it. There were too many memories. Even the good ones hurt.

"Let's be really corny and go to the Edwardian Room at the Plaza," Kate had said on the phone. "It's so damned Dickensian with its old-fashioned trimmings and fur-bearing tourists. I love it. I'll get us a nice, sedate table near the window where we can look at Central Park and the horse-drawn carriages and Bergdorf Goodman done up in Christmas lights. Okay?"

"Sure."

"I'm overwhelmed by your enthusiasm," Kate said tartly. "What are you rehearsing for—the road-company role of Scrooge?"

"I'm sorry. I know I'm not much fun these days." Susan tried to sound brighter. "It's a good idea. The Plaza, I mean. I couldn't stand looking at all those jaded faces at Caravelle."

"Not too many of them around. They've all fled in horror to Palm Beach. But I agree. To my dying day I will fight the efforts of the effete to make Christmas chic."

As she came through the revolving doors at the Fifth Avenue entrance and entered the crowded lobby of the hotel, Susan's heart sank. It seemed everywhere she looked there were women of her age, many of them holding the hands of bright-faced, excited children, chattering in high-pitched voices which their mothers tried to still. Don't hush them, Susan thought. Be glad you have them, well and happy.

Kate was already in the dining room. Susan saw there was a small package at the other plate and a bottle of champagne in a silver wine cooler standing next to the table. She clutched the big box that was her gift to Kate—a pale beige, hideously expensive Ultrasuede dress from Halston. It seemed strange to be giving a magazine editor a dress for Christmas, but it

431

was the newest, chic-est "status symbol," the fabric introduced only that fall and the designer already a favorite of Jackie Onassis and all the rich New York ladies. Besides, Kate never bothered much about clothes for herself. She loved them, but the stubborn streak in her made her dress almost dowdily in contrast to the fashion editors who pounced on every new trend the minute it came on the market. It had seemed a good gift for Kate, a change from the usual expensive handbag or perfume or jewelry of which her friend already had too much. Now Susan wasn't sure. Maybe Kate would think Susan was being patronizing about the way she dressed. Maybe the damned thing would be construed as an insult. Standing in the doorway, Susan toyed with the idea of pretending the dress was her own, apologizing that she hadn't had time to buy Kate's gift, rushing to Tiffany after lunch to find something "safer." No. Kate will like it, Susan thought. Why am I so indecisive about everything these days?

They exchanged perfunctory kisses and Susan sat down, the box leaning against her chair. She smiled warmly at her friend. It was good to be with Kate again. She hadn't seen much of her lately. It was unfair to burden even your nearest and dearest with your depression. Except Paul, she thought fleetingly. Paul didn't mind. At least he said he didn't.

Susan glanced at the champagne. "Heavens! How festive!"

"Why not? Christmas attacks us only once a year."

"Do you know I haven't had a drink in months? I'm not sure I should even now."

Kate shrugged. "Suit yourself. God knows I don't want to enlarge the membership of AA. I was one of the early complainers about your drinking, remember? But I don't think a couple of glasses of champagne will hurt you. Might even cheer you up. It's that heavy stuff I object to. The five-martini lunch scene. Unless you have a real drinking problem, Susie, I can't see how a little wine in moderation could do much harm."

" 'Moderation,' " Susan echoed. "That's the key to

432

everything, isn't it? I don't seem to understand the word. I love too much, hate too much, grieve too much, expect too much." She gave a little laugh. "Who was it who said, 'I'm moderate about everything except moderation'?"

"I don't remember. W. C. Fields, maybe. Or Dorothy Parker. Who cares? The point is, can you handle a little bubbly or would you rather have an appropriately named Virgin Mary?"

"Champagne," Susan said. "I don't expect I'll go straight from the Plaza to Skid Row."

Kate grinned. "For a minute you sounded like a girl I used to know. Open your present. I love watching people open presents. Except for some of those bitches at the office. You know how their greedy little eyes light up every time a messenger brings in a hunk of a loot from a grateful manufacturer. I'm secretly delighted that things have changed since your day, Susie. Remember the gold goodies we used to get? Now it's more likely to be a box of Godiva chocolates or a fifth of scotch. The pickings aren't what they used to be. Seventh Avenue is in a much more frugal period these days and we're no longer covered in caviar and Cartier baubles. Things have changed. Santa Claus has a smaller tote bag." She signaled the waiter to pour the wine and lifted her glass to Susan. "Here's to change. The good and the bad of it. At least it isn't stagnation."

Susan raised her glass in return, saying nothing. She took a sip and opened her package. Inside was a charming little hand-enameled Battersea box, delicately engraved "Remember the Giver."

"Oh, Kate it's beautiful! But so extravagant! You shouldn't have!"

"What the hell. It's only a week's pay."

"You're trying to make that a joke, but I know better. It *is* a week's pay! These antique English boxes are superb. And outrageously expensive. But I love it. Not only the box, but the message. As though I could ever forget the giver." Susan almost shyly handed the

433

big Halston box to her friend. "Merry Christmas. I hope you'll like this. It's exchangeable if you don't."

"A sable coat," Kate teased, untying the ribbon. "Susan, you *know* I find sable ostentatious and fat-making." She pulled aside the tissue and her face lit up with pleasure. "Well, did you ever? An honest-to-God Halston Ultrasuede! How on earth did you know I was dying for one and too damned cheap to buy it for myself? Speaking of extravagant! Thank God you have a rich husband!"

"I'm so glad you like it. I was afraid . . ."

"That I'd think it was a commentary on my usual unsnappy style? Don't be crazy. Those ladies at the office will faint when I turn up in this. Probably think I'm being kept. Hah! I should live so long! Even a hundred years ago when I used to get gifts from some poor benighted guy it was never anything this grand. I'm the only slob in New York who had to buy her own mink coat. No, now that I think of it, there was one other. But she looked like an orangutan by a gargoyle out of *The Hunchback of Notre Dame*. No hope for her, poor dear."

Susan was laughing now, actually wiping the tears from her eyes as Kate went on and on with nonsense about the magazine ("Did I tell you the office manager has given us all a new paint color called 'merciful oblivion'?") and stories about some of the people she'd recently interviewed ("There was this old movie star whose hair was so lacquered it wouldn't have moved in a hurricane. She kept assuring me it wasn't true she'd had her face lifted, while I sat there looking at enough scars to turn Zorro green with envy."). It was a gay lunch, Kate making light small talk, Susan even managing to counter with an absurd story of a cook, recently hired and fired, who thought the kitchen was full of demons and accused Susan of putting a curse on her.

But even as she told her little anecdote, Susan realized how restricted her life had become. Obsessed with Katie's death and Richard's infirmity, living a private, hidden life (for Richard wanted no one to know what had happened to him), she felt very narrow, very dull. Even the "old days" when she'd found the tours so boring and Richard so unpredictable seemed preferable to these endless days and nights of nothingness. Dear Lord, I have nothing interesting to say. My most lilting contribution is a stupid story about a domestic. I'm thirty-two years old and I'm as dreary as a dowager. Drearier. At least a dowager can talk about social events and charities. And children.

Kate watched sadness come over the face of the young woman she loved like a daughter. All the pretended gaiety was ridiculous. They couldn't sit here like casual strangers and make idle chitchat, even though she'd come to lunch determined to keep it light, to avoid talking about Susan's troubles.

"How goes it, really?" she asked. "Things are rough, aren't they?"

Susan nodded. "I don't know what I'm going to do."

"The doctor helping Richard?"

"I think so. There's no physical evidence of it, but I see slight changes in him. He's much more introspective these days, much more absorbed with himself."

"Is that news? Richard's always been absorbed with himself!"

"This is different. He always was automatically selfish, not broodingly obsessed with his actions. Therapy does do that to you sometimes. Makes you examine every move and motivation. I know. I've been through it. Even his attitude about Maria is slightly different. He seldom calls her. She does all the telephoning. He's still deferential, but it's not the same."

"That sounds like progress to me! God knows, if he'd kick his mama hang-up that would be a big step!"

"It's not as simple as that, Kate. It's going to be a long pull. He's thirty-eight years old. He has a lot of lifelong hang-ups to kick, and quite a few more recent ones. Like the collapse of his career."

"But that will be resumed in time."

"Maybe. Hopefully. But when? He doesn't want

435

anyone to know what's happened to his hands. We've put out word in the press that he is in temporary retirement following the death of his daughter. We had to make up some excuse when the tour had to be canceled, and we certainly don't want to indicate he may never play again. I think the use of his hands will come back, but what of the state of his mind? He's bitter and angry and pathetic and remorseful all at the same time. He says he can't live without me. Imagine, Kate. The very thing I used to dream of when I thought he didn't care." She paused. "But how real is it? Will he feel that way when he's well again? Or will the old Richard return? And if not, do I want this dependent one? God, I'm so mixed up! I know part of this is my fault. I tried to change him. Always a fatal mistake. And I was angry when I couldn't. And now I have a child leaning on me and I don't want that, either."

Kate was quiet, letting her spill out the doubts and fears that tormented her.

"I've been spending time with Paul," Susan said.

"Oh?"

"It's not an affair. I've been going to his apartment almost every afternoon since Katie died. Sometimes we don't exchange a dozen words, but it's so peaceful just to be there. He's a marvelous human being, Kate."

"He's more than that, Susie. He's in love with you."

"I know."

"Are you in love with him?"

"I don't know. I'm not sure. He's so unlike Richard. He's the kindest, gentlest, most undemanding man I've ever known. Yet he's so strong. He makes me feel protected, as though nothing could ever hurt me again."

"But you're not in love with him."

Susan seemed to rouse herself from this dreamy recital. "Damn all this talk about being in love! I was so crazy in love with Richard I would have died for him! And what has it gotten me? A few happy hours and more misery than anyone in her right mind could bargain for! If that's what being in love is all about, I

436

don't want to ever feel that way again! Maybe Paul *is* the right one for me. Maybe I should take the safe line I'm lucky enough to be offered."

"Don't be an ass! You're talking nonsense! No one is a bigger admirer of Paul than I, but he's not for you. You're too old for a security blanket and too young for placid companionship. You're a strong woman, Susan. You don't want to be wrapped in cotton wool. You need a man who'll challenge you; not an adoring protector! Why do you think you've stayed with Richard all these years when he's done everything unspeakable? Because it's been exciting, terrible as it is, to live with an ego like that! And why are you questioning your love now? Because the challenge has gone. He's changed. He's admitted his need of you. You've won. And you never wanted to win!"

Susan stared at her. "You're crazy, Kate! That's not true. I stayed with Richard because I was in love with him, even though he wasn't what I hoped for in a husband."

"Wrong. He was not what you hoped for but he was what you had to have. The very independence you hated was what intrigued and held you. That was the romantic, unrealistic side of you, always looking for a mountain to climb, a star to reach. Richard was your adversary and you played the game, pretending to despise it. Well, the game's over. You have a man now, with human weaknesses, with needs, and with the guts, finally, to see what he's been missing. You think the thrill is gone. It isn't, Susie. It's just been replaced by more honesty on both sides. If you want my opinion—and you'll get it, wanted or not—you and Richard can finally love each other as sharing people, not as individuals constantly spoiling for a fight. Richard grew up overnight. When are you going to begin?"

Chapter Thirty-three

Jacqueline watched silently as her mother-in-law stood impatiently in front of the big fireplace, her fingers drumming an annoyed tattoo on the big mantel. Maria was in a terrible mood and making no effort to hide it. Ever since Jacqueline and Walter had arrived late that morning of Christmas Eve with their children, followed in minutes by Sergio and Mary Lou and Gloria and Raoul with theirs, Maria had been in a foul humor. Even more brusque than usual, she'd dismissed all inquiries about what was troubling her.

"Are you feeling all right, Mother?" Walter had asked solicitously after she'd given all of them the same cool reception.

"Of course I'm feeling all right! Why shouldn't I be?"

"No reason. You just seem . . . preoccupied."

"I have things to be preoccupied with," Maria snapped. "Perhaps you think it's easy to put together a Christmas for sixteen people, but I assure you it's not!"

"Seventeen," Sergio corrected. "Joseph is bringing a friend, remember? Besides, it never used to faze you if there were seventy people in the house. What's wrong, old girl?"

"Nothing is wrong! And I'll thank you, Sergio, to remember that I'm your mother and do not care to be addressed in such vulgar terms."

"Sorry." Sergio suppressed a smile. It was heresy to

438

make even a flippant reference to Maria's years. Not that she was that old. These days, seventy-three was still a vigorous age and there was no one more vigorous than she. Her family was still amazed at the complete recovery she'd made from that stroke. "A miracle," they called it, and Maria had agreed.

"It was God's will," she'd said. "His will and the strength He gave me to be healed."

Maybe so, Sergio had thought at the time. Maybe God is on her side. She pays Him enough attention in church-time and money. But I don't think God could have stopped Mother from getting completely well even if He'd wanted to. She's the toughest creature, man or woman, I've ever met. She's a survivor, pure and simple. She'll bury us all.

"Well," he said now, "as long as everybody's here except Joseph and his young lady, who's for the woods to cut down our Christmas tree?"

All hands shot up in the air with the exception of Jacqueline's. "Count me out," she said. "Tradition or no tradition, I'm not playing lady-pioneer in a blizzard. You maniacs go ahead. I'll stay and keep your mother company while we wait for Richard and Susan." She gave Maria a steady, meaningful look. That was what was making her mother-in-law so testy: waiting the arrival of her precious and uncomfortably altered youngest son. Strange no one else realized why Maria was so edgy. But they wouldn't. They were all much too concerned with themselves.

"Say, you're right! Richard hasn't arrived." Gloria seemed genuinely surprised. "They coming by train or car?"

"The chauffeur is driving them."

"Oh, of course. I keep forgetting about Richard's hands. Well, maybe it's just as well they're late. It might be embarrassing for Richard, knowing he couldn't help with the tree-cutting."

There was unconcealed rage in Maria's response to her daughter's remarks. "Gloria! You are the most insensitive girl I've ever known! Forget about your

439

brother's troubles? How could you? How could you possibly forget we're witnessing the interruption of the greatest musical career in history!"

Gloria sounded like a sulky, chastised child. "I didn't mean I *forget*, Mother. Just for that *moment* I did. Anyway, Richard never did join us when we cut down the tree. Always afraid he'd get a splinter in his precious fingers."

"And rightly so," Maria said coldly. "And when he's recovered, he still will have sense enough to guard those priceless hands."

There was a tense silence. What are Walter and Sergio thinking? Jacqueline wondered. How can she so unfeelingly dismiss their talents and refer to Richard's that way? "Interruption," she said. I wonder whether she really believes Richard will regain the use of his hands. I'm sure she does. She's counting on God's help again. God's help and Richard's determination, which she likes to think is as great as her own. Only it isn't. Richard is weak and insecure, thanks in no small part to Maria herself. And Gloria. How does she endure the constant, contemptuous scolding? Forty-eight years of being the awkward ugly duckling in a family of talented swans. How she must hate all of them!

"Let's go," Sergio said as though nothing had happened. "Everybody set? It's snowing like crazy. Be sure you're all prepared for it."

There was a scramble for heavy coats and boots and mittens and then all of them, including Gloria's twins, streamed out the door, shouting and shoving with good-natured exuberance. Maria gave a small sigh of relief as they departed and she and Jacqueline were left alone in the big living room, but signs of her nervousness remained—the slight scowl and the incessant drumming of her fingers.

"Don't worry about the storm," Jacqueline said. "They'll make it all right. Phipps is a good driver."

"I'm not worried. You know I simply detest tardiness."

A lie. She was worried, but not about the driving.

440

Nor the lateness. She was worried that the doctor she had opposed was alienating her son, influencing him as even Susan had been unable to do. Jacqueline and Susan had talked often in these past months and it was clear that the analysis was forcing Richard to examine his whole life. Including his relationship with his mother. As she had to Kate, Susan mentioned to Jacqueline that Maria now instigated all the contact between herself and her son, hinted that Richard seemed almost unwilling to be in his mother's company these days. Maria was no fool. She sensed the change. She must be secretly frantic, Jacqueline thought. To see the dreams disappear, to lose control of the only one who could fulfill those dreams. I wonder if she ever takes any of the blame for this on herself? Of course she doesn't. The scapegoat would be Susan. Susan and her rebellion. Susan and her tragic child. Susan who interfered with Maria's methodical plans for Richard's life. Susan who convinced her husband to enter the therapy which presumably was separating him from his mother.

Jacqueline was relieved to hear the sound of a car pulling up to the front door. They were here at last, thank God. Maybe Maria would relax now.

"That must be Richard and Susan now," she said.

"Yes. I suppose it is." Maria did not stir from the fireplace, made no move to go and greet them. Typical. They'd have to come into The Presence, figuratively tugging at their forelocks, apologetic about keeping her waiting.

The old feeling of anxiety came over Susan as it always did when she entered this house. Not that she'd been here often in recent years, but the memory of that first weekend stayed with her. How young she'd been! How overwhelmed by the beauty of Richard's big, handsome family, the Old World courtliness of the maestro, the hypocritical temporary graciousness of a welcoming Maria. It hadn't taken long to be disillusioned about most of them, she recalled. She knew almost from the start that she had only two true friends among the Antoninis: Giovanni and Jacqueline. And

441

now one of them was gone and sorely missed by his daughter-in-law. She was glad he hadn't lived to see the tragedy of his grandchild or the professional and personal decline of his son.

As she watched Richard dutifully kiss his mother's cheek and apologize for their being late, she thought how much he'd changed in these past few months. There seemed to be no spark in him, he who'd always been the epitome of energy. He moved slowly, as though he were old and tired, his stiff hands hanging hopelessly at his sides. But he was more handsome than ever. The face had a drawn, ascetic quality that made him appear more sensitive, and the touches of gray that had appeared overnight at his temples gave him the look of a distinguished personality rather than a boyish matinee idol.

She could not dismiss that last luncheon with Kate. Was her friend right? Was there, perhaps, a masochistic streak in her, a need not to be needed but to be mastered? Had Kate touched on some facet of Susan's character that had eluded her even in her days with Dr. Marcus? Had she fallen in love with Richard because he was so full of assurance, even conceit? Did she love him less now that the overblown ego had been punctured by his losses?

Strange how she lumped the losses as though they were of equal importance: a child's life and the end of a career. As though the latter had any comparable importance. But it did. With the paralysis, Richard had lost his reason for being. Just as she had lost hers when Katie died. We've both been deprived of the things we love, Susan thought, and now we're alone though we're together. Love. Was it always such a lonely thing? Did one pay for every ounce of pleasure with a pound of pain?

Even while she searched for answers she went through the motions of "a well-brought-up girl," greeting Maria politely, adding her apologies to Richard's; kissing Jacqueline; even inquiring where the others were.

"In the woods, cutting down the Christmas tree," Maria said in answer to Susan's question.

"Such an exhausting group," Jacqueline added. "It makes me tired just to watch them."

Maria ignored the remark, her whole attention concentrated on Richard.

"Did you bring your valet, son? If so, I must make arrangements for his sleeping quarters."

"My *male nurse,* you mean, Mother. No. Susan generously offered to take over for the next couple of days. She's very good at being my surrogate hands."

"It's only temporary, dear."

Richard looked at her insolently. "Is that so? I didn't know you had a degree in psychiatry, Mother."

It was the first time Susan had ever seen Maria unsure of herself, almost frightened. She seemed startled by the rude remark, but she quickly recovered.

"One doesn't need to be a doctor to predict the outcome of this." She smiled confidently. "One needs only be a mother."

What an actress she is! Susan thought. What an accomplished performer. As though that ended the whole subject, Maria now chattered about the family. "Would you believe, Richard, that Sergio's Joseph has asked a girl up for the holiday! Dear heavens, I can't believe he's old enough to even think about girls!"

"He's twenty-three, Maria," Jacqueline said. "I imagine he's been thinking about them for quite some time. Who is she, by the way?"

"I haven't the faintest idea, but she can't be much. Any girl of a good family certainly wouldn't be anywhere but in her own home at Christmas. I don't know what Sergio's thinking of to let that child become involved at his age!"

"He's no child," Richard said flatly. "He's a man."

"Well, perhaps. Legally. But twenty-three-year-old boys aren't like girls of that age. They're immature until they're thirty or so, really. They should have time to find themselves before they seriously think of settling down."

"What makes you think Joseph is serious?"

"Richard dear, what a question! *You* know very well when any member of this family brings a *stranger* for a holiday it's more than a passing fancy."

Susan flushed. There was no mistaking the intent of that last remark. She was reminding Richard of that long-gone Fourth-of-July weekend. Damn her. She never gave up.

"May we go up to our room, Mrs. Antonini?" Susan asked quietly. "I'd like to unpack our things."

"Of course. But there's no need for Richard to go, is there? It's been such a long time since I've had a chance to chat with him, and there probably won't be another moment of peace after this." She looked appealingly at Richard. "Stay and talk a few moments, won't you, dear? There's so much I want to catch up on. I'm sure Susan doesn't mind. Jacqueline can help her get settled."

The daughters-in-law went up to the room Richard and Susan would share. Jacqueline flopped on one of the twin beds while Susan opened suitcases. One was completely filled with gifts, nearly two dozen of them for the family and staff.

"Christmas is a nightmare in a family this size, isn't it?"

Susan nodded. "An exercise in insanity. We should really stop exchanging gifts except for the children."

"I agree. That would cut the list down to nothing. They're all grown except Pierre and Claudette." She stopped, distracted by the look of pain on Susan's face.

"I'm sorry, Susan. I can imagine what you must be feeling this Christmas. I didn't mean to remind . . ."

"It's all right. You didn't do anything wrong. As for reminding me, nobody need worry about that. I never forget. Not for a single waking moment."

"How's Richard? I mean, *really.*"

"Discouraged. Depressed. Guilt-ridden. Confused." Susan shook her head. "I don't know what's going to happen to him, Jacqueline. I'm over my irrational hatred for him, the way I felt when it . . . first happened. Now I feel sorry for him. Imagine anyone feeling sorry for Richard Antonini. But I pity him. He's so helpless, in every way."

"Do you think he'll come out of the paralysis? Have you talked to his doctor?"

"Yes to both questions. I think he will recover the use of his hands, but no one can say how it will happen or when. Dr. Beekman is optimistic, though he says Richard is as complex a problem as he's seen since medical school." Susan gave a little laugh. "You'd know that would have to be so, wouldn't you? Richard Antonini was never one for an uncomplicated life." She paused. "Kate says that's what attracted me to him in the beginning. Do you think that could be so?"

"I wouldn't discount it. We're all rather alike in that way. Look at my crazy life with my once bisexual, now thoroughly homosexual husband. Look at Mary Lou with that arrogantly unfaithful Serge. Look at you, marrying a notoriously spoiled mama's boy. What do we all think? That we can change these men? Are we so conceited we still consider their flaws some challenge we'll eventually overcome? Probably. Women like us are so damned strong ourselves that we believe we can alter our husbands' personalities. What colossal nerve!"

"But you've accepted Walter's way of life," Susan said. "And Mary Lou has learned to live with Serge's cheating. You've both given up trying to change them."

"Only on the surface, my dear. We put up good fronts, but deep down we're still engaged in hand-to-hand combat with our stubborn spouses. You were too, until last September. What now? Are you still attracted to the docile, well-tamed Richard? *You* didn't accomplish the change in him. Does that make the victory hollow?"

"You sound as though you've been comparing notes with Kate."

"No. We both just know you. And love you." Jacqueline spoke the last words almost shyly.

"I love you, too," Susan said. There was a slight,

embarrassed pause before she said, "Oh Lord, I don't have a gift for Joseph's girl!"

"Not to worry. You and I will run into town tomorrow and pick up some perfume or something. It would have been nice if Mary Lou had bothered to let us know her son was bringing someone." Jacqueline rose. "I'll leave you to your chores. You still haven't answered my question, though. *Is* the victory hollow?"

"I don't know," Susan answered. "I don't even know whether it's a victory."

In the living room, Maria gazed indulgently at her favorite child. "I think you've been avoiding me, Richard," she said playfully.

"Not really. I haven't felt like seeing anyone."

"Except the doctor."

He sighed. "Look, Mother, I know you don't approve, but he's the only thing that's kept me from suicide these past three months. Don't nag me about the analysis, please. I don't want to have an argument with you."

Maria looked hurt. "Nag you? I've never nagged you in my life! What a terrible thing to say!"

There was no response. Maria kept control of herself.

"Why can't we talk together any more?" she asked. "We used to be so close, dear."

"Too close, perhaps," Richard said quietly. "And we never talked together. You talked and I listened."

"Richard!"

"It's true, Mother. I'm sorry to say it, but I've discovered that I spent my life trying to please you. Trying to atone for being born. I hated my father because of what I thought he'd done to you. I had no life except music because that's what you wanted. Oh, I wanted it, too. I still do. But I want it in perspective, as part of my life, not the whole of it. And God knows whether I'll ever have it again. Ironic, isn't it?"

446

Maria couldn't believe what she was hearing. "What kind of ridiculous talk is this? Atoning? I've never asked that of you! I simply acquainted you with facts! And because I recognized genius and encouraged you, does that make me an ogress? Because I didn't want you to saddle yourself with a wife and keep a handicapped child at home, does that make me a terrible mother? And I was right. Events have proved that! You don't know what you're saying. You're parroting all that stupid psychiatric jargon! You've been brainwashed by that doctor and, yes, by that selfish, hostile woman you married. You should get down on your knees and thank God for the background you've had. For the talent He gave you. And you should beg Him to give you another chance to use it. Turn to the real God, Richard, not to some white-coated charlatan who tries to impersonate Him!"

Suddenly he was no longer calm. "Listen to yourself! You still don't care about me. You never have. It was always my goddamned career that mattered. And even that wasn't for me. That was for you. So you could be the woman who gave birth to the famous man! So you could bask in the reflected glory and to hell whether there was any personal happiness in my life! You liked it when I had my 'little affairs.' They kept me from seriously devoting myself to any one woman. You hated the idea that a wife might steal some of the attention from you. You were ashamed to be the grandmother of a deaf-mute." He was raging now. "What a pity all your children turned out to be so second-rate, Mother! The least one of us could have done would have been to become President so you could ride down Pennsylvania Avenue in state!"

"Richard, I forbid you to speak to me that way!"

"You forbid me nothing! You've done your last forbidding. You've damned near wrecked everything with your interfering. You've given me a lifetime of guilt and a terrible feeling of inferiority that I tried to cover up by being Superman! No more, Mother! Not one

447

more second of it! Don't push me one more inch or I'
say all the terrible things I feel!"

"What more terrible than what you've already said?
Maria's fury matched his own.

"One thing more terrible! I hate you. I've alway
hated you!"

He stopped aghast. The blood drained from his fac
and he was trembling. But there was something else
He was almost afraid to look, terrified to trust his ow
eyes. But it was true. In his agitation and anger he wa
steadily clenching and unclenching his fists.

Chapter Thirty-four

Through the windows behind Dr. Beekman's desk
Richard could see Central Park and the skyline of th
East Side of New York. It was beautiful, this day afte
Christmas. The sky was crisp, clear blue and the build
ings silhouetted against it stood proud and tall, like .
row of sentinels guarding the sacred city. We live or
the wrong side of town, he thought irrelevantly. Th
"unfashionable" West Side has the spectacular view
while the "silk stocking district" pays dearly for th
privilege of looking toward grubby Tenth Avenue.

"I beg your pardon?"

"I said, 'And what happened then?' " the doctor re
peated.

"It's hard to remember. I recall seeing my hand
moving and being surprised. Not even excited o
happy. Just surprised. And then everybody was cryin;

and talking all at once. Even I was crying, I think. Just sitting there, looking at my hands and crying like a damned fool."

"There's nothing foolish about tears, Mr. Antonini. They're a sign of some emotion: sadness or sometimes happiness. Or rage. Even children seldom cry without a reason."

"I wouldn't know. I was never a child."

Dr. Beekman didn't answer.

"Did you ever play that game where people sit around at parties and try to see who never did the things most kids do?"

"No. I don't think I know that one."

"I always won," Richard said. "Nobody believed me, but I was always the only male adult in the room who'd never played ball or tinkered with the engine of a hot-rod or gone away to camp. I might have hurt my hands, you see," he explained carefully. "Mother lived in deathly fear of that." He looked thoughtful. "I was also the only one, usually, who'd never been spanked or even slapped."

Dr. Beekman waited.

"You were asking me about Christmas Eve, weren't you? When my hands started to work again. Yes. Well, let's see. There was a kind of 'slow take' about it all. It took me a few seconds to realize what had happened and I remember seeing Mother's face change from anger to astonishment. And then I guess I yelled for Susan and she came running downstairs and saw me moving my fingers. And Jacqueline came in and all the crying started, along with the hugging and kissing and shouting. We were like crazy people. Like we'd won the Irish Sweepstakes or struck oil in the back yard." Richard smiled sheepishly. "We must have looked like a bunch of lunatics, all of us."

"All of you?"

Richard frowned. "No. Not all of us. I remember being dimly aware that Mother didn't move. She was crying, I know that. But she didn't hug or kiss me. She just sat there looking at me as though I were a stranger." He reached for a tissue from the box next to his chair and blew his nose hard. "At that moment I didn't even remember the fight we'd had. I was so damned happy I didn't hate anybody. Not even Mother, though I'd just told her I did."

The doctor made a note. "And then?"

"Then I realized what I'd done. The things I'd said to her, I mean. I went over to her chair and tried to embrace her, but she pushed me away. She pushed me away," Richard repeated, "and then she got up and walked out of the room. She never said a word. Not a single, solitary word."

"What did you expect her to say?"

Richard thought for a few seconds. "I don't know. Was I waiting for her to compliment me?"

"She always did whenever you accomplished something great."

"Yes. That's stupid, isn't it? I didn't accomplish anything this time. It just happened."

"Why do you think it happened?"

Richard bristled. "You always said it probably would. It just did, that's all."

"You really think that's all, Mr. Antonini?"

The belligerency disappeared. "No. Of course not. All the while Mother and I were talking, this thing kept building up inside of me, like a steam valve that was going to blow. Nothing in the world could have stopped me from saying what I did. I didn't want to hurt her, I just couldn't help myself." He paused. "That's not true. I did want to hurt her. I wanted to punish her for everything she'd ever done since she went to bed with my father thirty-nine years ago. It all came boiling out, all the disappointments of my life, all the things I've been deprived of, all the bloody damned years I tried to be what she wanted. I was so angry. Angrier than I can ever remember being. I hated her. I hated that smug assurance that things would turn out exactly as she believed. I guess I always felt this hideous resentment. A few times in my life I came near to telling her, but I always backed off. I took my frustration out on something, or someone, else." He shook his head. "You know, Doctor, in a way you were directly responsible for what happened two nights ago. I've put up with her maneuvering and her slurs about people I love, but when she started attacking these sessions with you, mouthing platitudes about God and forgiveness, I realized she was the most coldly conniving, selfish woman who ever lived. I felt I had to protect myself from her, stand up to her because I'd never survive if I didn't. I knew if I let her talk me out of seeing you, I'd never make it. God! It's weird! I came here not believing in you or anyone like you. And you end up being the one thing I won't let my mother take away from me. When I think how I resisted the need for this therapy! I wanted to live with my guilt. I thought the paralysis was my punishment for letting Katie die."

"And now?"

"Now I suppose that tragedy was the match that finally lit the stick of dynamite that's been inside me for years." Richard spoke slowly. "I didn't lose the use of my hands just to punish myself for the neglect of my child, did I? I lost it to punish Mother, too. I wanted her to suffer, not for me but for herself. I wanted to take away the one thing she cared about. Is that possible? Is that what I really did? Was this paralysis as much revenge as guilt?"

"It's possible."

"But I still feel such terrible guilt about Katie! I wanted to be working and I was saddled with her that day." Richard's eyes misted. "Yet I remember feeling quite happy about being with her. She was so trusting, so adorable. It was the one time in her whole little life that I felt close to her. It didn't surprise me that I couldn't play after she died. I had to pay for her death. I couldn't look at the piano without seeing her face in the keys." He began to waver. "Maybe I was right in the first place. Maybe I couldn't move my hands because of that day, not because of all the resentment toward Mother."

"If that is so," Dr. Beekman said, "why do you

451

think movement in your hands came back at the very height of the attack on your mother? Was it coincidence? Why not sooner? Or later? Or never? You'll always be remorseful about Katie. So if you've been punishing yourself for that alone, what caused your recovery? In these sessions, Mr. Antonini, I haven't encouraged you to absolve yourself of blame for that tragic accident. We've talked about almost everything else in your life."

"But it's fashionable to blame everything on one's parents, isn't it?" Richard's voice was bitter. "Maybe that's all I'm doing now: looking for someone to blame for what I am. Child prodigies develop strangely. Look at stage kids or baby movie stars. They're screwed up, take drugs, kill themselves. And people always point the finger at a pushy parent. Maybe I'm trying to unload the mistakes of my whole loused-up life on Mother and convince myself that I couldn't get well until I told her I hated her."

Beekman was sympathetic though he tried to remain unemotional about his patients, objective and impersonal. It was the only way he could survive this daily onslaught of misery, these endless tales of self-recrimination and frantic searching by bewildered, unhappy people. He knew what Richard was going through; ashamed that he did not love and honor his parent, wishing he could deny what he now knew to be true. Look at the sudden reversal of thinking. Look at the still desperate desire to be a "good son." Poor bastard.

"You told your mother you hated her," the analyst said quietly. "You accused her of selfishness, of interference, of blind ambition that could be achieved only through you. Think about it now, Richard" (It was the first time, he realized, that he'd ever used his famous patient's first name.) "and tell me honestly how you feel."

The words seemed to come sadly and realistically from somewhere deep inside Richard. "She is a selfish, interfering, blindly ambitious woman, but I don't hate her. I can't love her. I can't even like her as a person.

452

But I suppose she did what she thought she had to do. She's always seen herself as the strong one in the family, the one who made the decisions and set down the rules. I can't really know her motives, can I? Maybe this is her kind of talent, making us all rich and famous. She grew up the daughter of a genius. She married one. Should I condemn her for expecting more of all her children than we possibly could give? She's a child herself isn't she? A spoiled, demanding child to whom we've all catered, my father, my brothers and sister, and, most of all, me. We let her run our lives. If she's run them badly, should we blame her for doing it, or ourselves for permitting it? She's been wrong, Doctor. But so have we." He straightened in his chair. "I hope I haven't alienated her forever. She's my mother and I'd like her to be my friend. I won't apologize for the things I said, because they were true. But I simply didn't see that all this suppressed anger toward her was also anger at myself for being less than a man. I've failed her, in her eyes. But I failed Susan and Katie in worse ways. I've disappointed friends like Paul Carmichael, and God knows I've failed myself. I *was* punishing myself for Katie. Nothing will ever make me believe otherwise. But I was also punishing myself for being stupid and superficial. The anger that ate at me is gone, Doctor. It came out of me like vomit. The knowledge of a thousand blunders remains, but at least I'm beginning to recognize them."

"That's what it's all about, Richard."

"Yes, I suppose it is."

"And now?"

"I have work to do. I have to try to make my wife love the 'real' me. I have to pick up my career, maybe in a less frantic way. I have to mend fences, eat crow, face the music. Choose your cliché. I have to do all of them, don't I?" The famous smile appeared, but this time it was more than a surface gesture. "I'm grateful to you, Dr. Beekman."

"Are you discharging yourself?"

"No. I don't feel ready for that. I'm going to need

453

your help for a long time to come. I have enough sense to realize that there are a helluva lot of hurdles still to clear, a frightening number of things I still don't understand about myself or other people. My father, for one. All my family, for that matter, not just Mother."

"I'm glad you feel that way about continuing the therapy. You must be the one who decides when you're well. But won't you start touring again? How can you see me and be away for months at a time?"

"I thought about that last night. I'm not sure I want to go on performing as regularly, now that the obsession is clear to me. We'll have to see. In any case, it will take months of practice to get back to playing as I used to." He smiled again. "The old hands have rusted with disuse. I'm not sure they'll ever be the same. Funny, it doesn't bother me that I might not be the big 'idol' again. There's so much more I want. I thought I had everything and I've missed a lot that really matters."

"You're still a young man."

"You mean there's time to catch up. Yes, I think so. God knows, I hope so."

❁

"Tell me exactly what happened," Bea Langdon said.

Susan described their arrival at Maria's on Christmas Eve and the few tense minutes that followed before she and Jacqueline went upstairs.

"I'd just unloaded all the gifts and Jacqueline had left when I heard Richard frantically calling. I rushed down and he was opening and closing his fists, staring at his hands as though they weren't part of him. Oh, Mother, you'll never know how I felt at that moment! So full of joy and gratitude that I couldn't stop crying. Richard was crying, too. And Jacqueline when she came in."

"Mrs. Antonini must have been beside herself with happiness."

454

"She was crying," Susan said, "but she was the most tragic figure I've ever seen."

"Tragic? Why on earth would she be tragic at a time like that?"

Susan recounted most of the bitter exchange as Richard had told it to her in the car on the way back to New York less than an hour later. "I didn't know until we were on the road home what had happened. Richard quietly told me to get our things, that we were leaving. He seemed so distraught I didn't even question our abrupt departure. I just did as he asked. I hadn't even opened our personal suitcases. I left the gifts there on the bed, called Phipps and we were on our way. The others hadn't even come back from the tree-cutting."

"Did she say goodbye or anything?"

"Mrs. Antonini? No, she left the room while the three of us were jumping around for joy. I didn't see her again. Later I found out why of course."

"Poor woman," Bea said. "I can't help feeling sorry for her. How terrible to have your child say you've ruined his life; that he hates you." She shuddered. "I know everything Richard said was true, but it must have been unbearable for her to hear, and just as hard for Richard to say."

"But he had to say it, Mother. It was what was eating at him. I'm sure the paralysis was partly Katie and partly the result of all that pent-up fury. Just as all the irresponsible things he did in his youth were more to defy his mother than to gratify himself. Even in our marriage he's been more concerned with her approval than with mine. God knows we saw that when she convinced him to take Katie away! And she kept him separated from his child even when the baby was home. For almost seven years, he acted as though Katie didn't exist, simply because Maria made him feel ashamed of a handicapped daughter!"

Bea was quiet for a moment. "There's something I want to tell you, Susan," she said at last. "Perhaps Richard or even Mrs. Antonini is not entirely to blame for that isolation from Katie." She repeated the theories Wil expounded the day they drove home from the funeral. "Your father loves you so much, but he can be more objective than I. I don't think it was deliberate, but perhaps, with reason, you were overly possessive about Katie. Maybe you shut Richard out of her life more than he might have really wanted, given a second chance. Darling, this is hard for me to say. You've always had all my sympathy, all my support. You still have it, from your father and me. But Susie, my dear child, perhaps you were unconsciously self-righteous about your situation. Oh, I know you tried in the beginning to involve Richard and you were terribly hurt when he wouldn't go along with your convictions about the right way to raise your child. I can't blame you for that. But you never tried to understand his side. You didn't work at the problem. When you saw he was unable to give of himself the way you could, you gave up trying. It wasn't fair to him or Katie. It wasn't even fair to yourself." Bea looked troubled. "It's easy to be wise in hindsight. Perhaps we should have raised you to be more sympathetic toward those who haven't your strength. You're so competent yourself that you have a low level of tolerance for those who are weak and easily influenced. We fostered independence in you. Perhaps in this case it backfired."

Susan was aghast. This, from her own mother? Was this how people saw her? The shock turned into anger.

"I can't believe you and Daddy feel such things! Shut Richard out? Mother, you saw it all! He shut himself out. I never wanted it that way. I wanted him to love Katie. I wanted us to be a family!"

"On your terms, darling. Without much thought of what was going on inside Richard. You didn't know all his private demons. You didn't really try to find out the real reasons for this unnatural rejection of one's child. It was easier to blame it on his mother, on his selfishness and vanity. It was easier to abdicate responsibilty for marriage and pour everything you had into your utter devotion to Katie."

456

With horror, Susan realized what Bea was really saying: If Richard had been forced to understand Katie that awful carelessness on the beach wouldn't have happened. No! It wasn't true!

"You're blaming me for the accident!"

"No, darling, of course not. I'm just saying . . ."

"You're saying I was the one with the overblown ego," Susan interrupted. "You're saying I should have demanded that Richard love his child. That I should have made him participate in her upbringing. That if he'd known how to handle her she'd never have drowned! Don't you think I tried? You saw it yourself. It was impossible. He didn't want to hear any of that, Mother!"

Bea was in physical pain, but she went on. "It doesn't matter what he wanted to hear. He would have heard. He would have known to watch her every minute, even if he didn't want to. Blame you for the accident? Of course no one blames you! But it's not right to blame Richard entirely, either. He didn't feel responsible for Katie's care. He didn't even know what he was supposed to do. I'm not excusing him, Susan. It was despicable for him to let his mother be horrible to you. It was wrong that he went along with her in most things. But you were guilty of unwitting bad judgment, too. Your assuming sole responsibility for your child was a kind of self-indulgence. You had faith only in yourself. None in Richard. I know. He's never done much to inspire faith. Quite the contrary. But you didn't even try to trust him or urge him to be trustworthy. You couldn't believe in him so you walked away. It's understandable. You didn't know he needed help as much as Katie did. How could you? But the truth is you were defying Richard and his mother as much as you were following your own heart. No one's all right in this, my dear, but no one's all wrong. A hard lesson. But life's full of hard lessons."

Susan was quiet for a moment, digesting the words that Bea found so painful to say. She didn't want to accept this surprising theory, but she could not dismiss it.

457

She'd simply never thought of it that way. Maybe I did cop out. Maybe I was so resentful of their opposition, so hurt and angry about all the things Maria and Richard did that I kept the biggest weapon for myself. Katie. Maybe I used that child as proof of my own capabilities. Evidence that I didn't need anyone. Not even Richard.

"Don't hate me, Susie." Bea's voice was soft and sad. "I'm thinking of the future. Yours and Richard's. He's trying to change. Don't let him feel alone. Let him know you understand. Let him see you've changed, too. Be patient, darling. Be loving and mature. You are, you know."

"Am I?" Susan was wistful. "I wish I could believe that. Perhaps you're right, Mother. Could be I *liked* being the only one Katie looked to for her life. Could be I enjoyed the secret revenge, the bittersweet knowledge of owning something the Antoninis couldn't touch, even if they wanted to. God, it's all gone so wrong! Everybody has made so many awful mistakes!"

"They can't be rectified," Bea said. "But they need not be repeated. Richard's in the process of purging himself. You love him still, Susan. And he loves you. Make it right this time. Make a few changes in yourself. If he can, you can."

Susan tried to smile. "Can I? You and Kate. Always making me look at my warts. Kate thinks I'm masochistic. And you see me as some kind of self-ordained avenging angel. I'm quite a creature, according to my two best friends."

"Darling, you *are* quite a creature. Quite a wonderful, human, fallible creature, thank heavens! I'd be terrified to think I'd given birth to a saint!"

"No danger of that," Susan said. "No danger at all."

On that Christmas Eve, for the first time since she was a little girl, Maria Antonini had wanted to hide. She heard the car pull away, knew Richard had left her house, maybe forever. Not that he could have stayed after the terrible, bitter words between them, ungrateful words she never dreamed she'd hear from her son's lips. He hadn't come looking for her, to apologize, after she'd walked out of the room. He must have known it would be useless. She'd never forgive him. She washed her hands of him.

Hands. Richard had regained the use of his hands. She knew he would. She knew the Almighty would see to it in His own good time. Hadn't she just told Richard that? She lay on her bed, thanking her personal God for this blessing, unsurprised it had been granted.

She'd have to tell the others about the miracle. But how would she explain Richard's sudden departure? I can't face them, she thought. I can't face that sea of inquisitive faces. But I must. My family is waiting for me. She rose and dressed carefully, taking special pains with her make-up. The Givenchy. Yes, she'd wear the new bright red Givenchy. It was beautiful, expensive and elegant, as she was. I look very well, she thought dispassionately. Not at all like a woman whose child has just told her that he hated her, that she was selfish and scheming.

For a moment she sat down, weakly. More than half a century ago, another man had said much the same to her. Her father had lashed out in much the same way when she'd announced she was going to marry Giovanni Antonini. She could still hear the words, still see the scornful look on his face.

"So you're going to marry the young Antonini, are you, Maria? Why? He's a nobody!"

"I love him, Papa."

"Love? Phah!" He'd spat out the word. "You don't love anyone. You're marrying him because he's weak-minded and manageable and you can get whatever you want through him. Silly young fool, he can't see how selfish and crazy for power you are! It wouldn't do to pick a strong man like your papa, would it? Not for you. You're too much like me, Maria. You must have your own way. You won't be like your mama. She is gentle woman as women are meant to be! Her pleasure in life is making her husband happy. Giovanni Antonini," he repeated. "You'll make him famous and miserable, won't you? Probably do the same to your children. You'll never make anyone happy. Not even yourself."

She'd run from him and hidden, as she wanted to hide now. He knew her so well. She was ambitious even then, and shrewd enough to choose a talent she could mold. She'd never have her adored father's genius, but she could have her own kind of fame if she worked things right. She'd be a celebrity's wife and the mother of celebrated children. It frightened her that her father understood her so completely, recognized his own ambitious, ruthless nature in her, knew how she despised her mother's complacent self-effacement. Papa knew she found power more desirable than love. Why not? So did he.

"I did it, Papa," she said aloud. "I made Joe immortal and turned my sons into great men. I was as strong and tough and successful as you."

Why, then, did she feel so empty and alone?

Susan picked up the telephone.

"I'm a little late," Paul said, "but Merry Christmas, Susan. I heard about Richard's recovery. That must be the best present any of you could have gotten."

Susan realized she hadn't thought about Paul for a single moment in these last three days. She'd told Bea and Katie the good news, but she hadn't even remembered to call the man who'd been her greatest comfort through it all. She was distressed and ashamed. She'd been so involved in examining her own reactions to this sudden change in her life that she hadn't considered the person who might also be drastically affected by it.

"Paul, I'm sorry I didn't call you right away! It was unforgivable of me."

"It's all right." (Was there a touch of reproach in his voice?) "Kate rang up this morning. I'm happy for Richard."

"Yes. Did Kate tell you how it came about?"

"Most of it, I guess. How's he doing?"

"It's been hard on him, but it had to come. It's been brewing for a long time. You know that even better than I. I'm only grateful that he finally got up enough courage to tell Maria the truth. He's free of her, Paul. It's saddened him, but there's also an obvious feeling of relief."

"And how are you?"

She understood what he meant. Now that Richard was self-sufficient again, what was she going to do?

"I'm all right," Susan said noncommittally. And in the next breath, "No, I'm not really all right. I've had to put myself under a microscope lately and the picture looks pretty damned unattractive."

"I find that hard to believe."

"It's true. My self-imposed halo is giving me a headache."

Paul laughed. "How's your time? Want to come by tomorrow? I'll be working at home. We could have a pre-New Year's Eve Coke, or a post-Christmas one. That is, if you're still on the wagon. Otherwise, I'll chill a bottle of champagne."

She hesitated. She wasn't sure she was ready to see Paul. It had been easy enough when she was feeling ill-used, when the future looked hopeless. But now she was at a crossroad and Paul knew it. It was the first time he'd ever issued a special invitation to visit, instead of waiting for her to drop in when she needed to get away from home. At their next meeting there'd be no long, undemanding stretches of silence. She was free to make a decision now, and Paul had every right to expect one.

"Chill the champagne," she said lightly. "I had some with Kate before Christmas and I didn't go straight to perdition."

She hung up, thinking about the conversation,

feeling confused and troubled. "Pre-New Year's Eve," he'd said. She'd almost forgotten it was only three days off. They'd made no plans this year, for obvious reasons. What will Richard want to do? she wondered. How will he wish to welcome in 1973?

Chapter Thirty-five

Jacqueline called the next morning.

"How are things?"

"Pretty good here. How were they in Pound Ridge after we left?"

"Not to be believed! Maria swept down, done up in Hubert's latest Paris creation, and announced that you and Richard had gone back to town so he could check with his doctor about the recovery which she, of course, knew was nothing short of an act of God! Everybody was stunned about Richard's hands, but not a damned one of us believed her story about your hasty exit. What doctor works on Christmas Eve? What *did* happen?"

Susan told her about Richard's terrible confrontation with his mother. "I didn't know, myself, why we were leaving so suddenly. We had to, of course. Those two couldn't look at each other. I'm not sure they ever will again."

"Lucky Richard," Jacqueline said. "Lucky you. Such a divorce from Maria should only happen to Walter and me."

"Was Christmas bearable?"

"Scarcely. Everybody was dying to know what really happened and nobody dared ask. So we played out the charade, complete with overpriced, useless gift-giving. You never saw so many blue Tiffany boxes in your life! We were Gucci-ed and Pucci-ed up to our eyebrows. I have your presents and Richard's here, by the way. And I distributed the ones you brought. And I even got a bottle of Weil de Weil for you and Richard to give Joseph's girl. You owe me seventeen fifty."

"Thanks so much. I'll send you a check. By the way, how was Joseph's girl?"

"Cute as a button. Maria hated her."

Susan smiled. It never stopped, did it? Any female competition was abhorrent to Maria. She only tolerated women and not even then if they threatened her. Why on earth would she care one way or another about a girl her grandson was interested in?

"Was there anything to hate?"

"I couldn't find anything, but don't go by me. I'm not programmed like our dear mother-in-law. But going back to Richard and her, I can see why she was so preoccupied the whole time we were there. Mutiny against Lady Bountiful! Dear me! And led by the most submissive member of the crew at that! Who'd have thought it! That doctor must be a magic man if he gave Richard courage to tell Maria what he really thinks of her. We'd all like to do that, but nobody has the guts. Maybe the rest of us should start with a shrink. Make it in an organized rebellion."

"I only hope it sticks," Susan said.

"Meaning?"

"It's hard to change the patterns of a lifetime."

"You think he'll go crawling back?"

"I don't know. I don't want to think so. But she's so powerful, Jacqueline. So difficult to anticipate. She'll do anything to get him back."

"I think you're wrong there. She'll never make the first move. It isn't her style. Too proud. Too haughty. She'd cut her tongue out before she'd say she's sorry for what she's done to him. For that matter, what she's done to them all. And I don't think Richard will back down either. He's stubborn in his own way when he chooses to be. As though I had to tell you! But from what you've said, I think he's burned his bridges and he's probably much too relieved to rebuild them. The others would be more likely to buckle under in this situation than Richard would be."

"Speaking of the others," Susan said, "I'm surprised we haven't heard from Sergio or Gloria. You'd think they'd ring up and say they're happy about his recovery. You already knew. You were there and Richard knew how delighted you were. But there hasn't been a word from the rest."

There was a long pause before Jacqueline said reluctantly, "Listen, Susan, I don't know that they're so all-fired happy, any of them. Except Walter and me."

She was incredulous. "I can't believe that! Anyone would be happy for him. Even a stranger!"

"More likely a stranger. A stranger hasn't had to compete for the last thirty years with Mama's little darling. My dear, Sergio and Gloria have always been consumed with jealousy over Richard's talent and Maria's obvious preference for him. I won't say they were glad when his paralysis put him out of business, but I can't honestly say I think they were sorry. I know that's almost too sick for you to accept, but you haven't known them as long as I have. They knew damned well that without his music Richard was only a minor threat. He wouldn't be more famous than Sergio or more loved than Gloria. Mama would love them as much as she did her baby boy. And then, by God, he goes and recovers! They don't know about the big fight. All they can see is that he also goes right back to being the center of Maria's universe. I'm sure they're sulking in their tents, rotten little beasts that they are."

"That's horrible! Their own brother!"

"Well, how would *you* explain their silence? Fortunately, Walter doesn't have those hang-ups. He's mixed up in a lot of other ways, but he doesn't crave fame or a pat on the head from Herself. He wanted to call you and Richard when we got home yesterday, but I thought we should let you catch your breath, particularly since you already knew how happy I was."

"I see," Susan answered. But she didn't see at all. It was hard to believe that children of the same parents didn't love each other. More than that, were jealous of each other. She supposed it was because, as an only child, she had no frame of reference for what was called "sibling rivalry." Until now, it had been a textbook phrase to her. Even throughout her marriage the one thing she'd been convinced of was the clannishness of the Antoninis, like an inbred mutual-admiration society. Wrong again, she thought. They put on a great show of solidarity for the public, even for "outsiders" such as I. But they have no real loyalty or affection, not even for their blood relatives.

She wondered whether Richard felt the same about them. Was the constant bickering between him and Sergio only brotherly teasing? And he'd been so fiercely determined to master the difficult concerto Walter had written. As though he was fighting an enemy.

What strange, pathetic people they were. For all the advantages they had, they were petty and insecure even among themselves. The Antoninis as a dynasty are no more than a myth perpetuated by public relations, Susan thought. They're not a close-knit family. They're a bunch of talented, scared-to-death individuals who fight each other for recognition. They don't even like their own.

Jacqueline was rattling on. "Any chance of you and Richard coming to us for New Year's Eve? I know you haven't been going anywhere, but maybe now . . . We're only having a few friends, about twenty, including Walter's newest, a very nice young man who does *not* wear yards of gold chains. We'd love to have you."

"I'll ask Richard. I'm not sure what he wants to do that night."

"Well, come if you can. The Sergios and Taffins are

not, underline *not*, invited! It's a buffet, so you can let me know later."

"Thanks, I will."

She moved slowly down the hall toward Richard's bedroom. Since their return from East Hampton they'd occupied separate sleeping quarters. For the first few days it was because Susan could hardly bear the sight of him. Later, the man who took care of a partially paralyzed Richard had to have constant access to him, so there was no question of their returning to a shared room. Had they stayed at Maria's, it would have been the first time they'd slept in the same room in months. But, at the time, the fact hadn't disturbed Susan, even though she would still physically reject him. Not that it mattered. He was too proud to come near her in his less-than-perfect state. He wouldn't have touched her while he was a "cripple," even if she'd wanted it. And in the few days since his recovery, there'd been no move on either side to change the arrangements.

She tapped lightly on the door and was told to come in. He was still in his pajamas, reading the *Times* and having a cup of coffee. He looked up at her and smiled, and Susan thought again what a beautiful specimen he was.

"Look!" he said. "Isn't it sensational? I can turn the pages of the paper and lift my own coffee up! Would you ever imagine a grown man could find such pleasure in little things?"

"It's wonderful, Richard."

"I swear I'll never take anything for granted again." He was suddenly very subdued. "Every time I turn a doorknob or eat a meal or strike a chord, I'll remember the days when I couldn't."

Will you? she wondered. Time has a way of dimming the memory of pain. When they're well and happy, people forget how sick they once were, or how sad. The old cliché about childbirth being the worst pain in the world and the most easily forgotten is true. Would Richard go back to being the way he was, before the paralysis, before Katie?

466

"I'm continuing with Dr. Beekman. Did I tell you?"

"Yes. I'm glad." She hesitated. "That was Jacqueline on the phone. She'd like us to come there New Year's Eve. Would you like to?"

"It's fine with me if you want to. But I hoped . . ."

"Hoped what?"

"I hoped we might spend it together. Just the two of us. It's a very special night this year. I'd like to celebrate quietly, if you wouldn't mind." He sounded almost embarrassed by his unusual sentimentality.

"I'd like that very much," Susan said formally.

"We have a lot to talk about."

"I'll tell Jacqueline." At the door, she paused. "Don't you think it's strange we haven't heard from Serge or Gloria?"

His voice was calm. "No. I didn't expect to. By now Mother probably has hinted that she wants no more to do with me. They'll take her side in any estrangement, no questions asked."

"But why? They're your brother and sister!"

"No, they're my mother's children. Maria's puppets. They belong to the lady who pulls the strings."

Her knees were shaking as she rode the rickety little elevator up to Paul's apartment. One side of her was eager to see this man who loved her, but another side dreaded the encounter. It was not because she didn't want to hurt him, though that was part of it. It was because she wasn't sure of the rightness of her choice. If she had an ounce of intelligence she'd run to Paul, now that in good conscience she could. He would care for her, give her other children, never be mercurial and infuriating. He was strong and sane and sweet and she loved him. But not enough, Susan thought sadly. He'd never have the whole of me.

Damn it, what was this irrational, ungovernable hold Richard had on her? Why did she go back, time and time again, for more punishment? She supposed she

467

was not unique by any means. The world was full of women in love with men they should never have chosen and were incapable of leaving. And the other way around. There was no explaining it. Call it masochism, as Kate did. Or call it love, as Susan preferred to. Whatever, Richard was the right man for her. And the wrong one, too. I must be one of those women who are fatally attracted to rotten men, Susan thought. And Richard may still be rotten. I can't yet make myself believe in that quiet person who says he'll be forever grateful for any motion he can make with his hands. Why do I grasp at the hope that he won't go back to being what he was? That he might not go back to Maria? Why can't I face the fact that this may be another mirage? That he may be physically healed but still emotionally disabled?

She felt a rush of affection for Paul, who stood waiting for her. But it was only affection. No excitement, no breathless, eager desire. She hugged him and stepped inside. The champagne was there and after he helped her out of her coat he opened the bottle and poured two glasses. Curled up in the corner of the sofa, Susan accepted one and waited for him to speak.

"What shall we drink to? A new year? A new life?"

He knows, Susan thought. He had only to look at my face to know I do not love him less but Richard more.

"I'll drink to you, Paul. To the finest, dearest, kindest man I know."

He did not respond to her toast. He simply gazed down at her steadily and said, "But not the man for you. That's it, isn't it, Susan? I knew it when you walked in. I'm not really surprised. I've always known it. There'll never be anyone for you except Richard."

Her voice was almost a whisper. "There can't be."

"Then I drink to you. To the happiness you hope for and the contentment you deserve."

Her eyes were full of tears. "Oh, God, Paul I wish it were different! We'd be so right. I know that."

"We'd never be right." There was no bitterness.

468

Simply resignation. "I told you I'd wait to see if I were your true love. I'm not. There's no 'rightness' about being in love, Susan. It doesn't come with a built-in guarantee of happiness. That's for fairy tales. And you and I are too old for fairy tales."

"And too old for happy endings?"

"Not really. One man's happy ending is another man's letdown. Or vice versa. I don't delude myself about perfect happiness. There's no such animal. It's all compromise and making the best of what we have. It's adult acceptance of reality. I've avoided it too long. So have you. It's time we grew up and faced the facts of life. Real life. It's never going to be all we want; all peaches and cream and strawberry sodas. Not for either of us. Not even for Richard. But we'll all be where I suppose we're meant to be in the scheme of things. We'll make do."

"Why can't I get over him, Paul?" Her voice trembled. "What's wrong with me?"

"Nothing's wrong with you. You just don't know what it is to take the easy way out. And you'd hate it if you did. You're a fighter, dear Susan. And love is really war." He pulled her to her feet. "You'd better get out of here while I'm still being so damned brave and noble."

The question framed on her lips would not come out. Paul smiled.

"You're afraid to ask if we can still be friends, aren't you? Ever the avoidance of the obvious! Yes, dear, we'll be friends forever, but don't come here again to test my strength of character. Or your own. Go home to your husband, Susie. That's what you want. But do me one last favor, will you?"

"Anything."

"Start working on your book again. You can do it now. And it's important for you."

She cringed. "I can't, Paul. That's one thing I can't do. I want to forget those years."

"You can't forget and you mustn't. You can't run from the memories of Katie as though they were some-

469

thing terrible. They were beautiful. *She* was beautiful and so was the life you gave her. Put it on paper, Susan. For her. For other people. For yourself. Put into it all the faith and tenderness you felt for that little girl, and all the love and courage she returned. Give her a memorial that means something. And give all your bottled-up hurt a chance to come out. Promise me you will."

She looked into the serious, pleading face that mirrored such concern for her. Concern greater than his own disappointment.

"All right," she said. "If you think I should, I'll try. I don't know if I can, but I'll try."

Rhett Wilson was delighted when she phoned and said she thought she was ready to get back to the book. She hadn't even spoken to him since September. He understood and hadn't pressured her.

"I'm so glad to hear it! I haven't wanted to bother you, of course, but I'm delighted, for many reasons, that you feel able to go on with it. It's important, Susan. It really is. It will be comforting to a lot of troubled people."

"That's what a friend of mine says."

"Your friend is right. We'll extend your deadline a few months. Plan publication in the fall of seventy-four instead of this coming year. I don't want you to feel pushed. Take it slowly. I know it won't be easy for you." His voice was full of compassion. "I'm so sorry about Katie. I hope the writing will give you a sense of release. It often helps to put things on paper."

She went almost fearfully to the dresser drawer where she'd shoved the beginning of the manuscript. She remembered that awful day in East Hampton, trying to pack a few personal things for the sorrowful return to New York. She recalled picking up the folder from her desk, moving like she, too, was no longer alive. She'd thought of destroying it, but she'd literally

470

not had enough strength to rip the pages to pieces. Instead, she'd tossed them into a suitcase and later, in unconscious imitation of Bridie's movements with Katie's doll, had hidden them away, out of sight and hopefully out of mind.

Slowly, reluctantly, she began to read what she'd written with such optimism, with such a feeling of dedication. The tears began again and she brushed them away. There were other little girls to think of, other parents and children to help if she could. Their stories might come out better than hers.

❖

On the afternoon of New Year's Eve, Susan was restless and uneasy. She'd spent the morning trying to write and it came hard. Richard didn't know she was working on the book again. She'd been almost afraid to tell him, not sure what his reaction would be. They still lived as harmonious, though wary, strangers, uncertain of each other. He might think she was resuming the story to punish him. That wasn't true. Forgiveness was not, perhaps, the proper word for what she felt. Shared regret was more like it. Or Paul's "adult acceptance of reality," including her own shortcomings.

I'll tell him about the book tonight, she thought. He'll see it's a step toward our new life, a reminder not to forget our child but to rid ourselves of bitterness and guilt.

She felt increasingly nervous and sad as the hours wore on. She tried to tell herself she always felt this way on the last day of any year. There was something gloomy about it, as there was about fall, when everything withered and died. No good reminding herself that things were reborn in the spring, or that the old year made way for the new. She still hated the end of anything. That about sums up my character, she thought. I can't bear to see things end: seasons, years, lives, marriages. I seem to want them to go on, even when they're worn out and useless. I didn't want to

471

stop seeing Paul. I wanted it both ways, and that's impossible. I'm like Richard, who thought he could have his affairs and his marriage, his freedom and his commitment. We should have taken different vows: "Love, honor, and betray." She smiled mirthlessly. "Till life do us part."

Soaking in a foamy bath, seeking relaxation in the warm, scented bubbles, Susan knew that part of her nervousness was caused by the prospect of spending this New Year's Eve alone with her husband. "We have a lot to talk about," he'd said. Like what? The past? The present? The future? Can we really communicate again? "Again" is the wrong word. We've never communicated, not even in our happiest hours. We've shared the same roof but not the same thoughts. We've made love, but only our naked bodies have touched. We've never truly bared our souls.

She glanced at the little clock on the bathroom shelf. Half-past six. Richard was never this late getting back from the doctor. Where was he? With a woman? He was a physical person and now that he could enjoy sex again perhaps he'd gone seeking the satisfaction he no longer found at home. I'm jealous, she realized. God help me, it's starting all over! No. I mustn't feel that way. But where could he be? Maybe with Maria? The thought came over her like a black wave. What if he'd decided to start the new year by making things right with his mother? It's sinful of me to want them estranged, but I do.

She was startled to hear his voice calling to her through the bathroom door. He'd not been in her bedroom since their return.

"Susie! Come out! I have some great news!"

"In a minute!"

She dried herself slowly, postponing the "great news." It's Maria. I know it's Maria. Wrapped in a thick, terry robe, she came out. Richard was barely visible in the darkness of the late winter afternoon. She could only make out the outline of him perched on the edge of the bed. She snapped on a lamp and saw the happiness in his face. Susan stood quietly, a little way from him.

"What's your news?" She tried to speak naturally.

"I've been thinking about it for the last few days, but I didn't want to tell you. I was afraid it couldn't work out. Or that you might not approve if it did."

Oh, dear God, no!

"But today I discussed it with Dr. Beekman and for once he broke down and told me he thought I'd made a good decision."

Would he never come to the point? It was like waiting for a bomb to fall . . . an explosion you knew would wipe you out.

"Come on," she said lightly. "This suspense is killing me."

"Susie, I've decided to handle my career differently. Spend less time away giving concerts, and more at home. I'm fed up with airports and lousy hotel food and literally sweating out every appearance. I'll take a few important bookings every season. I have no intention of retiring. But I'll do more recording. And," he broke into a big grin, "here's the best part. This afternoon I went to the Mannes College of Music and made them a proposition. I said I didn't want to join the faculty, but I'd be glad to take any really promising students who weren't already working with other teachers. I'd like to be responsible for developing talent. I won't take money for it and I won't accept anyone who doesn't show signs of tremendous promise. Maybe only two or three a year, carefully screened. They jumped at the idea, and I can't wait! Think of the satisfaction of seeing kids develop and knowing you've helped! God, I'm so excited! If it works out, I could do the same thing with Juilliard or the Manhattan School of Music. Maybe both. Of course, I'll need a few months of work myself before I begin. I need a lot of limbering up after such a long layoff." He was bubbling like a child. And then he abruptly subsided. "You do agree, don't you? You never liked touring. And we have no money problems. I'll still earn plenty, not that we need it. Father left us well fixed. It's okay with you, isn't it? You're not angry that I didn't tell you what I was going to do?"

She sank down on the bed beside him, too relieved and stunned to speak for a moment. The idea that Richard would not go back to his old life in music was the furthest thing from her mind. She was happy but bewildered, hardly able to believe it.

"Agree?" she said. "Of course I agree. It's fantastic! But I'm so surprised. I don't really understand. I thought you couldn't live without the constant applause, the endless excitement of performing. I thought you needed that limitless admiration. It's been your whole life, Richard. Thirty years of hard work to become one of the world's greatest artists. And now you've decided to give it up and teach?"

"I'm not giving it up. I'm simply cutting back to some degree of sanity. I told you, I'll still appear. I'm proud of my work. I'm young. I don't want to be forgotten. I won't be. But I don't want to be so driven, so possessed, that everything else is secondary to the next concert. I don't think that's necessary. I don't blame you for being surprised. The applause and admiration and all those things you mentioned have always been like food and drink to me. In a way, they still are. I like being famous. I'm not ashamed to admit that. But I don't like the one-dimensional life I've lived. I want to be more than a symbol. I'd like to try being a person, not the instrument of someone else's ambition." He stood up and began to pace the room. "Sometimes it takes a terrible shock to make you open your eyes to what you really are. Or what you thought you were. I thought I was the best of the Antoninis. The best of the best. I had to have the best treatment, the best publicity, even the best wife. I thought it was coming to me. When I heard about Katie's handicap I wallowed in self-pity. Yes. More pity for myself than for her. I didn't have the best child. I asked myself over and over how that could have happened to me. To me! Incredible! And even when she . . . died, my remorse

474

was clouded with a sense of the injustice of it all. How dared you and Bridie saddle me with a job I didn't know how to handle! Even then, Susan, I was angry. It wasn't only the end of her life that paralyzed me, it was the unwilling recognition of still another failure."

"Don't!" Susan said. "Don't torture yourself this way! It's not true. Especially the part about Katie. Nothing on God's earth could make me believe you didn't feel grief and remorse about her!"

"I felt grief. And certainly remorse. I was that human. I regretted a lot of things I'd done. And hadn't done. Of course I felt guilt for her death. Terrible guilt. But I also felt I'd been cheated somehow, and I didn't know by whom." He spoke slowly, carefully. "All this fall, with Dr. Beekman, I've been trying to get to the bottom of all this. And in the end, the answer was so simple: I've never known how to love. I thought success was a replacement for it; that you and Katie and, yes, Mother should be content with the only thing I could offer: the privilege of living in the shadow of the great man's triumphs. It was enough for Mother. It was all she wanted, because she doesn't know how to love either. But it wasn't enough for you, Susan. And in the end it wasn't enough for me."

She held her breath and let him continue, uninterrupted.

"You know all about my hang-ups. You recognized, long before I did, how they colored my life. I thought I hated my father. I didn't. I wanted him to worship me, too, the way Mother did. Or pretended she did. I had the insane idea that I could be to her all that he wasn't." Richard laughed. "Good old classic Oedipus. And even when I realized how crazy I was to blame myself for being born, even when I thought I hated Mother for making me feel guilty all my life, even then I knew I hadn't really gotten at the answer. I don't hate her. I don't think she realized how empty my life was because I didn't know how to give. She's a taker. Perhaps she'd be surprised if she found out how good it feels to do something for someone besides yourself.

475

The teaching is the only way I know to begin. That and trying to show you that I can love you."

He really means it, Susan thought. He doesn't yet realize the monumental step he's taken or all the reasons why. This is more than a break with Maria's values. More than a fresh start with me. He may not know it, but he's also doing this for Katie, to make up to young people for the attention and help he was never able to give his child. I write a book and Richard molds talent, and both are for Katie. She corrected herself. Not entirely for Katie. This is also for himself and for me. And, most importantly, for us.

He stood in front of her, waiting for her response. "I need you, Susie. I need to get back your love."

"You never lost it," she said simply. "God knows you tried. We both did. But nothing could make me stop loving you." Without thinking, she held out her arms and he knelt and held her.

"Happy New Year, darling," he said.

She reread the opening words.

"My darling, this is a love letter to you."

The book was finished. The book she'd written for Katie. *To* Katie. I do believe she knows, Susan thought. She must know how much at peace we are. As she is.

She looked down at her swollen belly. Another baby conceived like Richard, on New Year's Eve. But this one in happiness, in harmony and in desire. A new life, inside and out. Another child, welcomed and wanted and shared. A new chance in a new world.

Thank you, Katie, she said silently.

Thank you for the lessons you taught in the time you were here.

Thank you for helping us find ourselves. Forever.

B-12

Reading Fit For A Queen

QUEEN-SIZE GOTHICS are a new idea. They offer the very best in novels of romantic suspense, by the top writers, greater in length and drama, richer in reading pleasure.

- ☐ THE FOUR MARYS—Rinalda Roberts — 00366-9 — 1.25
- ☐ GRAVE'S COMPANY—S. Nichols — 00252-2 — 1.25
- ☐ GRENENCOURT—I. Charles — 00264-6 — 1.25
- ☐ THE HARLAN LEGACY—
  Jo Anne Creighton — 03206-5 — 1.50
- ☐ THE HEMLOCK TREE—E. Lottman — 00235-2 — 1.25
- ☐ ISLAND OF SILENCE—
  Carolyn Brimley Norris — 00411-8 — 1.25
- ☐ ISLAND OF THE SEVEN HILLS—Z. Cass — 00277-8 — 1.25
- ☐ KEYS OF HELL—L. Osborne — 00284-0 — 1.25
- ☐ THE KEYS TO QUEENSCOURT—
  Jeanne Hines (Empress) — 08508-8 — 1.75
- ☐ THE LAZARUS INHERITANCE
  (Large type)—Noel Vreeland Carter — 00432-0 — 1.25
- ☐ THE LEGEND OF WITCHWYND
  (Large type)—Jeanne Hines — 00420-7 — 1.25
- ☐ LET THE CRAGS COMB OUT HER
  DAINTY HAIR—J. Marten — 00302-2 — 1.25
- ☐ LUCIFER WAS TALL—Elizabeth Gresham — 00346-4 — 1.25
- ☐ MIDNIGHT SAILING—S. Hufford — 00263-8 — 1.25
- ☐ THE MIRACLE AT ST. BRUNO'S—
  Philippa Carr (Empress) — 08533-9 — 1.75
- ☐ OF LOVE INCARNATE—Jane Crowcroft — 00418-5 — 1.25

Buy them at your local bookstores or use this handy coupon for ordering:

ALL TIME BESTSELLERS
FROM POPULAR LIBRARY